Taming Blackhawk

by Barbara McCauley

How could he have known she was a virgin?

Grace was a grown woman, for crying out loud. It had never entered Rand's mind that she hadn't been with a man before.

But she hadn't. And though he wasn't proud of it, there was a part of him, that primitive male arrogance, that was actually glad he was her first. She'd said he'd made it special for her, but she'd made it special for him, too. Special in a way it never had been before.

He glanced over his shoulder at Grace. Her cheeks were flushed, her deep green eyes alert and sparkling.

Something slammed into Rand's chest. Lust, most definitely. But something more than that. Something that made him sweat.

There was no future for them, he was certain of that. But that didn't stop him from wanting her.

Michael's Temptation
by Eileen Wilks

The ground was hard. The woman he held was soft.

Michael didn't hold out much hope of sleep.

But Alyssa was asleep. Soundly, peacefully asleep. That baffled him. Oh, the exertions of the past day and night had been enough to make stone feel as comfortable as a feather bed…but she'd curled into him so trustingly. That's what didn't make sense.

He'd made it clear he wanted her. She'd made it clear she didn't want him. Oh, on a physical level she did. Michael wished he could take some satisfaction from that truth, but he couldn't. Not when it was *him* she rejected—his actions, his choices, his career. His life.

Yet she was snuggled up as warm and cozy as if they'd slept together for years. As if she trusted him completely. What was a man supposed to make of that?

Dear Reader,

Welcome to a wonderful New Year and a fresh selection of 2-in-1 volumes from Desire. As always, all these stories can be read alone and contain complete romances.

See an exotic sheikh and a bad-boy billionaire brought together in one volume with an atmospheric story from Alexandra Sellers's THE SULTANS—*The Playboy Sheikh*—and the second story in the BILLIONAIRE BACHELORS series—*Billionaire Bachelors: Stone* by Anne Marie Winston. Watch out for the third rich and sexy brother, Garrett, in March 2003.

We're just full of dangerously sexy men this month. Barbara McCauley's Blackhawk hero in *Taming Blackhawk* is a prime example, and she has another Blackhawk man coming your way in March, too. Also, in this volume is the final story in Eileen Wilks's TALL, DARK & ELIGIBLE trilogy, *Michael's Temptation*.

Finally, Metsy Hingle brings us an irresistible *Navy SEAL Dad*—funny how endearing a bachelor and a baby can be! Kristi Gold continues her MARRYING AN MD series with the delectable, delicious *Dr Desirable*.

Enjoy!

The Editors

Taming Blackhawk
BARBARA McCAULEY

Michael's Temptation
EILEEN WILKS

All the characters in this book have no existence outside the imagination of the author, and have no relation whatsoever to anyone bearing the same name or names. They are not even distantly inspired by any individual known or unknown to the author, and all the incidents are pure invention.

First published in Great Britain 2003
Silhouette Books, Eton House, 18-24 Paradise Road, Richmond, Surrey TW9 1SR

ISBN 0 373 04853 X

51-0103

Printed and bound in Spain
by Litografia Rosés S.A., Barcelona

TAMING BLACKHAWK

by

Barbara McCauley

BARBARA McCAULEY

has written more than twenty Silhouette romances and lives in Southern California with her own handsome hero husband, Frank, who makes it easy to believe in and write about the magic of romance. Barbara's stories have won and been nominated for numerous awards, including the prestigious RITA Award from the Romance Writers of America, Best Desire of the Year from *Romantic Times* and Best Short Contemporary from the National Reader's Choice Awards.

Books by Barbara McCauley in the SECRETS! series

Silhouette Desire

Blackhawk's Sweet Revenge
Secret Baby Santos
Killian's Passion
Callan's Proposition
Reese's Wild Wager
Sinclair's Surprise Baby
Taming Blackhawk

Silhouette Sensation

Gabriel's Honour

To Melissa Jeglinski, the best editor an author could ever hope to have. Thanks for keeping me focused, for trusting me, for making me laugh and, most especially, for just being you. This one's for you!

One

Rand Sloan had a reputation.

In fact, depending on who you asked and their gender, he had several. If you were a man, then *bastard*, *hardheaded* and *bad tempered* were a few of the words used to describe Rand. If you were a woman…

Well, there were so many words. *Amazing. Incredible.* And certainly the most popular overall—*extraordinary.*

But if there was one thing that everyone agreed on, men and women alike, it was that Rand Sloan was the best damn horse trainer in the entire state of Texas.

At thirty-two he had an edge to him, as if he'd already done and seen more than any other man his age. On Rand, though, the lines that etched the corners of his coal-black eyes and firm mouth only added to his appeal. His hair, thick, shiny and black, fell untamed down his neck. More often than not, his strong, square jaw bore the same dark stubble. He never hurried—a fact greatly appreciated by the women who knew him—and he always carried his entire six-foot, four-inch, lean, hard body with purpose.

Self-control and discipline were critical to Rand. When a man worked with a wild horse, those attributes could mean the difference between a nasty bruise or a broken leg. Even between life and death. Untamed horses were inconsistent and unpredictable, a few of the animals even teetered on the precipice of insanity. But all they needed was a little coaxing, a little patience, and he could pull them back, give them self-respect. Make them whole again.

Perhaps that was why he'd been drawn to wild horses, Rand thought absently. Why he'd chosen his profession—or why it had chosen him. Because he understood what those animals were feeling.

Because there were days, too many, when he also stood on that precipice.

"Here we go, sweetheart," he murmured as he led Maggie Mae out of her stall. The mare nuzzled the front pocket of his denim shirt, looking for a treat. He gave the animal a thick slice of crisp apple, rubbed the blaze of white on her forehead, then clipped her bridle to a ring on the redwood post outside her stall. The horse was small, but feisty and smart, a pretty two-year-old sorrel who would be auctioned off with the rest of the livestock and equipment when Rand's mother put the ranch up for sale next month.

Ignoring the hot, San Antonio breeze that swept through the barn, Rand set about his work. Work always cleared his mind, gave him balance. Today he needed that balance more than he'd ever needed it before.

It wasn't every day a man found out that his entire life—or at least his life from the time he was nine years old—was a complete lie.

That Seth and Lizzie, his precious little Lizzie, were not dead. They were alive.

Alive.

That one word wrapped around his chest like a steel band and squeezed. Alive. His brother and sister were alive.

Dust swirled around him as he raked numbly at the old straw, then replaced it with new. After he'd read the letter this morning from Beddingham, Barnes and Stephens Law Offices in Wolf River, Texas, he'd shoved it into the back pocket of his jeans. He hadn't looked at it since, but he knew every sentence, every comma, every word by heart.

But only one sentence mattered to him, only one that kept running through his mind, over and over…

Seth Ezekiel Blackhawk and Elizabeth Marie Blackhawk, son and daughter of Jonathan and Norah Blackhawk of Wolf River County, Texas, were not killed in the car accident that claimed the lives of their parents…

There were dates and the usual legal mumbo-jumbo, requests to contact the law firm as soon as possible in order to discuss the estate. But what the hell did he care about an estate? Seth and Lizzie were *alive.*

Seth would be about thirty now, Rand knew. Lizzie maybe twenty-five or six. Over the years, Rand had never allowed himself to think about his sister and brother or the night of the accident. But there were times, late at night, when even a bottle of whiskey couldn't chase the persistent demons out of his head.

And then he would remember—the lightning bolt, the sound of screeching wheels and crunching metal. His mother's scream and Lizzie's cries.

Then silence. A deafening, sickening quiet that pounded in his ears to this day.

How many nights had he woken in a sweat, the sheets ripped from the mattress, his heart racing and his hands shaking?

Too damn many.

Even now, as he thought about Seth and Lizzie, about the letter in his pocket, his hands shook and his heart raced.

"Rand?"

Startled from his thoughts, he glanced up at Mary Sloan's soft call. At sixty-one, she was still an attractive woman. Her raven hair was peppered with gray; her skin looked healthy and tanned, with deep lines around her blue eyes. She looked exhausted, he thought. But then, she usually did. Ranching was hard work, long hours and little pay. In her twenty-nine years of marriage, she'd never known any other life.

Mary and Edward Sloan had adopted Rand Blackhawk immediately following the accident. Mary had always been good to him, Rand thought. Raised him like her own, loved him.

Edward Sloan had been another matter entirely.

"Are you all right?" she asked, and took a step closer.

His first reaction was to say that he was fine. That everything was fine. Isn't that what everyone had always done in the Sloan family, pretended all was well, when in fact, it was anything but?

"I don't know what the hell I am, Mom," he said honestly. Or even *who* I am.

Mary knew about the letter, who it was from, what it said and what it meant to Rand. "It's one-fifteen," she said after a long moment. "Are you coming?"

Was he? His hand tightened around the handle of the pitchfork.

"Yeah." He stabbed at a flake of straw and tossed it into the stall. For her he would. "I'm coming."

"Rand—" She took another step closer. "I—"

She stopped again, not knowing what to say.

Hell, he didn't know what to say, either.

"It's all right, Mom. You go on. Soon as I finish here, I'll be in."

She nodded, turned slowly to leave, then stopped at the sound of car tires crunching on the gravel driveway outside. They both looked at each other.

"Are you expecting anyone?" she asked.

"Not me. You?"

"No." Her eyes, which had looked so tired just a moment before, now simply looked sad. "I'll go see who it is. Maybe it's one of Matthew or Sam's friends.''

They both knew that was doubtful. His younger brothers, Mary and Edward's birth sons, had both left the ranch years ago. Like himself, they'd come home only yesterday. No one knew any of the Sloan boys were back in town.

Once again she turned to leave, and once again she turned back. ''We'll talk later. All right?''

Rand nodded. He watched his mother suck in a deep breath, straighten her shoulders, then walk out of the barn.

He stabbed another forkful of straw and tossed it. They'd talk, no doubt about that. He had no idea what they would say to each other, but one thing was certain, they *would* talk.

Grace Sullivan pulled her rented black Jeep Cherokee in front of the two-story farmhouse and parked. Tipping her sunglasses up, she took in the name carved roughly on a strip of pine over the front porch: Sloan.

Finally.

She closed her eyes on a sigh of relief and cut the engine. She'd been all over Texas looking for the legendary Rand Sloan. Even if he didn't live here, maybe someone who did could help her.

If anyone lived here.

She stepped out of her car into the blistering August sun and slid her sunglasses back down to shield her eyes as she looked at the house. Its once-white paint had begun to peel, the screens were torn, and the composition roof needed repair. The flower beds had long turned to weeds and dust, and the corrals were empty. On the porch a wooden swing with faded blue cushions swayed slightly in the breeze.

Her gaze swept back toward the mile-long dirt driveway she'd followed off the main road. A cloud of dust still hung in the heavy air from where she'd driven in. The land was flat, dotted with cactus and thornbush, and stretched as far as the eye could see. Grace listened, but the only sounds she heard were a hawk shrieking overhead and the squeak of the wooden sign moving gently in the hot wind. The place looked and felt deserted.

Not that there would be much taking place in this heat at this hour on any ranch, she reasoned. Still, she would have expected *some* kind of activity. Maybe a ranch hand smoking in the shade of the large oak tree beside the barn, or a horse nuzzling a patch of grass. But she saw no sign of life at all. Not even the customary mangy ranch dog had rushed up to bark at her.

Not your typical ranch, she thought as she closed her car door and headed for the house. But then, from everything she'd heard, Rand Sloan was not your typical man.

''May I help you?''

Grace turned and saw the woman standing at the edge of the house, her expression wary but not unfriendly. She was a tall woman, Grace noted, slender, but not delicate. Her short, dark hair was starting to gray; she wore black slacks, a short-sleeved cotton blouse and black cowboy boots.

"Hello." Grace smiled at the woman. "My name is Grace Sullivan. I hope I'm not bothering you."

"Not yet you're not." The woman moved closer and offered a firm handshake. "Mary Sloan."

A wife? Grace wondered. Sister? She knew so little about the man. "I'm looking for Rand Sloan. Does he live here?"

The woman smiled, as if Grace had said something funny. "Rand hasn't lived here for fifteen years."

Disappointment stabbed at Grace. Not another dead end, she thought. She didn't have time for another dead end.

"Would you have any idea where I might reach him?" Grace asked. "It's important that I speak with him right away."

"Take a number," Mary said, then nodded over her shoulder. "He's in the barn."

He's in the barn? Grace swiveled a look at the barn, tried not to let her chin hit her knees. That simple? After dozens of phone calls and three wasted trips, had she actually found the mysterious Rand Sloan?

Excitement skittered up her spine.

"Is it all right if I go on in?" Grace asked.

"Help yourself." Mary walked past Grace and moved up the porch steps. The woman hesitated at the front door, then said over her shoulder. "But if you're from that lawyer's office in Wolf River, you best give him a wide berth."

Grace frowned. "I'm not from a lawyer's office."

Mary nodded. "Good."

The wooden screen door slammed behind the woman as she disappeared inside the house. Brow furrowed, Grace stared after her. Now *that* was odd, she thought.

But her excitement over finding Rand Sloan pushed the strange woman out of Grace's mind. Gravel crunched under the sturdy flat heel of her ecru pumps as she made her way toward the large, weather-beaten barn. She wished she'd had time to change her clothes earlier, but if she'd wanted to catch her flight from Dallas to San Antonio, she'd had no choice but to go directly to the airport from the board meeting this morning. The off-white skirt and jacket might fit in at the glossy, teak, ten-foot-long table at Sullivan Enterprises, but on an isolated, dusty ranch one hundred miles from The Alamo, silk and high heels were definitely out of place.

The story of my life, Grace thought with a shake of her head.

She quickly ran through her proposal in her head as she approached the open barn doors. From the time she was old enough to read and write, if she had wanted something, Patrick Sullivan had insisted his only daughter present her case in an organized written and oral form. When she was eight, she'd gotten Princess Penelope's Tea Party by demonstrating the usefulness of learning social skills; when she was sixteen and wanted her first car, she'd argued the necessity of independence and self-sufficiency. She'd used visual aids for that presentation. Even now, at twenty-five, she still had fond memories of that sleek, shiny black Porsche.

She pushed all thoughts of tea sets and cars out of her mind, then squared her shoulders and stepped into the barn.

"Hello?" she called out, hesitated when she saw the man bent over a stall in the corner of the barn.

When he glanced over his shoulder at her, her mind simply went blank.

Good Lord.

Grace had no idea what she'd been expecting. Someone older, certainly. Maybe middle-aged, with bowed, skinny legs, slumped shoulders and skin like crushed leather. Maybe a bushy mustache and graying temples. Your typical, well-worn cowboy.

There was nothing typical about Rand Sloan.

He was probably in his early thirties, she guessed, though there was something about his piercing black eyes that made him look older.

He straightened, pitchfork in his hand, and turned those eyes on her. Grace felt as if she'd been speared to the spot.

He was well over six feet, lean, hard-muscled and covered with dust. His jeans were faded, his denim shirt rolled to the elbows. Sweat beaded his forehead and dripped down his neck.

And then there was his face.

She thought of Black Knights and Apache warriors, could almost hear the distant drums of battle. The pitchfork he held in his large, callused hand might have easily been a lance or a sword. A dark stubble of beard shadowed his strong jaw. His eyebrows, the same dark shade as his hair, were drawn together in a frown.

His narrowed gaze swept over her, assessing, moving upward slowly, sucking the breath from her as he touched her with those eyes of his.

Her knees felt weak.

"Something I can do for you?" he asked in a raw, hot-whiskey voice.

Now *there* was a loaded question, Grace thought, and quickly dismissed all the options that jumped into her brain.

"Rand Sloan?" she asked, annoyed at the surprise in her voice and the breathless quality that accompanied it.

He stabbed the pitchfork into the ground and nodded.

"I...I'm Grace Sullivan. I've been trying to contact you for the past two weeks. You're a hard man to get a hold of."

Grace blushed at her words. What woman *wouldn't* want to get a hold of this man?

"Sometimes I am," he said simply. "Sometimes I'm not."

"You don't have an address or phone number and I tried just about—"

"Why don't you just tell me what you want, Miss Sullivan?" His eyes dropped to her hand. "Or is it Mrs.?"

"What? Oh—it's Miss. Grace, I mean."

He lifted a brow. "Miss Grace?"

"No." Dammit. There was that blush again. She rarely blushed, and now she couldn't seem to stop. "Just call me Grace."

He nodded, his expression telling her that he was waiting for her to answer his question.

And what was the question? Oh, yes. He'd asked her what she wanted. She had to think a minute to pull her thoughts together.

"I'm from the Edgewater Animal Management and Adoption Foundation," she finally managed. "Maybe you've heard of us. We rescue wild horses and care for them until they can be adopted out. We'd like to hire you to round up some stray mustangs in Black River Canyon and bring them out."

"You went to a lot of trouble, Grace." He turned his back to her and stabbed another flake of straw. "My answer is no."

No? Just like that? *No?*

Grace stared at him, did her best not to notice the firm backside he'd turned toward her.

"We'll pay you very well, Mr. Sloan, plus all expenses and travel costs." She stepped closer, and the scent of fresh straw, horse and sweat-covered male assailed her senses. Strangely, the combination was not at all unpleasant.

"You'll have to find someone else."

He continued to work, his muscles rippling as he tossed another forkful of straw into the stall.

She'd met some difficult people before, Grace thought in annoyance, but Rand Sloan took the prize.

"I don't want anyone else." She moved beside him, refusing to be ignored. "I want you."

Rand straightened and leveled his gaze on Miss Grace Sullivan. In a different situation, he might have taken the woman's comment and carried their conversation in a different, more interesting direction. But this was not the day, and—he took in her light-colored silk suit and heels and caught the scent of her expensive perfume—this was not the woman.

Not that she hadn't caught his attention in the looks department. That thick, tousled, auburn hair of hers was enough to catch any man's eye. It was the kind of hair a man could fist his hand into, then pull that long, slender neck back and dive in. Her skin looked liked porcelain; her eyes were bottle green, wide and tilted at the corners, with thick, dark lashes.

And that mouth. Lord have mercy. Those lush lips of hers were meant for a man's mouth.

She had long legs—he guessed her to be around five foot eight—narrow waist, full breasts…

He glanced at the fresh straw, then at the woman.

What a damn shame.

"Why me?" he asked.

"Everyone says you're the best," she said. "This is a difficult job. Probably dangerous. I heard that's your specialty."

Another time he might have been flattered, and he definitely would have been interested. He'd always enjoyed a challenge, and the danger part made his blood race.

Another time.

He unclipped Maggie Mae's bridle. "You're wasting your time, Miss Grace."

"You're my last hope," she said quietly.

Her words, spoken with such intensity, made something catch in his chest. He didn't want to be *anyone's* last hope. Didn't want anyone to depend on him. He closed Maggie Mae's stall door.

"That's too bad." He tugged his handkerchief from his back pocket and swiped at the sweat on his face. "But my answer is still no."

"Mr. Sloan," she said when he started to walk away, then, "Rand, please."

He stopped when she said his name so softly.

"Could you please just give me a few minutes?" she asked.

"I haven't got a few minutes, Miss Grace." He glanced over his shoulder at her. "Now, if you'll excuse me, I have to go to my father's funeral."

Two

The sound of a car door slamming startled Grace awake. She hadn't meant to doze off, but after only five hours sleep the night before, the early-morning board meeting, the flight to San Antonio, then renting a car at the airport and driving one hundred miles, her eyelids had simply grown too heavy to keep open.

She rose from the comfortable easy chair in Mary Sloan's living room and looked out through the lace curtains. Mary and Rand had already stepped out of an old, dust-covered tan truck. A second truck, newer, deep blue with dual cab, pulled up in front of the house, as well. Two men younger than Rand, also tall, with dark-brown hair climbed out.

Grace glanced at her wristwatch, surprised that the Sloan family was back so soon from the funeral. The service must have been a short one, and the reception, if there had been one, even shorter than that.

Grace hadn't intended to stay at the Sloan house. As badly as she wanted—needed—Rand's help, she knew she couldn't intrude at such a difficult time. But it was a long drive to San Antonio, and after Rand had left her standing in the barn, Grace had knocked on Mary Sloan's door to ask for a glass of water before heading back to the airport. Next thing Grace knew, Mary had sat her down at the kitchen table and asked point-blank what Grace wanted with Rand. Grace had told Mary about the foundation and the horses, then Mary had insisted that Grace stay and join them for dinner.

Grace had politely turned down Mary's offer, but the older woman had refused to take no for an answer. It had been a long time since she'd had any company, Mary had said, and she would certainly appreciate another female in the house tonight.

The genuine concern in Mary's eyes, the sadness, made it impossible for Grace to say no. Since Rand had turned her down, Grace had nowhere to go, no one else to turn to, anyway. So why not stay a few hours if Mary wanted her to? Grace could only imagine how devastated her own mother would be if anything happened to her father. If Mary Sloan wanted female companionship, then it was the least Grace could do for the woman.

She looked up when Rand opened the door and stepped inside. He'd obviously showered and shaved since she'd seen him last. He now wore black dress jeans, a white shirt and shiny black boots. He glanced at her, unsmiling. Obviously, Rand did not approve of his mother's request that Grace stay.

Well, the hell with him. The man was just going to have to deal with it.

Their eyes locked for one long moment, then he boldly slid that dark, intense gaze of his all the way down her body, then slowly back up again. It annoyed Grace when her breasts tightened and, dammit, her nipples hardened. She pressed her lips firmly together. She decided he was crude and coarse and…just about the sexiest man she'd ever met.

''I heard you're staying for dinner,'' he said at last, bringing his gaze back to hers.

''Your mother—''

''Mind your manners, Rand Sloan.'' Mary swept in the house behind her son and moved past him. ''I asked Grace to stay. A woman needs a breather with all that testosterone that'll be filling this house tonight. I need some feminine balance.''

''Matt and Sam will be here,'' Rand called after Mary, then turned and looked at his brothers as they strode through the front door. ''That should balance the femininity about right.''

Surprised, Grace glanced at Rand. The man had actually made a joke, she realized. A sarcastic one, true, but a joke nonetheless. She wouldn't have thought he had it in him.

''I'll give you feminine when I'm picking your teeth out of my knuckles.'' One of the brothers walked toward Grace and stuck out his hand. ''I'm Matthew Sloan,'' he said with a smile. ''This is Sam.''

Heavens, but the Sloan men were a handsome lot. Though Rand had darker hair and eyes than his brothers and his face was more sculpted, they were all rugged and tall, with killer smiles. Not that she'd seen Rand smile, she thought dryly.

''Grace Sullivan.'' She shook each of their hands. ''I'm sorry about your father.''

There was an awkward moment of silence, as there always was with condolences, then Matt said, ''Thanks for staying. After looking at Rand's ugly mug all day, my eyes could use a break.''

Rand frowned at his brother, but there was no malice in the look. If anything, Grace thought, it was the first sign of affection Rand had displayed.

''Matthew and Samuel,'' Mary called from the kitchen. ''Get your butts in here now. I need help.''

Matt and Sam excused themselves, leaving Grace alone with Rand. ''I...I should go help, too,'' she said.

He took her arm when she started toward the kitchen. ''In all the years I've known her, my mother hasn't asked for help in the kitchen once.''

Confused, she simply looked at him.

''She's thinking we need a minute alone.''

''Oh, I see,'' Grace said, then gave him a weak smile. ''I'm sorry. I'm sure the last thing you want is to be alone with me.''

''I wouldn't say that.''

Grace felt her throat go dry at the flare of interest in his black eyes. She looked down at the hand he'd laid on her forearm. A working man's hand. Large, with long fingers and tanned, rough skin. Against her smooth, cream-colored silk jacket, the contrast was amazingly sensual. The heat of his fingers burned all the way through the fabric.

She really needed to get a grip on her hormones.

"Rand," she said carefully, "your mother asked me to stay, but I have no intention of intruding on your grief. Just forget why I came here and think of me as you would any other guest in your mother's house."

It might be hard to explain to the woman that his mother rarely had guests in her house, Rand thought. But it really wasn't anything that Miss Grace Sullivan needed to know, anyway.

"Samuel Sloan, you get your fingers out of that potato salad right now!"

Rand watched Grace's head snap toward the kitchen. At the sound of a loud *thwap,* those deep-green eyes of hers went wide.

"Shoot, Mom, someone's gotta make sure it tastes right," Sam told his mother.

"You saying I don't know how to make potato salad?"

Another loud *thwap!*

Rand heard the sound of Matt's laugh, then again, *thwap!*

"Hey! What'd I do?" Matt complained.

"It's for what you're gonna do," Mary said. "I saw you eyeing that cake."

"You hold her, Matt," Sam said. "I'll grab the cake."

"You so much as—" Mary's reprimand was cut off abruptly and there was a lot of hollering.

A good sound, Rand thought. When Edward Sloan had been around, the family rarely joked. The best times in this house had been when the old man was gone, either on a business trip or one of his hunting and fishing excursions. Fortunately for everyone, Edward took those trips often. It was the only time they ever really relaxed, the only time they could have fun like this without Edward hollering they were all making too much noise.

"Matthew Richard Sloan," Mary yelled from the kitchen. "Get your fingers out of that frosting right this minute!"

Grace looked at Rand, her brow furrowed with concern. "Shouldn't you go help?"

"Why would I do that?" Rand shrugged. "Unless you want some cake. I could probably grab it while they're all busy and be out the back door before they even noticed. My mom bakes a chocolate cake that could make a grown man cry."

"Chocolate cake, you say?" Grace lifted a brow and glanced at the kitchen. "With chocolate frosting?"

"Is there any other kind?"

"I suppose I could start my car and you could jump in," she said thoughtfully. "I'd expect a fifty-fifty split, though."

Rand felt a smile tug at the corner of his mouth. It felt strange to joke with a woman, especially a beautiful one. His entire adult life, when there'd been interest between himself and a woman, there'd been few preliminaries. There'd been the usual amount of flirting and silly banter, he supposed. But there'd been no pretenses, no long courtships. If he wanted a woman, he simply said so. If she wanted him back, then fine. If she didn't, then that was fine, too. He respected a woman's right to say no. There were always more women in the next town he'd drift to.

Not to say that he slept with every pretty female that came along. In spite of the rumors, Rand had always considered himself a man of discriminating—and careful—tastes. He was no fool, and he wasn't stupid when it came to sex.

He looked at Grace, watched those big, green eyes of hers widen at the sound of a crash from the kitchen. She wasn't going to be around long enough for him to give it a lot of thought one way or the other, Rand knew. She'd be gone after dinner, and he would never see her again.

And that, he thought as he looked at those gorgeous lips of hers and killer body, was a damn shame.

Unlike the worn and neglected exterior, the inside of the Sloan house was neat and tidy and clean. The furniture was utilitarian: a plain brown sofa and chair in the living room, maple coffee and end tables. A bookcase filled mostly with history and ranching books. No TV, no DVD or video equipment, not even a stereo, that Grace could see. Simple and practical and down to the basics, would best describe the Sloan residence.

It wasn't a cold house, but it wasn't exactly a warm one, either. Except for the dining room, Grace thought, where the family had gathered around an oval pine table to eat. She felt comfortable here, relaxed. Well, not completely relaxed. It was pretty difficult to truly relax with Rand sitting across from her, those incredible black eyes of his watching her. Not that he was staring. In fact, it seemed that every time she'd looked at him, he was intentionally *not* looking at her.

Nevertheless, she *felt* his eyes on her, *felt* the intensity of that dark gaze. No man had ever made her so…aware. Of him, of herself, of everything around them. The feeling confused her, made her unsteady. It also annoyed her that she was being such a nervous Nelly. Such a scaredy-cat. A big, fat—

"Chicken?"

Startled, she snapped her gaze to Rand. "What?"

"Would you like a piece of chicken?" He held a large platter of fried chicken in front of her.

"Oh. Yes, of course." She helped herself to a leg and smiled at Mary. "This all looks wonderful."

A person would have thought that an entire football team was coming to dinner instead of three men, Grace thought. Mile-high, fluffy mashed potatoes beside a tureen of velvety brown gravy; a heaping bowl of baby peas; golden, steaming biscuits with a tub of honey-sweetened butter. The smell alone was enough to make Grace's mouth water.

And when she took a bite of the chicken, it was all she could do not to groan. Mary's sons, on the other hand, were not subject to the same restraint. Every one of them, including Rand, expressed their pleasure with sighs and groans and enough compliments to make Mary beam with delight.

"Lord, I've missed your cooking," Matt said around a bite of biscuit. "When you sell this place and move, I'm just gonna have to follow."

"You're selling the ranch?" Grace asked as she scooped up an extra ladle of gravy. She didn't care if she had to do three extra miles on her treadmill at home. This meal was worth every calorie.

"She's moving to Sin City," Sam said. "Las Vegas, Nevada."

"I have a brother there," Mary said. "I haven't seen him in ten years. It'll be nice to catch up."

Grace listened while they all talked about Mary's move and their uncle Steve. It seemed odd to her that not once was there any mention of the funeral or Edward Sloan. No shared memories of their life together. And not one person had stopped by to pay their respects. It was almost as if the man had never existed.

"My mom says you're from Dallas, Grace," Sam said, interrupting her thoughts. "What do you do there?"

She glanced at Rand, who appeared intent on buttering a biscuit. She'd promised not to mention the wild horses, but she supposed it was all right to mention the foundation. "I work with Edgewater Animal Management," she said.

"I saw an article in the *Dallas Chronicle* about Edgewater Animal Management." Matt teased his mother by reaching for her already buttered biscuit.

Without missing a beat, Mary slapped her son's hand and kept on eating. "If I remember correctly, the piece mentioned its founder was the daughter of some mega-millionaire Dallas businessman."

"Probably some spoiled, buck-toothed debutante who wouldn't know the backside of a mule if it stared her in the face," Sam muttered.

"I do believe I would know," Grace said curtly and stared at Sam.

There was a long beat of silence, then Sam's eyes widened, and he had the decency to blush. Matt and Mary both started to laugh, and even Rand had a grin on his face. Sam took his knife and made motions of cutting his wrists.

"Hot damn, Grace," Matt said, still laughing. "Any woman who can put my brother in his place is the woman I want to marry."

"The fact that she's beautiful and rich don't hurt, either," Sam added. "Come on, Matt, I'll arm wrestle you for her."

Mary shook her head at her sons' nonsense while she offered Grace more chicken. Grace declined, shocked that Matt and Sam actually had their elbows on the table and hands locked, ready to wrestle. Never in her life had she seen anything like this. Dinner at her parents' house was always quiet and sedate, a five-course meal prepared by a cook and served by a maid on fine china and linen tablecloths.

Dinner with the Sloan family was like getting on a roller coaster at Six Flags, Grace decided. An exciting, fun, adventure-filled ride that took your breath away.

Rand was the only one that held back, she realized. Not that he wasn't at ease with his family. He was. But there was something about Rand that Grace couldn't quite put her finger on. It was subtle, but he was different somehow from his brothers.

He was watching her now, she knew, ignoring his brothers' shenanigans and focusing his attention on her. The intensity of his gaze made her shiver. The worst of it was, she couldn't look away.

"If you want that chocolate cake," Mary said to her sons, "you boys best get your elbows off that table. I taught you better manners than that. And, Rand, stop staring at Grace. You're embarrassing her. Just look at her, she's all red in the face."

Grace dropped her gaze. She hadn't been embarrassed, she'd simply been hot and extremely bothered. But she couldn't very well tell Mary that.

The meal finished in relative peace—relative being a very broad term when it came to the Sloans. Sam and Matt flirted shamelessly with her, plus there were more wisecracks and insults between the brothers. Even Rand jumped in a time or two, but for the most part he was silent and thoughtful, as if his mind was somewhere else.

When Mary rose to get the cake, Rand told her to sit right back down, then looked at his brothers. Matt and Sam went out the front door, with Mary wanting to know what all the fuss was about. The two younger Sloan boys came back in a few moments later, carrying a large, blanket-covered box. They set it down at their mother's feet and pulled the blanket back.

"Happy Birthday, Mom," Sam said quietly.

It was a thirty-five-inch color TV with remote control and picture-in-a-picture feature.

Mary stared, then blinked furiously, got up without a word and walked out the front door.

Bewildered, Grace watched while the brothers all looked at each other and smiled.

It seemed that Rand wasn't the only Sloan family member who wasn't inclined to show emotion, Grace thought.

"Let's set it up," Matt said, then he and Sam carried it into the living room.

"It's your mother's birthday?" Grace asked Rand.

"Sort of," he said cryptically and looked at the door his mother had walked out. When he glanced back at Grace, there was a grin on his face. "She just might need a little 'feminine balance' right about now," he said. "Would you mind?"

She had no idea what he was talking about, but if Mary needed company, then Grace would be happy to sit outside with her. She looked at all the dishes on the table, but he took her by the arm and led her to the front door. "Never mind the mess. We'll take care of it."

It was the second time he'd put his hand on her today, the second time her body reacted with a mind of its own. Grace opened her mouth, but hadn't time to speak before he'd opened the door, gently shoved her outside, then closed the door again.

The light from the living room window illuminated the front porch, but beyond the porch railing, it was pitch-black. Grace could see Mary on the porch swing, staring out into the dark. Grace waited, not certain if she was intruding or not.

"Come sit by me, Grace," Mary said.

Grace sat and together they listened to the loud *er-rick-er-rick-er-rick* of an army of crickets and the rhythmic squeak of the swing. Inside the house, the sound of Mary's sons talking and laughing in the living room drifted out into the warm night air.

"Rand doesn't mean to be rude," Mary said after a few moments. "He's having a tough time right now."

"You mean because of his father?"

"Heavens, no. There was no love lost between Rand and my late husband." Mary sighed. "But that's not what I wanted to talk to you about or why I wanted you to stay."

"Why did you want me to stay?"

"Rand needs a woman like you right now," Mary said.

Grace missed a beat on the swing, then picked it up again. "Excuse me for saying so, Mrs. Sloan, but I don't think your son needs anyone, especially me."

Mary laughed softly. "That's where you're wrong, Grace. I know my boy and I know what I see. He might not even know it yet, but believe me, he needs you."

"Mrs. Sloan—"

"Mary."

"Mary," Grace said, shaking her head. "I came here because I need Rand's help. He turned me down flat. The only reason I'm still here is because you asked me to stay."

"And I'm glad you did." Mary patted Grace's hand. "It was refreshing to have another woman around. Sometimes living out here, without any woman friends stopping by for coffee or cookies, makes me forget I'm a woman myself."

The sound of a baseball game blasted from inside the house, and Mary's eyes lit up. "Well, I suppose I should go take a look at what they bought me," she said matter-of-factly. "Wouldn't want to hurt their feelings."

"Would you mind if I sat out here for a while?" Grace asked. "It's been a long time since I've been away from the city lights."

"Take your time," Mary said. "I'll make sure my boys save a piece of cake for you."

"No easy task, I'm sure," Grace teased.

Smiling, Mary went back into the house. With a sigh, Grace settled back in the swing and mentally went over the events of the afternoon and evening. The Sloan family perplexed her. The sons had buried their father, Mary her husband, but Edward Sloan's name had not been mentioned once amongst them. Mary had plainly said that Rand and his father did not get along. Then the boys had given their mother a television for her birthday, only it really wasn't her birthday.

Rand needs a woman like you.

That comment from Mary had to be the most perplexing of all. Though there was no question there was chemistry between herself and Rand, Mary certainly hadn't been speaking of need in a physical nature. She'd been speaking of something else, something on a deeper, more meaningful level. Grace couldn't imagine what Mary meant, but it really didn't matter at this point.

Grace couldn't put it off any longer. It was almost nine and she needed to leave in a few minutes. It was a long drive back to San Antonio. She'd need to find a place to stay for the night, then catch the first flight back to Dallas tomorrow.

She knew she was leaving her last hope behind her, but she refused to think about that right now. Grace knew that she was still foolish enough to believe in miracles, and she also knew that it would take one now to save those mustangs.

Three

When Rand first stepped out onto the porch, he thought that Grace had fallen asleep on his mother's swing. With her eyes closed and her hands resting lightly on her knees, she looked completely at peace.

He told himself to go back into the house, to leave her alone and let her enjoy the quiet. But he quite simply couldn't take his eyes off her.

Long strands of soft, auburn hair tumbled around her serene face. Dark, thick eyelashes rested against pale, delicate skin. There was a regal quality to her straight, sculpted nose, angular eyebrows and bow-shaped mouth. He could picture this woman in a past century, smiling and waving to her loyal subjects as the royal carriage carried her through the cobblestoned streets of her dominion.

It amazed him that after a day of airplanes and cars and the hot San Antonio desert, she stilled looked so fresh and neat. Her white suit had no smudges or wrinkles. Even those low heels of hers appeared as if she'd just taken them out of the box.

He had a strong, sudden desire to put his hands on her and muss her up.

She opened her eyes, smiled at him as she stretched, and he wanted to do a hell of a lot more than simply muss her up.

Desire slammed through his body. Pure, primal passion. He struggled to get a grip on it, to wrestle the beast down. But even when he did, he felt it pulsing, breathing inside him. Waiting for him to let down his guard even the tiniest fraction.

"I brought you some cake." He clenched his jaw when she stretched again, wished to God he'd stayed in the house.

"Thank you." Her voice had a low, throaty quality to it. "But it wasn't necessary. I was going to come inside in a minute."

When he moved in front of her, Grace's eyes widened at the huge slice of cake he handed her.

"Good grief," she gasped. "I can't possibly eat all that. I already had to loosen the button on my skirt after that meal your mother served."

The thought jumped into his head that he'd like to loosen more than a button, then slide that skirt down those long legs of hers. Or better yet, shove the skirt upward and save time.

He felt the beast jump inside him again, and he fought it down. ''Well, if you don't want it…''

Her hand snaked out and snatched the plate. ''Mister, men have died for lesser evils than depriving a woman of chocolate.''

She took a bite, closed her eyes and groaned deeply. The pleasure on her face bordered on sexual. Rand groaned silently.

Damn this woman.

''Will you sit with me for a minute?'' she asked when she opened her eyes again.

Bad idea, Rand, he thought.

But he sat, anyway.

''I like your family,'' she said. ''They're…''

''Obnoxious?'' he supplied when she hesitated.

She shook her head and smiled. ''Bigger than life.''

''That's a new one.'' Rand settled back on the swing, watched Grace slice another piece of cake onto her fork. He followed that neat little bite all the way to her mouth and instantly went hard.

He dragged his gaze away, forced himself to stare into the darkness. It had been a long time since he'd sat out here on this swing, the first time he'd ever sat here with a woman other than his mother. He caught the faint scent of Grace's perfume, something light and exotic, then cursed himself when he dragged the fragrance deep into his lungs.

Annoyed with his wandering thoughts and overactive libido, Rand turned his attention to the sounds coming from inside the house. His brothers arguing over who got the bigger piece of cake and his mother reprimanding both of them. Just like the old days, he thought with a smile, only better.

Much better, now that Edward Sloan was six feet under.

His smile faded as he thought about the letter he'd tucked into the back pocket of his jeans. He'd been carrying the letter since he'd opened it this morning. He hadn't read it again, he'd just wanted it close....

...Seth Ezekiel Blackhawk and Elizabeth Marie Blackhawk...were not killed in the car crash that claimed the lives of their parents

...not killed...not killed...

He heard the sound of Grace's voice, but it took a moment for her words to register. She'd asked about the television set.

"It was Sam's idea," Rand said absently. "We all figured it was about time she had one. When my brothers and I were little, we'd go into Maiman's Department Store and we'd see her staring at all the televisions on display, watching whichever show happened to be on. She always had a look of such longing on her face."

"You mean she's never had a television before now?"

"Not for twenty-nine years." Rand rocked the swing into motion with the heels of his boots. "To quote Edward Sloan, 'They weaken a man's mind and spew propaganda.'"

"So your father—"

"Not my father," he said sharply. "Edward and Mary adopted me when I was nine, after my real parents were killed in a car accident, but he was never my father."

The tone of Rand's voice alone spoke volumes, Grace thought. Mary had said there was no love lost between Rand and Edward. Grace was beginning to see more than a glimpse of that.

"Sam and Matt," she said carefully. "Were they adopted, too?"

Rand shook his head. "Sam came along a year after they adopted me, Matt a year after that. Quite the joke, isn't it?" he said dryly. "The doctors told Mary she could never have children, so she and Edward adopted me, then right away she has two kids of her own. Just goes to show you can't believe a damn thing people tell you."

Grace had the distinct feeling that Rand's last comment wasn't directed at the doctors. That there was something else behind that dark, mysterious mask of his, something that had nothing to do with Edward and Mary or being adopted.

Something that was none of her business.

In the dim light, Grace watched the play of shadow on Rand's face. She had to resist a sudden and overwhelming desire to reach out and touch that handsome face, to run her fingertips over the hard set of his jaw and lay her palm on his smooth-shaven cheek. The thought alone made her pulse skip; she couldn't imagine actually doing it. Not only were she and Rand practically strangers, she was certain he wouldn't appreciate the gesture at all. Rand Sloan did not strike her as being the kind of man who wanted, or needed, comforting.

"You wasted a trip here, Grace."

Her hand hesitated on the bite that was halfway to her mouth. Well, now, *that* was certainly to the point, she thought. No, "I'm sorry," or, "It's too bad," or, "Wish I could help you." Just, "You wasted a trip."

"Hardly," she said lightly, then slid the cake into her mouth and licked the frosting off the fork. "This cake alone made the trip worthwhile, not to mention that dinner your mother made. She should open a restaurant when she gets to Vegas. She'd make a fortune."

There was a light in Rand's eyes Grace hadn't seen before. When he turned that light on her, she felt her breath catch.

"What makes these horses so important to you?" he asked.

He wasn't the first person who'd asked her that question. Her father had, her mother, every person she'd ever hit up for a donation. She'd never been quite sure how to answer. Wasn't certain herself that she knew the answer.

She looked out into the night, heard the distant howl of a coyote, felt the loneliness there.

"Was there ever something you felt," she said softly, "something that went so deep and was so important, that words simply fell short?"

When he said nothing, she went on, "My uncle has a ranch in Austin and I used to spend three weeks every summer there, riding and taking care of his horses. I've been riding since I was eight.'' She stared at the plate in her hands and shrugged. ''Starting this foundation just happened. One morning I was sitting at my kitchen table, drinking orange juice and eating cinnamon toast, trying to decide what to wear to my mother's hospital charity luncheon that afternoon. If my pink pumps would look better with my floral skirt or my leather dress sandals.''

Rand lifted a doubtful brow. ''Pink pumps?''

''Hey—'' she pointed her fork at him and lifted her nose ''—these were serious decisions in my life. A girl can never be too careful about her footwear.''

Grace could swear she saw a smile tug at the corners of Rand's mouth. Shaking his head, he drew in a slow breath, then said, ''Somehow I've missed the connection between shoes and wild horses.''

''While all these important things were going on, I was watching the television, too,'' she said. ''A documentary about an organization in Nevada that was formed to save a band of wild horses outside of Reno. I ended up calling the number asking for donations and spoke to a man named Mitch Tanner. He invited me down to see what their group was doing. I accepted, then came back and started my own foundation. The rest,'' she said, stabbing another bite of cake and popping it into her mouth, ''is history.''

Rand's gaze rested on her mouth. That light she'd seen in his eyes a moment earlier turned dark and sensuous. There it was again, that heat simmering between them. Grace felt her pulse stumble, but she steadied herself before she did anything foolish.

''Why are you here?'' he asked, leveling his gaze back with hers. ''Why me?''

''These horses—'' she hesitated ''—this roundup, is a little more complicated.''

''Why?''

''The horses managed to break off from the main herd we've already rounded up and disappeared into Black River Canyon, a canyon that's notorious for flash floods. If they are still alive and we don't get them out soon, they will either starve or drown.''

He stopped rocking and looked at her. ''You're telling me you want to go into a dangerous canyon after a bunch of horses you aren't even certain are still alive? How many horses are you talking about?''

She swallowed hard. ''Four or five, maybe six.''

''You're kidding, right?'' He sat up straight now, his brow furrowed. ''You'd risk your life, or someone else's, to *maybe* save *maybe* six horses?''

''If they are there, and they are still alive, they haven't got a chance if we don't go down there and get them out.'' Grace closed her eyes. ''Everyone else has turned me down. Told me it was a waste of time.''

''They were right.''

She opened her eyes again, narrowed them at him. ''I refuse to believe that. You could do it. You're probably the only one who can. I've got two volunteers waiting to hear from me, two good horsemen who are willing to go down into the canyon with you and help.''

''Mother Nature can be brutal. Life is that way sometimes and there's no way around it.'' He sighed, then added more gently, ''Some things are best let go, Grace. Accept it.''

She shook her head, not certain if her overwhelming disappointment was that Rand wouldn't take the job, or that he didn't believe in it.

Whichever it was, the bottom line was that he wasn't going.

He was right, she thought sadly. She had wasted her time coming here.

As much as she wanted to, she *wouldn't* cry. At least, not now. Later, after she checked into her motel room and crawled under the covers, maybe then she'd give in to the pain in her chest.

Forcing a smile, she stood and looked down at him. ''Can't blame a girl for trying. I'll just say goodbye to everyone and be out of your hair.''

He nodded, followed her into the house where Mary sat in front of her new television, a soft smile on her face as she watched a rerun of *Frasier.* The Sloan family stood, and they all said their goodbyes, then Grace surprised Mary by hugging her and wishing her well with her sale of the ranch and her move to Las Vegas. When Grace shook Matt's and Sam's hands, they flirted shamelessly once again, making her blush.

''I'll walk you to your car,'' Rand said when she turned to shake his hand, as well.

''That's not nec—''

But he was already holding the door for her, waiting, so she said goodbye one more time to his family, then walked outside.

She stopped on the porch and offered her hand again. "Thank you for your time, Rand. I—"

"I said I'd walk you to your car."

He placed a hand on the small of her back and guided her down the porch steps and to her car. Her body betrayed her by responding to Rand's touch. Grace pressed her lips together in irritation. Damn this man. He frustrated the hell out of her, in more ways than one. Heat shimmered up her spine; her skin tightened; her pulse jump-roped.

There was no other word for her reaction to him than pure, man-to-woman, simple lust.

She'd had boyfriends; she'd been attracted to men before. But she'd never experienced anything like this. She suspected she might never again.

There weren't very many Rand Sloans in this world.

Grace wasn't certain if that was a good or a bad thing.

He opened the car door and she half expected him to pick her up and toss her inside, he seemed so anxious to be rid of her. Instead, he hesitated, looked down at her in the dim light that shone from the house.

"I appreciate you being nice to my mom," he said, his hand still on the door. "Things haven't always been easy for her."

Or you, either, Grace almost said. "She's a nice woman. I'm glad we met. If I get to Vegas, I'll look her up."

He nodded.

But still he didn't move.

"Well," she said awkwardly, then held out her hand again. "Thank you again."

He ignored her hand. His gaze fell to her mouth; Grace felt her heart lurch.

His jaw tightened. When he turned away from her, Grace's heart sank.

She nearly laughed at herself as she stood there and watched him walk back to the house. Good heavens, what had she thought? That he was actually going to kiss her? That would be ridiculous. Absurd. They'd just met, and he'd made it clear he wanted no part—

Oh, dear.

He'd whipped back around toward her, a determined, intense expression on his face.

Her breath caught.

As he approached, she opened her mouth to say something, but the words were lost when he reached out and dragged her to him.

"I have to know," he said fiercely, then covered her mouth with his own.

Nothing could have prepared Grace for the onslaught of emotions swirling through her. His mouth was hard, demanding. A little angry, even. She tried to hang on to reason, but it seemed as if the ground had opened up under her and sucked her into a world where reason and logic simply didn't exist. She held on to him, not just because she wanted to, but because she *needed* to. Her legs had turned to the consistency of overcooked noodles.

His kiss shocked her, but what shocked her even more was the fact that she was kissing him back.

She felt the heat of his long, hard body press against her, smelled the masculine scent of his skin. His mouth moved over hers; his teeth nipped at her bottom lip, then his tongue invaded. She welcomed him, met every hot, wet sweep of his tongue with her own.

She thought what she'd felt for him before had been simple lust. How wrong she'd been. There was nothing simple about this at all. It was the most complex, most complicated, most mind-blowing experience she'd ever encountered.

And then it was over.

Just like that, he released her and stepped away. She had to reach for the door frame or she would have slid to the ground.

''Goodbye, Miss Grace,'' he said, his voice rough and husky.

Then he turned and walked not to the house, but toward the barn. Still struggling to breathe, she watched him disappear into the darkness.

Two hours later Rand could still taste her.

Even as he swung the hammer and slammed it down on the head of the nail, the taste of rich, sweet chocolate lingered in his mouth. The scent of her perfume filled his nostrils. The feel of her soft, full breasts pressed against his chest sang in his blood.

He had to be the biggest fool that ever lived.

He'd thought that one little taste of her would put her out of his mind. That whatever attraction he'd been feeling toward the woman would dissipate if he wasn't left wondering what it would be like to give in, to wrap himself around her and just let himself feel.

Big, big mistake.

As if his life hadn't been difficult enough right now, he'd had to go and make it even more complicated.

Swearing under his breath, he reached for another plank of wood and fitted it snugly against the one he'd just hammered in place. Eleven o'clock at night might be an odd time to repair broken stalls, but what the hell. He wouldn't be falling asleep anytime soon, anyway.

He appreciated that his brothers understood his need to be alone tonight. They knew about the letter, too. He'd shown it to them when it had first come. Matt had whistled under his breath; Sam had sworn softly. They hadn't asked him what he was going to do. They both knew that Rand would tell them when he was ready.

"It's a little late for all this sawing and hammering, don't you think?"

He turned at the sound of his mother's voice. She stood at the open barn door, wearing a red-plaid robe over simple, white cotton pajamas and her black cowboy boots. She had a bottle of Jack Daniel's in one hand and two glasses in the other.

He straightened, gave a shrug of his shoulders. "Needs doing. Now's as good a time as any."

She walked toward him, set the glasses on the sawhorse, poured a healthy shot of whisky in each one. "It's been a long day."

He set the hammer down and took the drink she

offered. They clinked glasses. He tossed his back, while Mary sipped on hers.

"Do you hate me, Rand?"

He frowned at her. "Why would you ask me a dumb question like that?"

She stared at her drink. "You should. Edward Sloan was a first-class bastard to you. He rode you hard, never let up, no matter what you did or didn't do. I should have stopped him."

"You couldn't have stopped him." Rand reached for the bottle. "Nobody could have stopped him."

"If it had just been you and me," Mary said quietly, "I would have left him. But after Matt and Sam came along, he never would have let me go."

In all the years they'd never spoken of any of this. Of Edward's strict rules and discipline, the lack of love in the house. The fact that Edward had openly hated Rand, a half-breed Indian boy who wasn't Sloan blood. Rand knew that if Mary hadn't been there to temper her husband, to balance out his meanness, Rand would have left long before he turned seventeen.

But there was one question he'd wondered all those years, one question that had never been answered. Rand asked it now.

"Why did he ever adopt me?"

Mary took another sip. "I wanted to adopt, your father—Edward—didn't. I got a call one night from a lawyer in Granite Springs who'd heard I'd been looking into adoption. He told me about you, that your family had been killed in a car accident and we could meet that night and adopt you immediately, without all the usual red tape and waiting period.''

''Didn't that strike you as odd?'

''I wasn't stupid. I knew it wasn't legal, but I didn't care. You were so frightened, so lost, and I fell in love with you the second I laid eyes on you. I told Edward if he didn't agree to adopt you that I'd leave him.'' Mary sighed. ''I should have let you go to a better family, one where both parents would love you. But I was selfish. I'd hoped that Edward would come to care about you, learn to love you as much I did. I was a fool, and you paid for it.''

Rand shook his head. ''It doesn't matter now. There's good that came out of it. I have you and Matt and Sam.''

''And now you have your real brother and sister,'' she said softly. ''Seth and Lizzie.''

Rand sucked in a breath. Did he have them? At this late date, could he?

''You need to contact that lawyer in Wolf River, Rand,'' Mary said. ''At least talk to him.''

''I'll think about it.''

Mary nodded. ''And what about Grace?''

He looked up. ''What about her?''

''You should go with her,'' Mary said. ''Down into that canyon where those horses are. You could do a lot of thinking there.''

''Those horses are a lost cause,'' he said, and threw back another shot.

''The world is full of lost causes, son.'' Mary stood

and looked Rand in the eye. ‘‘Those are the ones that need help the most.’’

She turned and walked toward the barn door, then stopped.

‘‘Rand?’’ she said without turning around.

‘‘Yeah?’’

‘‘Thanks for the TV.’’

He couldn’t help but smile. ‘‘You’re welcome.’’

She took another step and stopped again. ‘‘Rand?’’

‘‘Yeah?’’

‘‘I love you.’’

Before he could answer her, she was gone. With a sigh he sat on the sawhorse and poured himself another drink, then pulled the letter out of his back pocket and opened it up.

‘‘Dear Mr. Rand Blackhawk…’’

‘‘We can do it without him, Tom,’’ Grace said into the phone as she paced back and forth in her motel room. She was still dressed in her pajamas, waiting for the coffee she’d ordered from the front office. She’d need it strong and black today. ‘‘I’ll get the supplies today and meet you at the canyon’s entrance in two days.’’

Grace listened as Tom argued with her over the wisdom of proceeding without Rand. They’d been going round and round for the past fifteen minutes.

‘‘There’s nothing supernatural about Rand Sloan,’’ Grace said irritably. ‘‘Don’t believe everything you hear. He’s just a man, a good horseman, yes, but he’s still just an ordinary man.’’

Liar, she said to herself as Tom continued to disagree with her. Rand was as far from ordinary as it gets. And she wasn't quite sure about the supernatural part, either.

Lord knew he'd put some kind of strange spell on her. Not only had she kissed the man like some kind of wanton, sex-starved hussy, she'd had dreams about him all night.

Hot, erotic dreams. His hands on her naked skin, his mouth on her neck, her breasts, and—

She blushed just thinking about it.

She got hot all over again, thinking about it.

Grace heard Tom calling her name and snapped her attention back to the phone. “Tom, we can do this. I know we can.”

Dragging a hand through her loose, tousled hair, she looked at her wristwatch. It was already ten o'clock, and she wanted to be out of here by twelve, loaded with supplies and on her way to Black River Canyon. If she hadn't overslept, she would have been gone already.

“Listen,” she tried again when Tom still refused to listen to her. “You and Marty are terrific horsemen and you're wonderful with the mustangs. You can—”

She stopped at the knock on her door. Thank God. She hoped the coffee came with an IV. “Hold on a second,” she said into the phone and opened the door.

Rand.

She heard Tom saying her name, but she was incapable of words. So she simply stared.

He stood in her doorway, leaning casually against

the doorjamb. His jeans were faded, his black, collared shirt rolled to the elbows. He wore a black Stetson, black cowboy boots and aviator sunglasses.

She thought he looked like Satan himself.

"Mornin'," he said.

She felt, rather than saw his gaze slide the length of her.

And still she couldn't speak.

Tom was frantic at the other end of the line now, thinking something had happened.

"I—I'll call you back," she managed and hung up the phone.

"Sweetheart," Rand said in a rough, hot-whiskey voice. "You've got five minutes to get dressed or I'm coming in."

Four

Grace managed to throw herself together in less than the five minutes he'd given her. She jammed her arms into a white cotton sleeveless blouse, yanked on a pair of jeans while hopping around the room looking for her boots, then grabbed a hair clip and clawed it into the mass of uncombed curls she'd piled on top of her head.

So much for the refined rules of grooming her mother had raised her on.

When she opened her motel room door, she saw Rand leaning against her car, drinking hot coffee out of a large foam cup.

Her coffee, unless she missed her guess.

The steam drifted around that rugged face of his, and she felt her heart trip. When he lifted his gaze to hers, butterflies danced in her stomach. This man should be illegal, she thought. Or, like a pack of cigarettes, come with a warning label: Rand Sloan is hazardous to the health of women everywhere.

Sucking in a breath, she squared her shoulders and marched over to him. ''Stealing a person's morning coffee is punishable by death in this state.''

He lifted a brow. ''The state of Texas?''

''The state of Grace.''

He grinned at her and there they were again, dammit. Those irritating butterflies.

''Didn't your mother teach you to share?'' he said, handing her the coffee.

''Not with men who show up unannounced at my motel room.''

''You showed up unannounced at my place,'' he reminded her.

''Touché.'' She raised her cup to him, took a sip, then handed it back.

She wanted to ask him what he was doing here, why he'd come, but instead, she waited. She understood Rand was a man who did things his way, in his own good time.

The morning was pleasant, with a few wispy clouds in the blue sky. The air was still cool, but quickly warming up. Grace had lived in Texas all her life and knew how fickle the weather was, how quickly it could change. In the summer, though, there were only two degrees of heat—hot and hotter. And because that was too easy by itself, Mother Nature threw in a good dose of humidity to make it more interesting. Years ago

Grace had given up trying to dry her hair straight and had resigned herself to the thick, unruly mass of curls she'd inherited from her father's side of the family.

A man and woman stepped out of the motel room across from hers, said good morning before getting in their car and driving away. Three giggling teenagers, all girls, wearing bathing suits and carrying beach towels, headed for the motel swimming pool at the end of the parking lot.

And still she waited.

It worried her that maybe he hadn't had a change of heart about going to Black River Canyon. That maybe he'd come here for her. Well, not exactly for *her,* but for sex. After the way she'd kissed him last night, there was no question she was attracted to him. Maybe he simply had an itch, and he thought she might scratch it for him.

The thought made her stomach twist. She hadn't meant to give him the impression that she jumped into bed with strange men, or even men she knew, for that matter. She most certainly did not.

But the way she'd kissed him, without even the tiniest protest, could easily have seemed like an invitation for something more intimate. She could hardly blame him if that was what he was thinking.

Still, she couldn't believe he'd drive a hundred miles for a roll in the hay. Rand Sloan wouldn't have to drive far to find a willing woman. He wouldn't have to drive at all, Grace reasoned. A man with Rand's smoking sensuality could pick up a phone and have a busload of women come directly to his door.

No, he wasn't here for sex, Grace decided. Something told her, if he was, he would have already said so.

It annoyed her that she almost felt disappointed.

But as the realization dawned why he had come, Grace felt her pulse begin to race with excitement. He *was* going to Black River Canyon with her. He *had* changed his mind.

Her first impulse was to throw her arms around him and hug him, but she quickly fought back the urge. That, she knew, would be a very bad idea. Even though Rand hadn't come on to her, the tension still simmered between them, and she didn't dare risk everything by encouraging anything personal between them. Going to Black River Canyon with Rand was going to be difficult enough. Any sort of intimacy between them—even an innocent hug—would only complicate their already delicate relationship.

She wasn't even going to ask why he'd changed his mind. If he examined the reason too closely, she was afraid he just might change it back again.

They finished the coffee in silence, then he handed the cup back to her.

"We should get going." He glanced at his wristwatch. "We need to make Dallas before night."

How like this man, Grace thought. He didn't say, "If you still want me for the job," or "I've given this some thought and decided to go with you." He just said, "We should get going."

Well, she certainly wasn't going to argue.

''We'll need to go into town for supplies,'' she said. ''I've got a—''

''Already done.'' He nodded toward the end of the parking lot to a dual-cab navy-blue pickup, complete with filled-to-occupancy double horse trailer.

And she thought this man couldn't still surprise her. She blinked at the truck, then looked back at him. ''You don't waste time, do you?''

''Not once I make a decision.'' He pushed away from her truck. ''You ready to go?''

His question hit her like a bucket of cold water. Was she? She'd been so sure of herself all along, so determined. Now that he'd actually agreed to go, she was terrified.

She sucked in a deep breath and nodded.

Five minutes later, after she called Tom and checked out of the motel, Rand followed her in his pickup while she returned her rental truck, then she climbed into his truck and they hit the road.

Late-morning sun shimmered off the unending ribbon of asphalt between San Antonio and Dallas. Rand was more than familiar with this long, lonely stretch of I-35. The dry, flat desert seemed to stretch forever, with cactus, tumbleweed and desert grass as far as a man could see. The landscape would change soon, though. They'd be coming into Austin before long, with all its cultural centers, skyscrapers and traffic.

But this was no sight-seeing expedition. Rand wanted to get to Dallas before it got dark, settle the horses and get a good night's sleep so they could be back on the road early tomorrow.

"Would you like me to take the wheel?" Grace offered. "It's only fair that we share the driving."

Rand pulled his attention from the highway and cast a sideways glance at Grace. She sat at an angle facing him, with one leg tucked neatly under her. She'd shucked her boots off when they'd stopped for fast food in San Marcos, then settled back and enjoyed a burger and fries. Her boots sat on the floor of the front seat. The seat belt cut across the front of her white blouse between her breasts and strapped across her lap.

Rand wouldn't mind being that seat belt right now.

He dragged his gaze back to the road and forced himself to concentrate on his driving instead of the woman beside him. But it wasn't long before an image popped into his head, one he'd been trying to push out of his mind all day—Grace in her pretty pink pajamas, her hair tumbling around her sleepy eyes.

The sight of her standing in her motel room doorway this morning, looking like she'd just slid out of bed, had caught him off-guard. Just like that, he'd wanted her. Wanted to step inside and close the door, slide his hands under that soft cotton and touch her everywhere.

He still wanted to, dammit.

Pulling his thoughts away from what he'd like to do with Miss Grace Sullivan, he asked, "You've driven a truck and trailer before?"

"Certainly," she said with a sniff. "Ranch House

Barbie came complete with a black pickup and horse trailer. Barbie and I went everywhere in that rig.''

He cocked his head and gave her his best that-wasn't-even-worth-a-smile look.

There was a glint of humor in her eyes as she brought her leg up on the seat and laced her hands around her knee. ''As a matter of fact, yes, I have, though usually short distances. I've transported several of the foundation's horses to their new adoptive owners.''

''How exactly does that work?'' he asked. ''The adoption process, I mean.''

''For the most part, the Internet.'' She leaned forward and searched the radio for a station that wasn't mostly static. When Travis Tritt came through the airwaves, singing about ''the best of intentions,'' she settled back. ''We also hold live auctions every two months at the Double S Ranch outside of Dallas where we corral and train the horses we round up or others that are brought to us.''

''Brought to you?''

''The horses that people don't want or can't afford to keep. Every horse has to be assessed and given a number on the adoptability scale.''

The adoptability scale. Rand's hands tightened on the steering wheel. He knew it was unreasonable, but it was impossible not to equate Grace's horses with what those bastards had done with him twenty-three years ago, and with Seth and Lizzie. They'd all been assessed and given a number that determined their worth to humankind. And while Rand understood that the system might work for horses, for human beings it was inherently wrong.

Rand knew that he'd been adopted out illegally; he knew it now, anyway. But he'd been told by the man and woman who had taken him away that night that his entire family had died, that he had been the only survivor.

Lies. All goddamned lies.

Why? His eyes narrowed as he stared at the long stretch of road in front of him. Why the hell would anyone do such a vicious, hateful thing—separate three young children after losing their parents and tell them their siblings were dead? How could anyone be that heartless, that cruel?

As if he didn't know. Money, of course. Money was the usual motivator for most men and women. Had there been some kind of black-market auction on his sister and brother? Rand wondered. They'd both been younger than him, certainly more adoptable. Especially little Lizzie. She would have been the child that anyone would want. Beautiful Lizzie, with her big blue eyes and shiny dark brown hair. She'd looked more like their mother than any of them, and the blend of Native American and Welsh had given her an exotic look.

The thought of his sister being sold to the highest bidder, like an unwanted horse, made him suddenly and violently ill.

He heard Grace calling him. He jerked his mind back to the moment, to his driving.

"Rand, what's wrong?" Grace asked, her voice heavy with concern.

"Nothing," he said through clenched teeth.

Breathe, he told himself. Slow, deep breaths.

"That's not true." She leaned toward him, her brow furrowed. "You're white as a ghost and you're sweating."

"I'm fine." He wiped at his brow with the sleeve of his shirt, willed his heart to settle back down to a normal pace. "Why don't you rest? We've got several more hours to go. Next time we stop, you can take over and I'll rest."

That way, there'd be no more talk. He could keep the demons away by concentrating on other things. He'd learned at an early age how to shut out the bad thoughts. The dark thoughts.

"Are you sure?" She watched him, a worried expression on her face.

"I could use some quiet," he said more firmly than he meant to, saw her pull away at his harsh words.

"All right."

She slid her leg off the seat and angled her back to him, rested her head on the back of the cushion. He could see the tension in her shoulders and back and had the strangest urge to touch her. To say he was sorry.

But he couldn't. Better to keep some distance, he thought. He'd already told her things about himself, about his parents dying and Mary and Edward adopting him, things he'd never told anyone else. Somehow, when he wasn't looking, she'd managed to get under his skin. Made him feel things he never had before. Things he didn't want to feel.

He wouldn't deny he wanted her in his bed, wanted his body to be inside hers. But on a physical level only. Not in his life, or in his heart.

That he simply couldn't let happen.

"Did you know that the best-preserved dinosaur tracks in Texas are close by here?" Grace asked while she and Rand studied the menu at Roger Bob's Rib House in Grandview. She'd read the trivia off the paper place mat on the table, but she doubted that Rand had noticed it. "The first sauropods tracks were discovered there."

"Is that a fact?"

"They also found tracks of the duckbilled dinosaurs," she went on.

He grunted, but did not respond, just kept staring at his menu and gave her no encouragement to continue. But then, he'd given her no encouragement to speak at all for the past five hours. He'd bluntly told her he wanted quiet while they'd been driving and though she'd admittedly been hurt by the cold shoulder he'd turned on her, she'd given him his space and his quiet.

But enough was enough, already. This lone wolf silent treatment of his was getting on her nerves. She was tired and hungry and she needed a conversation, dammit. With or without him.

"They were called theropods," she said with as much interest as she could muster. "Thirty feet long and twelve foot tall meat eaters."

"Well, let's hope they haven't ordered before us," Rand said evenly, and reached for the bottle of beer he'd ordered. "I wouldn't want to have to wrestle one of them for the last steak."

It wasn't much, but at least it was a start, Grace thought with relief. He'd been acting as if he'd had a sour drop stuck in his throat all day. And they said *women* were moody. Jeez.

They'd pulled off the Interstate less than an hour ago and found a small motel where Rand could care for the two horses he'd brought, a large-boned, dapple-gray gelding and a delicate pinto mare with the biggest eyes Grace had ever seen on a horse. He'd brought everything they'd need for the trip—canned food, drinking water and sleeping bags. He'd even brought her one of Mary's cowboy hats. It amazed her that he could be ready so quickly for an excursion like this, but at the same time, she had the distinct feeling that Rand was a man who was always ready to head out somewhere, always ready to move on.

Definitely not the type to stay in one place long, and definitely not the type to settle down.

She reached for the margarita she'd ordered and took a sip, then licked the salt from her lips. It had been a long day, and she needed something to unwind after spending eight hours cooped up in the cab of a truck with Rand. Every inch of that long, hard-muscled body radiated masculinity. He filled her senses. The earthy-male scent of his skin, the rugged profile of his handsome face, his large, callused hands on the steering wheel. And on those rare occasions when he had spoken, the deep, gravelly texture in his voice felt like the tip of a finger moving slowly up her spine.

If they hadn't stopped soon, she was afraid she might have thrown herself out of the truck. Or more likely, thrown herself on him.

"Rand Sloan!" A pretty blond waitress from another table hurried over. "You're a sight, cowboy. Where you been this time? Abilene or Del Rio?"

"El Paso," he said with a grin.

"El Paso! No wonder you been scarce as hen's teeth." The woman turned her big, blue eyes on Grace and stuck out a hand. "Hi. I'm Crystal. I'd wait for Rand to introduce us, but my Social Security check would probably get here first."

Considering the woman only looked about thirty, that would obviously be a long time, Grace thought. She smiled back at the waitress and shook her hand. "Grace Sullivan."

Grace couldn't help but notice that Crystal wore no wedding ring. And based on the way she'd greeted Rand, the two were very well acquainted.

And considering the amount of moving around he did, no doubt Rand Sloan was well acquainted with a lot of women in the state of Texas.

"Grace Sullivan." Crystal furrowed her brow, then her eyes widened. "I know who you are. You're with that horse adoption agency. I saw you on TV last week. That cute guy with dimples on Channel 8 news was interviewing you."

Normally one of the staff volunteers for Edgewater

Animal Management handled the PR, but no one had been available that day, and Grace had been forced to do the interview herself. She wasn't comfortable in front of a camera of any kind, but the spot on the news show had brought in a lot of donations, so she certainly wasn't complaining.

"Hey, Pinkie," Crystal called over her shoulder to the restaurant manager. "We got a celebrity here. Bring some free guacamole and chips out and make sure these drinks are on the house."

Grace felt her cheeks flame as several other people, restaurant workers and patrons alike, gathered around the table.

So much for having any kind of conversation or quiet meal with Rand, Grace thought. She could see the amusement in his eyes as he settled back in the booth and took a long pull on his beer.

Still, once she started talking about the foundation, explaining how the wild horses were rounded up and brought in, then adopted out, Grace forgot about Rand and concentrated on the growing crowd.

Rand, on the other hand, had not forgotten about Grace in the slightest.

He watched her, fascinated at the light that came into her eyes every time she talked about the foundation. There weren't many people who were truly passionate about their work, he knew. He'd been lucky. From the time he was five, he'd always known what he would do. He'd never even considered anything other than working with horses. He'd rather drink tar than put on a tie or a suit, or work indoors eight to five.

Handling and training horses came easy to him. People did not. Grace, on the other hand, was as easy with people as a duck swimming in a pond. Her face was animated as she rambled off statistics and talked about the horses and her organization; her skin literally glowed. When she laughed at something one of the local ranchers said, Rand felt something shift in his chest. When she took another sip of her margarita, then licked the salt from her lips, he felt something shift lower on his body.

Just that simple, innocent sweep of her tongue over her mouth made his blood heat up and his pulse pound.

When she did it again, his hand tightened on the bottle of beer in his hands.

Dammit, she was turning him on. Right here in front of a dozen people at least. He told himself to look away, to count backward by threes, but he couldn't get past eighty-eight before he was looking at her again, staring at that lush mouth still damp from her tongue.

He knew what she tasted like after she'd eaten chocolate cake; he suddenly wanted to know what she'd taste like now. A tangy mixture of sweet and sour, he was certain. And salt. Salt that would only make him thirsty for another taste. And another.

With tremendous effort, he dragged his gaze from her and glanced at the people who had gathered around their table. He'd been a regular at this restaurant when he'd worked a three-month stretch at the Rocking J in Waxahachie, a town five miles from here. That must have been three years ago now, he figured. Considering the number of ranches he'd worked for in the state, sometimes it was hard to remember what year he'd worked where. Sometimes he didn't know what year it was now, or where he was.

Or who he was.

That was the biggest question. Who the hell was he? Rand Blackhawk or Rand Sloan? He'd only been Rand Blackhawk for nine years. Could he go back?

Did he want to?

And Lizzie and Seth. Once they found out he was alive, would they want him as their brother again?

Could they ever forgive him?

He knew he'd never forgiven himself.

A burst of laughter dragged him from his thoughts. Dammit, he'd encouraged all these people to gather around Grace to give him a breather from making conversation. Now he simply wanted them gone.

Especially the guy in the white Stetson who'd been staring at Grace since he'd sauntered over from his own table across the aisle. Rand vaguely remembered him as a rancher who lived over in Brandon. Clay Johnson was his name, but as Rand recalled, everyone called him C.J. Last he knew, Clay was single with a couple of kids and looking. Apparently, based on the interest in the rancher's gaze as he watched Grace, the man was still looking.

As stupid as it was, Rand did not like it one little bit.

He'd never been the jealous type. He couldn't ever remember feeling possessive or annoyed if another man looked at a woman he was with.

Not that he was *with* Grace, he reminded himself. He might have kissed her, but that was before he'd agreed to work for her foundation. Their relationship was business now, and that's the way it needed to be. He needed to stay focused.

Oh, he was focused, all right, he thought sourly. On Grace's incredible mouth and long, curvy legs. Her tempting, full breasts that he'd love to—

He slammed his beer down on the table and drew a few looks from the group, including Grace.

"You think we might get our food sometime before Christmas?" Rand asked Pinkie, who had come out of the kitchen and was busy yakking with the rest of the party around the table. "Or do I have to go in the kitchen and get it myself?"

"Help yourself, Rand," Pinkie said, and pulled up a chair next to Grace. "Ribs are already cooked and sitting under the lamp."

That did it. Rand leaned forward and said in a low growl, "If I don't have my food in front of me in two minutes, *you're* gonna be under that lamp."

Pinkie sighed and straggled back to the kitchen, and seeing the mood Rand was in, the crowd scattered, as well, including C.J.

But not before he gave Grace his card and told her to call him if she could use his help with anything or if she were ever passing through.

Rand clenched his jaw so tight he thought he might crack a tooth.

"You all right?" Grace asked him with concern.

"I'm fine. Just fine," he snarled.

She raised an eyebrow, but didn't say anything, just settled back.

After a long moment of silence, she said, "Did you know that sauropods were plant-eating reptiles, more than sixty feet long, weighing thirty tons?"

"You don't say."

Rand suppressed a groan, listened to Grace while she spouted off dinosaur trivia and prayed this meal would be over soon.

Five

They arrived at the entrance to Black River Canyon late the next day, with barely enough time to set up camp before it got dark. While Rand took care of the horses, Grace gathered dried branches and bark from the surrounding red cedar and dogwood trees, piled everything into a small hole she'd dug beside a rock perfect for sitting on, then set a match to the leaves and twigs she'd layered underneath. It took almost an entire book of matches and several minutes, but when a flame finally sparked and the fire ignited, Grace gave a small yelp of joy.

She quickly bit her tongue and appeared nonchalant when Rand glanced over at her from where he was tying the horses to a nearby dogwood. He lifted a curious brow at her, then turned back to the horses.

Grace stuck her tongue out at him and made a face. She'd never admit it to Rand, but this was her first fire.

The truth be told, she'd only been camping two or three times in her entire life, but Rand didn't need to know that. She was certain he would never let her go down in the canyon with him if he was aware of her lack of experience with the rugged outdoors.

She knew what he thought of her, that she was a rich, bored city girl who had too much time and money on her hands. And maybe she was rich. She certainly didn't need to make excuses because her father owned and ran a large, successful steel-manufacturing company, or because she'd gone to the best schools and graduated with a business degree from UT. She certainly wasn't bored, and since she'd started the foundation, she definitely did not have too much time on her hands. She only wished there were more hours in a day.

She stared at her fire and smiled. Rand Sloan could just think whatever he wanted. What did it matter to her? She had to listen to her heart, and no one, especially some hard-nosed, temperamental cowboy, was going to stop her from doing what she needed to do.

High, jagged mountain walls surrounded them, a magnificent sculpture of carved red rock and sandstone. A slow-moving creek wound through a small stand of stunted oaks and the *ker-oke-ker-oke-ker-oke* of dozens of frogs filled the warm, smoke-scented evening air. Grace glanced around at the splendor of nature, at the wide, darkening sky and jutting cliffs and felt…full. She'd never been anywhere so completely remote before, and it was impossible not to feel the touch of something so much bigger than herself.

"Kinda gets to you, doesn't it?"

Her breath caught at the sound of Rand's husky voice close behind her. She'd been so engrossed in the scenery, she hadn't heard him come up.

She drew in a deep breath and nodded. "A person could forget everything here. The pile of bills to pay, the mountain of work, all the dozens of daily problems that fill a life."

"Like pink pumps or leather sandals?"

Grace heard the teasing tone in his voice and smiled. She didn't turn around, afraid if she did, the moment of magic they were sharing would be gone. After another full day's driving, with little more exchanged between them than a few grunts and an occasional token monosyllable from Rand, Grace was eager for conversation.

"Hey, a person can't help what they were born into," she said lightly. Then after a moment she asked, "What about you, Rand? What were you born into?"

He said nothing, and Grace worried that her question had stepped over that invisible line Rand drew around himself, the one that he never allowed anyone to cross.

A warm breeze drifted over them, carrying the scent of smoke and juniper brush. The sound of the crackling fire and the creek frogs faded into the distance, as if nature itself were waiting for an answer. The silence stretched, hovered between them.

When he finally spoke, she slowly released the breath she'd been holding.

''My father was Comanche,'' he said quietly. ''My mother from Wales. She was an exchange student her last year at the University of Texas. My dad was taking weekend classes in horse husbandry. They met at the cafeteria, so the story went. She said he was staring so hard at her, she went up to him and told him to either stop staring or buy her a cup of coffee. They were married two months later, bought a small horse ranch in the town where my father was raised and settled in.''

He paused, then went on. ''One of my father's brothers was furious that my father had turned his back on his heritage and married outside the reservation and his own people. There was a huge rift in the family. I remember when I was eight and one Saturday I went into town with my parents. We were at the hardware store. This man came in and stared at my father with more hatred in his eyes than I'd ever seen in all my life, then he turned around and walked out. My mother told me later that was my uncle.''

Though Grace had never been exposed personally to such prejudice, she wasn't so naive not to know it existed. It was just so sad, so incredibly sad. And the fact that it was family made it all the worse.

''Did you ever see him again?'' Grace asked.

''Once,'' Rand said, his voice tight. ''The night my parents were killed. He looked at me with that same hatred in his eyes, then turned his back on me, said something to a woman who was with him, then got in his car and drove away. The woman took me to her house, and two days later I was adopted by the Sloans. I never heard from or saw that uncle again."

Grace couldn't fathom turning her back on a child, let alone family. Her insides twisted with anger at a man she'd never even met. "And there was no other family to take you in? No place for you to go?"

"There was another uncle, but he had already died before my dad. My parents had led a fairly solitary life on the ranch."

She turned then and lifted her face to his, saw the pain in his eyes. "What about the funeral?" she asked. "Didn't you go to the funeral?"

"Far as I know, there was no funeral. Since my uncle was in charge, he had my father's body taken back to the reservation. I don't know about my mom." He looked down at her, frowned, then said softly, "Hey, what's this?"

He reached up and brushed a tear from her cheek with his thumb. She hadn't even realized she'd been crying. "I—I'm sorry for you, Rand. For your parents."

He cupped her chin in the palm of his hand, continued to lightly brush her cheek with his thumb. "It was a long time ago, Grace. Life goes on."

She closed her eyes, felt another tear slide down her cheek. "You were so little, you must have been so scared."

"For a while. The woman who took me to the motel with her was nice enough, and Mary Sloan was a good mother to me. I got through."

A child should do more than "get through," Grace

thought. She had such a wonderful, loving family and she knew that quite often she took them for granted, something she suddenly felt very ashamed of.

With a sigh she turned her cheek into Rand's hand. The rough texture of his callused palm against her skin, the scent of earth and horse and man, seeped into her senses.

He wasn't the only one who'd let his guard down, she knew. Perhaps it was the long, two days of driving, the fact that she was tired. Or maybe it was the spiritual and physical beauty of the canyon's entrance playing havoc with her mind. Probably it was a combination of both. But no man had ever made her pulse race with just a look, made her body respond to a simple touch. No man had ever looked into her eyes and made her feel that he knew exactly what she was thinking. Knew exactly what she wanted.

It terrified her that she wanted him. That he might know it.

There was so much more to this man than what he let people see. So much more than the lone, rough and rugged cowboy. He might have "got through," but not without scars.

His thumb, still lightly brushing her cheek, felt gentle and soothing. The hard edge around his dark eyes had softened, the tightness around the corners of his mouth had eased. What would happen, Grace wondered, if she pressed her lips to his hand, if she moved into the heat of his body and slid her arms over those strong shoulders?

She closed her eyes, and the innocent stroke of his

thumb on her face sent tiny vibrations of heat shimmering through her body. It seemed as if the air around them had turned heavy and thick, as if the ground underneath them was shifting and tilting. She felt the heavy, hollow thud of her heart in her chest, wondered if he could hear it, as well. Grace held her breath, felt the burn of Rand's gaze as he stared down at her.

It would be so easy to let go. Two people strongly attracted to each other, alone on a mountaintop, sharing a tender moment. It would be easy to give in to her feelings, she knew. What wouldn't be easy would be later, after that moment had passed and reality set in. That was the hard part. Or should she say the *heart* part. Because there was no doubt in Grace's mind that—for her—making love with Rand would involve much more than a joining of their bodies. Did she dare risk it, knowing that heartache was a certainty?

At the sound of the horses stomping their hooves, Rand dropped his hand, making the decision for her. Grace nearly protested, had to bite the inside of her mouth to keep from telling him that she wanted his touch on her. And more.

"I've got to finish with the horses," he said, his voice strained. "There's a duffel bag of canned goods in the trailer. Why don't you heat something up."

Grace might have laughed at his choice of words if her throat hadn't seized up on her. For the second time since she'd met the man, he turned and walked away from her, left her feeling as if she were on a tightrope, struggling to find her balance.

She watched him go, then let the breath shudder out

of her as she headed for the trailer on wobbly knees, to find something to "heat up."

Two hours later Rand sat on the rock beside the fire Grace had built and sipped at a cup of strong, black coffee.

This was the time of day he liked best. When the sun had just gone down and stars—millions of them—blinked in the huge night sky. He'd slept under those same stars dozens, if not hundreds of times, and each time he felt that same exhilaration.

That same peace.

It was probably the only place he'd ever found peace. Under these wide, open Texas skies. As far away from people and cars and paved roads as he could get. In a place like this, Rand could let himself relax. *A person could forget everything here,* Grace had said.

And a person could remember...

Rand Blackhawk, you stop fighting with your brother right now or I'll have your father hang both of you on a fence post and you'll eat your dinner there...

Hey, Rand, I found a garter snake, how 'bout you and me and Seth put it in Mom's bed and see how loud she screams...

How do you like your new baby sister, Rand? Her name is Elizabeth Marie. Isn't she the prettiest thing you ever saw...

He remembered the strong smell of lemon cleaner after his mother had washed the kitchen floor, the sound of his father's boots hitting the front porch when he'd take them off before coming in the house at night, his mother's stern look if her sons didn't keep their hands folded and eyes down when she said grace at the dinner table.

That was all he had left of his family. Memories. He'd taken nothing with him of his own that night, only the blood-stained clothes he'd been wearing. He'd been given new clothes, a new home, a new name. As if nothing before had ever existed.

That old, familiar ache spread across his chest. There were times he'd considered finding his uncle. Going to Wolf River and track the bastard down, confront him. Ask him why. But he never had. What good would it have done? Nothing would have changed. His parents would still be dead, and—so he'd thought—Seth and Lizzie.

But now things *had* changed.

Dramatically changed.

He'd have to deal with those changes when this job was done, but he'd made no decisions yet. Had no idea which road he would take or what direction. Since the night of the accident, Rand had sworn he'd never let anything frighten him again. And he hadn't.

Not until now. Now he was scared to death.

The fire popped, startling him out of his thoughts. He stared at the dancing flames, remembered Grace's excitement earlier when she'd finally managed to ignite that first flame. It was clear she'd never started a fire before, but if there was one thing to be said about

Miss Grace Sullivan, Rand thought with a smile, she was one determined lady.

One sexy, determined lady.

He'd always separated sex from business, never got intimately involved with any women he worked for or with. Women started to think they owned more of you than your time when things started to heat up. They started thinking picket fences, with little rug rat ranchers and ranchettes. He liked his life just the way it was. He went where he wanted, when he wanted, with whomever he wanted.

And that's how he intended to keep it.

Rand picked up a stone and tossed it into the fire, watched the sparks rain upward. Why was he having such a hard time keeping himself under control with Grace? He wasn't so stupid that he didn't know hormones were messing with his ability to stay focused and disciplined. He wanted the woman, he'd be a fool to deny that. But he'd also be a fool to act on his attraction to her. He'd been a lot of things over the years, been called just about every name in the book. But he'd never been a liar. Not to himself or any other man.

And never to a woman. He'd had a few short-lived relationships, but he'd been honest up-front. He wasn't the type to settle down. He never would be. He'd been on his own for too long to change now.

Grace was from that other world. That world where rose bushes grew behind picket fences, where bonnet-wearing babies cooed and home-cooked meals were on the table at six o'clock. The fact that she was rich only made it all the more complicated, but in the end it wouldn't be the money that would be the problem. It would be who she was, what she would need. What she deserved.

He'd already opened a door with her that he'd never opened with any other woman. Told her more than he'd ever told anyone about his past. It was time for him to close that door again.

That's exactly what he intended to do—keep his mind on his work and off pretty Miss Grace.

And then she walked out of the darkness like some kind of mountain nymph, a smile on her face, and his breath snagged in his throat.

She'd gone to wash up by the creek after dinner—dinner being a can of chili he'd brought and a bag of pull apart rolls Grace had picked up at a gas station convenience store earlier in the day while Rand pumped gas. She'd changed into a clean T-shirt, a fresh pair of jeans, and pulled her hair back into a ponytail. The smile on her face widened as she held out a paper bag.

''Dessert,'' she said, shaking the bag.

She sat cross-legged by the fire and dug into her cache.

He grinned and shook his head when she pulled out the contents—graham crackers, marshmallows and chocolate bars. He should have known it.

While she busied herself unwrapping and assembling everything, he watched her. Her fingers were long and slender, without rings. He wondered about that. Why she wasn't married, or at least engaged. She hadn't mentioned a boyfriend; he hadn't asked. He knew she'd made several phone calls to another volunteer named Tom. Her voice had softened every time he'd heard her speak to the man, and she'd turned away so Rand couldn't hear what she was saying. He'd say that was a strong indication that she might have something going on with the guy.

He was just making conversation, Rand told himself, when he asked, "So how long have you known Tom?"

She glanced up, clearly surprised by his question. "Tom?"

"Yeah, Tom. You know, one of the volunteers that's supposed to meet us here in the morning. That's his name, isn't it?"

"Yes, of course." Grace reached for a long, skinny stick she'd found earlier, stabbed a marshmallow and held it over the flames. "Tom will be here in the morning with Marty. They're both meeting us here."

She still hadn't answered his question, Rand noted. Was she being evasive? Well, fine, dammit. It wasn't as if she needed to explain anything to him, and it didn't really matter to him one way or the other, anyhow.

He gulped down the last of his coffee, waited for at least five seconds, then said, "So what's he think about you coming up here alone with me?"

"Who?" The marshmallow burst into flames. She yanked it out of the fire and blew on it.

Rand gritted his teeth. *"Tom."*

"He doesn't like it," she said, and slid the marshmallow onto a graham cracker already layered with chocolate.

"I wouldn't like it, either. If I were Tom, I mean."

Grace shrugged. "It's not his decision. It's mine. Here you go."

Rand took the graham-cracker-marshmallow-chocolate sandwich she offered him. He had no idea why, but she was starting to annoy him. "He must be a real understanding, patient kinda guy."

She laughed at that, and the sound rippled on the cool night air. "Understanding and patient would be the last words anyone would use to describe Tom," she said while she popped another marshmallow on the stick. "But I love him, anyway."

She loved him? Rand felt a muscle jump in his jaw. "If you *love* him, then what the hell are you doing gallivanting around Texas with me? How do you know I'm not some psycho socialite killer?"

"I am *not* a socialite," she said firmly, and stared at him as if he *were* psycho. "Rand, what's the matter with you?"

"If *I* had a girl, I sure as hell wouldn't let her take off for parts unknown, alone with some stranger." He knew he was out of line. But the thought of this guy she *loved* letting Grace run around and put herself in danger aggravated Rand to no end. "Sounds to me like Tom needs to find himself a little backbone."

Her lips pressed into a thin line. "Are you trying to make me mad?"

"Just making an observation." He took a bite of graham cracker. "It's your life, *Miss* Grace, but if I were Tom, I'd hog-tie you and lock you in the barn before I'd let you do something that just might get you killed.''

''First of all,'' she said tightly, ''you are *not* Tom. Tom is not a sexist, thick-headed, chest-thumping gorilla, which you *are.*''

''Now wait a—''

''Second of all,'' she went on, ''I checked you out carefully before I drove to your mother's house. I talked to at least six different men—and women—that you've worked for. If you're a psycho killer, then you've managed to fool every person who knows you, and you've hid the bodies very well.''

''I was just making an ex—''

''And *third,*'' she cut him off again, ''I'd like to see you just *try* and hog-tie and lock me in a barn, mister. I'm not as completely defenseless and fragile as you seem to think. I guarantee you that you'd come away singing soprano.''

Good God. He'd unleashed a tigress defending her cub. Obviously, she *was* in love with this Tom guy. But that realization only irritated him all the more. ''Look, just because I insulted your boyfriend doesn't mean that you—''

''Fourth,'' she snapped out, ''Tom is *not* my boyfriend. He's my brother.''

Oops. He sucked in a breath. ''Your brother?''

''My brother.''

Damn. He felt like an idiot. ''Well, why the hell didn't you say so before?''

''You were too busy criticizing and *making obser-*

vations about someone you don't even know to let me get a word in.''

''You never once mentioned that this guy, Tom, was your brother,'' Rand said. ''Why didn't you tell me before we set out?''

She yanked the marshmallow out of the fire, frowned at how black it was, then slapped it between two graham crackers, anyway. ''Because I knew you'd judge him, just like you judged me. You'd think because he wasn't born with a bridle in his hand and raised on a ranch, that he wouldn't know what he was doing.''

He stared at the graham cracker concoction she'd made him and shrugged. ''Maybe I would, maybe I wouldn't have. You still should have told me.''

''Why? What difference does it make to you who Tom is to me?''

Rand frowned. He didn't like that question. ''Did I say it made a difference? All I said was that if you were my girl, I wouldn't let you go.'' Dammit, that wasn't what he'd meant to say. ''Into the canyon, I mean.''

The cracker that Grace had lifted to her mouth stopped midair. She looked up at him, her gaze steady. ''I'm not your girl,'' she said evenly. ''Or anyone else's, either. In fact, I'm not a girl at all. I'm a twenty-five-year-old grown woman. Your concern touches me, but I'm doing just fine, thank you very much.''

''Fine.''

''Fine.''

They both turned their attention to the dessert Grace

had made. He watched those soft lips of hers nibble on a corner and felt his stomach clench.

As if he didn't know that she was a woman, for God's sake. Every thing about her was woman. The scent of her skin, the way she walked, the tilt of her pretty head. She sat here in front of him, those long, curvy legs crossed in front of her, with firelight shimmering in her auburn hair like fall leaves dancing in a breeze, and he sure as hell didn't need her to tell him that she was a woman.

I can keep my hands off her, he said to himself. I can.

She licked a spot of chocolate from the corner of her mouth, and he nearly fell off the rock he was sitting on.

"We should turn in," he said, looking at the two sleeping bags he'd already laid out beside the truck. "If Marty and Tom get here by eight, we'll need to be ready to move by nine."

"You go ahead," she said, still nibbling on her graham cracker. "I just need a few minutes."

He nodded. "I'm going to go wash up by the creek. If anything slithers your way, just give a call."

He saw the fear flash in her eyes, then she narrowed a look at him that said the only thing she saw slithering had two legs.

"I'll be fine."

He nodded and walked away. He glanced at Grace's sleeping bag, then at her stiff back.

...hey, Rand, let's throw a snake in Mom's bed and see how loud she screams...

Nah.

But the thought was enough to lighten his mood for the moment. He whistled all the way to the creek and back, then slipped into his sleeping bag while Grace still sat at the fire. He tipped his hat over his eyes, turned his back to her and fell instantly asleep.

Rain.

Icy cold, black rain. It pounded the windshield, the roof of the car. Rand felt his heart pound louder than the drum his grandfather had given him when he'd turned seven. ''I think you should pull over,'' Rand heard his mother say to his father.

''Soon as the road widens around this turn,'' he answered.

Beside Rand, Seth sat still as a stone, his eyes wide with fear. On his other side, Lizzie sat in her car seat, sleeping. Rand's mother turned and looked at her sons. ''We'll be fine,'' she said with a smile. ''Don't be afraid.''

Lightning.

Blinding white explosion. It hit directly in front of the car.

His mother's scream, and they went down into that black hole that Rand thought for sure was hell. The crunch of metal…Lizzie's cry…

Then nothing…

Absolute silence…

Heart racing, pulse-pounding, Rand sat. Darkness surrounded him. Where the hell am I? He felt a moment of panic, told himself to breathe slowly…

A dream, he told himself. Just a dream. Again.

"Rand?"

He snapped his head in the direction of the woman's voice.

Grace. It was Grace.

Relief poured through him. He nearly pulled her into his arms, had to clench his hands into fists so he wouldn't.

He stared at her for a long moment, waited for her features to clear in the dim light of the dying fire. She sat on her knees beside him, her eyes filled with concern. Shadows danced on her face and in her tousled hair.

"Are you all right?" she asked softly.

He still couldn't speak. The edges of the dream were still with him, hovering. He nodded, sucked in a breath.

She laid a hand on his arm and leaned closer. "You were dreaming."

"Go back to sleep," he finally managed, his voice hoarse and dry. "It was nothing."

"You're shaking," she said, and moved her hand up and down his arm.

Rand felt the heat of her skin seep through the light flannel shirt he wore. She smelled like sleep and fresh air and Grace.

He wanted her so badly he ached.

"Grace, for God's sake, just go back to sleep," he said roughly.

She shook her head.

Damn stubborn woman.

She moved in closer to him, kept rubbing his arm.

Rand ground his back teeth and closed his eyes. ''Dammit, will you stop that.''

He grabbed her by the shoulders and held her still. Her eyes widened for a fraction of a second, then her gaze dropped to his mouth.

His heart slammed in his chest, only this time it had nothing to do with the dream and everything to do with Grace.

On an oath he dragged her to him and covered her mouth with his.

Six

He'd kissed her before, so it wasn't the fierce, sudden rush of heat that shocked Grace. He'd held her in his arms before, so it wasn't the exhilaration of his muscled body pressed against hers that shocked her, either.

What shocked Grace was the *intensity* of the pleasure racing through her blood. The savage, hungry desire that had sprung to life at the first touch of his mouth on hers.

She'd never experienced such need before, would never have believed such depth of feeling even existed. Still wasn't certain that *she* wasn't the one having the dream instead of Rand.

But if this were a dream, she thought dimly, she didn't want to ever wake up.

His mouth moved over hers, deepened the kiss as his arms circled her shoulders and pulled her close.

On the edge of a cliff, only a fool does handstands.

The thought jumped into her dazed mind. Good heavens, she was not only doing handstands, she was doing cartwheels and flips. It would be a long fall over the edge of this cliff she stood on with Rand. A long, hard dive into certain heartache.

She was beyond caring. Beyond rational thought. She wanted this man like she'd never wanted before, and she was too far gone to stop what was happening. She didn't want to stop it.

He whispered her name between kisses, and the rough, husky sound of his voice made her pulse race even faster. His mouth, hot and demanding, slanted against hers again and again, the stubble of his beard sending sparks of electricity coursing through her veins. Grace opened to him, met the hungry thrust of his tongue with her own. She recognized the subtle taste of mint and the darker, more exotic taste of Rand himself. The masculine, earthy scent of his skin invaded her senses, heightened them, made her more aware of him and of the night surrounding them, the crescent moon overhead, the dim glow of the dying fire, the distant howl of a coyote.

The sensations all swirled upward in her mind and her body; they spun faster, and faster still. She wound her arms tightly around his shoulders and held on, let herself be drawn upward and carried away with the tornado of feelings he evoked in her.

From the first moment she'd seen him working in

the barn, she'd known it would be like this. Not in her head, she couldn't have imagined anything this intense. But in her heart, in her soul, she had known. She'd tried to tell herself she could manage her feelings for Rand, the physical and the professional. But she'd been wrong. So very wrong.

She'd seen something, felt something, the instant their eyes had met that first time. Something that went beyond understanding or explanation, and certainly beyond common sense.

His hands tightened on her shoulders, then he lifted his mouth from hers and looked down at her.

"Grace," he said raggedly, "if you want to stop this, you need to say so right now."

He offered no tender words, no soft whispers of endearment. What he did offer, Grace understood, was honesty. No lies, no promises. Nothing beyond this moment.

Was that enough for her? she asked herself. Could she make love with this man, knowing that this was all there was?

She looked into his dark eyes, saw an edge she'd never seen before, the same edge she heard in his voice. It was raw and primal, filled with need.

He frightened her.

He thrilled her.

Grace had waited all her life for this. For him.

She might be a fool, but her heart and her body simply wouldn't listen to her head. Lifting her hand to his cheek, she lightly traced the firm line of his mouth with her thumb. She felt a muscle jump in his jaw at her touch, watched those dark eyes of his narrow with passion.

"Make love to me, Rand," she whispered. "Please make love to me."

She was certain she saw relief in his eyes, then he caught her to him again and crushed his mouth to hers. She felt and tasted his desperation in the long, searing kiss he gave her.

Then he let her go.

Confused, she watched as he shoved the sleeping bag off him and rose.

"What—"

He bent down and kissed her again, a quick, heated brush of lips. "I'll be right back."

It took a moment for Grace to comprehend what Rand was doing, but when he walked to the cab of his truck and rifled through the glove box, she understood. She felt her cheeks warm with embarrassment. She'd been so completely lost in his touch, she hadn't thought about protection.

He kept his gaze on her as he walked back toward her. The pale light of the dying flames cast shadows over the hard, sharp angles of his face. His eyes narrowed with need.

She shivered.

When he knelt in front of her, she rose on her knees to face him. Slowly, hesitantly, Grace lifted her hand and laid it on his chest. She felt the wild beating of his heart under her palm and the heat of his skin through the light flannel shirt he wore.

Like an electrical current, desire vibrated from his

body to hers, then back again. When he covered her hand with his own, the voltage only increased.

"Grace," he said her name with velvet softness, "I don't want to hurt you. You need to be sure about this."

Didn't he know they were way beyond that? That the hurt was inevitable, and still she wanted him, wanted this, more than her next breath?

That wasn't something she could tell him.

But she could show him.

Grace laid her other hand on Rand's broad chest and splayed her fingers, moved upward, over his collarbone, felt the tension radiate from his body. She moved her fingers up his neck, then cupped his face in both of her hands. Her gaze held steady with his.

"Kiss me," she whispered.

His eyes narrowed with need, then he lowered his head to hers and captured her mouth. His kiss was gentle, yet insistent. His tongue lightly brushed over her bottom lip, then parted her lips and moved inside. She opened to him, welcomed him, and together they moved in a steady, primitive rhythm as old as time.

The kiss deepened. Grace felt her pulse pounding in her head, in her veins. She'd never felt so alive, so sensitive to every touch, every sound, every smell.

He pulled her tightly into his arms, held her close to the solid heat of his body. She shuddered. When his head dipped lower and blazed a hot trail of kisses down to the rise of her breast, she moaned.

"I want to see you," he said huskily, then slipped his hands under her T-shirt.

Grace sucked in a breath at the first glorious touch of his fingers on her bare skin. His rough, callused palms skimmed up the sides of her waist. Ripples of heat coursed through her body. She wanted those hands everywhere. Wanted her hands on him.

Breathing hard, she inched away from him, held his gaze with her own as she reached for the hem of her T-shirt and pulled it over her head.

She tossed it aside, and was naked from the waist up.

Rand's gaze dropped to her breasts; his eyes turned black as the night surrounding them, burned hot as the embers in the fire.

His hands slid upward.

She trembled at his touch. When his hands cupped her, she drew in a quick breath. Grace felt her skin tighten, felt the hot rush of blood pumping through her veins. Certain she would fall if she didn't hold on to him, she slid her hands up his forearms, felt the light sprinkling of coarse hair and the ripple of hard muscles.

"You're so damn beautiful," he murmured.

His thumbs brushed over her hardened nipples. Arrows of white-hot pleasure shot directly from her breasts to the juncture of her thighs. On a soft moan she closed her eyes and dropped her head back.

Nothing had ever felt so right to her before, so completely natural, and because of that, Grace felt no embarrassment or awkwardness. She simply let herself *feel,* and the sensations engulfed her. She wouldn't have believed it possible to experience pleasure this intense.

And then he bent and took her in his mouth.

Grace gasped at the feel of his tongue on her beaded nipple and the rasp of his beard on her soft flesh. She gripped his head in her hands and raked her fingers through his thick hair, struggled to drag oxygen into her lungs. Her heart slammed in her chest as he moved his hot, wet tongue in a sensual, rhythmic movement, then lightly scraped her sensitive skin with his teeth. Shock waves rippled through her, an electrifying, glorious raging river of need.

She hadn't had time to draw in a breath before he moved to her other breast and once again hungrily pulled her into his mouth. Pleasure bordered on pain. A steady, insistent throb pulsed between her legs. If it were possible to die from feelings this intense, then she was certain she would.

"Your clothes," she gasped between breaths and moved her hands restlessly over his shoulders. "I want to touch you."

He pulled away from her, his breathing ragged and heavy, then tore at the buttons on his shirt and yanked it off his shoulders. The firelight danced over his bronze skin and rippling muscles. He was the most magnificent man she'd ever seen: his shoulders were broad, his chest wide, his belly flat and hard. It was a warrior's body, marked with the scars of his battles. She laid her palms on his chest and splayed her hands, then lightly traced his flat, tiny nipples with the tips of her index fingers. He jumped at her touch, and she felt his shudder vibrate from his body to hers.

He caught her in his arms and his mouth swooped down on hers again, pulling her in, tasting, taking. Destroying. He demanded more, and she gave him everything. Bare flesh to bare flesh. She wrapped her arms around his shoulders and held on. Even as they fell backward on the thick sleeping bags, his mouth never left hers. Rand's long, muscled body pressed down on her, and she reveled in the feel of his weight on top of her. She wanted him closer still, and she hugged him tightly to her, moving her hips against him in a slow, sensual motion.

From deep in Rand's throat, Grace heard a rough sound, half growl, half moan. He grasped her hips with his large hands and held her still, then blazed hot kisses over her jaw and down her neck. Grace sucked in breath after breath with every nip of his teeth and sweep of his moist tongue. It seemed as if she'd been turned inside out, exposing every raw nerve to his touch. He moved down, over her shoulders, the swell of her breast, pausing to once again take each aching nipple into his mouth before moving lower still. His beard scraped at the soft skin on her belly; his tongue tasted hungrily.

He opened the snap of her jeans, and she heard the hiss of her zipper as the snug denim parted. While his mouth explored the valley of her hip, he eased the garment down inch by agonizing inch. When he nipped at the soft cotton-encased mound of her womanhood, Grace heard the sound of her moan. Gasping, her hands reached for his head, and she clawed her fingers into his hair.

It felt like a lifetime before her legs were finally free of her jeans. He linked two fingers under the elastic band of her underwear and in one swift, smooth move, they were gone, as well.

She lay naked under him, physically and emotionally, but it felt as natural to her as breathing.

He rose over her, his eyes intent and glinting with passion. He kept that dark gaze on her when he reached for the button on his jeans. Her chest rose and fell as she watched him slide open the zipper, then push denim down, moving away only momentarily to shrug the garment off. He stared down at her, the look in his eyes primal and possessive.

''Rand,'' she said his name on a ragged whisper and held her hand out to him. Flames from the fire reflected in his narrowed eyes.

Rand reached out and took her hand, linked his fingers with hers. He'd never seen anything more beautiful than Grace. Her hair fanned around her flushed face; sparks of red and gold danced in the wavy mass of shiny strands. Her lips were swollen from his kisses and softly parted, her eyes deep, deep green, glazed with desire. Her breasts were full, the tight buds of her velvet-soft nipples rosy. Her skin was like porcelain, a sharp contrast against his own.

He felt a need he'd never experienced with such intensity before, and the realization startled him. He quite simply had to have her or die.

His name was still on her lips as she pulled him

toward her. He took her other hand and linked their fingers, then lifted her arms over her head as he moved between her legs. He entered her slowly, watched her draw in a quick breath at the initial invasion, then closed her eyes on a soft moan.

"Open your eyes, Grace," he murmured. "Look at me."

Her eyes drifted open again, and she met his gaze. He brought his mouth to hers, brushed her lips with his, then began to move. When she sucked in another sharp breath and tightened her body, he stopped abruptly and lifted his head to frown down at her.

"What…?"

"Don't stop, Rand," she gasped. "Please don't stop."

With her legs wrapped tightly around him, Rand was finding it difficult to think. "Grace, I…wait…"

She shook her head, then surged upward, taking him deep inside her. She was so tight, so ready for him, and it was impossible not to move. Sweat beaded on his forehead; her fingers tightened in his. His entire body throbbed with need, a fierce pounding in his veins and his head that demanded release.

He moved faster, sheathed himself deeper still and she took him in, met him thrust for thrust, moan for moan. He felt her shudder under him, felt her inner muscles tighten and clench as she arched upward sharply on a cry. The shudder rolled from her body to his, intensified until he could hold back no longer. With a guttural cry, he drove into her. The climax shattered wildly out of control, as wild and primitive as the night surrounding them.

Her name on his lips, he gathered her in his arms and waited for his world to steady again.

Grace felt as if she were drifting, as if the breeze had swept her up and carried her away. Her head rested on Rand's chest and she heard the still, heavy beating of his heart, felt his chest rise and fall with each breath. She'd never known such contentment, such bliss, and to think that she'd found it here, in Rand's arms, on the edge of a steep canyon, seemed fitting.

"Grace." He said her name softly as he tucked a wayward strand of hair behind her ear. "Why didn't you tell me?"

She rose on one elbow and glanced down at him. He looked much too serious, she thought. "Tell you what?" she teased.

He frowned at her. "You know what."

She lifted a shoulder, then traced circles on his chest with the tip of her finger. "You mean that I was… inexperienced?"

"I made an assumption that you'd probably done this before."

"Well, that's what you get for making assumptions," she said, and nestled back into his arms. "And I'm in too good a mood to argue about it. If you have a problem with it, then it's your problem."

He rolled her onto her back, his eyes narrowed as he gazed down at her. "Did I say I had a problem?

I'm just a little...surprised. You're twenty-five years old.''

She rolled her eyes. ''You're making me sound like an old maid, for heaven's sake. Just because I waited a little longer than most women, doesn't mean I qualify for senior citizenship.''

He stroked a hand over her shoulder and down her arm, his expression thoughtful. ''So why have you waited?''

She shrugged, feeling a little foolish now. ''It just never seemed quite right to me before, that's all. That might sound old-fashioned to most people, but I wanted my first time to be special.'' She reached up and touched his cheek. ''You made it special for me. Thank you.''

Grace felt Rand stiffen, saw the mixture of uncertainty and hesitation in his eyes. She understood that what had just happened between them might not be special to Rand, that he'd been with lots of women before.

The thought felt like a knife in her heart, but she refused to let him see the hurt, and she also refused to let him spoil the moment.

She dropped her hand from his face and frowned at him. ''Rand Sloan, whatever you're thinking, stop it right now. I'm a big girl. I'm not asking or expecting anything from you, so stop looking as if I just locked the barn door behind you.''

He stared at her for a long moment, then sat and raked his hands through his hair. Certain that he was already turning away from her, Grace felt her throat thicken. She wouldn't cry, dammit. She wouldn't.

"Blackhawk."

She looked at his stiff back, not certain she'd heard him right. "What?"

"My real name is Rand Jedidiah Blackhawk," he said quietly. "My parents were Jonathan and Norah Blackhawk of Wolf River."

Blackhawk. The name was so familiar to Grace, but she couldn't place it at the moment. She pulled the sleeping bag up to cover her bare torso, then sat slowly.

"My brother was Seth Ezekiel Blackhawk," Rand went on. "My sister, Elizabeth Marie."

He had a sister and brother? She felt the tension radiate from him but said nothing, just waited for him to continue.

"I'd been told that they died in the accident that killed my parents." He stared into the darkness, his gaze fixed but unseeing. "Seth was seven, Lizzie was barely three."

"Are you saying they weren't killed?" she asked incredulously.

"Three days ago I received a letter from a lawyer in Wolf River telling me that they're alive," he said tightly. "Twenty-three years and all this time they've been alive, living somewhere else, like I was, with other families."

Grace understood now why Rand's mother had asked her if she were a lawyer and told her that she'd better give Rand a wide berth if she were. She could only imagine his shock at learning the sister and brother he'd thought dead were alive. ''Who would do such a horrible thing?'' she asked. ''And why?''

''My uncle was filled with hate,'' Rand said. ''I saw it in his eyes that night when he handed me over to that woman. He wouldn't have wanted his brother's half-breed children near one penny of whatever small estate my parents had, and he certainly wouldn't have raised us himself. So he farmed us out, sold us to the highest bidders and made sure each of us thought the other was dead so he'd never have to deal with any of us again.''

Appalled, Grace sucked in a slow breath and tried to absorb what Rand was telling her. Three small children had not only lost their parents, they'd been separated and told the others were dead, too. The injustice of it all sickened her.

''When I find my uncle,'' Rand said coldly, ''I'll kill him with my bare hands.''

Rand turned and looked at her, and Grace shivered under the murderous glint in his eyes. It frightened her that he just might follow through on his threat. While she couldn't blame him, Grace knew that no good would come of it. He stiffened when she laid her cheek on his shoulder, but he did not pull away.

''Your nightmare,'' she said softly. ''Was that what you were dreaming about? The accident and your family?''

He nodded. ''We were all coming back from town and got caught in a summer storm. A lightning bolt struck the road in front of our car and my dad lost control. We rolled over and went into a ravine.'' He closed his eyes. ''My memory is spotty after that. I was cold and wet. There was blood on my shirt and pants. The sheriff pulled me out of the car, and my uncle was there with a woman. He never even spoke to me, just told the woman to take me away.''

''Who was she?''

''I don't know. But she was the one who told me my family had died, that I had to go live somewhere else.'' He stared at the red-glowing embers of the fire. ''I wanted to die, too. I was angry that I hadn't.''

Rand's voice was so distant that Grace realized he truly wasn't speaking to her. The muscles across his back and shoulders were tight, his jaw clenched. She pictured him as a frightened child, alone and hurt, without his family, and she had a sudden, fierce desire to seek retribution on that horrible, horrible man who'd done this to him.

She steadied her own emotions, and gently stroked his arm and back. Slowly she felt him relax and lean into her. ''What are you going to do now?''

He shook his head and sighed deeply. ''It's been twenty-three years, Grace. Seth and Lizzie may not even remember me. They have their own lives now and I wouldn't want to disrupt that. I don't see where I can fit in.''

That had always been his problem, Grace realized. That after losing his family, he'd simply never fit in anywhere. He'd drifted from town to town, ranch to ranch. Never stayed in one place. Survivor's guilt, she'd heard it called. He'd never felt that he deserved a real home, or even love, for himself.

"But what if they do remember you?" she asked him. "What if all these years they've missed you, dreamed about you, too? You were their big brother, Rand. How could they forget you? Once they know you're not dead, they'll want you to be in their lives."

"Maybe." He sucked in a long breath and let it out. "Maybe not. Hey, what's this?"

He glanced down at her, at the tears that spilled from her eyes onto his arm. He turned and wiped at her eyes with his thumb. "Tears for me, Grace?" he said solemnly.

She shook her head. "For a nine-year-old boy who lost his family."

He smiled softly and gathered her in his arms. "Thank you," he said softly, tipped her face to his and kissed her tears, then brought his mouth to hers.

Grace tasted the salt of her own tears on his lips, the sadness, then, as the kiss deepened, the growing desire. When he pulled her into his lap, she slid her arms around his shoulders, wanting to give him so much more than her body. But as his kiss deepened, her body deceived her. The urgency to be close with him again, to make love with him and hold him inside her body, coiled tightly inside her. They were both breathing hard, their hearts beating wildly as he laid her back on the sleeping bag.

"Grace," he said on a ragged whisper, "I don't want to hurt you."

Did he mean physically, she wondered, or emotionally? Either way, it was too late, she knew. She answered him by dragging his mouth back to hers and arching her body upward to meet his. When he slid inside her, she nearly sobbed with the joy of the moment. There was no pain, only pleasure. Sweet pleasure that grew stronger with every thrust, with every kiss, with every whisper. For this moment he was hers, as she was his.

She held on to him; he held on to her, both of them driving toward that blissful end with a desperation that staggered the senses. When it came, they tumbled breathlessly, hopelessly, over that steep, jagged cliff together.

Grace woke early the next morning to the song of birds, a cool breeze on her face and the smell of a campfire. She was alone in her sleeping bag, but she could hear Rand close by, talking to the horses. She'd pulled her clothes on before they'd finally gone to sleep a few hours ago, and she snuggled in the warmth of her covers for a moment, letting herself enjoy the memories of the night before. A smile slowly spread on her face.

Rand had been a wonderful, exciting lover, and Grace knew she would always cherish the night they'd spent together. She'd be a fool to think that their relationship would ever be more, but she'd already been a fool once, so she couldn't stop herself from hoping. Wisdom and intellect seemed to take a back seat to matters of the heart.

She rose on one elbow, then stretched. She was

sore, but not overly so considering the night she'd had. She glanced at Rand, watched him lead the horses back from the creek where he'd taken them to drink the cool water. He wore a chambray shirt today and a pair of faded jeans. His dark hair was mussed, his beard more than a stubble. She could picture him with a star on his shirt, a Western marshall, on the hunt for escaped bank robbers.

The wave of desire that shivered up her spine startled her. Already she wanted him again, wanted her hands and mouth on him and his on her. When he glanced at her, leveled those black eyes on her, her breath caught.

Her heart pounded furiously when he dropped the horses' reins and started toward her. She felt her blood race through her veins.

The crackle of the two-way radio inside his truck stopped him. She saw the regret when he changed direction and walked toward his truck to answer the call. He kept his back to her as he talked, and when he turned to face her, his expression was somber.

''What is it?'' she asked, already afraid of his answer.

''There's a storm on the way,'' he said, keeping his gaze on her. ''We have to go back.''

Seven

"Go back?" Grace repeated. "You mean leave?"

"That was your brother on the radio," Rand said evenly. "He and Marty are stuck in a thunderstorm at the base camp."

The rosy blush that had been on Grace's cheeks only a moment ago vanished. Her face turned pale as she stared at him. "Are they all right?"

"Everyone's fine, but the storm has them penned in for now. They have no idea when they can get out."

She was already out of her sleeping bag and tugging her boots on. "So we'll go without them."

"Like hell we will. Even if we find those horses, and that's a big *if,* darlin', you haven't got the strength or the experience to bring them in."

"I'm stronger than I look, Rand," she said, pulling

her jeans down over her boots. ''And I'm a fast learner.''

She stood and closed the top button on her jeans, but not before he caught a flash of her flat belly. His heart slammed in his chest, remembering how he'd slid his hand over and kissed that smooth, soft skin. He was hard instantly, wanting her again with the same urgency as the night before. She was a fast learner, all right, he thought as he recalled how she'd felt in his arms and the way she'd brought him to a fever pitch.

It took a will of iron to force his thoughts back to their conversation. ''Dammit, Grace, this isn't a Sunday ride in the park. This could be dangerous. You could get hurt, and if that storm does come in while we're in the canyon, you could even get dead.''

''We can do this, Rand. I know we can.'' She reached for the blue denim shirt she'd laid out on a rock the night before, shook it vigorously, then pulled it on over the T-shirt she wore. ''There's not a cloud in the sky. We don't know the storm will come this way.''

''We don't know that it won't.''

''I swear to you,'' she pleaded, ''if it starts to look risky, I'll turn back without an argument.''

He shook his head. ''We're not going.''

She moved toward him, those long legs of hers encased in snug denim, and his pulse jumped. He clenched his jaw, refusing to let her see how strongly she affected him. How badly he wanted her. No woman had ever had that kind of power over him before, and he was determined no woman ever would.

"I mean it, Grace." He folded his arms, steeled himself against the look of determination in her eyes.

"We've come all this way, Rand," she said softly, and slid her arms around his neck. "We can't turn back now."

Damn her, anyway, Rand thought irritably. She wasn't playing fair at all, here. "Grace—"

She silenced him with her lips, and he felt the last of his resistance melt away.

Dammit, dammit, dammit.

"Please, Rand," she begged him. "I promise I'll do exactly what you say. We can't just leave them there to die."

She was right, dammit. In spite of everything he'd said, he knew she was right. He couldn't leave them. Not without trying.

On an oath, he took her arms and pulled them away from him. He felt a muscle jump in his temple as he stared down at her. "Be ready in two minutes or I'll leave without you. If we haven't found them within an hour, or at the first sign of bad weather, we're coming back. If you argue, I swear I'll dress you up like a Thanksgiving turkey and you'll ride back on your stomach instead of your butt. You got that?"

She nodded, a smile on her lips, but an edge of fear in her eyes, too. Good, he thought. He needed her to be afraid. It would keep her alert and focused and ready to move quickly.

He released her and turned on his heel. While he

saddled the horses, he alternately cursed her and himself. He was a damn fool, he knew, but he couldn't refuse her. She could have asked him to take down a charging bull with his bare hands and he would have done it.

She'd gotten to him, he realized with dread, and resolved that by the time this day had ended, he'd be back in control and Miss Grace Sullivan would be on her way home where she belonged.

It took them thirty minutes to get down the steep path to the bottom of the canyon. Dawn crept over the high cliffs in ribbons of pink and blue while a pair of hawks circled overhead and desert cottontails darted in and out of low-lying shrubs of mesquite and cottonwood. Rand searched the sky for any sign of clouds moving in. So far, so good, he thought with a sigh of relief.

Now if only they could find the horses that smoothly.

They hadn't spoken on the ride down, and he was thankful for that. He was still reeling, still unbalanced from the night they'd spent together, and he had no idea what to say to her. *Thanks Grace for letting me be your first, and see you around.*

How could he have known she was a virgin? She was a grown woman, for crying out loud. It had never entered his mind that she hadn't been with a man before.

But she hadn't. And though he wasn't proud of it, there was a part of him, that primitive male arrogance, that was actually glad he was her first. She'd said he'd made it special for her, but she'd made it special for him, too. Special in a way it never had been before.

He'd always been careful when it came to sex. Not only for health reasons, but he'd never wanted to worry that he'd left a woman pregnant behind him. The thought of a child—his child—without a father, was unthinkable for him. If he had gotten a woman pregnant, he would have had to settle down, get married, even. He never would have let any kid of his grow up without a father or be raised by another man. There were too many Edward Sloans in the world, and the thought of his own son or daughter living under that kind of harsh control made his chest tighten.

And what kind of father would he make, anyway? Rand thought. What did he know about babies and cuddling and bottles? Babies terrified him. They were so tiny and helpless. He'd rather bare-hand a rattlesnake than change a diaper.

He glanced over his shoulder at Grace when they were on level ground again. She rode maybe fifteen feet behind him on the pinto mare and had managed to keep up with him all the way down the trail, even when it had narrowed and grown steeper. She did know how to ride; he'd give her that much. She looked comfortable in the saddle, completely at ease. The white Stetson she wore was a sharp contrast to her dark, auburn curls. Her cheeks were flushed, her deep-green eyes alert and sparkling.

Something slammed in Rand's chest. Lust, most definitely. But something more than that. Something that made him sweat.

There was no future for them, he was certain of that. But that didn't stop him from wanting her.

He tore his gaze from her, then reined his own horse in and studied the canyon while he waited for Grace to catch up with him. The canyon narrowed behind them, so the horses had to be ahead. The map he'd studied had shown the canyon to be only five miles long, with fairly steep cliffs on either side. The trail they'd just come down was the only way in and only way out. With enough time and a couple of extra hands, it wouldn't be that difficult to box the herd in and capture them. But they didn't have time or extra hands. Though he didn't see any clouds, he'd already felt a subtle change in the air, and he suspected the weather would not stay as nice as it was at the moment for very long.

"We're downwind," he told Grace when she reined in beside him. "That will be to our advantage if we find them."

"*When* we find them," Grace said with conviction. "I know they're here. I can feel it."

Rand nodded. "They at least were here. I've seen some signs of grazing and some dried horse manure."

"So what are we waiting for?" she said impatiently. "Let's go find them."

"Grace." He put a hand out to steady her horse, wondered why he was having a difficult time saying what needed to be said. "You need to understand. Between lack of food and water and predators, they might be dead.''

Her lips pressed into a thin line, and she shook her head. ''I refuse to believe that.''

''You have to prepare yourself,'' he said. ''You have to be ready to accept whatever you find. And you have to accept what I'll need to do if they're sick or not strong enough to make the trip back out.''

Grace glanced at the rifle he carried in a saddle holster. She sucked in a sharp breath and nodded. ''I know.''

They rode in silence for the next few minutes, with Grace close behind. Rand knew she was thinking about what he'd said. She was worried about what he might have to do if the animals were too far gone to help. That part of his work had always been the most difficult, and he didn't want to dwell on the possibility right now. But the canyon appeared dry, and unless the horses had found water somewhere, they would most certainly be a lost cause.

The world is full of lost causes, Mary had said to him in the barn the night before he'd left. *Those are the ones who need help the most.*

His mother had known that he needed to take this trip not just for the horses, but for himself. He wasn't so dense as to not see the correlation between his own life and a lost band of horses, but he was a grown man. He had control of his life, he understood where he came from and accepted it. He'd never felt sorry for himself and he sure as hell didn't want anyone else to, either.

And what about Seth and Lizzie? What had their lives been like? Where did they live? Were they married, with a dozen kids between them? Did he have nieces and nephews? The thought made his chest ache, made him wonder things he'd hadn't truly allowed himself to wonder since he'd received that letter. And from that wonder came something else he'd never allowed himself before. Something he'd shut off the night that woman had taken him away.

Hope.

Grace had told him that his sister and brother could never forget him, not completely. Could she be right? Even if they thought he'd been killed, as he'd thought they had, did they still have memories? Would they welcome him into their lives? Or would they blame him? He was the oldest, he should have taken care of them, protected them.

The sudden splatter of raindrops on his hands brought Rand to a halt. Dammit! He'd been so lost in thought that he hadn't noticed how quickly the dark clouds were rolling in. He jerked his gaze to the sky and swore again, then turned to look at Grace.

"We're going to have to turn back."

The misery on her face said it all, but true to her promise to him, she didn't argue. Her shoulders slumped in defeat, and she nodded weakly.

He turned his mount, then froze at the sound of a high-pitched whinny. Grace's horse whinnied in response and stamped its front hooves. Eyes wide, Grace snapped her gaze to his.

"Rand," she said his name on a breathless whisper.

"I'll be a son of a gun," he muttered out loud. They'd found them! They'd actually found them!

The rain started to come down harder, and the large drops bounced off the dry canyon floor and began to puddle in the dusty dirt.

Grace looked at him, her expression anxious. She'd do whatever he said, Rand knew, even if it meant turning around now. He heard another distant whinny, and gauged the sound to be just around an outcropping of rocks no more than an hundred yards away.

And then he knew that there really was no decision. That probably there never really had been. Come hell or high water—and he hoped like hell there'd be no high water—he knew he couldn't turn back now.

"We won't have much time," he said roughly, keeping his voice low. "We're going to need the element of surprise. If the lead horse catches wind of us, he'll take off for the deep end of the canyon and we won't stand a chance."

"What should I do?" she asked.

"Stay here and be ready." He reached for the rope looped around the back of his saddle. "If I can get close enough to a mare and get hold of her, our only chance is that the stallion will follow, and the rest of the horses will follow him. It's a long shot, but it's all we've got."

He leaned over and reached for Grace, surprising her and himself both when he kissed her hard and quick. "For luck," he said, then took off at a gallop.

Stunned, Grace watched him ride off, her heart racing as he disappeared around the rocks. She pressed her fingertips to her mouth, her lips still tingling from his kiss. She barely noticed the rain coming down steadily now.

He'd gone after them, she thought, and the excitement and the thrill of it shimmered over her now wet skin. After all he'd said, he'd still gone after them. He wasn't as hard-hearted or as practical or logical as he wanted everyone to believe. She'd seen the look in his eyes when they'd turned to start back. He'd been just as upset as she had been, just as devastated.

She still wasn't completely clear what his plan was, but he'd told her to be ready, whatever that meant, so she kept her gaze on the spot where he'd vanished, listening, waiting.

But for what?

The rain fell harder still, and the distant sound of thunder had her horse prancing nervously under her. Grace kept a firm hold on the reins and her knees tight against her horse. The minutes ticked by, though it felt like hours. Rain poured off the brim of her hat, and she watched nervously as the water in the canyon began to rise and flow in the direction Rand had ridden.

Rand, she said a silent prayer that he was all right. *Hurry, please, hurry.*

The thought of anything happening to him terrified her. She told herself not to worry, that he was experienced and he knew what he was doing. But anything could go wrong, one wrong move and he could be lying with a broken leg or unconscious. The image made the knots in her stomach tighten.

He was all right, she told herself. He *had* to be.

She loved him.

God help her, but she knew that without a doubt now. She cursed herself for not telling him how she felt. He didn't have to love her back. She just wanted him to know, needed him to know.

She gripped the reins so tightly in her hand that the leather cut into her palm. "Where *are* you, dammit?" she said out loud.

As if he'd heard her, Rand came barreling around the rocks, splashing through the slowly rising river of water. A small bay mare, eyes wide with fear and confusion, galloped beside him. A rope around her neck kept her tied to Rand's saddle.

And chasing behind them, his proud neck held high and his mane waving, came the stallion. The animal was larger than most wild stallions, his coat pitch-black. He looked thin, but not emaciated. If it were possible to read an expression in the animal's eyes, Grace would have said that he was furious at the mare's capture and he intended to get her back. Behind the stallion came three more mares...and two foals!

Rand said nothing, just waved at Grace, signaled for her to get behind the small herd and follow. She swung her horse around and dropped in back of the animals. So intent was the herd on keeping up with the stallion, they didn't seem to notice her.

The group moved as one, the natural instinct of horses to stay with the herd keeping them all close together. The sky had opened up by the time Rand reached the spot where they'd come down. The ground was turning to mud, and Grace knew they'd have to get up the trail quickly, or they all would be in danger of slipping over the edges where it narrowed.

Rand went up first, dragging the mare he'd roped behind him. The horse balked when she first hit the trail, then followed. The stallion whinnied loudly and reared, then he followed, too, as did the other mares. It took every ounce of strength Grace had to keep her horse heading upward after the other horses. Her leg muscles screamed in protest, but she knew she had to hold tight in the saddle or she'd fall off for certain. Ahead of her, she watched Rand labor not only with his own horse, but the mare he pulled behind him. All of the horses pawed and struggled to get a footing in the mud and to keep together.

It was slow and dangerous, but they climbed upward, inch by inch, foot by foot, horse and humans together. The smell of wet leather and horse assailed Grace's senses; rain slapped at her face and poured off her hat. Eyes wide with determination, his nostrils flared, the stallion kept up with Rand's horse and the mare that had been stolen from him.

One of the foals slipped at the narrowest passage and its hind leg went out from under him. Grace bit her lip to keep from screaming as she watched the terrified animal slide over the edge, then catch its footing at the last minute and scramble back up with its mother.

Thunder rumbled, and the storm pounded at them. Grace made the mistake of glancing back down into the canyon, and the sight of the rising, rushing water nearly paralyzed her. Ten minutes more down there and they all would have been swept away. Clenching her jaw, she turned her attention back to the trail and what lay ahead, not behind her.

The rain blinded her, but her hat kept the worst of it off her face. She lost track of time, concentrating solely on staying in the saddle and keeping her horse on the disappearing trail. Rocks and mud slid down the trail and more than once the horse she rode stumbled, then gained her footing again.

When at last they hit the top, Grace slumped in her saddle, so exhausted she wasn't certain she could ride another foot. She let her horse take over now and carry her back to their camp. The herd followed the captured mare and Grace could do little more than watch as Rand quickly slid off his horse and roped the stallion, then tied him to a tree.

She knew better than to call to Rand or try to catch his attention. The wild horses weren't used to humans and their presence would frighten them. She closed her eyes and said a silent prayer of thanks, holding tightly to her saddle horn for fear she might fall off her mount. She barely noticed the rain anymore, she was already as wet as she could get, so it hardly mattered.

Her eyes flew open at Rand's touch on her leg. He reached up for her, and she slid off her horse into his arms.

"You did it, you did it," she said over and over and threw her arms around his shoulders.

Smiling, he lifted her up off the ground and hugged her tightly. "*We* did it," he said.

"Oh, Rand." Grace began to laugh. "I love you."

He stilled at her words, and she knew instantly that she'd made a mistake. But she didn't care. She *did* love him, and he was just going to have to deal with it. Or not. Whichever, the decision was his.

But she was too happy right now to let her slip of the tongue ruin this wonderful moment. She hugged him tightly, and the exhaustion she'd felt only a moment ago vanished. She felt like Gene Kelly at the moment—she could dance and sing in the rain and splash in the puddles and not give two hoots that she was soaked to the bone.

Rand carried her to the truck, then opened the door and set her inside. "I've got to get our saddles off our horses," he said, and closed the door behind her.

Grace felt useless, and she would have gone to help him, but she knew that he could do it faster than she could, anyway, and she would only be in the way. She felt an ache in her chest at the thought, knowing that was probably how he viewed her intrusion into his life, as someone who would only be in his way.

So here she was, head over heels for the first time in her life, and after today she would probably never see him again. Her throat thickened and her eyes burned, but she blinked back her tears. She was celebrating today, dammit! She would deal with the hurt and the pain later. Right now she was determined to enjoy the success of rounding up the strays.

Rand jumped into the truck a minute later, whipped his hat off and tossed it onto the back seat of the dual cab. Grace sat huddled against the door, her hair dripping, her clothes drenched.

''Are they all right?'' she asked, and realized her teeth were chattering.

He nodded, then looked at her in dismay. ''God, you're soaking wet.''

She had no idea why she found that funny. Perhaps it was his astute observation of the obvious, or the fact that he was just as wet as she was, but she started laughing. He looked at her as if she'd gone crazy. A smile tugged at the corner of his mouth and spread, and then he was laughing, too.

It was the first time she'd really heard him laugh, and the sound made her forget everything—that they could have died or been seriously hurt, that she'd told him she loved him. Even that she was wet and cold and her legs ached.

Still laughing, he reached for her, pulled her into his arms and hugged her. ''Ah, Grace,'' he said, shaking his head. ''What in the world am I going to do with you?''

She felt the heat rise from his skin, the hard play of muscle under her body as he held her close. A smile touched her lips as she lifted her face to his.

''Anything you want, Rand Blackhawk Sloan,'' she murmured. ''Everything you want.''

Eight

Grace's words sucked the air from Rand's lungs and sent heat flooding through his body. In that instant he wanted her with an intensity that shocked him. It didn't matter that they were both soaking wet, or that they'd both come close to dying down in that canyon. If anything, those things heightened his awareness of her and the need clawing at his insides.

He crushed his mouth to hers, tasted the rain and the passion on her. She parted her lips for him; he dived inside. Eagerly, she met the insistent rhythm of his tongue with demands of her own. Never before had the hunger been so keen or so sharp. It staggered his senses, blinded him from everything and everyone else but the woman in his arms.

He had to have her. Had to make her his, even if it were only for this moment.

With his mouth still on hers, he scooted to the center of the truck and pulled her on top of him. She pulled back from him, her chest rising and falling rapidly. Her T-shirt and bra were plastered to her skin, and he could clearly see the outline of her breasts and hard nipples through the wet fabric. His heart hammered in his chest.

On an oath, he clamped his mouth to her breast through the fabric while he kneaded the soft flesh with his hands. She raked her hands through his wet hair and dragged him closer to her.

"Take this off," he demanded and tugged her T-shirt upward. She peeled the wet garment off, and once again he brought his mouth to her breast, sucking the nipple through the thin cotton of her bra. Gasping, she let her head fall forward.

He found the front clasp of her bra and unsnapped it. Her skin was cool and damp, and he could smell and taste the storm still on her. He took her breasts in his hands and his mouth, wanting desperately to kiss and touch her everywhere at once. She writhed over him, moving her body against him until he thought he might go mad with the need pulsing white-hot through his veins.

He unsnapped the button of her jeans and pulled the zipper down. She brought her mouth to his and kissed him while he slid his hands between denim and skin and eased the wet jeans down her hips. They struggled together to free her feet of boots and her legs from her pants, but then she was naked on top of him, reaching for him. He lifted his hips as she tugged his jeans free, but they made it no farther than his knees before she straddled him and he slid inside her.

They both groaned.

And then she began to move, and he groaned again.

He gripped her bottom in his hands and guided her as she moved up and down, each time driving him deeper inside her. Her nails bit into his shoulders, holding tightly as she drove them both closer to their destination.

Rain pounded the roof and thunder rumbled close by. But the real storm, the true storm, was here, inside this truck, in their need for each other.

"Rand," she gasped his name and her nails went deeper into his shoulders.

The climax hit them both with all the energy and intensity of a lightning bolt. She threw her head back and cried out. He groaned, a rough, hoarse sound that came from deep in his chest.

She sank forward, dragging in deep breaths while the tremors still rippled through her. His heart pounding furiously, his breathing ragged, he held her close and waited for the storm to ease.

Grace listened to the pattering of the rain on the roof of the truck. The sound soothed her, and with Rand's arms around her, their bodies still joined, she'd never known such contentment before.

"You all right?" He pressed a kiss to her temple and slid his hand up her back.

"Mmmm," was the best she could manage. She felt his smile against her cheek.

"I take it that means yes."

"Oh, yeah. And you?"

"Oh, yeah."

Now it was her turn to smile. She snuggled against him, enjoyed the gentle slide of his hand up and down her back. "We really need to get your clothes off."

He chuckled. "Damn, woman, give me a few minutes, will you?"

Grace felt her cheeks warm at his implication. "That's not what I meant. Your clothes are soaked and I just thought you'd want to change into something dry."

"I'll get out of them, all right," he murmured and smiled at her. "You're so damn cute when you blush."

She blushed deeper and ducked her head so he wouldn't see. He pulled her against him and tucked a long strand of wet hair behind her ear.

"Grace," he said, his tone suddenly somber.

Not now, she thought, closing her eyes. *Please not now.* If he gave her the lone-wolf, I'm not the type of guy to settle down speech, she didn't think she could stand it.

"You did good down there in the canyon."

She looked up at him, saw the sincerity in his eyes.

"Between the horses coming at you," he said, "the rising water, and getting back up that trail in the storm, it would have been easy to panic. You didn't."

"I was too scared to panic," she said truthfully.

''You're an amazing woman, Miss Grace Sullivan.''

His compliment warmed her, though she truly didn't see where she'd done anything out of the ordinary.

''I was with you, Rand.'' She touched his lips with her fingertips. ''I knew you could do it. That's why I wasn't afraid.''

His eyes narrowed and darkened as he met her steady gaze, then he reached for her, dragged her mouth to his for a long, searing kiss that sent ribbons of heat curling all the way to her toes.

''How many minutes did you say you needed?'' she asked in a ragged whisper.

He answered her question by sliding his hands to her hips and moving under her. Breathlessly she followed his lead, then took over until they were both clutching each other, both gasping, both shuddering.

I love you, Rand Blackhawk.

But this time she didn't say it out loud. She kept it to herself, praying, hoping that somewhere in his life and in his heart, he might find even the tiniest place for her.

They slept in the cab of the truck, in each other's arms, until the storm passed over. When they finally woke, Grace pulled on a fresh T-shirt and jeans and struggled to do something with her hair while Rand shucked his damp jeans and shirt and dragged on dry clothes. The sun was already starting to peek through the clouds when they stepped from the truck. The scent of damp earth filled the clean, fresh air.

The stallion reared at the sight of humans; his mares and foals whinnied and huddled nervously close by. Sidestepping and without making eye contact, Rand slowly approached the horses and tossed them an armful of alfalfa before he retreated again. They scattered and snorted, but the scent of the alfalfa won the animals over and soon they were all pushing and nipping at each other to gain access to the treat. When Rand carefully tossed two flakes of hay down, they scattered a second time, but eased back to the food once again and ate hungrily.

From a rock on the other side of the camp, Grace sat and watched the animals eat. The mares were roans, the foals, one bay and one chestnut. They were all thin, with patches of hair missing on their dull coats. The mares and foals had bite marks on them, the method by which the stallion kept his herd in line.

Wild mustangs were not the most attractive horses, but to Grace they were beautiful.

Rand came up behind her and slipped his arms around her. He smelled like hay and horses and man. She breathed in the scent of him and smiled.

''They would have died down there,'' she said quietly.

''They didn't,'' he said simply.

''Because of you.''

''Not me, Grace. In case you've forgotten, I turned you down when you first asked me to come here with you. You were the one who never gave up, the one who really saved them, not me.''

She didn't agree with him, but she didn't want to

argue, either. It was too perfect a day, too perfect a moment. She laid her head back against his chest and simply let herself enjoy their success.

''He's pretty bossy,'' Grace said, watching the stallion move between his mares and foals while he ate, nipping at them and pawing the ground.

''He just wants to make sure they stay close,'' Rand said. ''He's stronger and smarter than they are. It's his job to protect them.''

''Spoken like a true man,'' Grace teased. In the horse world, though, what Rand said was true. The lead stallion was the strongest and usually the smartest animal in his herd. Grace, however, did not believe that axiom transposed into the human world. She watched the stallion shake his mane and bare his teeth at one of the mares and was quite thankful that she was not a horse.

''The foals are pretty little things, aren't they?'' Grace said absently. ''We shouldn't have any trouble adopting them out.''

She felt him stiffen. Furrowing her brow, she angled her head and glanced up at him. He stared at the horses, his lips hard and thin, the expression on his face solemn.

''Rand?''

He was silent for a moment, then sighed heavily. ''I was just thinking about Lizzie. That it would have been the same for her. She was so beautiful. I can only imagine there would have been a long line of people wanting to adopt her.''

It made sense that he would see the correlation between the wild horses and his siblings. And now, since he knew his sister and brother were alive, that he would wonder and worry what had happened to them.

''Who did she look like?'' Grace asked, turning her gaze back to the horses.

''She had my mother's blue eyes,'' Rand said softly. ''Her hair was lighter back then, not as dark as mine or Seth's. My mother used to say our sister had hair the same color as our Grandma Cordelia in Wales. Not a true black, but a deep, dark, sable brown. Even as a baby, Lizzie had an exotic look about her.''

''She'll remember you, Rand,'' Grace said with resolution. ''Maybe not as clearly as Seth will, but when she meets you, she'll know in her heart who you are.''

When she meets you. Grace's words made Rand's heart slam in his chest. He hadn't made that decision yet, hadn't even allowed himself to think about it since he'd told Grace last night about Lizzie and Seth.

Grace stroked his forearm with the tips of her fingers, and Rand felt himself relax under her touch. She'd cried for him last night, he remembered. In his adult life, no woman had ever done that for him before. There'd been tears of anger, tears of frustration and tears intended to manipulate, but never tears for *him.*

And she'd told him that she loved him.

He knew that she'd said the words in a moment of exhilaration after they'd brought the horses up from the canyon. Had she truly meant them?

Of course she hadn't. She'd just been caught up in the moment, he told himself. Even if she did think she loved him, he didn't believe she really did, or that she could. They were too different, from two different worlds. In time those differences would overshadow any feelings she thought she might have for him.

He'd be leaving soon, going back to San Antonio, and she'd be going back to Dallas. But he knew he'd never forget her.

He pulled her to her feet, and she went into his arms. Tenderly he kissed her. "Thank you."

"For what?" she said, her voice soft and breathless.

"I wouldn't have come here if it hadn't been for you. Mary was right when she told me I needed to do some thinking. A place like this puts things in perspective."

"Does that mean you've made a decision about going to Wolf River?"

He nodded. "I'll stop there on my way back to San Antonio. At least listen to what that lawyer has to say."

"Oh, Rand." There were tears in her eyes when she cupped his face in her hands and kissed him. "I'm so glad."

But there was sadness in her eyes, as well. He saw it, knew she understood they would each be going their own way soon.

The realization at how close that time was hit him like a two-by-four. He dragged her against him and kissed her hard. She clung to him, kissing him back with the same desperation.

There was only one place for this kiss to lead, but

he didn't back away from it. He welcomed it, deepening the kiss as he lifted her and started for the truck.

They'd gone no more than a few feet when the sound of an engine reverberated off the rocks and shook the ground. Rand froze, then swore and set Grace back on the ground. The horses lifted their heads and pranced nervously.

The truck came into view a moment later. A large black truck pulling an eight-horse trailer.

With a groan Grace dropped her head onto Rand's shoulder.

"They're here," she said weakly, then stepped away from Rand and watched as her brother and another man drove up, then parked their rig and got out of the truck.

"I've never heard anything like it," Tom said, shaking his head in amazement after Grace told him how they'd brought the horses in by themselves. "I wanna hear this again, only this time slow down and give details."

Arms folded, Rand leaned back against his truck and listened while Grace told her brother and Marty, in detail, what had happened down in the canyon. Her elaborate and animated description of the mare's capture embarrassed Rand a little, but the light in her eyes and the smile on her lips was worth hearing her account, not once, but twice.

Tom appeared to be a likable enough guy. He was tall, probably around six-two. He had Grace's green eyes, but his hair was dark-brown instead of auburn, and he had a face that most women would take notice of. Rand had sensed some hostility in him when they'd first shaken hands, but that was certainly understandable. Rand knew that if Grace were his sister, and she'd just spent the past few days gallivanting around Texas with a stranger, he'd be hostile, too. No doubt that if Tom knew what else had gone on, he'd be a hell of a lot more than hostile.

There were some things that brothers were better off not knowing.

Rand rolled his eyes when Grace embellished her description of him as he'd come galloping around the rocks with the mare beside him and the stallion on his heels. The only things she left out were his eyes shooting lightning bolts and his mouth spitting flames.

With the extra hands and equipment the men had brought, all the mustangs were now secured and the chance of any of them escaping was very slim. Tom and Marty had also brought enchiladas and rice from the base camp, plus homemade guacamole with chips and a six-pack of beer in a cooler. Marty, an older man with a bushy white mustache, had been busy laying the food out on a folding table beside the fire while Grace related the accounts of the day—minus what had happened in the truck, of course.

"Once we take these strays back and assess their condition," Tom said when they'd all filled a plate, "we can move the herd to an adoption ranch in Amarillo. Shouldn't take more than four or five days in all, then we can head for home." Tom swiveled a look at his sister. ''After this trip, Gracie, that must sound pretty good to you.''

Grace glanced up at her brother. She knew him well enough—the tilt of his head, the tone of his voice, the subtle narrowing of his eyes—to read between the lines of his casual comment. Tom wasn't dumb, and he wasn't blind. He knew her just as well as she knew him, and he obviously sensed something was going on between her and Rand.

He wanted a reaction, she knew, but he wasn't going to get one. She was a big girl, after all. The last thing she needed was her brother sticking his nose where it didn't belong. Whatever had happened between her and Rand was her business.

''A long, hot shower would be lovely,'' she said with a smile, and bit into a chip loaded with spicy guacamole. ''I just might feel human again.''

''How 'bout you, Rand?'' Tom turned his attention to Rand. ''You coming to the base camp with us?''

Grace felt her heart jump, then sink when Rand shook his head. Of course he wouldn't come along. He was going on to Wolf River. Which was exactly what he needed to do, she knew. She'd been a fool to hope for even a second that he wouldn't be on his way as soon as possible. And she was selfish to wish for anything different.

Well, so she *was* selfish, dammit. She attacked another chip. So she did want another few days with him. Another few hours, even. Everything between them had happened so quickly, and it wasn't enough. She wanted more.

Much more.

He didn't look at her, and she was glad. After the day they'd had, and as tired and strung out as she felt, she might have started with the tears again. That was all she needed to complete her humiliation. To start crying like a baby not just in front of Rand, but her brother and Marty, as well.

"Grace?"

"What?" She jerked her gaze up at the sound of Tom's voice. She'd been so lost in thought, she hadn't been following the conversation.

"The fund-raiser? You know, the one Mom and Dad are giving for the foundation?"

"What about it?"

He lifted a brow. One of those, so-there-*is*-something-going-on brow lifts. Terrific, she thought with a silent groan, and knew that the ride back to Abilene with her brother was going to be a long one.

"Mom thought you'd want to know that Bradshaw declined the invitation."

"I was hoping that the third time would be a charm," Grace said with a sigh.

She'd known that the man wouldn't come. Bradshaw was one of the wealthiest ranchers in Dallas, and the most mysterious. Rumors ran rampant about the man, from the story that he was disfigured and never went out in public, to the more romantic, though melancholy, version that he'd never left his house after his wife had died years earlier. His age was between twenty-five and seventy-two, based on who was telling the most current version of the man's life. Grace had invited Bradshaw to the last two fund-raisers, but he'd always declined, then sent an eye-popping donation the next day. But if she could get him to actually come to the event in person, she knew that the attendance would double, as would the donations.

She shook her head and shrugged. "I'll try him again next time."

"Dylan Bradshaw?" Rand asked casually. "From the Rocking B?"

Everyone went still and looked at Rand. Even Marty, who'd seen and done most things, Grace knew, looked surprised.

"You know Dylan Bradshaw?" Grace asked.

Rand took a bite of rice. "I know him."

"You mean you've met him," Tom said.

"It's pretty hard to know someone if you haven't met them," Rand pointed out, then added, "We worked together a while back."

Not, *I* worked for *him,* Grace noted. But *we* worked together. She wondered what "a while back" meant, but it would be rude and pushy to start grilling Rand with questions about his past and how he knew Dylan Bradshaw.

"Yeah, well, maybe you could give him a call and get him to change his mind," Tom said with a grin, clearly joking.

"Maybe."

Tom's grin faded. Even Marty had stopped chewing. Grace knew that her brother didn't really believe that Rand could just pick up a phone and get the man to go to the fund-raiser. Still, there was a mixture of awe and disbelief in both Tom's and Marty's eyes that she found extremely humorous.

But whether Rand could or couldn't get Dylan Bradshaw to attend the fund-raiser didn't matter to her. At the moment she wasn't concerned with or interested in any man other than Rand.

If Tom and Marty hadn't driven up when they had this afternoon, he would have made love to her again. It would have been their last time, she thought, knowing that there was no way they could be together now that her brother and Marty had joined them. Her body still tingled from earlier, and she could still feel the texture of his rough hands as they'd slid over her skin and the hard press of his mouth on hers. She was thankful they'd at least had those few hours alone.

She watched him talk with Tom and Marty, saw his expression change from serious, as they discussed the upcoming auction, to smiling, when Marty piped up and told a joke about a cowpoke and an amorous heifer.

All of this should have been perfect, the sun setting in ribbons of reds and golds, the soft nickering from the horses, the ripple of the nearby creek. Talking and laughing around a crackling fire. It *would* be perfect, except for the tiny little detail that the man she loved would be gone from her life by morning.

Damn you, Rand.

Needing to keep busy, Grace offered to clean up after they finished eating. While Rand and Tom settled the horses down for the night, Marty prepared the trailer to haul the mustangs out the next morning.

The frogs were out in full chorus when Grace went down to the creek with a metal bucket. The air had cooled, and a light breeze carried the scent of damp earth and mesquite. She bent to fill her bucket with water when a huge bullfrog jumped in front of her and croaked.

Grace frowned at the frog. "If you think I'm going to kiss you, just forget it, buster. I'm a little sour on fairy tales and happy endings at the moment."

She scooped up water, then stood. When she turned, she bumped into Rand. He reached out a hand to steady her when she stumbled.

"Talking to frogs now?" he asked her with a smile.

She felt her cheeks warm and hoped he hadn't heard what she'd said. But even if he had, she decided, what difference did it make? He already knew how she felt, and like the saying went, once the horse was gone, it didn't do much good to lock the barn door.

"I thought you were with the horses."

"I was. I'm here now."

She rolled her eyes. "I can see that."

There was a long, awkward moment between them. It was obvious that he wanted to say something but didn't quite know how.

With a sigh Grace ran a hand through her hair. "Just say it, Rand. Whatever it is, just say it."

"I'm leaving."

Her chest tightened, as did her grip on the bucket handle. It was one thing to know he was leaving, and another to hear him actually say it. "You mean now?"

''If I get out of here before dark, I can make Wolf River by two or three in the morning.''

''Okay.'' Only it wasn't. It wasn't okay at all.

''Tom and Marty can handle the mustangs without me,'' he said evenly.

''I'll put some coffee on,'' she said, surprised that her voice sounded so steady. ''You're going to need a thermos if you're driving half the night.''

She started past him, but he put his hand on her arm. ''Grace—''

She shook her head. ''Don't say it, Rand. I'll be all right.''

His hand tightened on her arm, and for a moment she thought that he might pull her to him and kiss her. But the sound of her brother's voice had him stepping away.

They walked back to the camp together, and while he loaded his horses she made strong coffee, hoping the extra caffeine would help him stay alert on the long drive across the Texas flatlands at night.

Tom and Marty shook his hand when he was all packed up and ready to go. When he turned to her, she offered her hand to him, as well, though she desperately wanted to throw herself in his arms and give him a kiss goodbye that he'd never forget. Their eyes met for a second, then he let go of her hand and turned away.

She watched numbly as he got in his truck, then started the engine and slowly drove away, his tires crunching over the rocks and debris.

And then he stopped.

He jerked open the door of his truck and walked back toward her. His dark gaze was on her every step of the way.

Her heart pounding, she watched as he marched up to her and stopped.

"Come with me."

That was all he said. *Come with me.*

She knew he just meant to Wolf River. For now that would have to be enough.

She nodded.

Grace saw the relief in Rand's eyes before he turned again and walked back to his truck to wait for her.

"Grace." Tom frowned. "What the hell is going on?"

"I'll be home in a couple of days," she said, releasing the breath she'd been holding. "I'll explain everything then."

Grace kissed her brother and said goodbye to Marty, then grabbed her bag and walked to Rand's truck. She got in and put her seat belt on, then stared straight ahead.

Neither one of them spoke.

In twenty minutes they were back on the highway and headed for Wolf River.

Nine

Rand woke early to the feel of cool, cotton sheets and warm, bare skin. Grace lay beside him in the hotel bed, her long, lovely back turned to him. He rose on one elbow and let his gaze travel slowly over her, the rise of her hip under the sheet, the sexy curve of her shoulder, her delicate, swan-like neck. All those glorious auburn curls fanning across the pillow she currently had her face half-buried in.

He picked one of those curls up and rubbed it between his fingers. Her hair was soft and had a silky quality to it. Without thinking, he brushed the curl against his lips, then frowned at the silly sentiment of it.

Damn, but he was getting soft. Since when did he think about swans and silk?

Must have been about the same time he'd completely lost his sanity and asked Grace to come to Wolf River with him.

He still wasn't certain how it had happened. One minute he'd been driving away, the next thing he knew he was saying, "Come with me."

If he'd have given it time, thought it through, he never would have brought her with him. She had her own life to go back to, her own world. A world he didn't belong in any more than she belonged in his. He had told himself that what had happened between them on the mountain and in the canyon would stay there, that he could leave all that, and her, behind him when it was time to go.

He'd been wrong.

Some strange, unexplainable force had brought them together. He simply accepted that without question, took each day as it came. He had feelings for Grace, as unfamiliar as they were confusing, but he had no delusions about tomorrow or the day after that. He might have lived his life on the edge, but when women were involved, he'd always been careful. And he'd always been honest. No pretense of marriage or babies or happily ever after.

He'd be careful now, too, he told himself. So maybe Grace had gotten to him. Maybe he was a little soft on her. So what? It didn't mean a damn thing. He'd wanted her to come to Wolf River with him. Wanted her to be with him for a little while longer.

He watched her stretch, then roll to her back. The

sheet slipped down, hovered precariously at the peak of her breasts.

Blood shot straight from his brain downward as he stared at her. His pulse pounded in his head.

He couldn't get enough of her. Couldn't stop himself from wanting her. When the time came, he would stop, he told himself. He would leave.

But the time was definitely not now.

She stretched again, and the sheet slipped lower. The pounding in his head increased, as did the ache in his loins. Her skin was pale and smooth, her rosy-tipped breasts full and firm.

He closed his eyes on a silent oath, swore that he'd let her sleep. Lord knew she needed it.

They'd rolled into town sometime around two in the morning and checked into a large, classy-looking hotel called the Four Winds that also had the facilities to care for his horses. Rand himself would have settled for The Silver Saddle Inn they'd passed on the outside of town, but Grace deserved something better than a hard mattress and lumpy pillow in a run-down motel. Grace deserved fluffy down pillows, smooth, satin sheets and room service.

And so many other things that he couldn't give her, too, he thought.

Her eyes fluttered open, and she turned her emerald-green gaze on him. Something shifted in his chest, swelled, then settled back down again.

Smiling, she pulled the sheet up and rolled to her side to face him. "Good morning."

"Mornin'." He grinned at her, tugged the sheet back down again. "I was enjoying the view."

Her cheeks turned pink, and she rolled to her stomach. "Show's over, mister."

"Hardly." He skimmed his hand down the curve of her back, taking the sheet with him as he exposed bare skin. When his hand cupped her bottom and squeezed, he watched her eyes darken with desire.

"You're insatiable," she murmured breathlessly.

"Complaining?" His hand slid lower, over the backs of her thighs. "Just tell me to stop, and I will."

She closed her eyes and stretched as if she were a cat. "I'll get back to you on that."

Chuckling, he explored the soft curves of her long legs and firm, round bottom. She moaned when he skimmed his fingertips along the sensitive skin of her inner thighs, sucked in a breath when he slipped one finger inside the moist heat of her body.

His own breathing was labored, his heart racing, but Rand forced himself to take it slow. They'd made love last night after they'd tumbled, exhausted, into the bed. But from the first time they'd made love by the fire that night, every time for them had been hurried, the need urgent and desperate. He wanted this time to be different.

Slow, he thought. He wanted this time to be slow.

He bent and pressed his lips to her shoulder, nibbled, then used his teeth to pleasure. He felt her shiver and squirm underneath him, but when she started to roll over, he slid his leg over the lower half of her body and held her pressed to the mattress. He kissed her neck, tasting, savoring every inch of smooth, soft skin, used his teeth on every sensitive spot, until she was writhing underneath him.

''Shh,'' he whispered as he gently bit the lobe of her ear, then slid his tongue inside.

Grace fisted the pillow under her face and buried the sound of her moan in the soft down. What Rand was doing to her was the most erotic, exquisite thing she'd ever experienced. His mouth and lips on her shoulders and neck were driving her mad. And his teeth—she gasped as he nipped lower, scraping and tenderly biting her shoulder blades. He lingered in one especially sensitive area and gave that spot his complete attention.

He was clearly taking his time.

''Rand, please,'' she begged him.

He straddled her, pressed her deeper into the soft mattress as he slid one hand all the way up her back until his hand fisted in her hair. Her entire body throbbed with raw, sharp need. He moved his free hand over her back and shoulders, and the feel of his rough palm and fingertips on her nerve-wakened skin had her struggling for breath. She couldn't move with him on top of her, yet that didn't frighten her, it only excited her all the more. She belonged to him, she thought. Completely.

With his hand still intertwined in her hair, he bent and kissed her neck again, then slid his free hand under her body to cup her breast. He found her nipple and rubbed the hardened tip between his thumb and forefinger. Intense pleasure shot from that spot to the already aching place between her legs.

She felt the hard length of him pressed against her bottom and thought she might go crazy with wanting him inside her. She moved against him, pleaded, but he barely seemed to notice her anxiety.

She swore at him, but still he took his time.

And then his hand slipped lower, from her breast, down her stomach, then slid lower, to the vee of her legs. When he slid his finger over the aching, throbbing nub of her womanhood, she cried out and arched her body upward. He stroked her, fueled the already out-of-control fire in her body, until she was sobbing his name.

He said something, though her mind couldn't comprehend what it was, then suddenly she was on her back and he was inside her. She reared up and met him, brought him deeply inside her, wrapped her arms and legs tightly around him.

When the climax exploded in her, he muffled the sound of her cry with his mouth, then groaned deeply as he shattered, too.

Unable to think, to speak, or even move, Grace fell back and took him with her.

It was a long time before they moved. A fine sheen of sweat covered both their bodies, and the only sound in the room was the wild beating of their hearts. Rand knew he should move, that he was much too heavy for her, but when he tried to roll away, her arms and legs tightened on him and held him still.

To ease his weight on her, he rose on his elbows, then pressed his temple to hers and kissed the tip of her nose.

"You were..." she said, still breathless. "That was..."

"Pretty damn amazing, Grace," he finished for her.

"Yeah." She smiled, then started to laugh.

It took him a moment to realize what he'd said, then he started to chuckle. She *was* amazing, he thought. He'd never laughed like this in bed with a woman before. This was a whole new experience for him. *Grace* was a new experience for him, as were the feelings he had for her. He'd thought that nothing could surprise him anymore, that he'd seen it all and done most of it, too.

And then Grace came waltzing into his life and turned everything upside down.

He wasn't sure he liked it, but there was nothing to be done about it now. Fool that he was, he couldn't let her go just yet.

But he would, he knew. He'd have to.

She ran her hands over his shoulders, then slid her palms to his chest. The expression on her face turned serious as she lifted her gaze to his.

"When are you going to call the lawyer?" she asked.

He'd known they were going to have to get around to facing that. He'd intentionally kept the lawyer, and the reason they'd come to Wolf River, out of his mind since they'd driven into town. He'd wanted to concentrate on Grace, instead. Wanted to remember the way her cheeks flushed after they'd made love, the soft, dreamy haze in her eyes, the breathy tone of her voice. He wanted to remember everything about her, knew that he'd carry even the smallest detail with him for the rest of his life.

With a sigh he rolled away from her and sat on the edge of the bed. He stared at the phone on the nightstand, felt as if his blood had turned to sludge in his veins. He was afraid if he reached for the receiver that Grace would see his hand shake.

''It's early,'' he said roughly, and dragged his fingers through his hair.

She rose up on her knees behind him and wrapped her arms around his neck, then pressed a tender kiss to his cheek. ''Leave a message, and he'll call you back when he gets into the office.''

''After I take a shower.''

Her lips moved to his ear and nibbled. ''Now.''

He frowned, but her hot breath and tongue on his ear made it impossible to be irritated. Or coherent.

He snatched up the phone and punched the hotel operator, then asked her to connect him with Beddingham, Barnes and Stephens Law Offices. He left a brief message on the lawyer's office machine, gave him the phone number at the Four Winds Hotel and the number of the room, then hung up.

His insides coiled, and his heart pounded. But he'd done it. He'd actually made the call.

Grace slid her hands over his shoulders and down his arms, then back up again in a gentle, soothing motion. Slowly he felt his muscles relax and his breathing steady.

"You go ahead and shower." She touched her lips to his shoulder. "I'll order some coffee and breakfast."

He turned suddenly, drew a gasp from her as he stood and swept her up in his arms. His mouth swooped down on hers, and he kissed her hard.

"I've got a better idea," he said, his lips still pressed to hers.

"What is it?" she murmured.

He smiled, then took her into the shower with him and showed her.

"Mr. Sloan, thank you for coming." Henry Barnes welcomed Rand into his office with a warm handshake, extended a hand to Grace. "Miss Sullivan, a pleasure to meet you."

"Mr. Barnes."

"We're informal here in Wolf River," the silver-haired, sixtyish lawyer said, then gestured for both Rand and Grace to sit in the armchairs opposite him. "Just call me Henry."

The smell of leather and freshly polished oak filled the lawyer's office. The carpet was navy blue, the walls oak wainscot, with dozens of certificates of education and awards mixed with various Barnes family photos. Rand noticed a copy of the *Wall Street Journal* on a small corner table, right beside a thick catalog of miniature trains and railroad accessories.

"Rand—may I call you Rand?" Henry asked as he

sat. When Rand nodded, Henry smiled. ''You're a difficult man to reach. I was beginning to think I might not hear from you.''

From his back pocket Rand pulled out the letter he'd been carrying with him for the past several days and laid it on the lawyer's desk. ''Tell me about my sister and brother.''

''Of course.'' The lawyer sat back in his chair. ''If I were you, I wouldn't want a bunch of small talk or legal blather, either. So I'll say it as simply and directly as possible. Your brother and sister are alive. Seth, who is now Seth Granger, is living in New Mexico. We haven't heard back from him yet, but we do have an address and it appears to be a reliable one.''

Rand had been in El Paso for the past six months. He'd been so close to the border he could have spit and hit New Mexico. He'd driven into Albuquerque at least a dozen times. The thought that he and Seth might have passed on the highway, or even been in a gas station or corner store at the same time, made Rand's pulse jump.

''And Lizzie?'' he asked through the thickness in his throat.

''Elizabeth has been more of a problem, I'm afraid.''

Rand gripped the arms of his chair, felt a muscle jump in his jaw. He didn't think he could bear it, to come all this way, to get this far, and find out that she didn't want to see him.

''What kind of a problem?'' he asked tightly.

''We haven't been able to locate her yet,'' Henry

said. "We have every confidence that we will, but for the moment, we only know that she's living somewhere on the east coast or, at least, that she was living there."

Rand let out the breath he'd been holding, then narrowed his gaze at the lawyer. "I want to know how this happened and why, after all this time, you're contacting me now."

Expression somber, the lawyer glanced at Grace.

Grace rose. "I'll just wait out—"

Rand took her hand and pulled her back. He wanted her here, with him. As much as it disturbed him, he *needed* her here.

"Whatever you have to say—" Rand kept his gaze on her as he pulled her back onto the chair, then looked back at the lawyer "—Grace can hear, too."

Henry nodded, then let out a long puff of air as he sat forward in his chair. "Twenty-three years ago, in a sudden and violent thunderstorm, your family's car went over the side of a ravine. Your parents were killed instantly, but you, your sister and brother were all still alive."

Rand pressed his lips into a thin line. "Tell me something I don't know, Henry."

"The first person on the scene was the sheriff in Wolf River, a man named Spencer Radick. He called your uncle William, who went to the scene of the accident with his housekeeper, Rosemary Owens."

Rosemary. Rand had forgotten the woman's name until now. She'd told him to call her Rose. He remembered the scent of onions and garlic had clung to her simple brown dress the night she'd taken him to the motel room.

''My uncle sent me with her,'' Rand said absently. ''She took care of me until the other man came and took me to live with the Sloans.''

''That other man was Leon Waters,'' Henry said. ''A seedy lawyer from Granite Springs who worked for your uncle. He arranged all the adoptions, but they were illegal, of course. With your uncle's help, Waters also had death certificates forged and paid off all the necessary people to make it appear that the entire family had indeed died. Sheriff Radick was paid for his silence, and he left town two months after the accident, though no one knows where he went. Not long after that, Leon Waters closed up his practice in Granite Springs and disappeared, as well.''

The list of people Rand wanted to pay a visit to was quickly growing. And the number-one person on his list was William Blackhawk. ''My uncle?''

Henry shook his head. ''He died in a small plane crash two years ago.''

Anger tore at Rand's insides, a searing, hot rage at the knowledge that he would never be able to face his uncle, to ask him how he could have done what he'd done to his own flesh and blood and still look at himself in the mirror.

Rand narrowed a gaze at the lawyer. ''What about the housekeeper? Where can I find her—talk to her?''

Henry shook his head. ''She died from lung cancer six months ago.''

Grace slipped her hand over his and squeezed. That simple gesture, and the look of concern in her eyes, dispelled the fury and disappointment spilling into his veins.

Rand linked his fingers with hers, then looked back at the lawyer. ''If everyone is dead or gone, then how do you know any of this?''

''Rosemary's daughter found a journal detailing everything that happened that night, including names,'' Henry said. ''Rosemary must have kept the journal for her own protection against William. No doubt she feared for her own life.''

After what his uncle had done, Rand thought, it was hardly a surprise that the man would be capable of murder if he had felt threatened. Rosemary had been smart to keep a journal as insurance.

Rand was anxious to see that journal. To see the words in black-and-white on the pages, to know every detail of what had happened that night, to his sister and brother.

Still, it felt as if something didn't fit, didn't make sense, and it dawned on him what it was. ''But if Rosemary's dead,'' he asked the lawyer, ''then who hired you to find me?''

''Lucas Blackhawk.''

''Lucas Blackhawk?''

Henry nodded. ''Your cousin.''

Rand furrowed his brow. ''I have a cousin?''

''Actually, you have two. But for right now, let's talk about Lucas. Your father had two brothers, William and Thomas. Lucas is Thomas's only son. He lives here in Wolf River.'' Grinning, Henry leaned forward. ''Why don't we give him a call and tell him you're here?''

Ten

Lucas Blackhawk's house was a few miles off the main highway, just outside of town. Rand pulled his truck up and parked in front of a pretty, two-story, blue-gray clapboard, with white shutters and trim and an inviting front porch with freshly potted containers of yellow daisies and orange marigolds. Beside the gravel-lined circular drive, there were a pair of child's plastic toy bikes, one pink, one blue. On the corner of the porch, a colorful wind sock of suns, moons and stars danced in the late-afternoon breeze.

Grace looked at the red roses blooming under the porch railing, the neatly manicured green grass and a painted wooden sign stuck into the ground beside the porch steps that said, Welcome. It was like a picture in a magazine advertising the perfect life, a dream home complete with two point three children and the proverbial station wagon.

Her heart swelled just looking at it all. The house, the children's bikes, the homemade welcome sign. She wanted this, too, she realized. All of this, even the flowers and that silly wind sock.

And the kicker was—life's little joke on her—was that she wanted it with a man who'd made it perfectly clear he had no interest in hearth and home or settling down.

She glanced over at him, saw him staring intently at the house, not with yearning but with apprehension. She set her own feelings aside, knew that she'd have plenty of time later to deal with them. Considering everything that was happening in Rand's life, she was being selfish to think about what she wanted.

He hadn't said more than a dozen words for the past hour. Not that being quiet was anything unusual for Rand. But the tension radiating from him had been almost tangible. Grace understood he was still trying to sort through and absorb everything he'd learned about what had happened the night of the accident, how Rand and his sister and brother had been the puppets in his uncle's cruel and sick plan. And now, finding out he had a cousin right here in Wolf River was only more fuel for the fire of turmoil burning inside him.

Though it had been subtle, she'd already felt him pull away from her, not just emotionally, but physically, as well. He hadn't touched her once since they'd left the lawyer's office, and it seemed as if he'd intentionally kept his distance.

Already she felt as if she didn't belong here. That he had too much in his life at the moment, and that she would only complicate matters even more. He'd been impulsive when he'd asked her to come with him, and she'd been impulsive when she'd agreed.

And even knowing all that, it didn't matter. Because if she had to do it all over again, she'd still say yes. She still would have come with him.

She would have gone to Antarctica with him if he'd asked.

She forced a smile on her lips and a light tone to her voice. "Here we are."

He nodded, then got out of the truck and came around to her side. She slid out before he could open her door, and together they walked up the porch steps. From inside the house Grace heard the sound of children screaming in laughter and a woman's voice saying, "I found you!"

Rand hesitated, then knocked on the door.

The door swung open a moment later. A woman, her face flushed and her short crop of pale-blond hair mussed, stood on the other side. Her eyes were smoky blue, large with excitement and pleasure. In her late twenties, Grace guessed.

She was stunning. Absolutely beautiful. And very pregnant, Grace noticed through the loose floral dress the woman wore.

Two point three children, Grace thought with a bittersweet smile. ''Lucas!'' the woman called over shoulder. ''He's here!''

Then she reached for Rand, took his hand in both of hers and pulled him inside the house. Grace followed hesitantly, feeling like an intruder at such a personal, important meeting between Rand and his relatives.

The house was beautiful inside, as well—white walls, shiny hardwood floors, polished oak banister on the stairway. And the intoxicating smell of baking cookies filled the air.

''I'm Julianna.'' The woman smiled brightly and nodded to her left. Two small children, one boy, one girl, stood perfectly still in the entryway of a dining room. ''That's Nicole and Nathan. You can't see them 'cause they're invisible right now.''

The children were undoubtedly twins, Grace realized. Probably around three or four, both with dark-brown hair, dressed in jean shorts and white T-shirts. Mischief sparkled in their big, dark eyes.

''Hello, Nicole and Nathan,'' Rand said, though he intentionally looked at the stairway directly ahead, instead of at the children, and Grace realized that he was actually playing with the children. ''It's nice to meet you.''

Nathan and Nicole giggled, but when a man dressed in paint-splattered jeans and a navy-blue T-shirt came down the stairs, wiping his hands on a rag, they both ran and jumped on his legs at the bottom step. ''Daddy!''

He was a tall man with black hair, both traits obviously dominant in the Blackhawk genes. He was a handsome man—another Blackhawk trait—with deep-brown eyes and a warm smile.

''Just finishing up the trim in the nursery,'' Lucas said, stuffing the rag into his back pocket. He scooped one child up in each of his arms, kissed both of them, then set them down again. Grinning, Lucas held his hand out to Rand. ''Is this the damnedest thing or what?''

''That's putting it mildly.''

Grace felt tears burn her eyes when the two men firmly clasped hands. She sensed both Rand's and Lucas's hesitation, their assessment of each other. But she also sensed their excitement, felt it herself as she watched them. Still, they were being cautious with each other, Grace realized, another Blackhawk trait.

''And this is?'' Lucas looked at Grace and raised a brow.

''Grace Sullivan.'' Grace offered her hand to Lucas. ''Just a friend.''

Lucas and Julianna both shook her hand, then Lucas furrowed his brow. ''Grace Sullivan? The same Grace Sullivan with the Edgewater Horse Adoption Agency?''

Surprised that Lucas would know about her and the foundation, Grace hesitated. ''Ah, well, yes, I am.''

''You sent us an invitation to your fund-raiser next week. I believe my office manager, Shelby Davis, RSVP'd that we'd be there.''

Lucas Blackhawk. No wonder the name Blackhawk had sounded so familiar to her. Grace had seen the list of people invited, but she'd been busy trying to track down Rand. Mattie, one of the volunteers with the foundation, had been in charge of organizing the event and handling the guest list.

Even after Rand had told her his birth name was Blackhawk and he'd been born in Wolf River, Grace hadn't connected him with the Blackhawk Ranch. How could she have missed such a blatant link between the two?

But she knew how she'd missed it. Since she'd met Rand, Grace hadn't been thinking clearly. She hadn't been thinking about the foundation or the fund-raiser or anything else besides Rand himself.

Embarrassed and at a complete loss for words, she simply said, ''I—I'm so glad you'll be able to attend.''

''Why don't you take Rand and Grace into the den, and I'll bring everyone something cold to drink?'' Julianna said. With a serious expression on her face, she looked around the room, right past her children, who stood shoulder to shoulder at the foot of the stairs. ''If I can find Nicole and Nathan,'' Julianna said, still searching the room, ''I might have some cookies for them in the kitchen.''

Grace watched the two children run to their mother, yelling, ''Here we are, Mommy. Here we are!'' then race off into the kitchen.

There it was again. That little *ping* in her heart. Grace drew in a slow breath to steady herself, then smiled at Rand. ''I'm going to see if I can help Julianna in the kitchen. Why don't you and Lucas go on?''

He'd need this time alone with his cousin, Grace understood. From everything the lawyer had told them, Rand and Lucas had a great deal to talk about.

"Take your time," she said, already turning toward the kitchen. "I'm going to see if I can beg a cookie or two from Julianna."

"Beg a few for us, too, will you?" Lucas said as Grace made her way toward the kitchen, then he turned to Rand and grinned. "My wife gains twenty pounds with this baby and puts *me* on a diet. Women."

Rand's thought exactly, as he watched Grace disappear into the kitchen. She'd been acting odd ever since they'd pulled into his cousin's driveway. He'd seen the longing in her eyes as she'd stared at the house, and he hadn't missed the soft, dreamy expression on her face when she'd looked at Lucas and Julianna's twins.

As he followed Lucas into the den, Rand glanced around the house, noticed the toys spilling from a yellow plastic toy box, the wedding photos on the walls, the balls of blue and pink yarn beside the half-knit baby blanket on the leather sofa.

Rand knew it all looked picture-perfect. The house, the kids. Roots. But what did he know about roots? Everything had been ripped out from under him when he was nine years old. Hell, everything he owned would fit in a suitcase, and even his suitcase had wheels.

He couldn't offer any of this to Grace. And she deserved it, all of it.

''I found this in a box of my mother's old photos.'' Lucas handed Rand a picture shot from an old Polaroid camera. ''I thought you might like it.''

The picture had faded with age; the edges had turned amber and brown. But clearly the smiling faces of Jonathan and Norah Blackhawk stared back at Rand.

His whole family was in the picture. Rand guessed he was probably around five or six, Seth maybe three or four, and Lizzie, wrapped in a blanket, looked like a newborn. They were all sitting on a hospital bed.

Rand felt as if a metal band were closing around his chest, squeezing every last drop of air from his lungs. He couldn't look at it now, not with Lucas watching him. Rand slipped the picture into the back pocket of his jeans, had to swallow the lump in his throat before he could speak. ''Thanks.''

''I'm sorry we didn't know each other when we were kids,'' Lucas said. ''Maybe if we had, things would have been different somehow.''

There were so many questions racing through Rand's mind at the moment. Why hadn't they known each other? What had happened to Lucas's parents? What did he know about Seth and Lizzie? He didn't know which one to ask first, so he chose the one that he'd been wondering about since he'd left the lawyer's office.

''Why are you doing this?'' Rand asked. ''Why, after all these years, would you go to all this trouble to bring me and my sister and brother together?''

"Why wouldn't I?" Lucas asked. "You're family. You and your sister and brother."

"You don't even know us," Rand pointed out.

"We're blood, Rand," Lucas said evenly. "I lost my parents when I was young, too. My mom when I was eleven, then my dad not long after that. He died in prison."

"Prison?"

"You would have only been around seven or eight at the time. Both of our families were busy with problems of their own during those years, not to mention our dear uncle William doing his best to cause upheaval wherever he could. He made sure the family stayed divided." Lucas sighed. "William was the only person who could have helped clear my father of the false charges against him. He never returned even one of my father's phone calls. He let my father die in that prison and me be shipped off to foster homes."

"Why?" Rand asked. "Why would a man tear his own family apart like that?"

"His brothers married off the reservation," Lucas said. "He hated them and all their children for that. And then, of course, there was the money."

Rand shook his head. "My parents had no money. We barely got by on a fifty-acre horse ranch."

Lucas turned his head at the sound of the women's laughter from the kitchen, then put a hand on Rand's shoulder and gestured toward the sliding French doors that led to the outside.

"Why don't I show you around my place while we talk?" Lucas said evenly. "This might take a while."

* * *

"You're staying for dinner." Julianna slid a roast into the oven, then set the timer. "I won't take no for an answer."

"I really don't think—"

"I insist." Julianna placed both of her hands on her lower back and stretched. "After being in this house day after day with two three-year-olds, I seriously need an adult to talk to. Just slap my hand if I start to cut your meat for you."

Grace glanced at the two children, who were sitting at their own pint-size table and chairs in a corner of the kitchen, eating chocolate chip cookies and drinking milk. "They're adorable."

"Put cookies in front of them and they're angels." Julianna brought a plate of still-warm cookies to the table and set them down, then slowly eased into a chair across from Grace. "Put carrots in front of them and they turn into little devils so fast your head will spin."

"They're so sweet." Grace accepted a cookie that Julianna offered. "I can't imagine them giving you any trouble."

Julianna gave a bark of laughter. "You should have been here last night. They wanted to see what was inside the vacuum cleaner bag."

Grace's eyes widened.

"And while I was cleaning that up," Julianna went on, "Nicole decided to shampoo Nathan's hair in the middle of my bedroom. Half the bottle was oozing down his face and back, the other half was on the rug. She was on her way for a cup of water when I walked in."

Grace knew nothing about babies or small children. She'd never thought about what kind of mischief they got into, or the destruction they could cause.

But she wanted to know. She wanted to know it all, experience it all. She wanted a dozen of them—well, maybe just three or four, she reconsidered, as the image of vacuum cleaner bags and shampoo popped into her mind.

''At least she used the no-tears,'' Julianna said with a sigh. ''Poor Nathan was screaming he didn't want his hair washed when Lucas tossed them both in the shower. Oh!'' Julianna looked down as she smoothed a hand over her stomach. ''Soccer time.''

Grace followed the rumbling movement across Julianna's stomach. While she had certainly seen a lot of mares ready to foal, Grace had never been quite this close to a woman who was quite this pregnant. Fascinated, she couldn't help but stare. ''Does that hurt?''

''Not usually.'' Julianna winced at the continuing ripple of movement, then frowned at one direct shot to her ribs. ''But he's definitely got my attention today.''

''You're having a boy?''

''That's what the ultrasound shows.'' Julianna glanced down at her stomach. ''Want to feel?''

Desperately, Grace thought. Not just Julianna's stomach, but she wanted to know for herself, wanted to experience that life growing inside her, a baby with the man she loved.

With Rand.

She might as well wish for the moon.

One prominent bulge on the side of Julianna's stomach moved and popped out directly in the middle. Grace hesitantly held her hand toward that bulge. "You...you really don't mind?"

"Of course not." Julianna took Grace's fingers and laid them directly on top of an undistinguishable baby body part.

When that body part moved under Grace's hand, she felt her breath catch. "He moved!" Grace laughed. "Oh, my heavens, I really felt it!"

Julianna smiled. "I take it you haven't been pregnant."

"No." Though it seemed rude, Grace couldn't bring herself to take her hand away. "I—I'm not married."

"That's not exactly a criterion today," Julianna said, then moved Grace's hand to another bulge. "So what's with you and Rand, then?"

"We, well, we're—" Grace avoided Julianna's eyes. "There's nothing between us."

"Grace, we just met, and you can tell me to butt out of your business anytime. But, honey, I saw the way he looked at you, and the way you looked right back. That's not nothing."

It was strange, Grace thought, how a person could meet someone for the first time yet feel as if they'd been friends for a very long time. That was exactly how she felt about Julianna.

With a sigh Grace reached for a cookie and sat back. "It's complicated."

Julianna laughed. "What relationship between any

man and woman isn't? Lord, someday I'll tell you about Lucas and me, but you better hold on to your eyeballs."

Grace took a tiny bite of cookie and shook her head. "It's different with Rand and me. You and Lucas obviously love each other very much."

Julianna absently stroked her stomach, a dreamy, soft expression on her face. "When I don't want to strangle the man for being so pigheaded, I love him so much it hurts."

"So pigheaded runs in the Blackhawk genes, too, huh?" Grace said with a smile.

"Lordy, yes. Prepare yourself. The Blackhawk men give new dimension to the word."

It was too late to prepare herself, Grace thought as she stared at her cookie. Rand was already in her head and in her heart. She'd asked him once how he'd managed after he'd lost his family. He'd told her that life went on. She wasn't sure how it did after you lost someone you love, but she did know she had to believe that was true. Otherwise, she'd end up begging him to at least give them a chance together, to try to love her.

As much as she wanted to do just that, she knew she couldn't. For these past few days she believed that he had truly needed her. She'd been with him as he'd faced the shock of learning his sister and brother were alive, then finding out what had really happened that night, and now, meeting his cousin.

But he didn't need her anymore. He had Lucas and Julianna to help him put the pieces together. And soon he'd have Seth and Lizzie. He'd have his family.

She might have been Rand's lover, but she wasn't his love. He'd made it clear he wasn't looking to settle down. And as she looked at Julianna and Lucas and at their children, Grace knew she couldn't settle for less than that.

It was time for her to go, she realized. Time for her to walk out of Rand's life as abruptly as she'd walked in. In the long run, it would be easier this way for both of them. He might be upset for a little while that she would leave without saying goodbye, but he would probably be relieved, as well. Goodbyes were always awkward. This way there'd be no pretenses that they would stay in touch, no dramatic exits.

And the truth be told, she knew she wasn't brave enough to do it any other way. If she said goodbye to him, to his face, she'd end up in a puddle of tears at his feet. That would only embarrass them both.

Grace forced her attention back to Julianna, but quickly changed the subject back to the twins and the Blackhawk Ranch.

Two cookies and six games of hide-and-seek later, Rand and Lucas still hadn't come back from outside, and Grace knew it was now or never. She swore she felt a migraine coming on and begged off dinner, then asked if Lucas would mind taking Rand back to the hotel later on that evening.

Grace returned Julianna's hug goodbye, then drove back to the hotel in Rand's truck. She packed her bags, left a cheerful note, then on legs that felt like rubber bands, she walked out of the hotel and Rand Blackhawk's life.

Eleven

The town of Wolf River looked different than Rand remembered from his childhood. A glass and brick official U.S. Post Office was now on the corner of Gibson and Main instead of in the back corner of the Rexall drugstore. A multiplex theater showing all the current movies was on Third Street where Drexler's Ice Cream used to be. A popular drive-through hamburger stand with the golden arches was now located directly across from another popular hamburger stand who made eating messy their motto.

Since when did Wolf River need *two* hamburger drive-throughs? Rand thought as he drove down Main Street. He felt a sense of relief when he spotted Papa Pete's Diner on the corner of Main and Sixth. Pappa Pete's made the best food in Wolf River, and on special occasions Rand's family had gone there to eat. On his eighth birthday, Rand remembered, he ordered a hamburger, French fries and a chocolate shake with whipped cream and a bright red cherry on top.

That was the best birthday he'd ever had, he thought with a smile.

There were a few other stores that looked familiar, too. Joe's Barbershop, Peterson's Hay and Feed, King's Hardware. All places Rand's dad had taken him when he was a kid. Places that Rand had forgotten about until now.

He stopped at a red light—something else the town hadn't had twenty-three years ago—and watched as an elderly woman crossed the street and waved at him. Like most small towns, people did that sort of thing. Waved at strangers, held doors for each other, smiled and actually looked you in the eye.

All these years he'd stayed away from Wolf River intentionally. He hadn't wanted to remember the town, the places he'd gone with his family or the people who lived here. Remembering those things couldn't bring his family back to him. Why would he come back?

In all these years he'd never called one place home. Never stayed in one place long enough to "let grass grow under his feet," as the saying went. The minute he started to feel settled somewhere was when he knew it was time to pack up his truck again and hit the road. There was always another ranch, always another horse to train.

Rand turned off Main Street and headed south out of town. The sky was deep blue, the day hot, but he kept his window down and let the wind blow through the cab of his truck as he took in the scenery. There were farmhouses and ranches that he remembered, though he couldn't recall the owners' names. But the names didn't matter. What mattered was that he needed something to hold on to, something with substance to keep him steady when it felt as if his world had been turned upside down.

And now, on top of everything else, Grace was gone, too.

She'd been his touchstone for these past few days. He hadn't realized how much he'd relied on her until she had left. He didn't know he *could* rely on anyone.

His first reaction when he'd come back to the hotel last night and found her gone was astonishment. Had he or someone else said something to her to make her leave without saying goodbye? Had something happened in Dallas and she'd had to get home right away? But her note had been cheery and simple. "I'm sorry I had to leave so quickly, but I really do need to get home and I hate goodbyes."

He'd stood there, staring at the words she'd written, and then the anger had come. He'd sworn, kicked his suitcase and the bed, then he'd slammed around his room and sworn some more. Enough time had passed that she might be home by now, he'd thought, and stomped to the phone to call her, to ask her what the hell she thought she was doing leaving like that.

He slammed the phone back down. He didn't even know her home phone number. He had an office phone number for the foundation, but that was it.

How could that be, he'd asked himself as he'd dragged both hands through his hair. How could they have shared what they had, and he didn't even know her damn telephone number?

He still swore, but there'd been no heat in his words when he'd sunk down on the edge of the bed. He didn't blame her for leaving. She'd given herself completely to him, but he'd given her nothing in return, offered her nothing. Why the hell wouldn't she leave?

He'd gone down to the hotel bar after that. The room was too quiet. Too empty. He thought he needed the company of Jack Daniel's, but two hours and half a bottle later, he knew he'd been wrong.

What he needed was something else entirely.

Rand slammed on the brakes. He'd been so lost in thought he'd nearly missed the turnoff he'd been looking for.

Cold Springs Road.

Hands tight on the wheel, he made a sharp right off the main highway. Oak trees and coyote bush lined the two-lane road. There were no houses out here, the creek bed flooded during storms and the land was too rocky, too unstable to build.

He realized he was driving too fast and he slowed down, forced himself to relax and pay attention to the landscape. It had been so many years, he wasn't certain he would remember.

Soon as the road widens around this turn…

His mother's voice came to him. The sound of thunder and rain on the roof of his parents' car pounded in Rand's head.

We'll be fine...don't be afraid...

There it was. Maybe twenty yards ahead of him. The turn where the road widened.

The turn his father never made that night.

Heart racing, Rand eased his truck off the road and cut the engine. His palms were sweating when he stepped out of his cab and looked down into the ravine.

This is where they'd gone over, he knew. This is where his life had changed twenty-three years ago.

Rand closed his eyes, saw everything again as it had happened that night, the flash of lightning, the car swerving off the road, that horrible sound of silence.

Breathing hard, he opened his eyes and looked around. Overhead, the hot August sun burned through his denim shirt and jeans, and a lazy hawk circled overhead. Puffy white clouds floated on the horizon.

And silence. Absolute, complete silence.

Only, this time the silence didn't frighten him. This silence relaxed and comforted.

Rand turned sideways and dug his boots into the side of the ravine. He slid down standing up; rocks and gravel tumbled ahead of him. A cloud of dust rose from the loosened dirt. At the bottom of the ravine, he looked around again, waited for his heart to slow, then pulled the photograph Lucas had given him from his back pocket.

His family. His only tangible link to the past, he realized. The impact of that knowledge and the importance of what he held in his hand overwhelmed him.

He remembered the day it was taken. Waiting for hours in a small room with his dad and Seth, watching TV and playing games, complaining because he was bored and why couldn't the baby just hurry up and be born?

And then, after she was finally born, they all got to see her, though just long enough for that picture to be taken by one of the nurses. He remembered everything now. The antiseptic smell of the hospital, the squeak of the nurse's shoes on the linoleum, the touch of his mother's lips on his cheek and her words, *Isn't she beautiful, Rand? Do you think you can help me take care of her?*

He'd promised he would. Always and forever, he'd told his mother.

He'd let his mother down. He'd let Lizzie down.

His hand tightened on the photo.

Mary and Matt and Sam had been an important part of his life. Rand was thankful that he'd had them, that he still had them. They were family to him just as much as if they'd shared the same blood.

But his first family needed him now, he knew. And he needed them. Rand had a second chance, a chance to make things right. This time he wouldn't let them down.

They had an address for Seth but not Lizzie. Yesterday the lawyer had asked Rand if he wanted to hire a private investigator to find Lizzie. Rand hadn't given Henry an answer. Lizzie had only been two at the time. What if his sister was happy where she was, with who she was? Would it only complicate her life to suddenly have two brothers she probably didn't remember show up at her doorstep?

But Rand knew that the decision had already been made, that there'd never really been a decision. Lizzie would be contacted by the P.I. who would tell her everything that had happened. Rand wouldn't force himself into her life, or Seth's, either. They'd both be given a choice if they wanted to meet. After that… well, they'd just have to take it one step at a time.

The silence in the ravine surrounded him. In the midst of the stillness, a soft breeze rose, whispered to him. *You'll be fine…don't be afraid…*

Rand listened to the breeze, felt it float over him like a velvet hand. He smiled, then slipped the photo back into his pocket and hurried up the ravine.

What he needed to do now had nothing to do with Seth and Lizzie. What he needed to do now was for himself.

Wearing a black velvet slip dress with V-neckline, spaghetti straps and a slit halfway up her leg, Grace stood outside the open French doors on her parents' brick patio and sipped her glass of champagne. Inside the house, the fund-raising party for the foundation was already in full swing.

By Texas standards, it was a pleasant evening, and Grace had stepped outside for a moment to take a few deep breaths of the warm night air and prepare herself for a very busy night ahead of her.

Normally she thrived on these affairs, knowing that

the money raised would help care for and find homes for so many horses. But nothing seemed normal to her since she'd come back to Dallas. Everything felt different. *She* felt different.

With a sigh Grace glanced across the patio and stared at the wavering pale-blue water in her parents' lit swimming pool.

She felt empty.

"Gracie, darlin', for heaven's sake," Roanna Sullivan said from the open doorway, "if that face of yours hangs any lower, y'all will be kissing your own behind."

It was her mother's favorite reprimand when Grace had been growing up, and, as a child, the silly expression had made her laugh. At the moment, however, Grace did not feel like laughing. However, to please her mother and the 150 guests laughing and talking and eating hors d'oeuvres inside the house, she did plaster a smile on her face.

Roanna—Ronnie to her husband and friends—cocked her head and looked at Grace thoughtfully. "Hmm. Can't decide which I prefer—the tick-fevered bloodhound expression or the I-just-ate-a-sour-apple look."

"You look beautiful tonight, Mom," Grace said, not only to change the conversation, but because it was true. She wore a long, silvery-green off-the-shoulder gown that complemented her short, pale-blond hair, sea-green eyes and slender figure. Even at fifty, the woman still turned heads and made men trip over their tongues and feet.

''Thank you,'' her mother said. ''You look stunning yourself. Now tell me why you haven't smiled once since you got back from your trip.''

So much for changing the subject.

Grace sipped from the glass of Dom Pérignon in her hand, though it might as well have been apple juice for all she noticed. ''Don't you have to check on the pâté? I heard that you were almost out of it.''

Normally a comment like that would have Roanna—a born-and-bred Georgia debutante—dashing away in horror at the mere possibility of such a social faux pas. Tonight she wasn't buying it.

''Gracie.'' The teasing tone in her mother's voice was gone now. ''You've been back five days. When are you going to tell me what happened?''

Five days. God, had it really only been five days? Grace thought. It felt more like five years.

Glancing away from her mother, Grace looked over the sea of shimmering gowns and broad-shouldered tuxedos in her parents' football-field-size living room. From a quartet in one corner of the room, strains of Mozart drifted over the buzz of conversation. Huge bouquets of red and yellow roses and white lilies scented the room and white-gloved servers with silver trays offered mushroom-cheese pastry puffs and salmon mousse toast squares.

A beautiful sight of elegance and wealth and privilege.

And Grace would trade it all in a heartbeat for canned chili over a campfire and one more night on a mountaintop with Rand Blackhawk.

She still felt that leaving the way she did was for the best. It would have been humiliating to burst into tears in the middle of saying goodbye, and would have only made Rand uncomfortable. So she'd made it easier for both of them.

She took another sip of champagne at the thought. Easy. Yeah, right. Leaving had been anything but easy. It had been the hardest thing she'd ever done in her life.

All the way from Wolf River back to Dallas, in the back seat of the car she'd hired through the hotel to drive her home, Grace had alternated between tears and rousing pep talks. *I'm still young,* she'd told herself. *I'll meet someone else. We were too different, I'm better off without him.*

Oh, and her favorite, *It's better to have loved and lost, than never to have loved at all.*

That was a big, fat crock. It *hurt* like hell, dammit.

And, fool that she was, she'd held on to the tiniest sliver of hope. Prayed that he might miss her even a little, that he might call, even to just say hello.

But he hadn't, and she knew she did have to move on. She hoped that everything went well for him, that he would reunite with his family and be happy. Because she loved him, she wanted him to be happy.

Grace felt her mother's gaze still on her, watching her, still waiting for an answer to her question about what had happened. Suddenly thankful that she had her family, her mother and father and brother, she gave her mother a hug.

"Later, Mom," Grace said. "Just you and me, in

the den, pj's and hot cocoa. Then I'll tell you everything.''

''Hot cocoa, huh?'' Concern narrowed Roanna's eyes as she touched her daughter's cheek. ''Must be serious.''

Inside the house, it seemed as if the room had quieted. A low hum, like bees in a hive, filled the house. Both Roanna and Grace turned to see what the buzz was about. A handsome dark-haired man at least two inches taller than anyone else in the room, wearing a black Stetson with a black tuxedo, was in the center of all that attention.

''Heavens.'' Roanna lifted one brow. ''Who is *that?*''

Grace stared, dumbstruck. Though she'd never met the man, she knew exactly who it was.

''I'll be damned,'' Grace said out loud. ''He did it. He actually did it.''

''Who did what, dear?'' her mother asked, her attention still on the man.

''Never mind.'' Grace turned toward her mother and kissed her cheek. ''Go say hello to Mr. Dylan Bradshaw, Mom.''

Roanna's eyes widened, then she smiled that devastating smile of hers and squared her shoulders. ''Let's see if the man's checkbook is as big as he is, shall we?''

''You go ahead,'' Grace said. ''I'll be there in a minute.''

So Rand *had* called the man, Grace thought in wonder, as she watched her mother move through the crowded room in Bradshaw's direction. Even with everything Rand had going on in Wolf River with the lawyer and Lucas and his family, he'd still remembered to make that call. Maybe he'd thought it was the least he could do for her. Sort of a final goodbye gift.

Odd, how a person could feel happy yet so miserable at the same time.

With a sigh she stared at her glass of champagne and knew that as corny as it sounded, it was also true. It *was* better to have loved and lost, than never to have loved at all.

In spite of all the pain and the heartache, she wouldn't have changed one thing that had happened between them. If she didn't have Rand, she would still have the memories. Every touch, every kiss, every laugh they'd shared, she would always remember. Maybe—and it was a big maybe—there would be other men in her life, but no man would ever take his place. No man could come close.

''Miss Grace?''

Startled, she glanced up at Jeffrey's call. Jeffrey, an elderly man with a British accent, had been the Sullivans' family butler since Grace was a little girl. He was more like an uncle than an employee, and Grace adored him.

''You have a package,'' Jeffrey said in that deep baritone voice of his.

''Would you mind putting it in the study for me?'' she asked. ''I'll take care of it later.''

Jeffrey—the calmest, most composed man on the

face of the earth, hesitated. ''I don't believe the study would be an appropriate place to put it, Miss. Nor do I believe you should wait until later.''

Grace shook her head. Jeffrey was much too formal, she thought. Not once in all her life had she seen the man let his hair down, so to speak, do the boogie-woogie or shake a tail feather. Life was just too damn short not to enjoy every moment.

Well, dammit, if it killed her, she was going to have a good time tonight. When the music changed later to something fast and fun, she intended to get out there and shake a tail feather of her own.

She might even shock Jeffrey and drag him out there with her.

For the moment, though, she would humor the man. She followed him to the front door, where he surprised her by taking the glass of champagne from her hands, then opened the door for her.

Her surprise turned to shock.

On her parents' front porch, were two foals. And not just *any* foals, but the foals that she and Rand had rescued from Black River Canyon. They bumped nervously into each other, but a lead line and bridle held them in place. Grace stepped outside, followed the ropes attached to those bridles to see who was holding them.

Rand.

Wearing a black tuxedo, of all things, he stood to the side of the front door, leaning casually against the house.

Grace felt her heart leap in her throat.

"Rand," she whispered his name. "What...what are you doing here?"

"Lucas and Julianna couldn't make it," he said. "They sent me in their place."

"Oh." What was she supposed to say? I'm so glad they couldn't come, and would you just please kiss me? "I...I hope everything is all right."

"Everything is great. Julianna had her baby early this morning, two weeks early, but she and the baby are both fine."

"I'm so glad." And she was, Grace thought, her mind reeling. Extremely glad. But with Rand staring at her with those black eyes of his, a smile lifting one corner of his mouth, looking incredibly and ruggedly handsome in the tux he had on, Grace simply couldn't keep a thought straight.

She'd thought she would never see him again, and here he was, standing two feet away from her. She stared at him, held her hands carefully at her sides because she was afraid she was going to leap into his arms and make a complete fool out of herself.

He was here for Lucas and Julianna, Grace reminded herself. Not for her.

She struggled to draw air into her lungs. "What are you doing here with the foals?"

"I adopted them."

"You adopted them?"

He nodded. "And the mares and stallion, too."

"You adopted *all* of them?"

"Yep."

Yep? He'd adopted five horses and all he could say

was "Yep?" The man was enough to make to her crazy. In fact, he already had.

"You said your mother was selling the ranch and all her horses," she said carefully. "Where will you keep them, and who's going to take care of them?"

"Actually—" he pushed away from the wall of the house and moved closer to her "—I was hoping you would."

"Me? You mean the foundation?"

"No. I meant you."

Confused, she looked at the foals. With their big, dark, watery eyes and sweet faces, she tried to think of a way she could keep them, but there wasn't. "Rand, I don't have a permanent place to keep them. That's why they're adopted out, to give them homes."

"What if you did have a place? A permanent place." He moved in front of her and stared down at her. "With me."

"Permanent?" Her pulse skipped, then starting to race. "With you?"

She knew she sounded like a silly parrot, repeating everything he said, but it was the best she could do under the circumstances.

"Yeah. With me." He touched her cheek with his fingertip. "I've got fifty acres in Wolf River. My parents' land. It's not much, but we can buy more later, after we build a new house."

"We?" she barely managed to get the single word out. "You and me, Grace," he said quietly. "A herd of horses, a passel of kids. Maybe even a dog and cat. I always wanted a dog."

A passel of kids? Terrified that her knees would give out on her, she grabbed hold of his arms and leveled her gaze with his. "Whatever it is you're getting at, Rand Blackhawk, *will you just say it?*"

He cupped her chin in his hand and looked down at her. "I'm asking you to marry me, Grace Sullivan."

Rand watched Grace's eyes widen and felt her jaw go slack in his palm. He'd expected her to be surprised, but hell, no one was more surprised than him.

She blinked, then stepped back from him. "You're asking me to *marry* you?"

Rand had never done this before, but still, he didn't think that her response was what anyone would call encouraging. He dragged a hand through his hair and frowned. "Look, I know I won't be the easiest person to live with, but I love you, dammit, so that's gotta mean something."

"That's how you propose to me?" she asked, folding her arms. "'I always wanted a dog. I love you, dammit'?"

"Yes." That wasn't what he'd intended. Somehow, that's just how it came out. "So what's your answer?"

"Yes."

She had him so damn flustered he wasn't certain what she was saying yes to. "Yes, what?"

"Yes, dammit. I'll marry you."

"Thank God," he said on a rush of breath, then dragged her to him and caught her mouth with his. Laughing, her arms came around his neck, and she kissed him back. He lifted her off the ground, smiled against her lips. ‘‘Thank God,’’ he said again, and held her tightly to him. ‘‘Thank God.’’

He deepened the kiss, felt a fierce and powerful emotion grip him. He’d never felt anything like it before, not before Grace, but he knew what it was. Love. He knew that she was his one true love, the woman he wanted to spend the rest of his life with.

‘‘Tell me you love me,’’ he whispered against her mouth.

‘‘I love you,’’ she said, breathless. ‘‘I love you, I love you.’’

She inched away from him and gazed up at him. ‘‘What happened in Wolf River, Rand? When I left, I thought I’d never see you again.’’

On a sigh he touched his forehead to hers. ‘‘For the past twenty-three years I’ve felt guilty. Not only because I hadn’t died with my family, but because deep inside of me I was *glad* that I hadn’t died. I felt I’d let my family down because I was happy I was still alive. So I didn’t believe that I deserved love, and I could never allow myself to love anyone back.’’

He brushed his lips against hers and smiled. ‘‘And then you came into my life, Miss Grace. I’ll never forget the way you looked that first day I met you, standing in that hot, dusty barn in your business suit and high heels. I wanted you so bad I hurt.’’

‘‘That first day?’’ She frowned at him. ‘‘You acted like all you wanted to do was get rid of me.’’

‘‘I did,’’ he said honestly. ‘‘Because I knew you were a threat to me. I knew I was looking at a woman—*the* woman—who had the power to get inside me. The power to make me feel. I'd spent a lifetime not allowing myself to feel, Grace. You scared the hell out of me."

"You scared me, too," she admitted.

"But you didn't back down," he said. "You hung in there, stood up to me, and stuck it out. I'd never met anyone like you before. You absolutely staggered me. You still do."

There were tears in her eyes as she kissed him, and when she drew back, she smiled at him. "And you mean it, about the fifty acres and horses and kids and everything? You really want all that?"

"Yeah, I really want all that," he said softly. "But only with you, Grace. Without you, none of it would mean anything to me." He grinned at her. "Not even the five million dollars I just found out I inherited."

Her eyes widened. "Five…*million*…dollars?"

"Yep." He was still trying to get used to it himself. "Seems my grandfather had a lot of money he'd made in oil and bonds and put in trust for his children. Since my uncle was the executor, he forged a new will when my grandfather died and took everything."

"And your parents died without any of what was rightfully theirs," Grace said sadly.

"The money didn't matter. My parents died happy, with each other. That was worth more than any amount of money." He pressed a quick kiss to her nose. "But don't get me wrong, darlin'. I intend to enjoy my inheritance. Build a ranch and a house and keep you living in the manner to which you're accustomed.''

She frowned at him. ''I would have lived in a pup tent if you'd asked me to, buster, though I should tell you I have a healthy trust fund myself, also from my grandparents. We wouldn't have needed to clip coupons to survive.''

''Yeah?'' He lifted a brow. ''I should have married you that first day and saved a lot of time.''

''Yes, you should have,'' she said primly, then the amusement in her eyes turned to concern. ''What about Seth and Lizzie?'' she asked. ''Have you found them?''

''We think we're close to finding Seth, but we've had to hire a private investigator to find Lizzie. They will both be free to do whatever they want with their trust funds, when and if we do actually find them, that is.''

''If? You mean you might not find them?''

''We never know what tomorrow brings, Grace.'' He pulled her into his arms and kissed her again. ''But with you by my side, sweetheart, I'm going to look forward to each and every day.''

The foals nudged Rand from behind, pushing him closer to Grace. Laughing, he pulled her into his arms and kissed her. ''Did I tell you how sexy you look in that dress you're wearing?'' he murmured.

''You look pretty damn good yourself in that tux, Blackhawk.''

He nuzzled her ear. ''So how long before this shindig is over and we can both get naked?''

"Soon," she whispered, then wrapped her arms around his neck and gave him a long, searing kiss that surely must have made smoke come out of his ears.

He whispered what he wanted to do to her later, felt her shudder in response to his words. Later he knew he would make her shudder again and again. And she would do the same for him.

Smiling, he held her close. It had taken him twenty-three years and the love of a special woman, but with absolute certainty, Rand Blackhawk knew that he had finally come home.

* * * * *

MICHAEL'S TEMPTATION

by

Eileen Wilks

EILEEN WILKS

is a fifth-generation Texan. Her great-great-grandmother came to Texas shortly after the end of the Civil War. But she's not a full-blooded Texan. Right after another war, her Texan father fell for a Yankee woman. This obviously mismatched pair proceeded to travel to nine cities in three countries in the first twenty years of their marriage, raising two kids and innumerable dogs and cats along the way. For the next twenty years they stayed put, back home in Texas again—and still together.

Eileen believes her professional career matches her nomadic upbringing, since she has tried everything from draughting to a brief stint as a ranch hand—Not until she started writing did she 'stay put', because that's when she knew she'd come home. Readers can write to her at PO Box 4612, Midland, TX 79704-4612, USA.

Books by Eileen Wilks in her TALL, DARK & ELIGIBLE series

Silhouette Desire
Jacob's Proposal
Luke's Promise
Michael's Temptation

This one's for Glenda, who wanted to read about a
woman minister who didn't fit the stereotypes,
with special thanks to my editor,
Mary-Theresa Hussey, and to Desire Senior Editor
Joan Marlow Golan, for making it possible.

Prologue

The sky growled. Lightning shattered the darkness, flashing an image of heavy wood and wet stone. The gargoyle flanking the door leered at him in the brief burst of light as he fitted his key to the lock.

Rain and darkness suited the old house, Michael thought as he swung the door open. Suited his mood, too.

The only light in the foyer came from a Christmas tree winking at him merrily from one corner. The wide stairwell was dark, and no light came from the hall that led to his brother's office.

Jacob wouldn't be in bed yet. The playroom, maybe. Michael's boots squeaked on the marble floor, reminding him that he was dripping wet.

Ada wouldn't thank him for tracking water all over. He stopped by a high-backed wooden chair that resembled a throne and pulled off his boots and leather jacket. Before tossing the jacket on the chair, he pulled a thick envelope from an inner pocket.

His steps were soundless now as he made his way to the back of the house. He paused in the doorway to the playroom.

The lights were off. A fire burned in the fireplace, hot and bright, tossing shadows along the walls. The windows were bare to the night, rain-washed, and the limb of one young elm tapped against the glass like fretful fingers. Jacob sat in the wing chair beside the fireplace, his legs outstretched, his face turned to the fire. He held a brandy snifter in one hand.

Michael smiled. "Snob. That expensive French stuff doesn't taste any better than what I can get at the grocery store for $12.95 a bottle."

If he'd startled his brother, it didn't show. Very little did, with Jacob. The face he turned to Michael revealed neither pleasure nor surprise, but the welcome was there, in his voice. "I have a palate. You drink like a teenager, purely for the effect."

"True." Michael moved into the room.

It was furnished in a haphazard way at odds with the elegance of the rest of the house. Every time their father had taken a wife, the new Mrs. West had redecorated. Michael and his brothers had gotten in the habit of stashing their favorite pieces here. The playroom had become a haven for castoffs in more ways than one.

There was a library table that had once been the property of a Spanish viceroy of Mexico. It made him think of his brother Luke and countless games of poker—which Luke had usually won. Michael's second-oldest brother might seem reckless, but he had always been good at calculating the odds. Luke was almost as at home with a deck of cards as he was on the back of a horse.

A chessboard with jade and jet pieces sat on the table now. Michael paused there to pick up the jet king and turn it over and over in the hand that wasn't holding the thick envelope. Chess had always been Jacob's game. The patience and planning of it had suited him when they were young, just as his careful accumulation of wealth did now.

Michael sighed and put the chess piece down. It was hard to ask, but worse not to know. "How's Ada?"

"Mean as ever." Jacob stood. He was a big man, Michael's oldest brother. Big all over, and four inches taller than Michael's six feet. His hair was short and thick, a brown so dark it almost matched Michael's black hair; his shirt, too, was dark, with the subtle sheen of silk. "She's doing well, Michael. The treatments are working."

The breath he hadn't realized he was holding came out in a dizzy rush. He cleared his throat. "Good. That's good."

"You here for a while?"

"I'll have to leave in the morning. I've been..." He glanced at the envelope still in his hand. "Taking care of business. You have anything to drink other than that fancy cologne you're sipping?"

"I think I can find something cheap enough to please you." Jacob moved over to the bar. "How much of an effect are you after?"

"More than that," Michael said when his brother paused after pouring two fingers of bourbon.

Jacob handed him the glass. "You can start with this. You won't be here long enough to nurse a hangover."

"I'll nurse it on the plane." He let his restless feet carry him to the pinball machine in the corner.

Pinball—that had been his game back when they all lived here. Flash and speed, he thought, and swallowed cheap fire, grimacing at the taste but relishing the burn. He'd been drawn to both back then. Lacking Jacob's patience and Luke's athleticism, he'd settled for the gifts he did have—a certain quickness of hand, eye and body.

He couldn't complain. Agility was an asset for a man who lived the way he did. So was a clear mind...but tonight he preferred to be thoroughly fuzzed. He tossed back the rest of the liquor.

Jacob's eyebrow lifted. "In a hurry?"

He shrugged and went over to the bar to refill his glass. What he'd done—what he intended to do—was for Ada, and therefore worth the sacrifice. Without the treatments administered by a Swiss clinic, she would die. But the treatments were experimental and very, very expensive.

There had been only one way for the West brothers to raise the money to keep Ada alive. The trust, the be-damned trust their father had left his fortune tied up in, could be dissolved and they could claim the inheritance none of them had wanted to touch...once they fulfilled the conditions.

Luke had already done his part. Michael intended to do his—that's why he was here. Jacob wouldn't be far behind...all three of them dancing to the old man's piping at last, five years after burying him.

Jacob set his snifter on the bar. "Pour me some more while you're at it. I'm not interested in a hangover, but I'll keep you company. What's the occasion?"

"What else?" He tossed the envelope on the bar. "That's a copy of the prenuptial agreement your lawyer drew up for me, duly signed and notarized."

"I see. Found someone already, have you?"

Michael lifted his glass, empty now, in a mocking salute. "Congratulate me. I'm getting married as soon as I get back from this mission. So tonight, I'm going to get very, very drunk."

One

Were they coming for her?

She sat bolt upright, thrust from sleep into wakefulness. The bed ropes creaked beneath her. The taste of fear was thick and dry in her mouth. *Dan,* she thought. *Dan, why aren't you here?*

There was, of course, no answer.

If it had been a sound that awakened her, she heard nothing now except the rhythmic rasp of Sister Maria Elena's breathing in the bed beside her. Darkness pressed against her staring eyes, the unrelieved blackness only possible far from the artificial glow of civilization.

Automatically her gaze flickered toward the door. She couldn't see a thing.

Thank God. Her sigh eased a single hard knot of fear. If they came for her at night—and they might—they would have to bring a light. She'd be able to see it shining around the edges of the door.

Her gaze drifted to the outside wall where whispers of

starlight bled through cracks between the boards, smudging the darkness. Soldiers had hammered those boards over the window when they'd first locked her in this room last week.

One week. When morning came, she would have been here a full seven days. Waiting for the man they called *El Jefe* to return and decide if she were to live or die…or, if the taunts of her guards were true, what form that death would take.

He would decide Sister Maria Elena's fate, too, she reminded herself, and wished the fear didn't always come first, hardest, for herself. But while the sister was a *religioso,* she was also a native of San Christóbal, not a representative of the nation *El Jefe* hated even more than he hated organized religion. She was old and ill. He might spare her.

A.J. pushed back the thin blanket, careful not to wake the nun, and swung her legs to the floor. Her knees were rubbery. Her breath came quick and shallow, and her hands and feet were chilled.

She ignored the physical symptoms of terror as best she could, making her way by touch and memory to the boarded-up window. There she folded her long legs to sit on the cool, dirty floor. Spaces between the boards let in fresh air—chilly, this far up in the mountains, but welcome. She smelled dampness and dirt, the wild green aroma of growing things, the heavier perfume of flowers. Even now, in the dry season, there were flowers here.

Wherever "here" was. She didn't know where the soldiers had brought her when they'd raided La Paloma, the sleepy village where she'd been working. San Christóbal had a lot of mountains.

The boards let in slices of sky along with air. And if the sky was clear…yes, when she leaned close she could see a single star. The sight eased her.

The night wasn't truly silent. Inside, there was the labored breathing of the feverish nun. Outside, frogs set up a staccato chorus, and the soft whirring of wings announced the hunt of some night-flying bird. Somewhere not too far away, a man cried out a greeting in Spanish and was answered. The distant scream of a puma rattled the night. Then there was only the sighing of wind through trees.

So many trees. Even without boards, without soldiers and fear, it had been hard sometimes to find enough sky here to feed a soul used to the open plains of west Texas.

A.J. tried not to regret coming to San Christóbal. That, too, was hard. Her eyes stayed open while her lips moved in a soundless prayer.

It shamed her, how deep and terrible her fear was. It weakened her, too, and she would need strength to get through whatever was to come. So she would pray and wait here, wait and watch as her slivers of sky brightened. In the daylight, she could remember who she was. There was Sister Maria Elena to care for then, and birdsong and monkey chatter to listen to. In the daylight, the slices of sky between the cracks would turn brilliantly blue. She could steady herself against those snatches of life.

But at night, locked into the darkness, she felt alone, lost, forgotten. In the darkness, she missed Dan intensely—and blamed him, too, as foolish as that was. In the darkness, the fear came back, rolling in like the tide of a polluted ocean. Sooner or later, *he* would be back. The one they called *El Jefe.* He would finish killing people elsewhere and return to his headquarters.

Being left alone was a good thing, she reminded herself. *El Jefe* was a man who believed in killing for his cause—but he didn't condone rape. Neither she nor Sister Maria Elena had been harmed in that way. A.J. watched her star and murmured a prayer of thanks.

If she hadn't been sitting with her head almost touching the boards, she wouldn't have heard the sound. Softer than a whisper, so soft she couldn't say what made it—save that it came from outside. From the other side of the window.

Her breath stopped up in her throat. Her eyes widened.

Something blacked out her star.

"Reverend? Are you there?" The voice was male and scarcely louder than her heartbeat. It came from only inches away. "Reverend Kelleher?"

It was also American.

Dizziness hit. If she had been standing, she would have fallen. "Yes," she whispered, and had to swallow. "Yes, I'm here."

A pause. "I'm going to kill Scopes," that wonderful voice whispered.

"Wh-what?"

"I was expecting a baritone, not a soprano." There was a hint of drawl in the whisper, a deliciously familiar echo of Texas. "Lieutenant Michael West, ma'am. Special Forces. I've come to get you out of here."

"Thank God." The prayer was heartfelt.

"How old are you?"

"Thirty-two." She bit back the urge to ask him how old *he* was.

"Are you injured?"

"No, I—"

"On a scale of couch potato to superjock, how fit are you?"

Oh—he needed to know if she would be able to keep up. "I'm in good shape, Lieutenant. But Sister Maria Elena is over sixty, and her leg—"

"Who?" The word came out sharp and a little louder.

"Sister Maria Elena," she repeated, confused. "She was injured when the soldiers overran the village. I'm afraid she won't be able to...Lieutenant?"

He'd begun to curse, fluently and almost soundlessly. "This nun—is she a U.S. citizen?"

"No, but surely that doesn't matter."

"The U.S. can't rescue every native endangered by a bunch of Che Guevara wannabes. And what would I do with her? Guatemala and Honduras aren't accepting refugees from San Christóbal, and Nicaragua is still pissed at the U.S. over the carrier incident last spring. They wouldn't let us land a military helicopter."

"But—but you can't just leave her here!"

"Reverend, getting you out is going to be tricky enough."

A.J. leaned her forehead against one rough board and swallowed hope. It lumped up sick and cold in her stomach. "Then I'm sorry," she whispered. "I can't go with you."

There was a beat of silence. "Do you have any idea what *El Jefe* will do to you if you're still here when he gets back?"

"I hope you aren't planning to give me any gruesome details. It won't help. I can't leave Sister Maria Elena." Her voice wobbled. "She's feverish. It started with a cut on her foot that got infected. Sh-she'll die without care."

"Lady, she's going to die whether you stay or go."

She wanted desperately to go with him. She couldn't. "I can't leave her."

Another, longer silence. "Do you know anything about the truck parked beside the barracks?"

She shook her head, trying to keep up with the odd jumps his mind made. "I don't know. They brought me here in a truck. A flatbed truck with metal sides that smells like a chicken coop."

"That's the one. It was running last week?"

She nodded, then felt foolish. He couldn't see her. "Yes."

"Okay. Get your things together. Wait here—I'll be back."

She nearly choked on a giggle, afraid that if she started laughing she wouldn't be able to stop. "Sure. I'm not going anywhere."

The moon was a skimpy sliver, casting barely enough light to mark the boundaries between shadows. Michael waited in a puddle of deeper darkness, his back pressed to the cement blocks of *El Jefe*'s house. A sentry passed fifteen feet away.

The sentries didn't worry him. He had a pair of Uncle Sam's best night goggles, while the sentries had to rely on whatever night vision came naturally. He also had his weapons—a SIG Sauer and the CAR 16 slung over his shoulder—but hoped like hell he wouldn't have to use them. Shooting was likely to attract attention. If he had to silence one of the sentries, he'd rather use one of the darts in his vest pocket. They were loaded with a nifty knockout drug.

El Jefe's headquarters was like the rest of his military efforts—military in style but inadequate. The self-styled liberator should have stayed a guerrilla leader, relying on sneak attacks. He lacked the training to hold what he'd taken. In Michael's not-so-humble opinion, San Christóbal's government would have to screw up mightily to lose this nasty little war. In a week or two, government troops should be battling their way up the slope *El Jefe*'s house perched on.

But what the guerrilla leader lacked in military training he made up for in sheer, bloody fanaticism. A week would be too late for the soft-voiced woman Michael had just left.

What was the fool woman doing here? His mouth tightened. Maybe she was no more foolish than the three U.S. biologists they'd already picked up, who were waiting nervously aboard the chopper. But she was female, damn it.

One sentry rounded the west corner of the house. The other had almost reached the end of his patrol. Michael bent and made his way quickly and silently across the cleared slope separating the compound from the forest. Then he paused to scan the area behind him. The goggles rendered everything in grays, some areas sharp, others fuzzy. Out in the open, though, where the sentry moved, visibility was excellent. Michael waited patiently as the man passed the boarded-up window. He wouldn't move on until he was sure he wouldn't lead anyone to the rendezvous.

He was definitely going to kill Scopes.

It was Scopes who'd passed on word from a villager about some do-gooder missionary who'd been captured by *El Jefe*'s troops. He must have known the minister was a woman, damn him. Andrew Scopes was going to strangle on his twisted sense of humor this time, Michael promised himself.

Maybe the minister's sex shouldn't make a difference. But it did.

He remembered the way her voice had shaken when she'd whispered that she couldn't go with him. She'd probably been crying. He hated a woman's tears, and resented that he'd heard hers.

She was scared out of her mind. But she wasn't budging, not without her nun.

A nun. God almighty. Michael started winding through the trunks of the giants that held up the forest canopy. Even with the goggles the light was poor here, murky and indistinct, but he could see well enough to avoid running into anything.

Why did there have to be a nun?

Since he'd joined the service, he'd had more than one hard decision to make. Some of them haunted him late at night when ghosts come calling. But a *nun!* He shook his head. His memories of St. Vincent's Academy weren't all pleasant, but they were vivid. Especially his memories of Sister Mary Agnes. She'd reminded him of Ada. Mean as a lioness with PMS if you hadn't done your homework, and twice as fierce in defense of one of her kids.

Dammit to hell. This was supposed to have been a simple mission. Simple, at least, for Michael's team. His men were good. True, Crowe was new, but so far he'd proved steady. But gathering intelligence on the deadly spat brewing between *El Jefe* and the government of San Christóbal, rounding up a few terrified biologists on the side, was a far cry from snatching captives from a quasi-military compound.

Still, the compound wasn't heavily guarded, and the soldiers left behind when *El Jefe* left to take the mountain road weren't well trained or equipped. Michael and his men had watched the place for two days and a night; he knew what they were up against. No floodlights, thank God, and the forest provided great cover. Once they got their target out, they had three miles to cover to reach the clearing where the Cobra waited with its cargo of nervous biologists. An easy run—unless you were carrying an injured nun with fifteen armed soldiers in hot pursuit.

But *El Jefe* had thoughtfully left a truck behind. And, according to the Reverend, it had been running a week ago, when they brought her here. There was a good chance it was in working order.

If the truck ran…

She'd giggled. When he'd told her to wait there—meaning for her to wait by the window so she would hear him when he returned—she'd answered with one silly, stifled giggle. That sound clung to him like cobwebs, in sticky strands that couldn't be brushed off. He crossed a narrow stream in the darkness of that foreign forest, his CAR 16 slung over his back and memories of Popsicles melting in the summer sun filling his mind.

Her giggle made him think of the first time he'd kissed a girl. The taste of grape Nehi, and long-ago mornings when dew had glistened on the grass like every unbroken promise ever made.

There was no innocence in him, not anymore. But he could still recognize it. He could still be moved by it.

He could knock the Reverend out. It would be the sensible thing to do. Downright considerate, even, since then she'd be able to blame him instead of herself for the nun's fate.

Of course, he'd blame himself, too.

When was he going to grow up and get over his rescue-the-maiden complex? It was going to get him killed one of these days. And, dammit, he couldn't get killed now. He had to get married.

That wasn't the best way to talk himself out of playing hero.

He'd reached the fallen tree that was his goal. He stopped and whistled—one low, throbbing note that mimicked a bird call. A second later, three men melted out of the trees. Even with his goggles, he hadn't spotted them until they moved. His men were good. The best. Even Scopes, though Michael still intended to ream him a new one for his little joke.

He sighed and accepted the decision he'd already made, however much he'd tried to argue himself out of it. He couldn't leave the Reverend to *El Jefe*'s untender mercy. Or the nun.

The Colonel was going to gut him for sure this time.

The wheeling of the earth had taken A.J.'s star out of sight. Now there was only darkness between the slits in the boards.

Getting her things together had been easy. They hadn't let her bring any of her possessions, not her Bible, not even a change of underwear. She had a comb and a toothbrush tucked in her pocket, given to her a few days ago by a guard who still possessed a trace of compassion. Of course, he probably expected to get them back when she was killed. Still, she asked God to bless the impulse that had moved him to offer her those tokens of shared humanity.

Waiting was hard.

He was coming back. Surely he was. And if he did…*when* he did, he would take her and the sister away with him. He had to.

She touched the place between her breasts where her cross used to hang and wished she knew how long she'd been waiting. How long she still had to wait. If the sun rose and he hadn't returned…oh, she didn't want to give up hope. Painful as it was, she didn't want to give it up.

Time was strange. So elastic. Events and emotions could compress it, wad up the moments so tightly that hours sped by at breakneck speed. Or it could be stretched so thin that one second oozed into the next with boggy reluctance. *Slow as molasses,* she thought. Into her mind drifted an image of her grandfather's freckled hand, the knuckles swollen, holding a jar of molasses, pouring it over a stack of her mother's buttermilk pancakes….

"Hey, Rev."

Though the whisper was so soft it blended with the breeze, she jolted. "Yes." It came out too loud, snatching the breath from her lungs. "I'm here."

"In a few minutes there will be an explosion at the east end of the compound. Are you familiar with the setup?"

An explosion? Her heart thudded. "I didn't see much when I was brought here, and I've been kept in this room ever since. Are you going to...Sister Maria Elena, will you...?"

"Yeah." He sighed. "We'll take the sister. You ready? Got your things?"

"There's nothing." Her hand went to the place her cross used to hang. A soldier with pocked skin and a missing tooth had yanked it off her neck. "Just Sister Maria Elena."

"Is she ready to go?"

"She doesn't hear well. I didn't want to wake her to tell her what was going on. I would have had to speak too loudly."

"Explanations will have to wait, then. The sentries are taken care of, but there might be other guards inside the house."

The sentries were "taken care of"? What did that mean? She shivered. "Why an explosion? Wouldn't it be better to sneak out?"

"We need a distraction. One of my men is going to blow up the barracks at the other end of the compound. When it goes—"

"No." In her distress she rose to her knees, putting her hands against the boards as if she could reach him through them. "No, the soldiers—they're sleeping. You can't kill them when they're sleeping."

"It's a shaped charge, just a little boom. Noisy enough to get their attention, but most of the force will be dispersed upward, taking out the roof. It probably won't kill anyone."

He sounded matter-of-fact, almost indifferent. As if death—killing—meant little to him. ''Probably?''

''Keep your voice down,'' he whispered. ''Look, this is war. A small one, but the rules aren't the ones you're used to. These men would shoot you and the sister without blinking. That's if you're lucky. They've done worse.''

A.J. swallowed. The area where she'd been working had been peaceful at first. She wouldn't have come to San Cristóbal if she'd known...but after she'd arrived, she'd heard rumors of atrocities in the mountains. Men shot, tortured, villages burned. In Carracruz, the capital city, they blamed outlaws. In the rural villages, they whispered of rebels. Of *El Jefe.*

''Maybe so. That doesn't make it right to kill them in their beds.''

''You worry about right and wrong, Rev. I'll worry about getting us out of here. Here's the plan. There's a helicopter waiting three miles away. While the *soldados* are busy worrying about the explosion, we get you and the sister out of here and run like hell. There's a trail that runs into the road about half a mile from the compound. We'll meet the truck there.''

''What truck?''

''The one my men will liberate. It will get us to the copter. If everything goes well, we'll be airborne about fifteen minutes after Scopes's bomb goes off. Got it?''

It sounded good. It sounded so good she was terrified all over again at the sheer, dizzying possibility of escape. ''Got it.''

''One more thing. From this point on, I'm the voice of God to you.''

''That's blasphemous.''

''It's necessary. You have the right to risk your own life, but you don't have the right to endanger my men. You do what I say, when I say. No arguing, no questions. If I say jump, I don't want to hear any nonsense about how high. Just jump. Understood?"

"I'm not good at following orders blindly."

"You'd better learn fast, or I'll knock you out and make my job easier."

She swallowed. She didn't have any trouble believing Lieutenant Michael West would knock her out if he considered it necessary. "You're supposed to be one of the good guys."

"They don't make good guys like they used to, honey."

"A.J."

"What?"

"You've called me Reverend, Rev, lady, and now honey. My name's A.J."

"Sounds more like—"

It was like being inside a clap of thunder—end-of-the-world loud, floor-shaking, ear-bursting loud.

His "little boom" had gone off.

Two

Michael had the first board popped off before his ears stopped ringing. He'd brought a tire iron for that chore, borrowed from the shed that held the truck Scopes and Trace were stealing at this very moment. He worked quickly, his SIG Sauer in its holster, the CAR 16 on the ground. He'd drugged the closest sentry before approaching the window; he could count on Hammond to take care of the other one.

The nun had let out a screech when the bomb went off. The Reverend was explaining things to her now—loudly.

A voice that was all bone-rumbling bass sounded behind him. "Do I get the one that's yellin'?"

"Nope." Michael pried off the last board and stepped back. "You get the one that screamed when Scopes's toy went boom. In you go."

"She'll start screamin' again when she sees me," Hammond said gloomily. The team's electronics expert did look like the Terminator's bigger, blacker brother, especially in camouflage with night goggles. He sighed and eased his six-feet-six inches of muscle through the small window.

Michael tossed down the tire iron and picked up his CAR 16, keeping his back to the window as he kept watch. He heard Hammond's low rumble assuring the Reverend she could trust him with the sister; seconds later, he heard the Reverend climbing out the window. He slid her one quick glance, then jerked his gaze back to the clearing and the trees.

She sure as hell didn't look like any minister he'd ever seen.

That momentary glimpse hadn't given him a lot details, and his goggles robbed the scene of color. But he'd noticed a slim, long-fingered hand that shook slightly. A tangled wreck of curls that hung below her shoulders. A wide mouth in an angular face, and big eyes fixed on the weapon he cradled. And about six feet of legs.

Lord, she must be nearly as tall as he was. And ninety percent of her was legs.

What color were her eyes?

Hammond was at the window, ready to pass out a blanket-wrapped bundle. Michael traded a CAR 16 for an armful of old woman.

Even through the blanket and the material of her habit, he felt the heat from her fever. She was tiny, so light Hammond could probably cradle her in one arm and still handle his weapon. She'd lost her wimple. Her hair was thin, short and plastered to her skull. Her face was small and round and wrinkled...and smiling.

She looked nothing like Sister Mary Agnes. Michael smiled back at her, told her in Spanish that they would take good care of her, then passed her to Hammond.

The scream of automatic fire shattered the night, coming from the other end of the compound. Good. The others were keeping the soldiers busy. His quick glance took in the preacher's pallor and shocked eyes. He didn't know if it was the gunfire that spooked her, or if she could see the huddled shape of the sentries a few feet away.

He didn't have time to coddle her. "We'll go single file. Reverend, you're the meat in the sandwich. Hammond and I can see where we're going. You can't, so hook your hand in my utility belt. We'll be moving fast."

"A.J. My name is A.J."

He turned away. "Hang on tight." As soon as he felt her hand seize the webbed belt at the small of his back, he moved out.

They crossed the clearing at a dead run and didn't slow much when they hit the forest. The ground was rough, and the night must have been completely black to her, but she didn't hold them up. A couple of times she stumbled, but her grip on his belt kept her upright, and she kept moving.

Good for her. He blessed her long legs as he wove among the trees, listening to the diminishing blast of gunfire behind them.

"Where are we going?"

"This trail intersects the road. We'll meet the truck there. There's a log here you'll have to jump." He leaped it.

She followed awkwardly but without falling. "This is a trail? Are you sure?"

He grinned, pleased with the trace of humor he heard in her voice. "Trust me. It's here." He'd found and followed it last night. Fortunately, the canopy wasn't as thick here as it was in some places—part of this forest was second-growth. But that meant that there was more underbrush.

"Hammond," he said. "Anything?"

"No sign of pursuit, Mick."

Everything was going according to plan. It made Michael uneasy. Yeah, it was a good plan, implemented by good men. Problem was, he'd never yet been on a job where everything went according to plan. The truck might not start, or any of a dozen things could go wrong with getting it out.

When they reached the road Michael's pessimism was rewarded. The truck wasn't there. A fistful of soldiers were. And they were coming *up* the road, not down it from the compound.

One second A.J. was running a step behind her rescuer, her hand locked for dear life in the webbing of his belt while plants tried to trip her. The next, he stopped so suddenly she slammed into him.

He didn't even wobble. Just spun, shoved her down and hit the ground beside her.

She couldn't see a thing. Her hip throbbed from her rough landing in the dirt. A stick was poking her shoulder, and she didn't know where Sister Maria Elena was. The other soldier, the one with the face of a comic book villain and the Mr. Universe body, wasn't beside them. When A.J. lifted her head to see what had happened to him, a large hand pushed it back down so fast she got dirt in her mouth.

He kept his hand on her neck. She felt breath on her hair, warm and close to her ear. His whisper was so soft she barely heard it. "Soldiers coming up the road. Not the ones from the compound."

Oh, God. More soldiers. Now that she'd stopped running, she felt cold. So cold. Or maybe it was his thumb, moving idly on her nape, that made goose bumps pop out on her shivery flesh. Or fear. She tried to keep her whisper as nearly soundless as his had been. "The truck?"

"Listen."

She heard it now—a motor laboring, moving toward them. And from the other direction, voices of the soldiers he'd seen, coming up the rough dirt road. How could they have gotten in front of the truck?

No, she realized, these soldiers weren't from the compound. They must be some of *El Jefe*'s other troops. Was *El Jefe* himself with them? Fear, sour and brackish, mixed with the flavor of dirt in her mouth. She tried to breathe slowly, to calm her racing heart.

Headlights! They splashed color against the dense black backdrop of trees just up the road as the truck rounded a curve.

"We'll have a few seconds before they realize the truck isn't part of their team anymore." His hand left her nape, and she felt him move, crouching beside her, his weapon ready. "I've signaled Hammond. When he moves, you follow. Head for the back of the truck."

The truck was closing the distance rapidly. Its headlights picked out three men on the road ahead—ragged, but unmistakably soldiers.

"I'll lay covering fire if needed, then—hell! *Damn* that Crowe!"

Shots—machine-gun fast and deafeningly loud—came from the truck. One of the soldiers jerked and fell. The rest scattered, leaping for cover. And firing back.

The gunfire hurled her back in time, to a place and moment she never wanted to see again—past blurring the present with horror and blood. Her ears rang. Terror spurted through her like flames chasing gasoline.

Someone yelled—it was him, Michael, the lieutenant—but she had no idea what he was yelling. He waved his arm and the other soldier leaped right over her, huge and dark and graceful. Then he was running toward the truck, the sister in his arms, with the roar and hammer of gunfire exploding everywhere.

The truck had slowed, but it hadn't come to a complete stop. The soldier leaped again and landed in the back of the rolling truck, the sister still in his arms. Oh, God, it was still moving. It would pass them by. She had to get up, had to run—but noise and terror, gunfire and memory smothered her, pressing her flat in the dirt.

The lieutenant grabbed her arm and jerked her to her knees. *"Run!"*

She gulped and shoved to her feet. A shadowy form loomed suddenly up out of the darkness. Moonlight gleamed on the barrel of his gun—pointed right at them.

Gunfire exploded beside her. The shadowy form jerked, fell. Someone screamed—was it her? Shots burst out all over, seeming to come from every direction. Dirt sprayed up near her feet.

He seized her hand and dragged her after him at a dead run—into the forest.

Away from the truck.

She pulled against his grip and tried to make him let her go. Maybe she cried out those words, *let me go, let me go to the truck*—but he dragged her after him, into the forest. She stumbled, tripped, crashing into the loamy ground. He jerked her to her feet and growled, "Run like the fires of hell are after you. They are."

She heard renewed gunfire. And she ran.

What followed was a nightmare of darkness and noise. The soldiers came after them. She heard them crashing through the underbrush, heard them calling to one another. And she heard their guns. Once, bark chips flew from a tree, cutting her cheek, when a bullet came too close.

They ran and ran. The lieutenant gripped her hand as if she might try to get away, but she no longer wanted to, no longer thought she *could* let go. She ran as if her feet knew the ground her eyes couldn't see, trusting him because she had no choice, relying on him to steer them both through the trees. She ran, images of death following her, of the man he'd shot to save them both—the body jerking, falling. Images of another man, shot under bright lights, not in darkness. Images of blood.

She ran, grieving for the truck and the lost chance of escape, fleeing ever deeper into the forest instead of being in the truck rolling rapidly away from guns and blood and bullets. After a while her entire being focused on running, on the dire importance of not falling, on the need to drag in enough breath to fuel her. There was only flight and the strong, hard hand that held hers. Pounding feet and a pounding heart and the sound and feel of him, so close to her, running with her.

Gradually, she realized she could see the black bulks of the trees and the vague outline of the man who ran with her. There were grays now as well as blacks, and dimness between the trees instead of complete darkness. She had an urge to look up, a sudden hunger for the sky. If she could see a star, just one—receive the sweet kiss of the moon, or glimpse the power of the sun pushing back the night…

He was slowing. As he did, the fear came rushing back, making her want to run and run, to run forever. She made herself slow along with him. And stop.

They stood in the gray light, motionless except for their heaving chests. The sound of her breathing shocked her. It was so loud, so labored. How long had they been running? Where were they?

Then she heard something else. A distant, mechanical thrumming. Coming from above? From the sky? A *helicopter,* she thought with all the wonder of renewed hope.

She turned to him, seeking the paler blur of his face. ''Is—that—yours?'' She was badly winded, making it hard to get the words out.

''They're looking for us. We have to get out from under these trees.'' He gave her hand a squeeze. ''C'mon. Unless I'm lost, the trees end up ahead.''

The air lightened around them. And it was lightest in the direction they were headed, as if they were walking toward morning. Another sound replaced the whir of the helicopter—the thrumming roar of water falling. She smelled it, too, the wild liquid scent of water.

So suddenly it shocked, they left the trees behind.

The air shimmered with morning and mist. The sky was slate fading to pearl in the east. There was dampness on her face, and she could see the ground she walked on, the spearing shapes of trees behind her, and the bulk of rocks—a short, blunted cliff—rising off to her left.

And she could see *him.* Not with much detail, but at last she could see the man who had rescued her. He was tall and straight and carried his gun on his back. His face was partly hidden by the goggles that had let him lead their flight through the trees.

The sight of him, which should have reassured her, made her feel more lost. Fleeing through darkness with only his hand to guide her, she'd felt somehow connected, as if she knew him in some deep, visceral way. The reality of him, so straight and military and unknown, shattered that illusion.

The water-noise was very loud now. In the muted grays of predawn she saw it falling from the top of the cliff. Her breath caught as her feet stopped.

A yard away the ground ended, sheared off neatly as if cut by a giant's knife. And below—far below—was the destination of the falling water, dark and loud.

A river. Which one? She tried to summon a mental map of the country, but her weary brain refused to make pictures for her. Whatever the river's name, it was hearty, swollen with rain from the recently-ended wet season. Hemmed in by stone banks, water churned and rushed far below.

''Where are we?'' she asked.

Maybe he didn't hear her over the noise of the waterfall. He was scanning the sky, the goggles pushed down. Was it getting too light to use them? Biting her lip, she looked at the sky, too, but didn't spot the longed-for shape of a helicopter.

''Come on, Dave,'' the man beside her muttered. ''Where else would I be but—*yes!*''

She looked where he was looking and saw it—a dark shape flying low, coming out from behind the trees well down the river. Heading their way. She laughed, releasing his hand at last, wanting to jump up and down.

Safety was flying up the river toward them.

A.J. had excellent hearing. Her other senses were no better than ordinary, but her hearing was unusually keen. It was she who heard the shout over the racket the waterfall made.

She spun. There—coming out of the trees—a soldier. No, *soldiers.* She gasped and grabbed the lieutenant.

He was already in motion, turning, his gun lifting.

Again, the impossibly loud sound of gunfire. Bullets spitting up dust at her feet—the soldiers fading back into the trees, save for one, who lay still on the ground. And hands at her waist, digging in, jerking her off her feet—

Throwing her off the cliff.

She fell. And fell. And fell. It seemed to go on forever, or maybe it was only an instant before the water slapped her—a giant's slap, stunning and vicious. Water closed over her head so quickly she had no time to get a good breath, though instinct closed her mouth as she plummeted, expecting rocks that would crush and break, tumbled by the water until up and down were lost.

But one foot hit the bottom, mushy with silt. She pushed off, her lungs straining. The current was strong, but she kicked and clawed her way up, up, and at last her head broke the surface. She gulped in air.

Stony walls rushed past. The river moved even faster than she'd realized, and it took all her energy to keep her head above the churning water—but not all her thought. Where was he? She could see little but the dark rush of water. A rock loomed ahead, and she struck out with legs and arms, trying to avoid it. It clipped her hip as she tumbled by, but speed, chill and adrenaline kept her from noticing the blow.

Where was he? He'd thrown her from the cliff—and she would have fought him if she'd had time to understand what he was doing, but he'd known. All along, he'd known what to do. Somewhere in the back of her mind, while the rest of her fought the current, fought to breathe and stay afloat, she knew why he'd done it. The two of them had been out in the open, nowhere to go to escape the bullets spitting around them.

Nowhere but down.

So he'd thrown her off the cliff—but where was *he?* Had he made it over the edge, too? Or was he lying back in the clearing, bleeding and dying?

Again, it was her ears that gave her answers. Faintly over the noise of the water she heard her name. She opened her mouth, swallowed water, choked and finally managed to cry out, "Here! Over here!"

But the torrent didn't allow her a glimpse of him until it slowed, until the stony banks gave way to dirt and the river widened and her arms and legs ached with the fierce burn of muscles used beyond their limits. The sun had finished pulling itself up over the edge of the world by then. She glimpsed his head, some distance farther downriver from her. She called out again.

He answered. She couldn't make out the words, but he answered.

That quickly, the energy that had carried her was gone. Her legs and arms went from aching to trembling. Weakness sped through her like a drug, and she wanted, badly, to let the water carry her to him, let him do the rest.

Stupid, stupid. Did she want to drown them both? She struck out for the nearest shore, her limbs sluggish and weak.

At last her foot struck mud when she kicked. Silty, slimy, wonderful mud. She tried to stand, and couldn't. So she crawled on hands and knees, feeling each inch won free of the water as a victory worthy of bands and trumpets and parades.

The bank was narrow, a stretch of mud, twigs and rotting vegetation. She dragged herself onto it. And collapsed.

For long minutes she lay there and breathed, her muscles twitching and jumping. Never had she enjoyed breathing more. Birds had woken with the dawn, and their songs, cries and scoldings made a varied chorus, punctuated by the chatter and screech of monkeys.

He *had* made it to shore, hadn't he?

She had to look for him. Groaning, she pushed herself onto her side, raising herself on an arm that felt like cooked spaghetti, preparing for the work of standing up.

And saw him, for the first time, in the full light of day.

He sat four feet away with one knee up, his arm propped across it. Water dripped from short black hair and from the wet fatigues that clung to muscular arms and thighs. He wore an odd-looking vest with lots of pockets over his brown-and-green shirt. His face was oval, the skin tanned and taut and shadowed by beard stubble; the nose was pure Anglo, but the cheekbones and dark, liquid eyes looked Latin. His mouth was solemn, unsmiling. The upper lip was a match for the lower. It bowed in a perfect dip beneath that aristocratic nose.

Her heart gave an uncomfortable lurch. The stranger watching her was the most beautiful man she'd ever seen. And he was looking her over. His gaze moved from her feet to her legs, from belly to breasts, finally reaching her face.

''Basketball?'' he asked.

Three

A.J. blinked. Maybe the vision of male beauty had taken a blow to the head? "I, ah, didn't bring a ball."

He grinned. "I must have swallowed more river water than I thought. No, I haven't taken leave of my senses. I was thinking of your legs. I thought I'd lost you..." His grin faded as his mouth tightened. "The current was rough. I couldn't get to you, and I didn't think you'd be able to make it on your own, not after the run we'd just put in. But obviously you use those legs of yours for more than kneeling."

"Oh." She processed the sentence backward to his original question, and answered it. "Track in college, baseball for fun, running for exercise, swimming sometimes."

"When you said you were fit, you meant it. Which relieves my mind considerably. We have a long walk ahead of us, Rev."

Annoyance flicked a little more life back into her. She pulled her weary body upright. "I've asked you not to call me that."

"Yeah, I know. The thing is, if I stop calling you Reverend, I'm apt to start paying attention to the wrong things, like those world-class legs of yours. They look great wet, by the way."

It occurred to her that her legs weren't the only part of her that was soaked. She glanced down—and quickly pulled her shirt out so it didn't plaster itself against her breasts. Heat rose in her cheeks. "Then you can call me Reverend Kelleher, and I'll call you Lieutenant West."

He shook his head. "I'll do better to think of you as one of my men for the next few days. We don't lean toward much formality on the team, so you need to be either Rev or Legs. I'm better off with Rev, I think." He reached for a canvas kit that hung from his belt. "Especially since the next thing we have to do is take off our clothes."

She stiffened. "I don't think so."

"You're cute when your mouth gets all prim."

"Refusing to strip for a man I don't know isn't prim. It's common sense. And a man who would ask me to—"

"Whoa." He held both hands up. "I might tease, but you're completely, one hundred percent safe with me. No offense, but you're the last type of woman I'd make a play for."

"Good." She might be superficial enough to react to his looks, but that was all it was—a silly, superficial reaction. It would fade. He was a man of war. Nothing like Dan.

He nodded and unhooked the kit. "Okay, now that we've got that straight…you'll find that I don't give a lot of orders. And never without a reason. When I do give one, though, you'd do well to follow it. And that was an order, Rev. Take off your shirt and pants."

"I'm not jumping without an explanation this time."

"Visual scan," he said briskly. "We need to check each other out for scrapes, scratches, anyplace the skin is broken. After being tumbled around in the river, we might not notice a small scratch, and between infection and parasites, even the smallest cut is dangerous.''

She thought of Sister Maria Elena's foot. He made sense...unfortunately. ''You first.

''I can wait.''

She inhaled slowly and prayed for patience. It was not a virtue that came naturally to her. ''What will happen to me if your misguided sense of chivalry kills you off before we get out of here?''

He didn't respond at first. His eyes were dark, steady and unreadable. Finally he pulled a small first aid kit out of his kit and handed it to her. ''Use the ointment—it's antibacterial. You'd better take care of my leg first.''

''Your leg?''

He nodded and unfastened his belt.

She tried not to gawk as he levered his hips up so he could pull his pants down. She was a grown woman. A widow. She'd seen male legs before. And her reason for looking at this particular pair of legs was strictly medical, so— ''Oh, dear Lord.''

''A bullet clipped me when I made my swan dive off the cliff.'' He bent to look at the long, nasty gouge dug into the flesh of his upper thigh. It was still oozing blood. ''Doesn't look too bad. The way it's been burning, I was a little worried.''

It looked bad enough to A.J. She dug out the tube of antibiotic cream. ''I don't see peroxide or rubbing alcohol to clean the wound.''

''Chances are it bled itself clean.''

They would have to hope so, it seemed. She uncapped the ointment and squeezed out a generous portion.

''Hey—be stingy with that. We don't have any more.''

''Shut up. Just shut up.'' Grimly she bent over his leg. ''I have no patience with blind, stubborn machismo. I can't believe you were going to let this wait while you looked for scratches I don't have.''

"A man has to take his pleasures where..." His breath caught when she stroked ointment into the shallow end of the wound. "Where he finds them. I expect I'll enjoy looking for your scratches more than what you're doing now. I don't suppose you were part of a medical mission?"

"Teaching." She bit her lip. She'd had little experience with nursing, and not much aptitude for it. Too much empathy. Her hands were already a little shaky. "You might want to start praying. Or cursing. Whatever works."

His muscles quivered when she pulled the torn flesh apart so she could get the dressing into the deepest part of the wound. His breath hissed out. But if he did any cursing or praying, he kept it to himself. "Nice hands. I don't see a wedding ring."

"I'm a widow."

"Pity."

What did he mean by that? "Okay. That's the best I can do." She sat back on her heels. "It needs to be bandaged, but the gauze is damp."

"Damned kit's supposed to be waterproof." He grimaced. "So was my radio, but I lost it and my CAR 16 in the river. Use the gauze. It won't be sterile, but it's better than letting flies lay eggs in my leg."

She bit her lip. "There's this plant...the villagers I worked with called it *bálsamo de Maria.* Mary's balm. I think it's a mild antibiotic. I don't see any nearby, but if I could find some, we could make a pad of the leaves."

"We don't have time to look for leaves." He grabbed the first aid kit, pulled out the gauze and began winding it around his leg. His mouth was tight, bracketed by pain lines.

"Here, let me."

Those dark eyes flicked to her. He handed her the roll of gauze.

His boots were on, and his pants were bunched up around his ankles. He should have looked silly. That he didn't might have had something to do with his briefs, which were undoubtedly white when they weren't soaked. At the moment they were more skin-toned. As she wound the gauze around his thigh, she could feel the heat from his body—and a slow, insidious heat in her own.

It was embarrassing but only natural, she told herself. She was a healthy woman with normal instincts. And he was so very male. "I think that will hold." She tied off the gauze and hoped she didn't sound breathless. "I'll check out the back of your legs now. If you could stretch out on your side...?"

He was remarkably obedient, moving as she'd suggested. The gleam in his eyes suggested he'd picked up on her discomfort, though. And the reason for it.

Oh, he knew he was beautiful. "Peacock," she muttered under her breath, and set herself to her task.

His legs were muscular, the hair dark and coarse. No cuts marred his calves, or the tender pocket behind his knees, or the stretch of skin over the strong muscles of his thighs. She did her best not to notice the curve of his buttocks, so poorly hidden by his shirttail and the wet cotton of his briefs.

Dan's thighs had been thicker than this, she thought, the muscles more bunchy, not as sleek. Hairier, too. Oh, he'd been hairy all over, her big, red giant of a man. And his calves had been freckled from the days when he'd worn shorts and let the sun scatter spots on his pale Irish skin, not dark like this man's was....

He looked over his shoulder at her. "Enjoying yourself?"

She jerked back. "I'm finished. No cuts."

He rolled into a sitting position. Levering his hips off the ground, he pulled his pants up. If the movement hurt, it didn't show. "Lighten up, Rev. I told you, you don't have to worry about me jumping you."

"I'm not." Automatically reaching for comfort, she started to touch her cross. But it, like Dan, was gone.

His fingers unfastened the many-pocketed vest. His eyes stayed on her face. "Something's wrong."

''Nothing that concerns you.'' Annoyed—with him for noticing, with herself for tripping once more over the past—she blinked back the dampness and the memories. ''Do you have any idea what we do next?''

''Start walking.'' He tossed the vest aside and began unbuttoning his shirt. ''I scraped my shoulder. You'd better have a look.''

He was sleek all over. Not slim—his shoulders were broad, the skin a darker copper than on his legs—but sleek, like an otter or a cat. His stomach was a work of art, all washboard ripples, and his chest was smooth, the nipples very dark. Her mouth went dry.

She moved behind him. There was a scrape along his left shoulder blade, and in spite of the protection of his shirt, the skin was broken. ''I'll have to use some ointment.'' She squeezed some onto her fingers. ''Where do we walk?''

''Over the mountains, I'm afraid. To Honduras.''

''Honduras?'' She frowned as she touched her fingertips to his lacerated skin, applying the ointment as gently as possible. ''I haven't known where I was since they took me and Sister Maria Elena out of La Paloma, but I thought we were closer to the coast.''

''The river we just body-surfed down is the Tampuru. I'm guessing we're about forty miles upstream of the point where it joins the Rio Maño.''

She wasn't as familiar with the mountainous middle and north of the country as she was with the south. Still… ''Shouldn't we follow the river downstream, then? The government is in control of the lowlands, and Santo Pedro is on the Rio Maño.'' Santo Pedro was a district capital, so it must be a fair-sized city. *Telephones,* she thought. Water you didn't have to boil. And doctors, for his wound.

''Too much risk of running into *El Jefe*'s troops. Last I heard, there was fighting around Santo Pedro. If the government is successful—and I think it will be—the rebels will be pushed back. They're likely to retreat this way.''

She shivered. "And if the government isn't successful, we can't wander into Santo Pedro looking for help." At least *she* couldn't. He might be able to, though. "You could probably pass for a native. None of the soldiers saw your face, and from what I heard, your Spanish is good."

"Wrong accent." He shrugged back into his wet shirt. "As soon as I opened my mouth I'd blend in about as well as an Aussie in Alabama. We're going to have to do this the hard way."

She sighed. "I'm sure we'll run across a village sooner or later. This area is primitive but not uninhabited."

"We probably will, but we can't stop at any of them."

"But we don't have any food! No tent, no blankets—nothing!"

"We'll eat. Not well, but I can keep us from starving. We can't risk being seen. Some villagers will be loyal to *El Jefe.* Most are afraid of him. Someone might carry word of our presence to him."

"Even if they did, why would he care? He has better things to do than chase us. Especially if his campaign is going badly."

"If it is, he and his ragtag army may be headed this way. And he won't be in a good mood. Do you want to risk having him punish a whole village for helping us?"

That silenced her.

"Your turn. Take off your shirt, Rev."

Her lips tightened. "If you want me to follow orders like a good little soldier, you're going to have to call me by name. And my name is *not* Rev."

Unexpectedly, he grinned—a crooked, very human grin that broke the beautiful symmetry of his face into something less perfect. And a good deal more dangerous. "Stubborn, aren't you? All right, A.J. Strip."

There was a path away from the river. It wasn't much, just an animal trail, and not meant to accommodate six feet of human male, but it was the only way into the dense growth near the river. Michael found a sturdy branch he could use as a walking stick—and to knock bugs or snakes from overhanging greenery.

At first, neither of them spoke. It took too much energy to shove their way through the brush and branches. Soon they were moving slowly up a steep, tangled slope.

A machete would have been nice, Michael thought as he bent to fit through a green, brambled tunnel. Hacking his way with one of those long blades couldn't have been much noisier than the progress they made without one. He had his knife, but it was too short for trail-blazing. It was also too important to their survival for him to risk dulling the edge, so he made do with his walking stick.

His leg hurt like the devil.

He'd really done it this time, hadn't he? He should never have complicated the operation in order to rescue a native. Even if she *was* a nun.

But Michael remembered the round, wrinkled face smiling up at him, and sighed. Stupid or not, there was no way he could have left Sister Maria Elena in the hands of a madman who made war on innocents.

His white-knight complex had put him in one hell of a bad spot, though. He hadn't exaggerated the danger of seeking help in a village. They wouldn't have to encounter *El Jefe* himself to be in big trouble. This area was smack dab in the middle of the easiest line of retreat for *El Jefe*'s troops if the action at Santo Pedro went against them, and soldiers on the losing side of a war were notoriously apt to turn vicious. The rebels already had a name for brutality. If *El Jefe* was defeated, his control over the worst of his men would be gone, leaving only one thing standing between the pretty minister and rape, probably followed by death: Michael.

And he was wounded.

He pushed a vine aside, set the end of his stick into the

spongy ground and kept moving. Already he was leaning more heavily on the stick than when they'd first set out.

His lips tightened. Pain could slow him down, but it wasn't a major problem. The real worry was infection, and there was damned little he could do about it. When the Reverend had made a fuss about treating him first he'd let her have her way, but that had been for her sake. She needed to feel useful, to feel in control of something. The few minutes' difference in getting his leg treated wouldn't have mattered. Not after his long soak in the river.

"Watch out for the branch," he said, ducking beneath an overhanging limb.

"Tell me, Lieutenant," said a disgruntled voice behind him. "Do you have any idea where you're going?"

In spite of his mood, Michael felt a grin tug at his mouth. He knew why he'd been demoted to a title. Her legs had looked every bit as delicious bare as he'd hoped. Better. He'd enjoyed looking them over—enjoyed it enough to make the first part of their hike uncomfortable in a way that had nothing to do with his leg.

That kind of discomfort he didn't mind. "I'm looking for high ground so I can figure out where we are and plan a route."

"How?"

"I've got eyes, a map, a compass and a GPS device." If he had to be saddled with a civilian, at least he'd drawn one with guts and stamina. She didn't complain, didn't insist on meaningless reassurances. She just kept going.

Couldn't ask for more than that. "What does A.J. stand for?"

"Alyssa Jean. I'm not fluent in acronym. What does GPS mean?"

"Global Positioning System." His brother Jacob had given him the gadget for his birthday, saying that this way Michael would know where he was, even if no one else did. "It talks to satellites and fixes my location on a digital map."

''Is that the thing you were fiddling with back at the river?''

''Yeah.'' He'd set the first waypoint after checking her out for scratches. He smiled. Man, those were great legs.

''I hope it's more watertight than your first aid kit.''

''Seems to be. Why do you go by A.J.? Alyssa's a pretty name.''

''First-grade trauma,'' she said, her voice wry and slightly winded, ''combined with stubbornness. There were three Alyssas in my class. I didn't want to share my name, so I became A.J. It suited me. I was something of a tomboy as a kid.''

''How does a tomboy end up a minister?'' A minister with long, silky legs and small, high breasts…and blue eyes. That had surprised him. Somehow he'd thought they'd be brown, a gentle, sensible color. But they were blue. Sunny-sky blue.

''Same way anyone else does, I guess. I felt called to the ministry, so after college I enrolled in seminary.'' There was a scuffling sound, and what sounded suspiciously like a muffled curse. He paused, glancing over his shoulder.

She was climbing to her feet. ''A root got me. Maybe I need a stick like yours.''

''I'll keep my eye out for one.'' They were near the top of the hill. Maybe he would let himself rest for a few minutes while he plugged in the new waypoint. His thigh was throbbing like a mother.

''How's your leg?''

''Not bad.'' He ducked under a hanging vine, grabbed the limb of a small tree to pull himself up a particularly steep section, straightened—and froze, his breath catching.

A small, scared whisper came from behind him. ''What is it?''

In answer, he moved aside, gesturing for her to come up beside him.

The pocket-size clearing in front of them was coated in

blue. Fluttering blue, brighter-than-sky blue, bits of sunny ocean floating free, their wings sorting air currents lazily.

Butterflies. What seemed like hundreds of butterflies flooded the little clearing, many with wingspans as large as his two hands.

A.J.'s shoulder brushed his. A second later, the butterflies rose—a dipping, curling cloud of blue swimming up, up through the air, lifting above the surrounding trees. Then gone.

"Ooh..."

Her soft exclamation was filled with all the wordless awe he felt. He turned to look at her. "Yeah," he said, because he had no words for what they'd just seen...or what he saw now in her shining eyes.

Blue eyes. Not as bright as the butterfly cloud, maybe, but clear and lovely.

A smile broke over her face, big as dawn. "I've never seen anything like that."

He hadn't, either. A child's delight on a woman's face...was there anything more lovely? Without thinking, he touched her cheek. "You've got a spot of dried mud here."

Her smiled faded. "I've got dried mud in a lot of places."

"Brown's a good color on you." He rubbed lightly at the spot on her cheek. Surely the butterflies' wings couldn't have been any softer than her skin. His fingers spread to cup her face, and rested there while he looked for something in her eyes. Permission, maybe.

"Michael..." Her throat moved in a nervous swallow.

"I'm going to kiss you." At that moment, it sounded wholly reasonable to him. "Just a kiss, no big deal."

"Bad idea." Her eyes were wide and wary. "Very bad idea." But she didn't move away.

"Don't worry. I don't let my—ah, my body do my thinking for me." He bent closer to her pretty lips.

One kiss couldn't hurt, could it?

He kept it simple, the most basic of connections—no more

than the gentle press of one mouth to another. No big deal. Her lips were smooth and warm, her taste was salt and subtle spice. Her eyes stayed open. So did his.

And his hand trembled.

He straightened. The hand that had cupped her cheek dropped to his side. He stared down into eyes as wide with shock as his own.

What had he done? What the hell had he just done to himself?

Four

The sun was high in the sky, and it was hot. Headachy-hot, the kind of sullen heat that drains the body and dulls the mind. They moved among brush, oak and *ocotino* pines now, not true rain forest. Here, sunlight speckled the shade. Parrots screeched, monkeys chattered, and insects scuttled in the decaying vegetation underfoot. Sweat stung A.J.'s eyes and the scrape on her hand, picked up while scrambling over rocks earlier.

Like they say, it's not the heat, she told herself as she skidded downslope after Michael. *It's the blasted humidity.* Or maybe it was exhaustion making her head throb. Or hunger. Or dehydration. Her mouth and throat were scratchy-dry.

Best not to think about that.

At least the rainy season was over. The mercury dipped slightly during the wet months, but the increase in humidity more than made up for that small drop. Afternoons became steam baths. Daily rains turned every dip into a puddle and roads into mud baths, and the mosquitoes bred like crazy.

Not that roads were a consideration, she thought wistfully. They hadn't seen any. They'd followed a shallow stream for a while, and that had made the going easier. It had also made her thirsty enough to drink her own sweat.

She paused to wipe the perspiration from her face. Probably she should ask for Michael's water bag, a reinforced plastic sack from one of his many pockets.

Without a pot they couldn't boil water to make it safe to drink, but he had iodine. He'd assured her it disinfected water as well as wounds, and he had treated water from the stream with it. Unfortunately, it tasted as nasty as it looked. She hadn't been able to force down as much as she probably needed.

He was angling to the left now, moving across the slope instead of straight down. With a sigh, she followed.

His leg had to be hurting like a rotting tooth. He'd grown awfully quiet, too. Worried, she let her attention stray from the endless business of finding her footing to the man in front of her.

The back of his neck was shiny with sweat; his hair clung there in damp curls. She wanted to touch those curls. To taste the salt on his skin. She wanted—oh, she wanted to stop thinking of that kiss.

Why had she let it happen? One kiss shouldn't complicate things so much…but it did. It left her hungry, needy, too aware of him. She didn't want to come to life now—not here, not with this man. Oh, be honest, she told herself. The thought of becoming involved with anyone scared her silly. Such a coward she'd become! Dan would have hated that.

Of course, the soldier in front of her hadn't been thinking of getting involved in a relationship when he kissed her. He'd been thinking of sex, pure and simple. She was making too much of it.

Yet she remembered the look in his eyes when he'd raised his head. Maybe it hadn't been simple for him, either. And maybe, she thought as she skirted the trunk of a fallen giant, it wasn't pain that had kept him quiet ever since he kissed her.

Tired of her thoughts, she spoke. "How's your leg?"

"It's holding up." He glanced over his shoulder. "How about you? You've been quiet."

The echo of her thoughts about him made her smile. "Keeping my mouth shut is one way to avoid whining."

"Do you whine, then? You haven't so far. Maybe you're saving it for when things become difficult?"

"As opposed to merely miserable, you mean?" The path widened, letting her move up beside him instead of trailing behind. "Whining is an energy-sapper, and I don't have any of that to spare. And I don't really have any business complaining. When I compare where I am now to where I was yesterday, my calves almost stop hurting."

"I guess a minister would be into counting blessings. Like, for example, not having stepped on a snake."

"Or into a fire ant bed," she agreed. The bite of the tiny red forest ants hurt worst than a bee sting. "Then there's the size of these mountains. We could have been stuck in the Andes—"

"Not in San Christóbal, we couldn't."

She grinned. "The point is that these aren't terribly high. Compared to the Rockies back home, these are mere foothills."

"Are the Rockies home for you?"

"No, I'm from West Texas—the little town of Andrews originally, and San Antonio most recently. I'm not used to all this up and down. It is gorgeous here, though—when I look at something other than the ground. Dirt looks like dirt everywhere."

"So it does. What brings you to this particular patch of dirt?"

"I signed up for a year's service with UCA."

"Now you're the one speaking in acronyms."

"UCA is the United Churches Agency. It's a nondenominational organization that sends teaching missions to undeveloped countries in Central and South America.''

''So you're a teacher as well as a preacher. What made you decide to give a year of your life to San Christóbal?''

''A promise.'' It had come out without thinking. Her forehead wrinkled. ''You're deceptively easy to talk to.''

''Better than the monkeys, at any rate. They interrupt too much. What kind of a promise?''

''One I made to my husband. After he died.'' She slid him a look, daring him to call her foolish.

He didn't answer at all, just kept walking. Something in his silence made her want to go on, to speak of things she'd kept wrapped up tightly inside. ''He was killed in a convenience store holdup two years ago. We'd stopped to pick up some milk.'' The sheer freakishness of Dan's death clogged her throat. ''It was senseless. So horribly senseless.''

''Death seldom makes sense to the living.''

''I suppose not.'' She'd revisited that night too often in her mind, in her dreams. Rewriting the script. Fixing things so that they didn't need milk, or went to the grocery store instead. She didn't want to go back there again. ''So, what brought you to this patch of dirt?''

''War.''

Well, that closed off one topic nicely. ''And what made you choose war as your career?''

His eyebrows lifted. ''You do have claws, I see.''

His amusement mortified her more than her sarcasm. ''I shouldn't have said that.''

He shrugged. ''I poked at your sore places. No surprise if you take a jab back. Believe it or not, I didn't choose the army because I enjoy war.''

They were angling down again. She had to watch her footing, but her conscience wouldn't let her give it all her attention. ''You wanted to be of service,'' she said after a moment. ''That's what they call it, isn't it? The armed services. Serving in the army. You felt called to serve.''

"I also liked to make things go boom. Here, watch out for the ant bed." He took her hand.

His palm was hard and callused. Hers tingled. "I didn't—wait a minute." She peered down through the trees. "Look! Isn't that a road?"

"Yeah." He dropped her hand and stopped. "Looks like one."

It wasn't much, just a pair of muddy ruts twining up the little valley—but those ruts promised much easier going than they'd had so far. She sent a quick prayer of gratitude and started to move ahead of him.

He took her arm. "No. If any of *El Jefe*'s *soldados* are around, that's where we'll find them."

Impatient, she shook him off. "We're more likely to run across a bored *carbonero* who'd be glad to share his cooking fire. And your leg—"

"Isn't a consideration."

"Of course it is. Ignoring the wound won't make it go away."

"I'm not ignoring it. But I'd rather limp than get a bullet in my head because I tried to stop five or ten men from raping you."

Nausea rose in her belly, and the blood drained from her head. "Don't you dare. Don't even think about playing the hero, about—I'd rather be raped, you understand? I won't see it happen again. I won't!" The trembling hit then, a flood of weakness she despised and couldn't stop.

The tight grip on her arm turned gentle. So did his voice. "Is that how he died, Alyssa? Your husband? Was he trying to protect you?"

Unable to speak, she nodded.

He slipped his arm around her waist. Casually, as if they were strolling in a park, he guided her down the slope.

It took her a minute to get her voice back, and when she did, it wobbled. "I thought you didn't want to take the road."

"You're right about my leg. It's slowing us down."

"But..."

"Don't worry. If a horde of bloodthirsty bandits shows up, I'll let them have their way with you."

She nearly choked on a laugh. "That's awful. Promise?"

"On my honor as a graduate of St. Vincent's. Of course, I didn't quite manage to graduate. And I wasn't exactly their star student. But when they asked me to leave, at least one of the nuns still had hopes that I would avoid prison."

This time her laugh was freer, more real. She pulled away from the seductive warmth of his supporting arm. "You went to parochial school?" She shook her head. "You definitely don't seem the type."

"My mother's Catholic. It mattered to her, and my father didn't care."

She sensed layers of meaning in that last statement. *Later,* she thought, too tired to sort it out now. Later she'd find out what he meant.

They'd reached the road, what there was of it. "This is a good time to take a reading," he said, and pulled his GPS gadget out of a pocket. While he pushed the buttons on the tiny pad, he asked casually, "What was his name?"

"Who?"

"Your husband."

"Oh. Dan. The Reverend Daniel Kelleher."

"Good G—grief. He was a minister, too?"

She smiled. "You don't have to edit your language because I'm a minister. I'm hard to shock."

"I don't do it because you're a minister. You're also a lady."

That moved her. Flustered her. She was used to people—especially men—seeing the collar, not the woman.

"So how did you and Dan meet?"

"He was the youth minister at my church. He was great with the kids, and he loved working with them, but...this was his dream, you see. Missionary work. If he hadn't married me..."

"Pretty pointless to blame yourself for someone else's decision."

"I suppose. But we were married for three years, and for three years I put him off. Finally I agreed to take a year's sabbatical—soon." She'd been so sure, so arrogantly sure they had plenty of time. "If not for me, he would have been following his dream, not walking in on a holdup."

"And maybe died even younger. 'If only' is a dangerous game. You can play it forever and never win."

Her mouth crooked up wryly. "I'm wondering which of us is the preacher."

"Advice is always easier to give than to take." He slid the gadget back in the pocket of his vest. "Seems like he could have come on his own if it was that important to him."

"He didn't want to be separated for a year. Neither did I. But I was new to my ministry, just getting established…oh, I had all kinds of reasons we should wait. And then it was too late."

When he started forward, he seemed to be leaning more heavily on the staff. It worried her, but she knew better than to say anything. He'd just insist his leg was fine.

"I guess you came here for him."

"In a way…no," she corrected herself. "That's not true. I thought I did, but really I came for myself, looking for…I don't know. A way to stop grieving. To finish something left dangling. One thing about being a prisoner," she added wryly. "It gave me plenty of time to think."

"And you spent that time thinking about your dead husband."

She stopped. "Gee. For a couple of minutes there, I mistook you for a sensitive man."

"That was definitely a mistake. Look." He stopped, too, and ran a hand over his hair. "I'm not crazy about being jealous of a dead man, but there it is."

"No." She took a step back. "No, you can't be."

His smile came slow and brimming with suggestions. "Sure I can. You're a damned attractive woman, Alyssa."

"A.J.," she corrected him, distracted. "I'm not your type. You said so."

"I changed my mind."

"I haven't changed mine." She started walking. He found her attractive? The idea brought an insidious warmth, a subtle and frightening pleasure.

"Haven't you?" He caught up with her easily in spite of his limp. "Tell me that you aren't attracted to me. That you haven't been looking at me the way a woman watches a man she wants."

"I'm a big girl. I don't have to act on every impulse my hormones send my way."

"This is more than impulse." His fingers curled around her arm possessively. He moved close to her, crowding her. Making her aware of his body. "Were you raped?"

"What?" She shook her head. "Oh, you mean when—when Dan died. No. That's not…look, if I gave you the wrong idea earlier, I'm sorry. I'm not ready for a relationship, and I don't believe in flings or quickies."

"Quickies?" His mouth tilted in a wicked smile. "Naughty talk from a minister."

"Don't." She tugged her arm free. "Don't tease, don't smile like that, don't…hope. I'm not interested."

He was still smiling, but in his eyes she caught a glimpse of another man—the warrior who'd gotten her out of the compound, and killed at least one man doing it. "But I am," he said softly, and let go of his walking stick, thrust his hands into her hair—and kissed her.

This was no sweet sharing, but a wild ride. His mouth was hard, rough. Insistent. Her own mouth had dropped open in shock or to make some protest. He took immediate advantage, stroking his tongue deep.

Her mind blanked. Longing rose, swift and merciless, a blind need to touch and be touched. Her eyes closed. She clutched his arms, holding on, holding him, bringing the warmth and fierce life in his body nearer. And in the darkness behind her closed eyes she saw a man's form, shadowed by night, jerking as bullets tore into it.

Her eyes flew open. She made a small, distressed sound.

He lifted his head. His eyes were hot and hard. "You're interested."

Her head jerked back. Her heart was pounding madly. "When my eyes closed, I saw him. The soldier you shot back by the truck. Your mouth was on me, and I saw you killing him."

His hands fell away. His expression smoothed into blankness. Without a word he bent and picked up his walking stick, turned and started limping up the rutted road.

The water was cold, and his hand was growing numb. Michael waited, his bare arm submerged in the swiftly flowing water of the stream, his eyes fixed on the fish inches from his elbow.

They'd climbed back into true rain forest as the day wore on, leaving the scraggly undergrowth behind. The sun was sinking on the other side of the dense canopy overhead. The light was green and dim. Trees crowded close, but the ground was bare. Finding a campsite had been a problem, but finally they'd run across a spot where *carboneros* had felled a few trees to make charcoal.

Another fish was already on the stringer he'd fashioned from a length of string. Farther downstream, A.J. was scouting around for dry wood. He hoped she found some. He didn't relish raw fish for supper.

Supper. He was good for that, he supposed. She wouldn't object to his skill at killing when it came time to fill her belly.

And that, he knew, was unfair.

The fish drifted, lazy and unalarmed, around the bend in his arm. He waited.

She hadn't called him names, hadn't accused him of anything. She'd stated a fact: when he kissed her, she saw the image of the man he'd killed.

He could have argued with her. In his head, he had. For the next hour, walking in silence down the rutted road, he'd argued bitterly. Yes, he had killed—to save her life as well as his own. Would she rather be dead herself? Maybe she'd prefer to see him bleeding his life out in the dirt.

But in his heart, he'd known she was right. He had no business putting his hands on her. God, he'd kissed her right after she told him how her husband, the saint, had been killed—gunned down in front of her eyes.

Good move, he told himself savagely.

He was drawn to her. Powerfully drawn. He might be jealous of her dead husband, but he was fascinated by her loyalty to the man. If there was one virtue Michael believed in, it was loyalty.

Then there was her innocence. Oh, not sexual innocence. That was a fleeting quality, not especially interesting. But Alyssa was untouched in a deeper way, one possible only to those rare souls who truly believe in right and wrong. People who saw the line clearly—and didn't cross it.

He'd crossed too many lines in his life. Sometimes because that's what it took to prevent a greater wrong. And sometimes, when he was younger, he'd been so purely mad at the world he hadn't cared what he did. After a while, the line between right and wrong had blurred. After a while, he wasn't sure there was a line, just a gray no-man's land where you did whatever you had to do.

The fish poked along the streambed. Close now, very close, but on the wrong side of his hand. He waited.

No, he didn't have any business touching her. The sweetness that drew him was the very reason he couldn't have her. He knew it. And knew he would kill again to protect her, if he had to.

Now. A flash of silver, a quick movement—and his hand

closed around a slippery fish. He stood, holding on to the meal he would offer the woman he couldn't have, and headed for the stringer.

Technically, he was engaged. Technically, he had no business kissing anyone but his betrothed—a woman he'd never kissed, much less taken to bed. He didn't want Cami, didn't like her, didn't intend to have anything to do with her aside from the necessary legal transaction. And that wouldn't matter to Alyssa. If she knew about Cami, she'd think he was scum.

Maybe he was. The lines had blurred a long time ago.

Yeah, he'd keep his distance, he thought, threading the string through the fish's gills. But he didn't have to like it.

Five

"What else is in those magic pockets?" A.J. asked. She sat on a fairly dry patch of ground, her knees drawn up to her chin, her feet bare. Michael had insisted they remove their shoes and socks and dry them by the fire he was building, using matches he'd carried in a waterproof pouch in one of his pockets. "A color TV? Or an air mattress, maybe."

"Aside from my transporter, you mean?" A whisper of flame flickered along the shredded bark.

"I guess it would be cheating to use that."

"We don't want to take all the fun out of things."

The brief jungle twilight had closed in, erasing clarity, leaving them wrapped in dimness and sound. The frog chorus was in full swing, and a breeze rustled the leaves overhead. There were no walls, nothing between them and the animals whose home they had invaded....

An unearthly roar shattered the night.

She jumped. "What was that?"

"A howler monkey." He fed twigs into his small flame. "Surely you've heard them before."

"Of course. I've never heard one bellowing at night, that's all. I wasn't expecting it." She'd thought it was a jaguar or puma—or maybe a monster. Oh, but she was silly with exhaustion, her mind tumbling from thought to thought without the energy to connect them rationally. Everything ached. She would be in real pain tomorrow, she thought, after sleeping on the ground overnight.

Her gaze strayed to the bed she'd cleared while he was catching supper, picking out all the small stones and twigs to make the dirt as comfortable as possible. One of the treats from his magic pockets was a silvery "space blanket" that was supposed to trap body heat. They'd climbed enough that day that the night would be chilly. Already it was cool.

One blanket. One bed. It was the only reasonable way for them to sleep—and it made her itchy from the inside out. She jerked her gaze away.

He'd sharpened a stick with his knife earlier; now he thrust the stick through one of the fish and held it near the merry crackle of the fire. A.J. watched the flames and sighed.

She was accustomed to thinking of herself as rather athletic, but compared to the man who was cooking their supper she was a couch potato. Michael knew what to do and how to do it, while she knew nothing. She felt useless. That, too, was new and unwelcome.

She glanced around their small campsite, but everything was already done. "I should reapply the ointment on your wound."

"I'll take care of it."

So much for that idea. He took care of everything.

How had he managed to keep going with a bullet wound in his thigh? Sheer determination, she supposed, coupled with the extraordinary degree of fitness necessary to a young man whose career was war. "How old are you?" she asked suddenly.

He looked up. The fire painted his face in shadows and warmth. "Thirty. Why?"

She shrugged, embarrassed. So he was two years younger than she. It didn't matter. "Just wondered how long it had been since you and St. Vincent's parted ways."

"A long time." His voice was soft and a little sad. He turned the speared fish slowly. "I was fifteen and, according to a lot of people, bound for hell or jail. Whichever came first."

"Did you stay out of jail?"

"Yes and no." He grinned suddenly. "My father sent me to military school. Some would say it was a lot like prison."

"Good grief. Were you really such a hard case?"

"I had a problem with authority. My brother Jacob used to say he didn't know how I managed to stand upright with all that attitude weighing me down. If someone told me to go right, I'd break my neck turning left. I didn't want to be at St. Vincent's, didn't want to hang around with a bunch of rich preppie types, and I made sure everyone knew it."

"Ah." Her ready sympathy was engaged. "You felt like an outsider."

"I'm Mexican on my mother's side, and that made a difference to some. Mostly, though, I made my own trouble. I didn't like snotty-nosed rich boys." He chuckled. "Probably because I *was* a snotty-nosed rich boy."

He came from money? She blinked, her picture of him doing a sudden one-eighty. "I was a Goody Two-shoes up through high school," she admitted. "Straight A's, teacher's pet."

"Never colored outside the lines, or took a walk on the wild side with a bad boy?"

"Heavens, no." She grinned. "But like a lot of good girls, I liked to look, as long as they didn't catch me at it. I didn't cut loose until college."

"Somehow I doubt you cut loose then," he said dryly. "Unless you call having a beer on Saturday night getting down and dirty. Here, hold out your plate. Your fish is ready.''

She held out the huge leaf she'd rinsed off in the stream earlier. He eased the fish off the stick. The meat flaked apart at his touch. ''It's hot,'' he warned her.

''Good.'' Her stomach growled. ''And thank you for feeding me first, before I embarrassed myself and started gnawing on your arm. I won't make any cracks about chivalry this time. I'm too hungry.''

She made herself eat slowly while he punched the stick in the other fish and held it near the flames. The flavor was strong and smoky and delicious.

''I really did get a little wild in college,'' she said between bites. ''All that freedom went to my head. My parents had me late in life—I was an only child and had been pretty hemmed in until then. This is incredibly good,'' she said, licking her fingers. ''Either you're the best cook on the face of the planet, or what they say about hunger being the best spice is true. What do your folks think about you being in the army? Do they worry?''

''My father died a couple years ago, but it's safe to say he was greatly relieved when I decided I liked the service. Surprised as hell, but relieved. My mother…'' He shrugged. ''She's not always in close touch with reality. Too much self-medicating. Liquor, mostly.''

''Oh.'' Her hands fell to her lap. ''I'm sorry. Is she depressive? Bipolar?''

He gave her a funny look. ''You know the lingo.''

''My bachelor's degree is in sociology. Before I decided to go to seminary, I was planning on being a therapist.''

He grunted—one of those all-purpose male grunts that can mean anything—and slid his fish off onto his leaf-plate. ''The water bag is right next to you. Drink. You need at least a gallon of water a day.''

She made a face, but picked up the bag and swallowed quickly.

Darkness had closed in while they ate and talked. The cheerful dance of their little fire was the only light now, and the air felt chilly after the day's heat. She hugged her knees closer and wished she didn't like him so much. Wanting him was bad enough. Discovering she liked him, too, made her feel even more of a fool.

At least he was talking to her again. He'd been silent for hours after that kiss. Not that she blamed him. He'd saved her life at great risk to his own, and she'd all but called him a killer.

He wasn't a killer, not in the sense most people meant the word. Yet he had killed. And that bothered her—no, it went deeper than that. It troubled her soul. Why? He'd done it to save her life, and his…

Oh, she thought. Oh, yes. Because of her, a man was dead. He'd died at Michael's hand. Michael was the link between her and violent death. Just like Dan, who had died because of her…no, what was she thinking? He'd died because he'd been in the wrong place at the wrong time. Hadn't she worked that out for herself slowly, painfully, over the last two years?

Nothing made sense. Not her thoughts, not her feelings. Maybe she shouldn't try to sort things out, anyway. A relationship with Michael could go nowhere, and she couldn't indulge in a brief physical relationship. Of course, no one would ever know….

The whispery thought shamed her but wasn't hard to answer. *She* would know. She tried to pray, to seek guidance, but couldn't hold her thoughts together. They were scattering, drifting away….

"Hey. You're falling asleep sitting up. Better make a trip to the bushes before you nod off."

A.J.'s head jerked up. She blinked. "Right."

She didn't go far. The night was dark, the rustlings in the bushes scary. When she came back, he had his pants down and was spreading ointment on his leg. She averted her eyes quickly, moving to their bed. "How's your leg?"

"It'll feel better when I've been off it a few hours." He rewound the bandage. "Go ahead and lie down. I'll take care of the fire when I get back."

He took his gun with him. She didn't think it was a conscious decision; keeping his gun handy was automatic.

How different they were. How totally, unbridgeably different.

A.J. stretched out with a sigh, fully dressed except for her shoes and socks. Probably, she thought, if she weren't so tired she'd be vastly uncomfortable. As it was, her eyelids drifted down the moment she was horizontal.

She barely woke when he joined her. His body curved around hers, big and warm and solid. He pulled the lightweight cover over them both, and rested his arm on her waist. She breathed in his scent, feeling safe, mildly aroused. And guilty.

Her eyes opened onto the darkness. "Michael?"

"Yes?"

"I'm sorry."

She was nearly asleep again before she heard him whisper, "So am I."

The ground was hard. The woman he held was soft. Between the fire in his leg and the one in his groin, Michael didn't hold out much hope of sleep.

But she was asleep. Soundly, peacefully asleep. That baffled him. The exertions of the last day and night had been enough to make stone feel as comfortable as a feather bed...but she'd curled into him so trustingly. That's what didn't make sense.

He'd made it clear he wanted her. She'd made it clear she didn't want him. Oh, on a physical level, she did. He wished he could take some satisfaction from that truth, but he couldn't. Not when it was *him* she rejected—his actions, his choices, his career. His life.

Yet she was snuggled up as warm and cozy as if they'd slept together for years. As if she trusted him completely. What was a man supposed to make of that?

Women were always a mystery on some level, he supposed. Maybe it was the estrogen-testosterone thing—one flavor of hormones produced a vastly different chemical cocktail from the other.

Still, for all her mysterious femaleness, Alyssa would have made a good soldier, he thought, trying to find a comfortable position for his throbbing leg. She had what it took—dedication, compassion, humor. And guts. A woman with the sheer, ballsy courage it had taken to refuse to be rescued unless they took the nun with them wouldn't flinch at other unpleasant necessities, like sharing a blanket with him.

But courage didn't banish fear. It might triumph over it, but couldn't erase it. And there was no fear in the warm body he held.

The night was black and restless, filled with small sounds. Brush rustled. A breeze plucked at the leaves overhead, and from off in the distance came the howl of some night-roamer. The pain in his leg was strong, a vicious red presence dulling his mind. The woman in his arms slept on, her breathing easy and slow. Her hair tickled his chin. It smelled good, he thought fuzzily. She smelled good.

Funny how soothing it was to breathe in her scent as his eyes closed…did she like the way he smelled? Pheromones, he thought fuzzily. Maybe there were trust pheromones as well as sexual pheromones, some mysterious alchemy of scent that could make a woman fall peacefully asleep in the arms of a man whose kiss repelled her.

He was still puzzling over that when exhaustion dragged him gently into oblivion.

Shortly before dawn, it started to rain.

It was Alyssa who remembered their footwear. She bolted upright and dashed to the extinct campfire.

"How wet are they?" he asked, holding the blanket up so she could climb under it again with his boots, her shoes and their socks.

"Not bad."

She sounded a bit breathless. Maybe that was because of her sudden movement. Or maybe she was noticing all the things he was noticing, like how perfectly they fit, snuggled close together beneath the silver cover. And how much his body appreciated the round shape of her rump, tucked up against him.

The leafy canopy overhead filtered the rain; it reached them only in stray drops, a cold trickle here and there. She shifted. Her movement had an immediate and enthusiastic effect on his body—which he didn't think she could have missed.

"Luke 12: 6 and 7," she said in a disgruntled voice.

He stiffened. "And your meaning is?"

"He keeps track of every sparrow—but He doesn't promise to keep them dry."

His laugh surprised him almost as much as she had. "We'll dry off eventually," he said. "Once it stops raining."

The rain faded to a drizzle about the time the road petered out into a trail, and dried up completely by midmorning. It was dim and green and warm beneath the canopy, an enormous plant-womb brimming with life. The rain forest was supposed to be home to sloths, anteaters, tapirs, armadillos, peccaries, and deer. The only wildlife they saw that morning had six or eight legs.

They didn't find any fruit, either. A.J. was feeling hollow all the way to her toes when they spotted the village at noon.

"I will not let you steal from those people," she whispered fiercely.

About one hundred meters below them, barely visible through the trunks of giant trees, lay a ragged cluster of huts in a narrow valley. The five huts probably belonged to *colonos* who, desperate for land, had chopped down or burned off enough of the forest giants to clear the small fields they worked communally. The soil beneath the rain forest was so thin and poor that in a year or two they'd have to move and do it all again...and more of the rain forest would die. It was slash-and-burn agriculture at its worst, but it was the only way they knew to survive.

A.J. and Michael had been arguing ever since they'd spotted the huts and he'd dragged her off the trail and up this hill.

So far, she was losing.

"Yeah?" he said. "How do you plan to stop me?"

"They have so little—anything we take could make the difference between survival and starvation."

"And you see our situation as being different in what way?" He shifted impatiently. "I'll leave them some money, more than the few things I take will be worth. I just want a couple of blankets, a little food, a cookpot."

"Taking things without permission is stealing."

"Give your overactive conscience a rest, Rev. Money is rare for these people. They'll be glad to get it."

She bit her lip. "If you're caught—"

"I won't be."

Maybe not. If everyone was in the fields, he might manage to slip in and out without being seen. But if he did, he wouldn't get any help for his leg—which was one reason she wanted to deal with the villagers, not steal from them. Not that she'd used that argument. He wouldn't admit his leg was worse. "You're being paranoid."

"That's one way of looking at it. From my point of view, you're dangerously naive."

She turned her head to study him. There were lines of strain along his mouth, and he was leaning against the smooth trunk of one tree. He'd been limping heavily for the last hour. "Your leg—"

"Don't worry about my leg," he said curtly. "It might slow me, but I can still move quietly."

Maybe so, but he needed to stay off of it. Since he couldn't, he needed *something,* some kind of help, and some of the folk remedies she'd run across while living in La Paloma were surprisingly effective. Of course, there might not be anyone down there who could help, even with folk medicine. It wasn't much of a village.

A. J. tried one last time. "These people don't care about politics, and they aren't going to spare an able-bodied man to carry word of our existence to *El Jefe* on the off chance he might care."

"They won't have to, if any of *El Jefe*'s troops are in the area. And trust me—*El Jefe* would definitely care about getting his hands on a U.S. officer who carried out an assault on his headquarters."

Cold touched the base of her spine. "We haven't seen any of his troops."

He shrugged. "We haven't seen anyone at all until we came to this village. Doesn't mean no one's around. Look, I'm going. You can sound the alarm on me, I guess—that would stop me. But since they usually chop off the hands of thieves, I hope you'll decide to wait up here."

She was angry, scared, hating what he was going to do—and unable to stop him. Or help him. "You'll be careful?"

He nodded, checking the strap that held his gun at his waist.

"You won't need that."

He shot her a hard look. "Don't worry. I'm not going to shoot anyone over a blanket. Over a steak, maybe, but only if it came with a side of fried potatoes and onions."

She shook her head, impatient with them both. "I know that. Michael..." She took his arm. His sleeves were rolled up, so her fingers closed around bare skin. "You're burning up!"

"Your hands are just cold." He shook her off.

Her hands were cold, cold with fear for him. And yet…maybe it was because she'd slept with him the night before, however chastely. Maybe it was because he was the only other person in her world right now, and so much depended on him. Whatever the reason, she'd been acutely conscious of him all morning, as if some subtle thread connected them. She'd found herself noticing the way his hair curled up at his nape, and the dark hairs on his forearms. The shape of his hands, and the signs of strain around his eyes. All morning, she'd been aware of the sheer physical presence of the man, strong and sure and warm.

But not this warm. She was sure of it. "You've got a fever."

"I'm fine." He picked up his walking stick. "Stay here and stay quiet. If I'm not back in an hour, you should…" He stopped, frowning, looking down at the village.

She looked, too.

Something was going on. People were running—the women and children, she realized. They were fleeing into the jungle. The men stayed in the fields, but they weren't working. They were watching the trail.

She didn't realize she'd clutched Michael's arm again until he moved away. His face was closed, his attention wholly on what was happening below them. Her hand fell to her side. "You can't still intend to go down there now. They're alerted. They'll see you."

"Something spooked them. I need to know what. Information can be more important than food." His smile was probably meant to be reassuring. "I shouldn't be long. Twenty minutes, maybe. Don't worry, okay?"

Don't worry?

He was right. Wound or no wound, he could still move silently. She watched him melt into the trees, moving slowly but surely. And she didn't hear him at all.

* * *

Going down the hill had hurt. Coming back up was a bitch.

Michael paused halfway up, breathing hard. Entirely too hard for such minor exertion.

Yeah, he had a fever. He wasn't sure why he'd denied it, except that he couldn't stand the thought of being fussed over. And he hadn't realized he was feverish at first. He'd been hot all morning, but they were in the tropics, weren't they? His wound had seemed explanation enough for his growing weakness. Finally, though, he'd had to accept that his temperature was climbing faster than the trail. He'd wanted to curse the air blue, but he'd kept moving. Not much else he could do. The aspirin in his kit had been contaminated by the river.

On a scale of one to dead, his fever rated around seven. What he'd just learned was worse. It wasn't on the same scale.

He glanced up the hill. She'd be worrying. He'd stayed away longer than he'd told her he would—first so he could get into position. Then to make a decision.

Not about grabbing blankets and food. That possibility had gone out the window as soon as he'd verified that the arrivals in the village were *El Jefe*'s men. He'd overheard enough to know that the self-styled leader had suffered some major reversals. Professionally, that pleased Michael. San Christóbal's current government wasn't great. There was corruption, inefficiency, plenty of problems. But it was democratically elected, and it was making an effort to observe basic human rights. *El Jefe* would be a hundred times worse.

Personally, though, the news stunk. Adding what he'd heard to the implications, he came up with an unpleasant sum. *El Jefe* was getting desperate. To survive, he would have to gather more support quickly. He thought he'd found a way to do that.

Alyssa had some more worrying to do, he thought grimly

as he started uphill again. Oh, he'd offer her a choice. That was only right. But he was pretty sure which way she'd jump.

Alyssa Jean Kelleher. The Reverend Kelleher. She wasn't what he'd expected, that was for sure. In her own way, she was as tough as they came. Tenderhearted, though. And she didn't know squat about how to move through hostile territory—hell, she barely realized she was in hostile territory. She didn't know how to get by with a knife, a map, a length of string and a few other odds and ends when she had mountains to cross.

Which was why he'd made the decision he had before starting back up this blasted hill. He just hoped like hell he'd chosen right.

''Of course I'm staying with you.''

Michael shook his head. Hadn't he known she'd say that? Still, he had to make sure she knew what she was risking. ''You do understand? *El Jefe*'s soldiers are after me, not you. He wants to embarrass the U.S. and drum up support from his neighbors. Without it, he doesn't stand a chance, and he knows that. He plans to use me to make it look like their *Norteamericano* Big Brother has been interfering in little brother's business again, and there are some who will back him, based on that.''

Her brow pleated. ''Does he have to take you prisoner to do that? I mean, he can say whatever he wants. And probably will.''

''Without me to display, he has no credibility.''

''Then you can't afford to be caught.''

No, he couldn't. Though he doubted she understood what that meant. ''The point is, if we split up they'll probably ignore you. You could stop in the next village we come to, send word to the authorities in the capital. Sooner or later, someone would come for you.''

''And you'll probably die of that infection you insist you don't have.''

"You going to lay on hands and cure me, Rev? If not, I can probably move faster without you. And my best hope of getting treated is to get the hell out of this country."

Her cheeks lost some of their color. "Oh. I...hadn't thought of that. Of course. If you could let me have some of the matches, and maybe—no, you'll need the knife." She did a good job of keeping her voice even, but the fear fairly screamed from those big blue eyes.

Damn. Why was he swiping at her? He ran a hand over his hair. "I'm not trying to ditch you. I haven't gone to this much trouble to get you out just so I could jump ship. But I want you to make your decision based on what's best for you, not on my goddamned leg."

For some stupid reason she smiled. "God didn't damn your leg, Michael. A bullet did the damage, and a man pulled the trigger on the gun that put it there. I'll be better off with you, I think."

Relief swelled in him. He ignored it. "Then we won't have to decide who gets this." He reached behind him and retrieved the one thing he'd brought back from his scouting trip—a battered five-pound coffee can. "Our new cooking pot. Don't say I never gave you anything."

They made camp early, well before dark. This time he let her help, directing her in laying the fire, showing her how to make their bed.

She knew why. His fever was up, his cheekbones sharp and flushed. He was too weary to do everything himself—and he was planning ahead. If he died before they got to safety, he wanted her to have some idea of how to go on without him.

The thought made everything inside her tighten. She wasn't going to let him die. Though what she could do...oh, she'd do something, she vowed. She'd find a way.

God, please don't let him die. Show me what to do.

They ate fish again. Her share tasted wonderful but didn't fill her up. He must have been even hungrier than she was, but he insisted on splitting the catch evenly.

Maybe tomorrow they'd find some fruit or see some kind of game. A.J. wasn't comfortable with the thought of killing an animal, but she wasn't foolish enough to pay attention to her squeamishness. Her stay in La Paloma had begun her education in that respect. Animals of all kinds went into stewpots there, and the process wasn't clean or pretty.

Survival was a messy business, she was learning, and seldom kind.

At least they'd been able to boil water. She hadn't needed to be nagged into drinking her share, and she'd watched to make sure he drank plenty, too. His fever would have dehydrated him.

When twilight hit she made a trip to the bushes, just like last night. And, just as before, when she came back he was redressing the wound on his leg. She frowned. He'd waited until she was out of sight—again. She didn't think his timing had anything to do with modesty.

This time she walked up to him. "How bad is it?"

He kept right on winding the worn gauze around the wound. "I'll be okay."

"Dammit, don't treat me like a child who needs to be reassured!"

He looked at her, brows lifted. "Cursing, Rev?"

"You only call me 'Rev' when you want me to back off."

"Yeah? And your point is…?"

"That you should level with me about what shape you're in. I might be able to help. I'm not a nurse or doctor, but I have had some first aid training."

"So have I." He went back to his bandaging, tying off the dirty, tattered gauze. "Save those nurturing instincts for your congregation. I prefer to take care of myself."

"I figured that out." She clenched her hands in frustration.

"What happens if you become too sick to go on? Will you hold me off at gunpoint rather than let me help you?"

"Depends on whether I've shot anyone that day or not. I wouldn't want to bag over my limit." He jerked his pants up and levered himself to his feet with his stick. "I'm going to get some sleep. Feel free to stay up and work on your sermon some more. It's a little rough."

A.J. stood in the deepening dusk and watched him hobble the few steps to their makeshift bed, her fists still clenched.

She'd always thought the fable about the mouse taking the thorn from the lion's paw was unrealistic. A great, proud beast like that was a lot more likely to swipe the mouse into oblivion with one huge paw, lashing out against its own helplessness.

Good thing she wasn't a mouse, she decided.

Her fists relaxed and she moved to join him, settling beneath the thin blanket without speaking. His body was as hard and reassuring as it had been the night before. It was also warm. Much warmer than last night.

A.J. stared out at the gathering darkness, listening to the frogs' serenade, the calls of the other night creatures, and the steady breathing of the man whose body heated hers like a furnace. He'd fallen asleep almost immediately.

She didn't. Long after exhaustion should have dragged her down, she lay there sorting her options, wondering, worrying. Praying.

She shouldn't have pushed. The harder she tried to make him admit he needed help, the harder he was going to shove her away. Some people were like that. Accepting help made them feel vulnerable, and they couldn't handle it. She wasn't sure why she'd tried to force things earlier—except that it had hurt. It had hurt a great deal more than it should that he wouldn't let her help, wouldn't let her *in.*

Well, she'd have to get over that. She wasn't doing either of them any good by trying to force a level of intimacy and trust he didn't want. And he had no reason to trust her, she reminded herself. They didn't really know each other…if it seemed as if they did, that was due to their situation.

But whether he wanted to admit it or not, Michael needed her. He was ill, injured, and he was going to have to depend on her, just as she depended on him. Or neither of them would make it out of this jungle alive.

Six

"My temperature's down this morning," Michael said when she returned from brushing her teeth at the creek.

Fortunately, Michael's magic pockets had held a toothbrush for him and a small tube of toothpaste, and she still had the toothbrush the guard had given her. The small ritual of brushing her teeth possessed amazing restorative power, as did being able to comb her hair. She felt more like herself when she was done.

Michael sat on a rock, tying the laces of his boots. He did look better. Less flushed, and his eyes were clear. Of course, fevers often went down in the morning, only to climb during the course of the day. It didn't mean he was well.

But there was a spark of relief in his eyes. She wouldn't take that away from him. "That's good," she said, folding their blanket, smoothing the air out and refolding it until it would fit in the pocket of his vest once more. "A good night's sleep must have helped."

Not that he'd slept well the first part of the night. He'd

been restless, moving often enough to wake her. Some time before dawn, though, she thought he'd fallen more deeply asleep.

"I'm not used to being sick." He picked up his stick and straightened. "I can't remember the last time I was. Probably when I was a snot-nosed kid."

"If that's your roundabout way of apologizing for acting like a cranky child last night, apology accepted."

"A cranky child, huh?" He grinned.

And she was in trouble all over again.

She was falling for him. It was temporary, she was sure—the product of isolation, danger, the fact that he'd rescued her…and her unfortunate susceptibility to male beauty. She'd been down that path in college, tumbling into one hormone-driven infatuation after another. She knew better now. She'd get over this.

But oh, how the world lit up when he grinned at her.

His fever came back by noon.

Michael didn't try to deny the growing heat and weakness this time. He cursed silently for a few hundred yards, then stopped for rest sooner than he wanted to, when they ran across a stream. He sent Alyssa to gather wood for a fire so he could boil more water.

He was going to need extra fluids.

She didn't nag, didn't ask annoying questions about how he was feeling. Quietly, efficiently, she did as instructed. Perversely, that irritated him, too.

While she scrounged for wood, he pulled out his topographic map. He'd entered their campsite in the GPS device last night and checked it against the topo map, so he knew where he was: about thirty miles from the border, another thirty from the nearest Guatelmalan town.

Those miles translated into a lot of mountain. If he'd been in good shape, he could have made the pass he was aiming for in a couple of days, and the town in another two or three. As it was…he refolded the map carefully.

As it was, he'd be lucky to make it at all.

A shiver went through him. He didn't want to die. Not like this, with so much left undone… What would happen to Ada if he died here? Would Jacob and Luke still be able to dissolve the trust? Michael had no idea what the legal ramifications would be if he died unwed…*Luke is already married,* he thought, *and I wasn't there to see Jacob's face when he learned who Luke had wed—Maggie, the woman Jacob had been dating. And Jacob…he might be married, too, by now. He'd sure been taking dead aim at that gorgeous new assistant of his…*

No, he didn't want to die from some stupid fever that made him sick and weak, unable to take care of himself, much less the woman he was supposed to be rescuing.

Some rescue. Quite the hero, wasn't he? Maybe he should have let her think she was slowing him down. She would have agreed to split up if she'd thought she was endangering him.

But he still didn't believe she could make it on her own. He'd just have to push himself. The fever wasn't that bad, and he was strong. His body might yet throw it off. He could keep moving. He had to.

"I couldn't find much," she said cheerfully. "Is this enough?"

Alyssa stood there, a small armload of sticks distributing a fresh serving of dirt on her already-grungy shirt. Her face was smudged, and her chinos were beyond dirty. Her abundant mess of curls was tied back with a scrap of cloth torn from the sleeve of her shirt. And she was smiling.

"You should have seen this bird," she said. "I only caught a glimpse of it before it flew away, but it was gorgeous—bright red, with long yellow feathers in the tail."

Something stirred inside him he couldn't name, something

odd and warm and disturbing. ''Let's see if you remember your fire-building lessons.''

What would happen to Alyssa if he died before getting her to safety?

He heaved himself to his feet, leaning heavily on his walking stick. ''I'll fill the water bag.''

''You should stay off your leg. I can get it.''

A black rage descended out of nowhere. ''Dammit to hell, would you quit arguing with everything I say? I'll do it.''

The fury faded almost as quickly as it had hit, but the black feeling remained, clinging like cobwebs. She was right. He knew that even as he limped toward the thin trickle of the stream. If she'd been one of his men, he would have sent her for the water without a second thought. She was more fit than he was right now.

Only he couldn't stand being so damned weak. Depending on her. It made him want to claw the bark off the nearest tree and howl.

When he came back she had the twigs and small branches in place, ready for his matches. He took a deep breath, let it out. ''I'm sorry.''

She gave him a smooth, hard-to read glance. ''We've both got a lot to learn, I guess. What do you think of my fire-building?''

It wasn't perfect, but it would do. They didn't have to worry about the smoke showing—the forest canopy would dissipate that. He showed her again how to light it, then forced himself to rest while she boiled water in the coffee can. And while the water was cooling, he showed her how to use the GPS device and topo map. Just in case.

They made camp at another little stream, stopping well before dark. Supper was simple and not very filling. Earlier they'd run across a mango tree, which A.J. had climbed, leaving Michael white-lipped on the ground. The fruit was green but edible, and they had a couple of mangos apiece left to go with the *plátanos* they'd found later. The thick, rather bready bananas were usually fried, but turned out okay when baked on hot rocks near the fire.

Before they ate, A.J. had taken Michael's shirt downstream and washed it as best she could. He needed to use the sleeves for bandaging; the gauze could still serve as a pad, but was too worn to work alone. She'd washed herself, too, and her panties and bra, though the stream was so shallow it was mostly a sponge bath.

Michael had said it was too shallow for fish. That was probably true. A.J. thought it was also true that his hand wasn't steady enough for fishing.

"It's a good thing it's December," she said after swallowing the last mouthful of *plátano.* "We wouldn't find as many streams in the dry season."

Michael grunted. She looked up, biting her lip.

He didn't look good. Fever glittered in his eyes and flushed his cheekbones, but there was a gray, pallid look to his skin otherwise. His hair clung damply to his forehead and nape and gleamed on his shoulders—his *bare* shoulders. He was using his knife to cut the sleeves off of his shirt.

She leaned back on her heels. "Hot compresses."

He glanced up. "What?"

"For your leg. I don't know why I didn't think of it before. We'll use part of your shirt and hot water. The heat should draw out some of the infection."

He hesitated, then handed her one of the sleeves. "It can't hurt. No, I take that back. It's going to hurt like hell, but maybe it will do some good."

"The water's simmering now. Are you ready for me to do this?"

He grimaced, nodded and unfastened his pants.

She looked away. By now she should have been used to him casually stripping in front of her. She wasn't. Using the hem of her shirt as a hot pad, she picked up the coffee can and poured some of the steaming water over the flat rock they'd cooked on, cleaning it as best she could. Then she folded the sleeve into a pad and poured more hot water over it. "It needs to cool a bit. The water was almost boiling."

"It needs to be hot to do any good." He reached over, picked up the pad and held it briefly as if testing the temperature. Then laid it on the red, angry wound in his thigh.

His lips peeled back. The breath hissed out between his teeth. "Mother Mary and all the saints. That ought to do something. Remove a few layers of skin, if nothing else. Keep the water hot. We'll need to repeat it."

There was a lot of skin showing right now. Michael was wearing briefs and a small pad of cloth, and nothing else. "Here." She handed him the silvery blanket. "This may help hold the heat in."

He spread the blanket over his legs while she moved the coffee can next to the fire. "You sound very Catholic when you're trying not to curse," she said as lightly as she could.

"You can take the boy out of the parochial school, but you can't take the parochial school out of the boy." He reached for the water bag. "Talk to me. I could use the distraction."

"You've pried all my best stories out of me already." He'd kept her talking most of the afternoon, probably for the same reason he'd given now. It helped take his mind off the pain. "Except for the tales of my misdeeds in college, and I'm not about to spill those."

"I'll bet I can top them. C'mon, let's trade—you tell me one of your deepest, darkest secrets, and I'll tell you one of mine."

A.J. looked at him thoughtfully. "You don't think I have any deep, dark secrets, do you?"

"You said you were a Goody Two-shoes."

"That was in high school. I made my share of mistakes in college."

He gave her a lazy, disbelieving grin. "Right." He tipped the water bag to his mouth.

"When I was a freshman, I lost my virginity in the men's locker room."

Water sputtered out of his mouth. "The hell you say."

She grinned. "I was dating the captain of the basketball team, and he had a key. I'd always wondered if their facilities were better than ours—I think I mentioned that I was in track? Well..." She spread her hands. "Late one night, he showed me around."

Amusement glinted in his eyes now, along with the fever. "And did you enjoy checking out the facilities?"

"Um..." She busied herself rolling up the leaf "plate" she'd used, tossing it into the trees and wishing she'd resisted the urge to shock him. "I've told you a secret. It's your turn."

"I was more traditional than you. I lost my virginity at seventeen in the back seat of my Jag."

What kind of a hell-raiser waited until he was seventeen to lose his virginity? Certainly he wouldn't have lacked for opportunity. She opened her mouth to tease him about that, but at the last second common sense stepped in. Enough talk about sex. "You had a Jaguar at seventeen?" She shook her head. "You did say you were a rich boy."

"Jacob gave it to me—my oldest brother. It was a bribe so I'd stick it out when my dad gave up and shipped me off to military school. Jacob bought the Jag used and rebuilt the engine while I was learning the joys of close-order drill." He moved the blanket aside and lifted the pad from his thigh. "Better hit me again. It's cooled off." He handed the cloth to her.

His big brother had bought him his first car after his father gave up on him? A rapid, dangerous softening in the vicinity of her heart made A.J. look away and tested the water with her fingertip. Hot, but not scalding. "Your brother rebuilt the engine himself? I'm impressed."

"Jacob's second passion is old cars. He gets off on grease and lug nuts."

''What's his first passion?'' She wrung out the pad, put it on the stone and poured water over it again.

''The money game. He plays it well, and plays to win. Not that different from Luke, really, for all that they use a different set of counters for success. Luke—'' He stopped, hissing as she put the pad on his leg. ''That wasn't as hot as the first time.''

''Hot enough. Second-degree burns won't speed the healing process. Who's Luke? Another brother?''

Michael nodded. ''He's an athlete. Picked up a gold at the Olympics for three-day eventing before he settled down to train horses.''

''Sounds like you come from a family of overachievers.''

His mouth turned up. ''Two out of three of us, at least. I'm the ordinary one.''

A.J. stared at him. ''Amazing. You can say that with a straight face while sitting there with hole in your leg and a fever burning you up after spending the last few days keeping both of us alive in a jungle while being hunted by an army.''

His gaze flickered away. ''This is what I'm trained for. If I were like my brothers, I'd be—oh, at least a captain by now.''

The light was going, dimming from shadowy green to the hush of twilight. The silvery blanket across his legs seemed to glow in the half light. Michael himself seemed to grow darker, his coppery skin blending with the deepening dusk. His expression was lost to her in the fading light, but there was tension in the stillness of his body.

This was important to him, she realized. For some reason, he had no clue what a remarkable man he was. For some reason, she couldn't stand that. She leaned forward, determined to make him listen. ''You play to win, too, Michael. Just like your brothers. Only you play for higher stakes than they do—lives, freedom, the precarious balance that passes for peace. Definitely an overachiever. You are,'' she finished softly, "one of the two most extraordinary men I've ever known. Real heroes are rare."

His head jerked around to face her. He was scowling. "Don't expect me to believe that. I've heard enough about Daniel Kelleher today to know you thought he was some kind of saint. And I know what you think of me."

No, he didn't. She wasn't sure herself, except that her ideas—of him, of a lot of things—were changing. "Daniel was hardly a saint." It was surprisingly easy to smile. "He was always late. He could be self-absorbed, and he had a lousy memory for anything that didn't interest him. I can't tell you how many times I'd ask him to pick up something on the way home, and he'd forget. That's how—" Her breath caught. "That's how we wound up at that convenience store that night. He'd forgotten to pick up the milk earlier."

Michael seemed to study her for a long moment, though she couldn't make out his expression. Then he pulled back the blanket. "This has cooled off again." He handed her the pad.

Hurt rushed in, making her as silent as he had been earlier. She took the cloth and turned away. Apparently she'd said too much, gotten too close to some invisible boundary, and he intended to pretend she hadn't spoken.

The fire had died down some, and the water wasn't as hot as it needed to be. She moved the can closer to the flames, hugged her knees closer to her chest and waited.

Long moments later, he spoke. "When my father died, he was a week away from marrying his sixth wife."

That pulled her head around to look at him. "He was married six times?"

"Seven, actually, to six women. He married Luke's mother twice." Michael grimaced. "I don't know what to say to you. I can tell that you had a real marriage. Solid. To me, that's like walking on the moon. I know some people have done it, but it doesn't have much to do with me. It's not something I'll ever experience. My mother was Dad's fourth wife. I had three stepmoms before he died, and that doesn't count the women who hung around between marriages. I can't imagine what it was like for you to lose someone you'd built a real marriage with."

"Michael." She got that far, then stopped and swallowed. Now she was the one who didn't know what to say. Her eyes stung, and she wanted to believe it was the smoke from the fire making them burn, but she knew better. Nor was it anything as unselfish as sympathy. "I, uh, think the water's hot now."

She bit her lip as she prepared the compress, getting herself back under control. When she turned to hand him the pad, she thought she had her expression evened out.

Their fingers brushed when she handed him the pad. "Damn. You got it hot enough this—" He broke off when he put the pad on his leg. His head tipped back and the cords in his neck stood out. For a few seconds he just sat there and breathed hard, riding out the shock of pain.

When he continued, his voice was lower, slightly husky. "The real heroes are the men like your Dan, you know. The ones who know how to handle the daily stuff. The ones you can count on, day in and day out. That takes a kind of guts I don't have or understand."

Her heart was pumping hard, as if she'd rounded a familiar corner and found herself face-to-whiskers with a tiger. "Are you by any chance warning me?"

The ghost of his usual grin touched his mouth. "Why would I do that? You're not crazy enough to fall for a man like me. But if you change your mind about taking that walk on the wild side you missed out on when you were a teen—"

"Never mind." Suddenly she pushed to her feet. "I'm going to wash my face and make a trip into the bushes before it gets any darker."

Michael was asleep when she got back. Not pretending sleep—though he might have done that to save them both embarrassment, he would have put the fire out first. She took care of that chore, then lay down next to him.

He was lying on his back. He hadn't put his pants or vest back on. He was all but naked, and his skin was dry and hot. Fear was becoming as familiar as aching calves and thighs, but the furnace of his body notched it up another level. She curled around him protectively.

Why had she kept him awake so long? Such a pointless conversation, too. She'd been doing it again—probing, trying to create an intimacy he didn't want. She was angry with herself for putting them both through that.

He *had* been warning her, however carelessly he'd denied it. And he'd been right to do so. And if she'd hadn't been so crazy with worry for him right now, she would have been horribly embarrassed. He'd picked up on her emotions before she'd let herself acknowledge them…and had gently let her know how hopeless those mute, newborn longings were.

She closed her eyes, too tired for the tears that had threatened earlier. Somewhere along the line, she'd come to realize that they weren't as different as she'd thought. They were both hopeless idealists. Oh, he chased his ideals differently, with guns and a capacity for violence that dismayed her. But his choices were as shaped by ideals as hers were.

He was an extraordinary man, just as she'd said—a weary knight in tarnished armor. He was also damaged. Wise enough to know the damage existed, and kind enough to warn her about it.

They were more alike than she'd realized, yes. And still so far apart in so many ways. He came from wealth, from a family fractured so many times she could scarcely imagine it. She came from loving if overly protective parents, the placid normalcy of Saturday Little League, Sunday pot roasts and a budget that only occasionally stretched to a vacation to someplace exotic…like Six Flags.

And she ached for him anyway. Lying on the hard ground,

surrounded by night and its creatures, with his ill, feverish body in her arms, she ached with desire for him.

She sighed and stroked the damp hair back from his face. He didn't stir. Michael was as wrong for her as she was for him, but he was a man who needed and deserved to be loved. After this was over, when she went back to her safe, ordinary life and he went on to find other dragons to slay, she might find the strength to pray that he found a woman who could give him everything she didn't dare.

But right now he slept beside her, gripped by the twin fists of fever and pain. Right now—however temporarily—he was hers.

It was around noon two days later that A.J. admitted the truth.

Barring a miracle, they weren't going to make it.

For two more days they'd tried. The hot compresses seemed to help his wound—the angry red streaks had retreated slightly—but the infection must have already been systemic. His fever didn't go away. At night it climbed alarmingly. For two more nights, A.J. had slept next to him as he burned, tossed and turned before falling into a deep, exhausted sleep that scared her worse than his restlessness.

She was hungry. Gut-gnawingly hungry in a way she'd never experienced. They'd found some more fruit—guavas last night, small and green and hard—but Michael hadn't let her eat much of it. An all-fruit diet, especially when the fruit was green, was likely to throw their digestive systems into revolt. Diarrhea and dehydration were more immediate dangers than hunger.

Earlier today, they'd seen a small deer, and A.J., who still cried when the hunters killed Bambi's mother, had been eager for venison. But Michael's hand had been shaking too badly to get a shot off. He'd stood there afterward, his head down, cursing the air blue.

She didn't know how he could still be moving, putting one

foot in front of the other. She didn't think his temperature had been below a hundred since yesterday morning, and they were still at least a day's journey from the border, farther than that from the tiny Guatemalan town he'd said was their goal.

A.J. was scared all the way down to her toes. And trying desperately not to let it show, because the last thing Michael needed was to have her fears to deal with as well as his own. However much he pretended he wasn't scared spitless, he *had* to be.

Overhead, in the hidden sky, clouds must have moved in. The light was dim. She thought it might be around noon. This part of the trail was narrow and steep and frequently obstructed by vines, shrubs and roots. They were high now, entering the range where conifers dominated, though the leaves of encina oaks still mixed with the knots of feathery needles on the towering ocote pines.

Michael was in the lead. He had the gun, the map and the know-how, even if he was wobbly and fuzzy with fever. Sweat lent a slick sheen to his skin. He wore only his vest, unbuttoned, and his camouflage pants; two nights ago he'd fashioned his stick into a crude crutch, lashing a second branch to it with vines and using his shirt to pad the top.

He was moving very slowly.

She wanted to prop him up, to let him use some of her strength. Tired and sore and hungry as she was, she still was in better shape than he. But she'd already offered the use of her shoulder, and received a polite refusal—along with a look of such flat fury that she hadn't mentioned it again.

If the only thing keeping him going was stupid, stubborn pride, she wouldn't kick that crutch out from under him.

He stopped. She kept going, closing the distance between them, thinking dully that he'd paused to get his breath—something he'd been doing fairly often today.

But he didn't start moving again. Something in his stillness alarmed her. "What is it?" she whispered.

He shook his head and turned slightly so she could move up beside him. She stopped with a whisper of space between them and put her hand on his shoulder.

Dear Lord, he was hot.

Over his shoulder she saw that the path dropped off all at once, winding down precipitously. They'd run across one of the little hidden valleys again—and this one held a village.

A *real* village. Thirty huts, maybe. She could see cleared fields and people in those fields, moving between the huts. A shout drifted up to them, vague and wordless at this distance, but sounding so human, so cheerful and ordinary that her eyes abruptly filled.

"It's remote," he said abruptly. "*El Jefe*'s men may not come this far, and if they do, they probably won't be looking for you. This is your best chance."

Her insides skittered unpleasantly, like nails on a chalkboard. "*Our* best chance," she corrected him.

"I can't risk it."

"You'll risk more by not getting help." She grabbed his shoulders, willing him to be sensible. His eyes didn't glitter now, but were dulled by illness. Hunger had dug hollows beneath his cheekbones. "You can't go on like this. You need rest, food, whatever help these people are willing to give."

He jerked himself away, turning his back to her. And he wobbled, damn him. "I'll be okay. I can move faster once I know you're taken care of."

He could barely move at all! She gritted her teeth against frustration. Or despair. He had to face the truth. "Michael, you're going to die if you don't get help."

"If I go on alone, I'm only risking myself. If I go into the village, I risk falling into *El Jefe*'s hands. I can't let that happen."

He knew. Oh, God, he knew he wasn't likely to make it, yet he still intended to go on alone. "This place is so remote—you said so yourself. No roads in or out, no reason to think *El Jefe* even knows about this place, or cares."

"I can't risk it."

She blinked furiously, trying to keep the tears in. He'd said he couldn't let himself be captured, but she hadn't realized what he meant—that he wouldn't take any chance of that happening. No matter what. A.J. tried to care about all those nameless, faceless people who would be hurt if *El Jefe* found a way to drag the war out. She wanted to care. She couldn't. Not enough to sacrifice Michael for them.

Michael cared. He cared enough to die, if necessary, for people who would never know his name. Was there any truer definition of *hero?*

In that moment, something small and simple and complete fell into place inside her, quietly and without fuss. She took a deep breath, balanced between painful calm and near hysteria.

What a moment to realize all her sensible decisions had been as effective as the sand walls children build to hold back the ocean. It was too late for fears, reasonable or otherwise. She was in love with him.

"All right," she said after a moment. "You know your duty better than I do. If you can't risk it, you can't. Do we take a break now, or keep going?"

He turned. His eyes narrowed. "*We* don't do anything. You go down there, make friendly with the natives."

"No."

Michael fought dirty. He told her he didn't want or need her tagging after him. She was a burden. She was more likely to get him killed than she was to help him.

"I don't think so," she said calmly. "And I don't care what you want. I'm going with you."

He dragged a hand over his hair. "Look, if you come with me, we'll probably both die. You want me to die knowing I caused your death?"

"You gave me some good advice a couple days ago.

There's nothing more useless than blaming yourself for someone else's decision. This is my choice, not yours.''

Finally, his eyes bleak and wild, he turned and started moving—back up the path. Away from the village.

A.J. followed.

Her decision had been quite simple, really. If she left him, he would die. Oh, he'd keep going as long as he could, and she didn't doubt his will, his drive. He wouldn't give up until the breath left his body.

But will and drive weren't always enough.

He might die anyway, of course. Her knowledge and skills were limited. But she'd do everything she could, and if it wasn't enough...if it wasn't enough, she thought, swallowing hard, she could at least be sure he didn't die alone.

Seven

Heat. Pain. Both beat at him, throbbed through him. Fire raged in his leg and pulsed through his body. His head and heart pounded in rhythm with the furnace. He tried to take a step with every beat. But it was growing darker.

Damned sun, he thought. Hiding behind a cloud when he needed to see. Couldn't trip. If he went down, he wasn't sure he'd be able to get up.

Unless…maybe it was night?

That seductive thought made him stop. He contemplated darkness, swaying and blinking at the sweat stinging his eyes. Night meant peace, rest. Lying down with Alyssa. Her hand on his skin, her body curled around him…

"It's not dark yet," he muttered, clenching his hand on the crutch-stick that held him upright.

"No, not yet," her soft voice agreed. And then she was taking his stick from him, lifting his arm. She put it over her shoulder, tucking her own shoulder under his arm. "Come on, soldier."

That's right. He was a soldier. He had to keep going, keep away from the village…keep Alyssa safe. But she was supposed to have stayed in the village. Safer for her there. ''You're supposed to be back there,'' he said, trying to focus on her face. ''In the village.''

''I decided to stay with you.'' Her voice was so soothing. ''Can you go a little farther, Michael? If we can find a stream, I can bathe you, maybe get the fever down.''

A stream. Yes, that was good. They needed water.

He started moving again. It was a little easier now, with her shoulder supporting him on one side.

The first time he went down, she helped him stand. The second time, she begged him to stay where he was. He didn't curse or argue. He didn't have the energy. It took everything he had to get to his feet. Then walk. Keep moving. If he stopped…he was no longer sure what would happen if he stopped. Something terrible. His world narrowed until all that remained was heat, pain, the necessity of putting one foot in front of the other.

After some brief eternity, his knees buckled. She was right there—lowering him to the ground.

''Have to rest,'' he muttered, closing his eyes. ''Be okay in a minute.''

''That's right. You rest.''

Something settled on top of him. His eyelids lifted slightly—the blanket. ''Is it night? Time to camp?''

''Close enough.'' Her voice sounded funny. ''You sleep, Michael. I'll be back soon.''

Back? His hand shot out, capturing her wrist more by instinct than aim. ''Where are you going?''

''To the village.'' Her hand was cool on his forehead, smoothing back his hair. ''I'll be back as soon as I can.''

She was going. Leaving him. That was what he'd wanted—wasn't it? For her to go to the village, where she'd be safe… ''You aren't coming back.''

"Yes, I am. I will." Her face was a fuzzy oval, but her voice was clear. And her hand was blessedly cool on his skin…he didn't want her to go. He needed her.

No. No, he couldn't need… "Don't come back."

"I'm sorry. I know you have your duty. I have to follow my own conscience. Or maybe I'm just not as strong as you are. I can't let you die because there's a *chance* you would be captured. Maybe you wouldn't be. Maybe…oh," she said, hurrying over the words, "I'm not putting this well, and you're too sick to know what I'm saying. Rest." Her hand again, stroking him, soothing him. "Sleep. I'll be back."

Then the comforting hand and the soothing voice were gone.

He almost cried out. But he remembered that she was supposed to go, to be safe…and that he shouldn't be heard, seen, found.

Couldn't be seen…but he was in the middle of the trail. That was wrong. He heaved himself onto his hands and knees. His head spun. *Keep moving,* he told himself, and crawled until he saw a great, spreading bush. He dropped to his stomach and rolled, aiming to get under those sheltering branches, and bumped his injured thigh.

The pain was fierce and violent. *Don't cry out.*

After a moment his breathing steadied. He would rest. He would lie here and rest until he had some of his strength back. Then he'd keep moving.

Keep moving…

"Mikey, can't you move any faster?"

"I don't want to go." He sat on his bed, his mouth sulky, his jaw stubborn. "Why do we have to go?"

"Because your father will be home soon. I have to get away. He's swallowing me. I—oh, you're just a kid. You can't understand. Never mind, honey." His mother smiled, but her lips trembled. "Be a good boy and put your things in the suitcase. I'll explain…oh, I forgot my necklace. I'll be back,'' she said, already moving. ''Pack your things, there's my good boy.'' She whirled out of his room on jasmine-scented air.

Michael sat beside the open suitcase she'd put on his bed. He wanted to cry, but he couldn't. He wasn't a little kid anymore.

He didn't pack. It made his insides knot up to disobey, but he didn't want to leave his father, his brothers. Where would they go? Who would take care of his mom if they left? The tears almost won when he thought about that, about having to take care of her by himself.

He wasn't a little kid anymore, but he wasn't really big, either. Not big like Jacob, or even Luke. Luke was eight, four years older than him. And Jacob was really big, thirteen and awfully bossy, but he always seemed to know what to do. And Ada…he sniffed. He really, really wanted Ada.

But his brothers were at school, and Ada was at the store. Michael was home alone with his mom.

He didn't know what to do.

''Mikey?'' She was back. ''Oh, Mikey, you haven't *moved.* We have to go *now.*''

''I don't want to go. My brothers are here. If you don't like Dad anymore, you can just stay away from him.'' His brothers would help him take care of her. She might be just their stepmom, but they loved her, too. He could count on them to help—if he and his mom stayed here.

''It's not that simple, sweetheart. Here, you'll want your new jeans, won't you?'' She began folding his clothes, her movements jerky.

''It's a big house. You could move into the yellow bedroom, the one in the east wing. You like yellow.''

''Oh, Mikey.'' Her hand trembled when she stopped moving, the small, telltale tremor he knew too well. She'd be drinking soon. ''How selfish I am. I understand, sweetheart.'' Swiftly she bent and kissed him.

She always moved fast when she was like this, as if there was too much of her crammed inside her skin and she was trying to get away from herself. "You stay here, sweetheart. He's not a bad father, and you'll have Jacob and Luke and Ada...you'll be better off here. Lord knows I'm not—not—" Her breath hitched and she straightened. "I'll come see you soon, all right? I just have to—to pull myself together. I'll be better soon," she said, spinning and heading for the door. "When I'm away from *him.*"

"Mama?" He shot off the bed. "Mama, you can't go without me!"

"It's for the best." She picked up her suitcase, stretching her mouth in a too-bright smile. "You'll see, darling. I love you so much...tell Jacob and Luke I love them, too, will you? I don't like leaving without seeing them, but I have to go. I'll be better soon," she promised, turning and walking quickly down the hall. "You'll see. Everything will be better soon."

"Mama?" He ran after her. "Mama, don't go! Mama..."

Don't go. Don't... Michael's eyes jerked open.

Leaves. There were leaves above him, ground below. And pain, terrible pain in his leg and his head. The light was dim, but it wasn't night...the rain forest. He remembered now. He'd been hurt, shot, and Alyssa had left him. She'd gone back to the village.

He was alone. And he was dying.

No! He struggled, got his elbow under him, levered himself up—not sitting, not quite, but it was a start. Only the effort made him pant, made his head spin. Darkness fluttered, frothy and inviting, at the edges of his vision. He collapsed onto the dirt once more.

He had to keep moving....

Where? How? *God,* he thought, but couldn't think of what to pray for, except for life. He wanted to live so badly.

Alyssa, he thought, or maybe he said it. She'd said she would be back.... Alyssa of the gentle hands, incredible legs and soothing voice. If only he could hear her voice again...funny. He couldn't hear her, but he could see her...the awe on her face when she'd seen the butterflies. The smudge of dirt on her cheek. The single, sweaty curl that kept straggling into her face in spite of the way she kept shoving it back...

She wasn't here. He knew that. She'd left him, yet he could still see her. Wasn't that strange?

Keep her safe, he thought, and let the darkness have him.

"We're almost there," A.J. said in Spanish, scrambling up a short, steep slope.

How had Michael made it up this part of the trail? Her own heart was hammering so hard she barely heard the murmured reply from behind her. That, too, was in Spanish, but the dialect was so thick she caught only some of the words. The tone, though, was clear—comfort, reassurance.

She made herself slow down. Sister Andrew might seem sturdy, with her broad face, shoulders and hips, but she had to be at least sixty. Señor Pasquez, the village's *tepec,* or headman, was even older. He looked like a strong gust of wind would blow him away.

At the top of the rise, A.J. looked around frantically. Here. She was sure she'd left Michael here. So where...? "Oh," she cried, hurrying to grab the silver material snagged on a branch. Their blanket. She'd covered him with it before she left.

Where was he?

She didn't realize she'd spoken aloud until Señor Pasquez answered in his colloquial Spanish. "Your man was out of his head, you said. He's moved a little, maybe. He won't be far. We will find him."

She flashed him a worried smile. "Yes. Yes, of course. He—I see him!"

He was several feet off the trail, half hidden beneath a bush. What instinct had prompted him to crawl under there, to hide? She hurried to his side, pushing the branches back. Sister Andrew went with her; Señor Pasquez and his donkey followed more slowly.

He was so still. But his chest moved. Life still breathed in him. "Michael." A.J. forced a calm she didn't feel into her voice, stroking his hair. He was very hot. "Michael, I've brought help."

Slowly, his eyes drifted open. He smiled up at her. "Hey." His voice was weak. "How about that. I can hear you now, too."

Then he passed out again.

Hands pulled at him. Michael roused from the dark ocean to fight.

"Shh, it's all right. We have to move you, Michael. Señor Pasquez's donkey can pull you once we get you on the travois."

Alyssa's voice? She wanted him to move. Yes, he remembered now. He was supposed to keep moving.

He tried. His wounded leg wasn't working, but he managed to push with the other one. Strong hands gripped him under his arms and dragged him. It hurt. He gritted his teeth. Did he still have to be silent? He couldn't remember. "Alyssa?"

"Here," she said. "Right beside you. It will take a while to get you back to the village, and I'm afraid you'll be bounced around. But they've got penicillin." She sounded excited. "Sister Andrew has had some medical training, too, and she knows the local remedies. She'll help you."

But the nun was named Sister Elena, not Andrew. Andrew was Scopes's first name. Was Scopes here?

No, that was silly. His eyes closed again. If he was going to hallucinate, he wished he'd dream up a soft bed and air-conditioning, not this hard jolting. It hurt. It hurt so much....

At some point the jolting stopped. There were people, voices—but he couldn't make the sounds break up into words. Children? Did he hear children's high, piping voices? Where was he?

He tried to focus, but everything blurred—people, light, movement. But Alyssa was there. She was holding his hand while other hands and arms lifted him, carried him... darkness. Something smooth beneath his back. A hand behind his head, and a cup held to his lips. He drank—cool, sweet water.

Another voice. A woman, but not Alyssa. She spoke English with a thick Irish brogue, which made no sense. Scopes had a touch of brogue in his speech...but Scopes wasn't here. Wherever *here* was.

Michael frowned. Hands tugged at the top of his pants. He struggled to sort the whirl of images, sensations, thoughts... "Why?"

"The sister needs to look at your wound," Alyssa said.

"No..." He shook his head weakly. "Why did you come back?"

"I couldn't leave you. And it will be okay, Michael, you'll see. These are good people. They insisted on bringing you here so the sister could take care of you." Her lips pressed a blessing to his forehead. "You're going to be all right now. You'll see."

Somehow that's when he knew. She wasn't a hallucination. None of this was. Alyssa was really there with him—in a hut. In the village. She'd done exactly what he'd told her not to do, jeopardizing his mission.

She'd come back. And they were safe.

Relief crashed in, a huge wave that swept him back out into that black ocean.

Eight

The water was waist-high and cool. Dirt squished between her toes. A.J. scooped soft soap out of the wooden bowl, luxuriating in the clean, slippery feel of it. She hummed as she rubbed the soap into her hair. The air was alive with birdsong, with the coppery tang of the river and the blended smells of earth and green, growing things. Trees leaned out over the water, but there was a long strip of unobstructed sky above the river, as blue as every promise ever made—and kept.

She looked up at that strip of sky, breathed it in and thought of Michael.

His fever had broken yesterday. Last night, though, it had peaked. He'd been delirious, and he'd babbled about many things. *Not all promises are kept,* she thought sadly. And when promises made to a child are broken the pieces can't always be put back together again.

She dunked beneath the water, then surfaced. Water streamed from her face, hair and shoulders.

"You look very clean now, *señora,*" a polite young voice said in Spanish.

A.J. smiled at the fourteen-year-old girl who'd accompanied her to the river. It wasn't considered safe or seemly to bathe alone. "Yes, I'm clean now."

"You certainly do enjoy bathing." Pilar handed her the length of cloth that would serve as a towel.

"It's considered very important where I come from."

A.J. dressed quickly. The air was warm, but she wasn't used to being outside in the nude, though they were screened by trees from the homes and fields.

Pilar chattered happily as they headed back to Cuautepec. The girl was as tolerant of A.J.'s oddities as the rest of the villagers. A.J.'s passion for frequent baths was only one of her peculiarities; more baffling was her status. Who had ever heard of a woman priest? She wasn't a holy woman like the sisters, nor was she like the priests who came to marry, baptize and offer communion every couple of years. The villagers didn't know what to make of her, so they called her Señora Kelleher.

Widowhood, they understood all too well.

She and Pilar parted by the well. A.J. unfastened the peg, let the bucket drop and heard it splash. It was certainly nice not to have to boil the water anymore. Or dose it with iodine, as Michael had done that first day.

Michael.

Love ached in her so strongly she rubbed her chest, trying to ease the pain. After their adventure was over, they'd never see each other again. A.J. knew that. Accepted it.

But oh, how scary and hard and beautiful it was to be in love.

She thought of the names he'd called out when he was feverish—his brothers, mostly. Jacob and Luke. He'd talked to someone named Ada, too. She frowned as she winched the bucket back up. Who was Ada? Someone important, she thought, pouring the water into one of her buckets. A stepmother? Aunt?

Girlfriend?

He hadn't cried out for his parents. But he had cried. The fever had sent him back in time at one point, way back, to when he'd been a little boy, crying for a mother who had left him. Other times, he'd spoken to one or another of his brothers about the need to take care of his mother.

"¿Su novio, il esta mejor hoy?"

A.J. blinked back to the present. An older woman, her black hair covered by a faded red cloth, her eyes kind and curious, waited patiently to take her turn at the well. A.J. flushed, embarrassed at being caught drifting off into her thoughts. She'd done that a lot the last two days. *"Perdone me, Señora Valenzuela. Si, il esta mucho mejor."*

Novio meant fiancé. The rural people of San Christóbal were relaxed about sexual matters; still, a woman, even a widow, didn't travel alone with a man who wasn't a relative. Therefore, Michael was A.J.'s *novio.* Sister Andrew had gently suggested that A.J. not argue with the assumption, which was at least partly a polite fiction.

A.J. emptied the water into her other bucket. "He isn't used to being sick, though," she went on in Spanish, "and he's restless. He thinks he should be well overnight."

The older woman chuckled. "Men. They are such babies about sickness. And so much trouble! Do this, fetch that. But how we miss them when we don't have them underfoot!" She shook her head.

Señora Valenzuela had a husband and a grown son that she longed to have underfoot once more, A.J. knew. "Perhaps Rualdo will be able to return for a visit soon."

She shrugged. "God willing. My girls work hard, but they haven't a man's muscles. If only…ah, well. Complaining doesn't make the pot boil faster." She took her place at the well.

A.J. positioned herself beneath the yoke that balanced the

water buckets across her shoulders. They were heavy when full. Straightening, she headed back to the biggest building in Cuautepec—the orphanage.

She and Michael had drawn more than their share of luck when they ran across this particular village three days ago. Compared to others in the impoverished north, little Cuautepec was prosperous. The fields produced crops regularly, due in part to a system that let the villagers dam a small river annually, flooding the fields and depositing valuable sediment. Many of the villagers had goats or chickens; there was good, clean drinking water from a well and even a crude sawmill, though it wasn't in use now.

The reason for all this prosperity was twofold: Sister Andrew and Sister Constancia. The two nuns had established the small orphanage fifteen years ago. That hadn't been enough to keep them busy, however. Over the years they'd done much to improve the lot of the villagers.

The one thing the village sorely lacked was able-bodied men. Many of the younger men traditionally left the village for a few months each year to work on a coffee plantation on the other side of the ridge. Then *El Jefe* had started "recruiting" by force, and several of the village men had been impressed into his army. Some had managed to return. Some—like Señora Valenzuela's husband—hadn't.

She exchanged greetings with three children, an old man, a goat and two more women before reaching the orphanage.

The small building that housed the nuns and their charges possessed many advantages, too. The roof was tin, the floors cement, and the exterior walls were cement blocks. There were four rooms. One took up half the building, and in it cooking, eating, work, play, prayer and lessons took place. The other half was divided into bedrooms for the children—one for the boys, one for the girls—and a tiny room at the back shared by the sisters.

A.J. went around back, stepping up on the plank porch, where a pretty girl with a missing front tooth flashed her a smile, then went back to grinding corn with a stone mortar and pestle. Inside, a six-year-old girl was shelling beans while two boys argued over whose turn it was to bring in firewood. A smaller boy sat on a stool in one corner, his back to the room, his shoulders slumped in dejection.

Manuel. A.J. smiled. The boy had enough energy and curiosity for an entire schoolroom. Unfortunately, he hadn't developed think-ahead skills yet. His curiosity often landed him in trouble.

"You don't have to get the water," Sister Andrew scolded in her lilting English. "We have many hands and backs for such chores."

"I drink it," A.J. said, bending at the knees until the buckets sat on the floor. "I should take a turn fetching it."

In the far corner, Michael sat on his pallet, whittling at something with that long, lethal knife of his. He wore his vest and pants. His chest looked hard and strong. The muscles in his arms shifted as he plied the knife.

He looked up when she spoke.

His skin still had the drawn look of illness, but his eyes—oh, his eyes. Why did he keep looking at her that way? Had he guessed how she felt? Flustered, A.J. bent her attention to unhooking the buckets from the yoke. "Looks like our patient found something to do."

Sister Andrew smiled. "He promised that if we let him work with his knife he wouldn't try to chop firewood."

"Firewood?" A.J. straightened, giving Michael a hard look. "He'd better not."

A smile played over his mouth. His eyes never left her. "I'm behaving. Come feel my forehead and see if I'm too warm."

"I should help with supper."

"Nonsense," Sister Andrew said. "The girls don't need help to cook beans."

"Sister Constancia—"

''Doesn't need any help teaching the little ones their catechism, either. Go, spoil your man for a few minutes.''

Pressed, she did as she'd been told, pausing long enough to dip him a cup of water.

His pallet consisted of two blankets folded lengthwise to cushion the hard floor. Two more blankets, folded more compactly, waited against the wall. They were what A.J. slept on—next to him. When she could sleep.

Even when he'd been sick, he'd aroused her. Now...well, now she no longer slept snuggled up to him, but it didn't seem to matter. Lying beside him, even without touching, made her ache. But she wouldn't act on her feelings. Just thinking about it—about him, about caring and intimacy—made her stomach constrict in a sick, nervous knot.

When she reached him, he smiled and put down the wood and his knife so he could take the wooden cup from her. ''Thanks.''

She sat next to him on the folded blankets, keeping several inches between them. Her foolish body ignored that, reacting as if she'd done what her palms itched to do and stroked the firm muscles of his arm. ''It's nice to see your hands steady again. What are you making?''

''It's supposed to be a bowl. Sister Andrew is indulging me by pretending she needs one.'' He finished the water and set the cup down. ''I see you've been scandalizing the villagers by bathing again.''

She felt her cheeks warm. ''What gave me away? The fact that I'm several shades lighter now?''

He touched her hair. ''Your hair is damp. And it shines like polished copper.''

''I wish you wouldn't flirt.''

''Why? Don't ministers flirt?''

She gave him a wary glance. Before, when he'd referred to her calling, he'd used it as a way to put walls between them. Now he was plainly, gently teasing. ''It makes me uncomfortable.''

"That isn't why you're uncomfortable, Alyssa. I can't do anything about the real problem. Yet."

Uh-oh. She was *not* having this conversation in a room with one nun and three children. "I need to get more water." She started to get up.

He caught her wrist and pulled her back down. "I'll behave. Promise."

His eyes were laughing at her. It annoyed her. "You and I have different ideas about what constitutes behaving."

"Your mouth sure is sexy when you prim it up like that."

She didn't mean to laugh. It just slipped out. "Keep it up and you'll have an opportunity to tell me I'm beautiful when I'm angry, too."

He smiled and picked up the lump of wood he'd been shaping. "Did I tell you that when I was feverish I thought Sister Andrew was Scopes?"

"No, you didn't." She relaxed slightly. "Who's Scopes—one of your men? You were ordering him around something fierce that first night we got here, when your fever was so high."

"Was I?" He frowned. "Did I babble a lot?"

"Some." He'd said more than he would want her to know, she felt sure. "So why did you think the sister was Scopes?"

"He's half Irish with a trace of brogue, and his first name is Andrew. I was afraid he'd suffered some terrible transformation." He chuckled.

A.J. smiled and smoothed their silvery blanket, which lay on top of the others. "The sisters have been good to us. The whole village has. I can hardly believe how lucky we were to stumble across them."

"Was it luck?"

"I'd call it God's grace, but I thought you might prefer to think in terms of luck."

"I'm not a complete disbeliever, even if I'm not sure what to believe in." He picked up his knife and started digging at the wood. "I'm worried about the trouble our presence could cause these people."

"Me, too." A chill touched her at the sight of that long, wicked knife in his hands—a foolish reaction. A knife was just a tool, and he'd used it often enough on the trail.

Had he ever used it to kill?

She shook her head, trying to shake off the morbid thoughts. "Sister Andrew was determined to help as soon as I told her about you. She's like that. The other villagers have been amazingly generous, considering how little they have."

"I'll see that they don't suffer for having helped us." A long wood curl spiraled off his knife. "I should be strong enough to move on in another two or three days. Are you going to go with me or stay here?"

Two or three days? Her heart gave a funny little hop in her chest. It was so soon. Too soon. And yet, hadn't she expected him to want to leave even faster?

Once he began to mend she'd expected all sorts of reactions from him that she'd hadn't seen, though. Anger, because she'd brought him here against his wishes. Maybe some gratitude mixed in with it. The one thing she'd been sure of was that he'd be antsy, anxious to leave.

He hadn't been angry. Or antsy, as far as she could tell. He just watched her all the time with those calm, intent eyes. Hunter's eyes.

He was confusing the heck out of her.

"Hey." He used his thumb to smooth her forehead. "What's the frown for?"

"I thought you'd try to leave as soon as your fever went down, even if you had to crawl. Instead you sound content to wait around."

"I was out of my head with fever when I insisted on continuing instead of getting help," he said mildly. "Now that we're here, I'd be foolish to leave before I'm strong enough."

He'd been so determined to avoid coming here that he'd

nearly killed himself—and now he was okay with staying a few more days? "So you're not going to try to slink away before your wound is healed?"

"I can't wait until it's fully healed, but I won't be doing any slinking." His knife stroked another long curl out of the center of the wood. "What about you, Alyssa? What do you want?"

You. The word echoed so strongly in her mind she had to pause before answering. "Why are you calling me Alyssa?"

"Why not?"

"I'm used to A.J."

He started another curl of wood with his knife. "It's human nature to hang on to whatever we're used to. When the Allied armies liberated the concentration camps, some of the prisoners walked out the gates, then turned around and walked back in. They weren't used to freedom anymore."

"You make it sound as if wanting to be called by my own name is like living in a concentration camp."

He paused and touched her arm lightly with the hand that held the knife. "But your name *is* Alyssa."

She moved her arm away.

"The knife bothers you?" He pulled it back, his eyes steady on hers. "I won't pretend to be other than what I am."

"I'm not asking you to. But I can't pretend it doesn't trouble me."

He nodded. "Fair enough. Honesty is a good starting point."

Hope and heat fluttered inside her. So did fear. "We're not starting anything, Michael."

"I think we already have. Doesn't anyone call you Alyssa?"

"My mother." Thinking of that warm, busy woman made her smile. "When I told her I wanted to be called A.J., she hugged me and said that was fine—but she liked the name she'd given me."

"What about your father? What does he call you?"

"Oh, I'm A.J. to Dad." Affection and memory chased each other, making her chuckle. "Since he didn't have any sons, he was delighted when I turned out to be a tomboy he could teach to pitch, bat and field a fly ball."

"A baseball fan, I take it."

"An addict." They would be so worried about her. They must know she'd been taken prisoner. Would they be told about the attempted rescue? Restless, anxious over what she couldn't change, she rose to her feet. "I need to get more water."

"Alyssa."

She paused, looking over her shoulder at him.

"Did your husband call you A.J.?"

Her brows knit in a quick, warning frown. "Yes."

He nodded and went back to his whittling. "That's what I thought."

She was all grace and light. Michael watched Alyssa as she helped the others put their simple supper together that night. She paused to wipe a child's dirty face, then to admire the pretty rock another had found.

He knew he made her uneasy. He wanted to. He wanted—needed—for her to be aware of him.

She might not know it yet, but the rules had changed for both of them. *Everything* had changed. He was feeling his way in this new landscape, unsure of a great many things—but very sure of his goal.

When the others were gathered at the big table near the fireplace where the cooking was done, Michael pushed to his feet. He still used his walking stick, but every day he needed it less.

Sister Constancia said the blessing. The two oldest girls served. One—Pilar? Yes, that was it—brought the beans to the foot of the table, where he sat as guest of honor. She was a pretty girl, clear-skinned, with a gap between two of her teeth that gave her smile a certain lopsided charm. At fourteen, she was ready to practice beguiling whatever male moved into range. She set the beans in front of him with a ducked head, shy smile and sideways glance. He thanked her gravely, took a portion and passed the bowl to his right.

Alyssa sat there. Their fingers brushed when she took the bowl. She glanced at him. Her smile came and went too quickly.

She didn't trust him. He knew that and he hated it, but he understood. She had no reason to trust. She had saved his life, while he had very nearly cost her hers.

He should never have let her go on with him after they'd seen this village. If it had taken him longer to collapse, she might have died, too, lost in a wilderness she didn't have the skills to cope with. But she'd been determined to stay with him. When he'd been out of his head with fever and unable to do either of them any good, she'd stayed. Then she'd left...but she'd come back. And changed everything.

Michael shifted on the hard bench. His leg ached. He'd used it more than anyone except himself had thought wise today. But he knew his limits, and he hadn't done any damage. He had to get his strength back. He couldn't stay here much longer.

In truth, he should have already left.

He glanced at the woman on his right. She hadn't said if she was going to leave with him. And he wasn't leaving without her.

"¿Señor West?" a small voice to his left said, going on in rapid-fire Spanish as soon as Michael turned his head, "Will you tell me about the television again, where the pictures move? And the electricity that makes this happen, and makes the lights work?"

He smiled at Manuel, who always had questions—especially about the marvels found in that mythical land, the U.S. It occurred to Michael that if he lived, he would soon be a very rich man.

Funny. He'd never cared about the money, never counted

on it. His father's bizarre will had come as a nasty surprise, but not because he was interested in wealth. There would be advantages to having money, though, he thought as he tried to explain the mysteries of electricity to a six-year-old. A boy as bright and inquisitive as Manual deserved a chance to soak up all the learning he could.

One of the girls chided Manual for not letting their guest eat. The boy reluctantly returned his attention to his supper, giving Michael a chance to scoop up beans with one of the soft tortillas they used in lieu of silverware.

"You're good with him," Alyssa said quietly in English.

"I like kids. You do, too, from what I've seen."

She nodded, looking down at her bowl. "That's another thing I put off: Having children. It made sense at the time, since we intended to put in at least one year of missionary work."

"Regrets?" He captured her hand. "You can still have children, you know." *My children.* The thought startled him. And aroused him. Yes, he thought as another part of this new landscape became clear. He wanted to see her big with his child.

Awareness flashed through her eyes, sharp and hot. She pulled her hand away. "You'd better eat," she said lightly. "Seconds only go to those who finish their first helping quickly."

Michael obeyed with an easy docility that would have warned his brothers to keep an eye on him. He'd gotten what he wanted—for now. She was aware of him.

Alyssa was going to be his. She just didn't know it yet.

There was a great deal of laughing and bickering while the table was cleared and dishes were washed. Michael joined the friendly chaos, insisting he was well enough to scrub the bean pot. Pilar looked shocked. Manuel wanted to know why he would wash a pot when there were girls to do such things. He told the boy that a real man always did his share of the work. Since he wasn't fit enough to chop wood yet, he would wash pots.

Finally, after Sister Andrew had dressed his wound again, the children were sent to bed and the sisters went to their own room. By the time Michael returned from a trip to the facilities behind the building, the fire had burned low in the fireplace. The room was warm and dark, and he had Alyssa to himself.

She leaned out the window near the front door, pulling the crude shutters closed. Someone had given her a nightgown. The yards of much-washed cotton nearly swallowed her.

"How's your leg?" she asked when she turned around. "You've been using it a lot today."

"Sore, but mending." He propped his stick against the wall and lowered himself onto his pallet.

"Thank God for penicillin. When I think of how ill you were..." She shook her head and knelt to unfold her blankets. "It's a miracle."

"Close enough. Of course, it helps that I'm so tough."

She chuckled. He settled on his side, his head propped on one hand. He loved watching her by firelight. The hints and shadows, the shapes shifting as she moved, the whisper of fabric and the quiet intimacy of bare feet—it all fascinated him. Aroused him. "Do you realize I'd never seen you indoors until we came here?"

"What a strange thought." Quickly, competently, she spread her blankets a foot away from his. "We haven't known each other very long, have we? Though it seems..." She shook her head, lay down and smoothed one blanket over her. "I was indoors when you found me at *El Jefe*'s compound."

"I wasn't. And I didn't see you until you came out the window."

Their eyes caught. Held. "I've wondered about Sister Maria Elena and your men. If they made it out okay."

"I'd put money on it. They're good men." Her eyes were

luminous in the dim light, her shape more sensed than seen. There was an easy intimacy to lying side by side this way. There was also a foot of space between their blankets. ''I liked it better when you slept tucked up against me.''

She looked away. Her fingers plucked nervously at the blanket. ''That was necessary on the trail. It isn't necessary now.''

He wondered if her pulse was pounding as wildly as his. It would be easy to find out—all he had to do was stretch out a hand and touch the smooth skin of her throat.

He sighed. She'd probably jump up and move her blankets to the other side of the room. ''Do you only do what's necessary, Alyssa Jean?''

''Oh.'' Her laugh was shaky. ''I haven't heard that in ages. My mother only called me Alyssa Jean when I was in trouble.''

He smiled at her through the deepening darkness. The fire was down to coals now. ''I don't think I remind you of your mother.''

For a long moment she didn't answer. ''No. Which is why I'm over here and you're over there, and it's going to stay that way.''

He could have told her that his intentions were honorable, but that was only partly true. And she would probably have scurried over to the other side of the room anyway. Yet she could do that now, couldn't she? He no longer needed a nurse in the middle of the night.

She stayed near because she wanted to. Frustration, keen and sexual, gnawed at Michael, but satisfaction was stronger. ''How about a picnic tomorrow?''

''What?''

''You know—dirt and ants. Finger food. Eating outdoors.''

Her voice was low and amused. ''We've done plenty of that.''

''I'm trying to be good, but I'm bored out of my mind. I thought a little walk tomorrow might let me exercise my leg without straining anything. I need to see how well I can manage. And I'd like some company."

"Oh...well, okay. I guess."

She sounded dubious. He smiled at the darkness. Her instincts were good. If she'd known how right she was to be wary of his invitation, she'd never have accepted it. "Good. I'll arrange it in the morning. Good night, Alyssa."

Her answering "good night" was soft and, whether she knew it or not, a little wistful.

It was funny, he thought as he rolled onto his back. A week ago, he would have sworn that he liked women. He'd been sure he'd gotten over the confusion his childhood had created about the female half of the species.

But you couldn't tell a man who had never seen the sun what light was like. Trust was the same, he'd learned. He hadn't known he was missing something until he'd been forced to depend on a woman—and learned what it was to trust her. Wholly, but without blinders. The same way he trusted the men on his team, or his brothers. He knew them well, understood their flaws, and knew he could count on them anyway.

He couldn't have guessed it would matter so much to trust a woman.

Until now, Michael had snorted at the idea of men and women being friends. Friendly, yeah—he liked a lot of women. But Alyssa was different. Like his brothers, like the men on the team, she was someone he could count on. She was a real friend.

Of course, she was a friend he wanted to have sex with. Badly.

Time was short and the stakes were high. For the first time since he'd put on his uniform, Michael was putting something ahead of duty. He had no business hanging around this village even one more day, but he would. Even though his leg was probably strong enough to carry him out of here now.

Probably wasn't good enough. Not when he had every intention of taking Alyssa with him. He had to be sure he was fit enough to keep her safe. Tension tightened the muscles across his shoulders.

He meant to have her. To keep her. But he wasn't underestimating the problems ahead. First and largest loomed her beloved ghost, Daniel Kelleher. She mourned him still and would resist taking another man in his place—especially a man like Michael, trained for war and death instead of healing and peace.

But Dan was dead. Michael was alive, and so was she. That was his biggest advantage.

There was also the matter of the woman back in Dallas who expected Michael to marry her upon his return.

Michael was used to walking in the blurred grays, where right and wrong were vague directions instead of sure and certain guides. Alyssa wasn't. She would never let herself become involved with a man who was engaged to another woman, no matter what the circumstances were. And if he explained those circumstances, she'd think he wanted to marry her to get his hands on the trust. She might sympathize with his motives, but she'd never agree to marry him.

She would want to be loved. Unease tightened the muscles at the base of his spine. He could offer her a lot, but love? The kind of strong, healthy love she'd known with her husband? Michael had never seen that kind of love, never come close enough to touch or smell it. How could he build something he'd never seen? All he knew of love was the destruction it wreaked when it was bent, twisted, when two people got their needs tangled up so tight they nearly choked the life out of each other.

He heard his mother's thin, shady voice in his mind… *I'm sorry, Mikey. I tried to stop loving him, but it never worked. Nothing worked….*

She'd swallowed a medicine cabinet's worth of pills out of love—or what she called love—that time. Then she'd called Michael to say goodbye.

He'd been fourteen. His father had been on a business trip and Jacob had been in his last year of college, but Luke had been home. He'd gotten Michael there in time, though for the last few blocks the flashing lights and siren of a police car had screamed up the street after them. Not surprising, considering their speed and the red lights Luke had run.

The cop had come in handy. He'd radioed for an ambulance.

They'd pumped Felicia's stomach and she'd spent the next year in a quiet place down by Houston with grassy lawns and flowers twining up the high iron fences. His father had paid for it. He'd paid for all of his fourth wife's medical care, never grudging the money. In some ways, Randolph West had been an admirable man—a disaster as a husband, but a steady friend, generous with his money, if not his time.

The psychiatrist had told Michael that she'd called him because part of her still wanted to live. She'd unconsciously cast Michael in the role of rescuer because her love for him had kept her alive in the past.

Maybe so. Sometimes, though…sometimes when he was growing up, he'd hated her. Now she mostly made him feel sad and tired.

Michael closed his eyes and shut the door on the past. It was a trick he'd gotten good at over the years. The present was what counted. And the future.

He wanted to spend that future with Alyssa. Friendship, he thought—he could give her that. He knew how to be a friend. Then there was sex. Oh, yeah, he thought, shifting slightly to ease the way his pants constricted his arousal. He could handle that part, too.

With luck, Alyssa would never know about his fiancée. All Cami really wanted was the money guaranteed her by the prenuptial agreement they'd signed. Once he gave her that, she'd slink off to spend it happily enough.

He would make it work. Somehow. Life called to life, and Alyssa wanted him. She didn't like it, didn't intend to act on her desire, but it was there, simmering beneath the surface of everything she said, everything she did. He could use that.

For a woman like Alyssa, bed and marriage went together. Michael didn't have time to persuade her to trust him, to ease her into a relationship slowly and gently. He had to move fast, and, yeah, he had to be ruthless or he was going to lose her. That was unacceptable.

He'd use whatever he had to. That's the kind of man he was—not her kind, and they both knew it. So he'd use sex to get to her. Then he'd persuade her to marry him.

Nine

Village time was different. Smoother than civilized time, it flowed and eddied without the jerky pace imposed by clocks and daily planners. Still, A.J. was shocked when she realized it was only twelve days until Christmas.

Twelve days until Christmas, and she was walking through a rain forest, not a shopping mall, on her way to a picnic breakfast with a man she loved and couldn't have. A.J. shifted the sack that held fruit, goat cheese and a round of coarse bread rather like a thick, nutty tortilla.

"You're quiet this morning."

She glanced at Michael. They'd followed the cheerful flow of the river for several minutes after leaving the village, then veered off on a path cut into the tangled growth. Vegetation was fierce here, with vines, plants, saplings and larger trees competing for space. The light was warm and green. "I was thinking about snow and shopping malls."

"Having a seasonal moment?" Michael still used his walking stick, but it seemed more of a prop than a necessity as he moved easily beside her. ''How would you celebrate the holiday if you were home?''

''Usually I don't get to go home for Christmas. Not home to my parents' house, that is. They live in Andrews, and my church is in San Antonio, about seven hours away.''

''I guess your duties keep you busy at this time of year.''

She chuckled. ''You could say that. There are a lot of church functions, of course, and the season is hard on people who are depressed or alone.'' For the last two years, she'd had to try to minister to those fighting grief, loneliness and depression while enduring the same battles herself. ''My folks drive down to spend Christmas with me sometimes.''

The last two years, they'd made a point of being there. Because she'd lost Dan, and they knew what she went through when the holidays approached.

Yet here she was, walking beside another man, one who made her heart pound and her body ache. A man who wore a gun on a holster at his waist. Yearning and fear twisted together. What was she doing? How could she be in love again? It was too soon. Too sudden, too—everything. Quickly she asked, ''What do you do to celebrate?''

''Pretty much the usual. Get together with family, open presents, eat too much.'' He smiled. ''Ada likes to stuff my brothers and me so full of turkey and fixings we can't do much except groan, then complain if we miss a speck when we clean up her kitchen afterward.''

''Ada? You mentioned her when you were feverish. I wondered who she was.''

''She used to be my father's housekeeper. When he died, Jacob wanted the house and Luke and I didn't, so he lives there now. Ada takes care of the place for him.''

''A housekeeper?'' Surprise lifted her voice and her eyebrows. The woman seemed like an important piece in the puzzle that was Michael. ''Ada sounded important when you spoke about her. I thought she was a girlfriend or a relative.''

His glance was cool and measuring. ''She *is* important. She's also a housekeeper.''

''I'm not criticizing her. My aunt Margaret was a housekeeper for thirty years. None of the families she worked for ever cleaned up the kitchen for her, though, on Christmas or any other day.''

He chuckled. ''It isn't as if Ada gives us a choice. Hey—I think we've arrived.''

A.J. followed him into the tiny clearing—and stopped. ''This is the place Señor Pasquez told you about?'' she asked softly.

''Yeah.'' His voice, like hers, was quiet. ''It's special, isn't it?''

Like a cathedral, the tiny clearing called for hushed voices and awe, but this was reverence on an intimate scale. The green wall of the forest breathed all around. There was a tiny trickle of a stream, so small and perfect in its tumble over stones that it seemed placed there for effect. Grass, a rarity in the poor soil and perpetual shade of the rain forest, carpeted the ground. And there were flowers. An orchid bloomed in singular splendor on a branch overhanging the little stream, and tiny blue-white flowers nodded on short stalks here and there. A foot-long lizard, green as spring, stared at them unblinkingly from a rock, then vanished in an emerald streak.

And there was sun. The canopy was broken overhead and sunshine fell, warm and mellow, on the grassy patch. She laughed in delight. ''Oh, this is wonderful. A fairy grotto.''

He smiled and spread a blanket on the ground.

They sprawled on the blanket, spread the cheese on the nutty bread, and talked. About anything and nothing—everything except war and passion and the choices that loomed in front of them.

She'd been humiliated by a D in English her third year in high school. He'd gotten D's in everything until he went to military school and discovered what it meant to have a goal.

He liked rock music. She preferred country western. They both liked fast cars, which made him raise his eyebrows and ask what other weaknesses she had. She laughed and admitted she loved dancing—two-step, square dancing, ballroom dancing, anything that got her moving to music. He claimed to have two left feet, which made her snort. ''No one who moves the way you do would have any problem on the dance floor.''

''You like my moves?'' He waggled both eyebrows at her. ''Want to see my etchings?''

She laughed again and leaned back on both elbows, tilting her head so she could breathe in the sky. ''It's good to see blue overhead. All this green is beautiful, but I start feeling hemmed in.''

''You'd have been used to wide open spaces in Andrews. San Antonio has plenty of green, though. It's a fascinating city.''

''You've been there?'' The idea pleased her.

''Went to visit Stephanie there once, before she married a politician and moved to Tennessee.''

''Ah—who's Stephanie? An old flame?'' She sat up and reached for one of the guavas they'd brought for dessert.

He chuckled. ''Hardly. Stephanie is Luke's mom. She's the one who married Dad twice, poor woman. Put in nine years altogether as Mrs. Randolph West. A record.''

''You must have had a good relationship with her if you went to see her after she and your father were divorced.'' Maybe, she thought, he'd found someone to mother him. From what she'd been able to piece together from his ramblings when his fever was high, his own mother had been in and out of treatment centers and hospitals for years.

He shrugged. ''Stephanie's okay. Not exactly Mom material, as she says herself, but a friendly sort. Very tolerant. She had to be,'' he added wryly. ''She was around during my wild days. In fact, it was her idea to send me to military school. That's one reason I went to see her later. I was mad as hell at her at the time, and I wanted to let her know it had worked out.''

She looked down, turning the guava over in her hands. It was green and about the size of a plum. ''Did you and your brothers all have different mothers?''

''Yeah. Here, let me dig out the pit for you.'' He took the fruit from her and pulled his knife from the scabbard at his waist. He'd set his gun down on the blanket earlier, but she'd noticed that the knife didn't leave his side. ''We weren't exactly the Cleavers, but I think you're imagining all sorts of traumas that weren't part of the picture.'' He handed her the halved fruit and dug into the sack for another. ''I had my brothers. We're pretty tight. And I had Ada.''

Ada again. She bit into the fruit. Green or not, it was tart and tasty. She finished both halves and reached for another one.

A twig cracked loudly.

He moved so fast her mind scarcely registered the motion. One moment they were eating. The next he was crouched, handgun ready, scanning the wall of green surrounding them. She hadn't even seen him retrieve the weapon.

A flurry of birds took off from the tree to her right. Otherwise, there was silence—then the shrill complaints of capuchin monkeys somewhere off to their left.

Something was out there. The second guava rolled, unnoticed, out of her limp hand.

Then she heard a squeal followed by thrashing noises and furious grunting from many throats. Animal throats. A.J. remembered to breathe. ''Peccaries,'' she said with relief.

''Mmm-hmm.'' He didn't put his gun down or stop watching the forest.

''I think they're moving away. Unless you want to hunt them down and shoot one for supper, you won't be needing your gun.''

''Probably not.'' His voice was soft. ''But something could have spooked the peccaries.''

She swallowed. ''Jaguars hunt at night. I can't think of anything else big enough to be a threat to a bunch of bad-tempered pigs.''

''Men hunt day or night.''

''Come on, Michael. How likely is it that some bandit or renegade soldier is out there?''

''Not likely. I wouldn't have brought you here if I thought there was much danger. But *unlikely* and *impossible* are not the same.'' He studied the trees a moment longer, then slipped his gun back in its holster. His smile lacked humor. ''Kind of spoiled the mood, didn't I?''

She took a steadying breath. ''You never completely relax, do you?''

''Not on a mission.''

She'd forgotten. She was a mission, wasn't she? Or part of one. A disastrous last-minute addition to his real mission here, which she assumed involved gathering data. He hadn't even known who he was rescuing when he'd shown up at her window. He'd thought Reverend Kelleher was a man.

How long ago was that? It seemed another life, but it was…she counted back. Nine days? Only nine days.

Surely she couldn't fall in love in nine days. It had to be infatuation.

''Look,'' he said, sitting down beside her. ''I think we'd better talk about this.''

''This?'' She shook her head, disoriented. ''About what?''

''The way you feel about my gun, my training. My career as a soldier.''

''I don't see the need,'' she said stiffly.

''Yeah, well, you haven't seen the look on your face every time I handle a weapon.''

Guilt made her bite her lip. ''I'm sorry. I don't mean to…I'm not used to guns. To any of this.''

One of the guavas had rolled near his foot. He picked it up. ''I think it's more than that. Your husband was shot to death in front of you. Seems like that would give you a pretty powerful hatred for guns. Maybe for men who use them, too."

"No! No, I don't feel that way about you. Truly." In her need to convince him, she made a big mistake. She touched him.

Her heart began a slow, hard pounding.

He knew. He felt it, too, for his eyes darkened, his voice deepened. "How do you feel about me, Alyssa?" He covered her hand with his. "Do you ache for me the way I ache for you?"

Her mouth went dry. Her heart thudded. "This is too fast for me. Much too fast."

"Fast, maybe, but not sudden." He took her hand from his arm and carried it to his mouth, and pressed a kiss to the center of her palm. "This has been growing between us from the first."

"It can't. We can't." She was near panic, yet couldn't bring herself to pull her hand away and lose the sweet touch of his mouth. "There's nowhere for us to go with—with what we're feeling."

Wickedness lit his eyes, curving his mouth in the shape of sin. "I can think of someplace I'd very much like to go with you."

She grabbed for sense, for reason—for all those reasons that seemed so important when he wasn't touching her. He made her feel so alive.

He made her feel too much. "I don't believe in flings."

"I know that." He released her hand, only to thread his fingers through her hair. "How about kisses, Alyssa? Do you believe in kisses?"

Yes. Her body shouted it while her heart quivered, small and aching and frightened, longing to hide. And still she didn't move, didn't pull away.

His smile faded. With utmost seriousness, as if the simple act of bringing his mouth to hers called for his entire attention, he laced his other hand on the right side of her head, tilting her face just so. And he kissed her.

Soft. The lips she'd seen tight with pain, curved in pleasure, hard with determination and—just now—tilted with wicked suggestions, were amazingly soft.

For a moment—just for a moment—she would let herself savor that surprise, and the warm delight of his mouth.

Her breath sighed out. When she inhaled, she breathed him in.

He smelled like Michael, like closeness and warmth in the night, teasing and companionship by day. And when his lips parted, urging hers open, he tasted like the fruit they'd both eaten. Tart, tangy…and living. The vivid male heat of him flashed through her, calling to everything female and alive in her. And it was sweet, so sweet, to feel her body sing with desire.

She'd forgotten how intimate a kiss could be. How it could blend two people, so that their needs touched, parted, and joined again, just as their mouths did.

Deeper this time. Hotter. He made a noise low in his throat and thrust his tongue inside—and broke through the sweetness, cracking open the need.

Oh, yes, she needed this, needed him. Her hands searched for the places on him she didn't yet know—the smooth skin on his cheek, the muscles taut beneath. His neck, and the pulse that pounded there. The flex of his shoulders as he slid his arms around her, drawing her close.

And his body. He eased her down onto the blanket, holding her close, and he was warm and hard against her. His leg slid between hers as he kissed her and kissed her—not pressing aggressively up against the juncture of her thighs, just resting there, his body and hers finding a fit.

His hand moved to her breast and kneaded it. She was the one who made a sound this time, a low croon of pleasure and approval.

At the back of her mind, a voice cried out warnings. There

was a reason, a very good reason, she couldn't do this...but this was what she'd dreamed of every night. Waking dreams that kept her from the comfort of sleep, kept her aching and aware...though this was better than dreams, better than anything she'd felt or imagined since...

Since Dan died.

The thought shot through her, stiffening her body, bringing a rush of feelings too huge and tangled to grasp. They swept through her, making her moan. And she put a hand between them to push him away.

"Shh," he murmured, his hands gentling now, caressing her breast, her throat. "Shh. It's all right. He wouldn't want you to mourn forever."

Whatever it was she felt, it wasn't guilt. "Michael," she whispered, confused. "I'm not ready for this."

"Who is?"

He sounded wry, even whimsical, but his eyes held darkness, a need so vivid and real she felt it lapping at her, a private ocean spilling from his shores to hers. Moved, she touched his cheek.

His jaw tensed—and he crushed his mouth to hers.

Huge, swelling chords of emotion and sensation made her body thrum and her heart yearn. She slid her tongue inside his mouth, seeking...and in the taste and scent and feel of him, she lost something. And found something else. Her shoulders relaxed.

It was all the signal he needed. His mouth left hers, but only to journey over cheeks, throat. He murmured to her, low, encouraging words about how good she felt, how right.

Yes. This was right. She wove her fingers into his hair, the rhythm of her breath breaking as he slid his hand inside her shirt and found her breast. He teased the tip, quick, feathery brushes of fingers, then squeezed it. The muscles of her thighs tensed as desire shot its electric arc from breast to belly to groin.

More. She needed more—of his skin, his taste. She needed

his muscles shifting, straining, as he answered the wild call drumming in her blood. Her fingers fumbled at the front of his vest, shoving it aside so she could explore his chest, his stomach. His muscles jumped at her touch.

When his mouth came back to hers this time, there was no wooing, no gentle soothing. On his part, or hers.

She tore her mouth from his and ran her hands down his sides. "You walk around in this damned vest…you've got the sexiest stomach. Did you know that?" she demanded, bending to press a kiss to his hard, flat stomach. "Did you guess how often I've thought of doing this?"

He groaned, his hands fisting in her hair. "If you've thought of it as often as I have…" When her tongue wandered from belly button to the smooth, tight muscles of his chest, pausing to circle one flat nipple, he jerked her head away.

"My turn." His voice was hoarse. "Let me show you what I've been thinking of doing to you. Dreaming of doing."

"Clothes," she said, tugging at his vest. "Clothes first."

Her shirt, his vest, her bra. Her shoes, his boots—oh, footwear made a foolish pause in the midst of such heated action, a time-out in the bottom of the ninth with the bases loaded. Sanity should have caught up with her then. But when her laces defied her and doubts nibbled at her mind, she pushed the thoughts away.

He got his boots and pants off while she still struggled with knotted shoelaces. She made the mistake of looking at him then, and forgot her shoes, her doubts, everything.

He was magnificent.

She'd seen his body before, but only in parts. Every time she'd tended his wound she'd seen the power in his thighs. Following him on the trail she'd been aware of the fluid strength of his back and shoulders. His hands had fascinated her from the first.

Now she saw all of him. Naked. And aroused.

He didn't wait around to let her admire him. As soon as he tossed his pants aside, he knelt and yanked off her still-tied shoes, then her socks—and then he kissed her foot. His tongue flicked the tender arch of her sole. She gasped.

He smiled a dark, pleased smile, hooked his fingers in the waist of her pants and tugged them, and her panties, down.

Naked was better. She had his skin against hers, sweat-slick and hot. The hard male shape of him pressed against her, the wall of his chest eased the ache in her breasts, and she had his whole body to explore.

He would have slowed down then. She wasn't having it. She wanted the haste and the heat and no room for thought. But he wouldn't be rushed too much. He had to lick here, touch there, press a kiss to the tender place beneath each breast.

At last, he rose over her, his upper body propped up by one arm, his other hand guiding him to her opening. She wrapped her legs around him, welcoming him, urging him to come in, into her.

He stopped at the very threshold. She felt him there, pulsing against her. The pupils of his eyes were huge, the lids heavy. Strain drew grooves along his cheeks.

''Marry me,'' he said. And began to sink slowly home.

Her eyes went wide. He hadn't said that. He couldn't have—oh, he was stretching her, entering so slowly, yet still she could barely take him in. He was big, so hard and thick. And it had been so long. ''What?'' she gasped, her fingers digging into his shoulders.

He shoved, one short, hard thrust, and was fully seated.

She moaned, her muscles contracting around him. ''Michael, what did you *say?*''

''Querida,'' he murmured, and bent and kissed her gently as he started to move. ''Beautiful Alyssa. Wise, strong A.J. Marry me.''

She shook her head, refusing to hear, to believe—and met his movement with her own. Slow motion at first, as they found each other's rhythm—hips rising, falling, hands gripping, sweetness and sweat rolling over them both. Body, heart, hands and lips, she rejoiced in the ancient dance, the sound of flesh meeting flesh, the rolling, rocking motion of the sweetest union this side of heaven.

And her mind stayed locked. Blank.

The slow motion didn't last. They were both too close, too eager, near the edge from the moment of joining. Heat and haste overtook her even as his thrusts grew harder, faster, until she cried out—one thin, high cry—and body, mind, world, contracted in a single knot of pleasure. And burst.

Ten

Michael lay on his side with his arms around her, her head pillowed on his arm, his chest heaving, his sex wet from her body. And cursed silently.

It had gone wrong, all wrong. Oh, not the sex. *Incredible* didn't begin to describe that.

She'd surprised him. Amazed him. He hadn't expected shyness, but neither had he expected such earthy appreciation. When she'd licked her way up his stomach…desire stirred, waking what he'd thought was down for the count for the time being, a fresh current binding them.

His arms tightened around her. Alyssa was right for him…but he was going to have a helluva time convincing her he could be right for her, too. Especially after the way he'd just screwed up.

God knows it wasn't the way he'd planned to propose. He'd meant to ask her afterward, when she was sated and happy. When his brain was functioning, dammit. Instead, he'd just blurted it out. And seen her eyes go blank with shock.

He'd tried. With everything in him, he'd tried to hold back, to gather his mind so he could give her words. Women needed words, and he thought Alyssa in particular would need coaxing, persuasion. Reasons. But he'd been inside her. She'd been pulsing around him, the fit perfect, her scent in his nostrils and her taste on his lips.

He couldn't have stopped then if *El Jefe* had jumped out of the bushes and held a gun to his head.

She hadn't spoken. Hadn't said a word since he'd asked her to marry him.

How was she going to play it? Would she pretend he hadn't asked her to marry him? Give him a kiss, maybe, a smile, then get dressed as if nothing had happened except a quick, hot romp? Or maybe she'd just continue to lie there, silent, her body so intimately his…every other part of her distant.

Not if he could help it.

He didn't know what to say, though, so he pressed a kiss to her hair. She stirred, then turned in his arms. Her hand came up to touch his cheek, then trace his lips. Her expression was calm.

Her eyes weren't. "Michael," she said sadly, "I can't marry you."

The pain was unexpectedly strong. He'd known what her answer was. Still, it hurt like blazes to hear it, to see the look on her face as she rejected him. So calm…as if she had regrets but no real doubts. "I need a little more than that. Like a reason." *Give me a reason so I'll know what I'm up against.*

"I'm not ready."

"You didn't think you were ready for this, either." He ran his hand down her side, curving over her hip, her bottom. "You were wrong about that."

He saw the flicker of heat in her eyes. And the way her

lips tightened. "You don't want an explanation. You want a hook to hang an argument on." She pulled out of his arms, pushed to her feet and grabbed her clothes.

Dammit to hell. "So that's it? That's all you're going to tell me—you're not ready?"

She moved over to the little stream, and bent down to wash him off. She wanted to wash away the stickiness of their joining, and as reasonable as that was, it made him furious. He pushed to his feet. "I just asked you to marry me, dammit! I want to know why you won't."

"Don't curse at me." She yanked her panties on, then reached for her pants. Her hand was shaking.

Good move, West. Yell at her enough and she's sure to agree. Michael lowered his head and stood quietly, struggling to get a grip on things he couldn't close his hands around. Finally he exhaled, turned his back to her and began dressing.

When he had everything back in place, from boots to SIG Sauer, he faced her again. She was dressed and shod, but fumbling with her buttons. He went to her and pushed her hands away.

She looked up. Her eyes were swimming with tears.

"Oh, hell." He sighed, put his arms around her and pulled her to him. "Seems like I should be the weepy one here."

She sniffed. "Right. When's the last time you cried, soldier?"

"I might be a little out of practice," he conceded, and sighed. "You were right. I do want to change your mind. But I also deserve to know why you gave yourself to me if you don't want me."

"I don't know!" She pushed out of his arms. Her shirt hung open, and her hair was wild. So were her eyes. "I've got reasons. All sorts of good, logical reasons. Practical reasons. Only there are too many of them, and they don't make sense. Nothing does." She jammed a hand into her hair as if trying to tame it, then winced as she hit a tangle. "God, I'm a mess. In more ways than one."

He reached into his pocket, pulled out his small black comb and held it out.

She stared at the comb as if he'd tried to hand her a snake. Then she laughed. It was shaky, rueful, but it seemed to smooth some of her other tangles.

"Thanks," she said, taking the comb. Instead of using it, though, she turned it over in her hands. "You're a good man, Michael. One of the best I've ever known. And I do want you. I guess I proved that, didn't I? But this has all happened so fast. I can't imagine..." She sighed and started working the comb through her hair.

He reached for her shirt. She jumped.

"Hey, I'm trying to have a meaningful conversation here. Can't do that when your breasts are peeking out at me." He pulled the sides together and tucked a button into its buttonhole. "So what can't you imagine?"

She was yanking the comb through her hair as if she was going to be graded on how fast she finished. "I can't picture you attending ninety-nine church potluck suppers a year. Or living in the cozy brick house that goes with my church. Or—ouch." She grimaced and plied the comb a little more carefully. "This—this whatever it is between us—how much is it a product of everything we've been through? I've got another world waiting for me back home, one that doesn't—Michael? What is it?"

He'd gone still, his hands stopping halfway up her shirt.

Then he heard it again—a low, throbbing bird call.

"My God," he said, and meant it. A grin broke out. He stepped back, cupped his hand around his mouth and returned the call.

Two men wearing grungy fatigues, with wicked-looking guns slung over their shoulders, stepped out of the bushes that marked the entrance to the grotto.

Alyssa gasped—then her hands flew to the job that had been interrupted. Hastily she fastened the last two buttons.

"You've been one hard son of a bitch to find, Lieutenant,"

the taller and darker of the two men said in the crisp tones of upper-class Boston. He nodded at Alyssa. "Good to see you're all right, ma'am."

"Jeez, Mick." The red-headed one shook his head mournfully as the two men came into the clearing. His accent was peculiar—Deep South touched by a hint of old-country brogue. "Here I've been picturing you neck-deep in all sorts of calamities. Instead, looks like we interrupted a little R and R. Sorry about that."

"Scopes," Michael said, "put a sock in it."

It could have been worse, A.J. told herself. Michael's men might have found them when she had a lot more unfastened than a couple of buttons.

Still, it was mortifying. Michael took her hand when he introduced her to his men, and she pretended she had no idea what they were thinking. Banner—the tall black man—made that easy with his gentle courtesy. Scopes was another matter. Though his grin was good-natured, it was obvious he intended to give his lieutenant a hard time about his "R and R."

The three men were obviously close. Tight, Michael would say. She listened to their easy banter and tried not to mind the way the sunlight dimmed when they left the little clearing, Banner in front, Michael and her in the middle, Scopes in the rear.

Michael still held her hand. She was too dizzied by everything that had happened to know if that was wrong or right. Probably foolish, she decided—and left her hand in his.

What was one more folly after what she'd done?

Apparently Scopes and Banner had been looking for Michael all along. Their colonel had feared the same kind of repercussions Michael had if he were taken prisoner—at least, that's what she assumed, reading between the lines of Banner's brief explanation.

Scopes put it more colorfully. "You know what a skinflint

the Colonel is. Worries about every penny as if it was his own. He wasn't about to let you wander around playing tourist on Uncle Sam's ticket. 'Fetch me that idiot,' he told me—''

''That's not quite the way I remember it,'' Banner broke in dryly.

Scopes ignored that. ''So off we went. Been wandering around this godforsaken jungle—pardon, ma'am—so long my toes have grown mossy. That's when Banner wasn't scaring me silly in his damned chopper. I'd have found you a lot sooner if they'd given me a *real* pilot.''

Banner snorted. ''Or if you could read a map.''

A.J. broke in. ''Pardon me, but—I've wondered for so long about Sister Maria Elena. The nun who was with me. Is she all right?''

Banner glanced over his shoulder at her. He was a long, narrow man with a basketball player's big hands and a bass voice that would have had her choir director salivating. His eyes were the same shade of brown as his skin, and as kind as they were curious. ''Just fine, ma'am. Treated and released at the base hospital, they told me. I think she went to a convent in Guatemala.''

A load lifted from her heart. ''Oh, good,'' she murmured. ''That's wonderful.''

''How did you find me?'' Michael said. ''Especially if Scopes was navigating. I'm surprised you didn't end up in Costa Rica with him handling the map.''

''Hey, I can read a map,'' Scopes protested. ''We'd have found you a lot sooner if you hadn't stopped off to do a little sightseeing at a village so small it wasn't *on* the map.'' He chuckled. ''Boise is gonna be so pi—ah, ticked off. He bet me a century he'd find you first.''

''He drew a rough section to search,'' Banner pointed out in his rumbly bass. ''Been a lot of fighting by Santo Pedro.''

''What's going on?'' Michael asked sharply. ''Has the government retaken the main road into the north yet?''

''Better than that, boyo.'' Scopes's voice was gleeful. ''*El Jefe* got his butt kicked, big time. Broke his so-called army into little pieces.''

A.J. listened with half an ear while they passed on details of the battle—which Banner refused to dignify by that name, saying it had been a pathetic excuse for a fight—and argued about whose fault it was that they hadn't located their lieutenant sooner.

She was amazed they'd found him at all, in several hundred square miles of jungle. They'd guessed Michael would head for the border, and had divided into pairs to search. Scopes and Banner had been quartering their section by chopper, stopping frequently to question the natives when they found a village or settlement. They'd almost missed Cuautepec, but Scopes had seen a flash of light—sunlight reflecting from the orphanage's tin roof, probably—and they'd decided to check it out.

She was thankful. She really was, especially for the news about *El Jefe.* She just wished...A.J. sighed. Her wish list was absurdly long, and lamentably contradictory. She wished Michael's men had found them sooner, before she lost her mind and made love with him. Only she wouldn't give up the memory of their union in that clearing for anything, so she wished they'd come a few minutes later.

She wished—oh, if only she knew what to wish for, she might be able to get somewhere in sorting out the jumble of thoughts and feelings.

She'd made love with him. After all the times she'd assured herself she wouldn't let her attraction take her farther than she could afford to go, she'd let him kiss her—no, she'd welcomed his kiss.

From kissing to lovemaking had been one short, hard fall. How could she have done it?

She glanced down at their joined hands. There were calluses on his palm. She could barely feel them now, but when he'd drawn that palm along her inner thighs...

Who was she trying to fool? She knew why she'd made love with Michael. She was in love with him, and she'd craved him, pure and simple.

Only she *couldn't* be. How could she love a man she'd only known nine days? Lust might hit that fast, or infatuation, but love didn't work like that.

Though she'd never before experienced anything like the last nine days. Or anyone like the man she'd spent them with.

She thought of him on the trail—the humor in spite of pain, the determination. Then she thought of the way he'd offered her his comb such a short time ago, and tears stung her eyes. She'd said she was a mess. He hadn't argued, had just given her what he could—a comb to untangle her hair. In that second, she'd had a flash of what it might be like to be married to him. He'd tackle leaky toilets and snarled schedules with the same step-by-step determination he used to cross a jungle, she thought.

He was a good man. An incredible man. And she'd hurt him, she was sure of that. Though he hadn't said anything about love…a cramping ache around her heart made her bite her lip. *Be fair,* she told herself. She hadn't exactly encouraged him to speak of love.

Soon, very soon now, they would be flying back to their real lives. The ones they lived in different cities.

Would she ever see him again?

Did she want to? Yes.

No.

Great. She was in love with him, but she wasn't sure she wanted to see him again. What kind of sense did that make?

It was his career that made her so uncertain, she thought. He might be an honorable killer, but still he killed. She was repulsed by his capacity for violence. No, not repulsed…bothered? Upset? Oh, she didn't know what she was. She needed time. Time to figure out what was wrong with her. Time…if he came to see her in San Antonio, maybe…but would he? She'd just turned down his proposal.

Dammit, he'd rushed her. Relationships took time. She couldn't just jump into one the way she might dive into a pool and swim laps. She'd known Dan for nearly a year before they even went out together, and they'd been dating for six months when he proposed.

Dan. A sudden shaft of feelings tore through her—guilt, sorrow, and an odd flutter of panic unlike the hasty fear she'd felt a moment ago, when she thought of never seeing Michael again. This felt as if she'd already lost something, an important piece of her that was gone now, forever gone. But that made no sense. She'd lost Dan more than two years ago, so what—

"I'd offer you a penny for them, but I'm low on cash. Do you give credit?"

She looked up, startled, into Michael's eyes. They'd reached the river, and his men had moved slightly ahead. Scopes was talking on a radio or walkie-talkie of some kind.

"None of my thoughts are worth going a penny in debt for right now."

"Say something stupid, then."

In spite of herself, she chuckled. "What are you trying to do—spoil a good brood?"

"If it takes that expression off your face, yes." He ran his thumb back and forth in her palm. "Why so unhappy? We're going home."

Just that. Just that simple, intimate brush of his thumb on her palm, and she wanted him again. Still. A.J. lowered her eyes, hoping to shield her reaction. "And what happens next?"

"Banner flies you out of here."

She stopped. "But what about you?"

"We don't have the Cobra here—the big helicopter," he explained. "They've been using a recon helicopter because it's smaller, lighter, covers a lot more territory without having to refuel. Sets down in a lot of places the Cobra can't, too. But it's strictly a two-man bird." He chuckled. "One-and-a-half men, according to Scopes. The passenger seat is directly behind the pilot, and it's cramped.''

She bit her lip. ''And...when I get home?''

''What happens with us, you mean?'' He framed her face with both hands, smiling that wicked smile. The one that ought to come with a warning label. ''Well, I'll probably propose again.''

Her heart leaped—and that horrid flutter of panic came back. She swallowed. ''Before we go any further, there's something I need to know.''

He drew his hands down to her shoulders. ''Okay. Shoot.''

''What...'' She couldn't say it. Couldn't come out and ask what he felt about her. ''Why do you want to marry me?''

''At last I get a chance to speak my piece.'' His thumbs circled under her jaw, lightly, as if he couldn't just touch. He had to savor. ''I had this great proposal all worked up. Forgot the whole thing when you seduced me.''

''Me?'' She tried to look indignant, but a smile slipped out. ''I didn't—''

''Hey, Mick.'' Scopes was headed back toward them, his expression for once serious. ''Just heard from Boise. The Colonel's had him and Smiley tracking the largest splinter that's left of *El Jefe*'s forces—some of the real bad asses. His signal was breaking up pretty bad, but I think I got the gist of it.''

Michael frowned. ''And?''

''They're headed this way, and they're not happy campers. Damned maniacs, sounds like.'' He shook his head, looking sour. ''If there's anything I hate, it's a bunch of damned wannabes doing the rape-and-pillage thing. Gives us real soldiers a bad name.''

Michael had gone very still. ''How far away are they?''

''They just hit a village about twenty miles away, horizontally. Not that anything is horizontal around here. It didn't have much for them to loot, which made 'em—'' He glanced at A.J. and cleared his throat. ''Anyway, if the natives of this flyspot have someplace they can hide out awhile, they might want to head there. Quick."

Choices and chances. Life was full of both, Michael thought as he left the *tepec*'s hut, his stride long and impatient. But sometimes the only choices were between the bad and the unbearable. And all too often, the chances only came once.

It looked as if his chance with Alyssa had already passed.

All around him, people hurried—women calling instructions to children, children chasing livestock into the jungle. Women and children and a few—a very few—men, most of them over fifty.

El Jefe's men were coming—without *El Jefe*.

As soon as they'd returned to the village, Michael had sent Banner up in the copter, high enough that the mountains wouldn't interfere with the radio reception. He'd gotten a more complete report on the portion of the broken rebel army that was headed this way.

Bad asses indeed. About forty men who had taken too large a part in some of the worst of *El Jefe*'s activities, men who couldn't go home again. Men with nothing to lose—not even their humanity. Considering what they'd done at the last village they'd encountered, that was already lost.

He'd told Señor Pasquez and the village elders. They'd chosen to evacuate, to head for the plantation where some of their men worked. The plantation had guards and weapons. More important, it was foreign-owned so the government would be forced to send troops if there was trouble. San Christóbal couldn't afford to lose foreign investors.

But it would take the villagers two days to get there, and there was a good chance the plantation was the renegades' goal, too. It was the only place between here and the border worth looting.

Michael spotted his quarry—Andrew Scopes's rangy figure, bent to help an old woman adjust the sling holding a sleepy baby on her back. "You've got what you'll need?" he asked tersely when he reached the sergeant.

"I'm good to go. You?"

"I will be once I've talked to Banner. He's by the copter?"

Scopes nodded. His shrewd blue eyes studied Michael. "You still intend to send the copter back to the base?"

"Yes." For several reasons—some of them tactical, one not. Michael felt another wave of doubt hit, tinged by guilt. "Are you sure—"

"If you ask me again, I'm gonna be offended." Scopes spat to one side. "Fine opinion of me you seem to have."

Michael didn't argue. There wasn't time. "I'll meet you at the head of the trail, then, in fifteen minutes."

Scopes glanced around. "Think they'll be ready to go that quick?"

"They have to be," Michael said grimly. "The renegades are less than two hours away." He turned away.

The copter waited in a field at the other end of the village. Michael increased his pace to an easy jog. Time was short, but he wasn't leaving without telling Alyssa goodbye.

She was going with Banner. Michael and Scopes were staying with the villagers, who didn't have a hope in hell of making it without them if the renegades headed for the plantation. Their chances weren't great, even with two soldiers guarding their rear. Two armed men against forty-five weren't good odds.

As for Michael's chances…

Choices and chances, he thought again. He couldn't choose any differently than he had. At least she would be safe. Knowing that made his other choices bearable.

Eleven

"What the hell is this crap you gave Banner about not going with him?" Michael stood in the doorway to the girls' room, hands on hips.

"Sounds like you got my message. Now, please step out of the way or else help me pack." A.J. spoke more calmly than she felt. She looked around, biting her lips. "What am I forgetting?" Something. Undoubtedly she'd forgotten several important things, but there was so little time…

"Alyssa." A pair of hard hands landed on her shoulders, turning her to face him. "Banner is waiting for you at the chopper. There's no time to debate the subject. You're leaving now."

"I'm ready." She hoped she was. "But I'm not going with Banner. I'm going with Sister Andrew, Sister Constancia and the children. They need me."

"No, they don't. They've been taking care of those kids for years without you."

"Michael." A hint of amusement filtered through the pervasive urgency. ''It's obvious you've never traveled with children. There are thirteen of them, and Sister Constancia is fifty-seven, Sister Andrew even older. I can help.''

''This isn't a blasted car trip to see the Grand Canyon!''

''It's not a forced march with trained infantry, either. My skills will be needed as much as yours will.''

''Dammit, you are not—''

''Keep your voice down. You're frightening the children.''

The nuns and most of the children were in the main room, packing food. Two of the smallest children had followed A.J. into the girls' bedroom and watched with big, bewildered eyes while she grabbed blankets and clothes and tried to shape them into packs the older children could carry. One—little Rosita—started to cry, more in confusion than real distress.

''There, sweetheart.'' A.J. stroked the toddler's head but didn't stop to pick her up. There was too much to do, and too little time. She met Michael's eyes. ''You're doing what you feel you have to do. So am I.''

Michael cursed under his breath. Then he kissed her once, hard. His eyes were bleak. ''Forget the rest of the stuff. We're moving out *now.*''

Two hours and five minutes after Scopes first told him about the rebel soldiers, Michael had his ragged troop moving down the trail. They'd done well, extraordinarily well, to move as quickly as they had, he thought. Especially since the thirty-some adults were responsible for three times that many babies, children and adolescents.

Manuel had nearly managed to be left behind. He'd been very disappointed when A.J. found him hiding in the big mango tree at the start of the trail.

A smile touched Michael's mouth. Alyssa had been right. This wasn't going to be like any forced march he'd ever been on.

His smile didn't last. They might have pulled off the evacuation faster than he'd expected, but they were still cutting it close. Too close. Soldiers could move a lot faster than the villagers. Even if they amused themselves for a couple of hours by torching huts and killing livestock, they'd still catch up with the villagers before nightfall.

So the bastards had to be slowed down, or diverted entirely.

Fifteen minutes after the last of his charges had vanished around a bend in the trail, Michael uncoiled from his position next to a pine that leaned out over a deeply cut gully, where he'd been watching for any sign of the rebels. He shouldered the CAR 16 that Banner had left with him and moved a little farther up the trail.

"How's it coming?" he asked Scopes.

"She's ready," the smaller man said, straightening. "Didn't have time to put her deep, but she'll do the trick. Bring down plenty of dirt."

Scopes always referred to explosives as female, for what he claimed were obvious reasons. "We don't want half the mountain falling on the trail," Michael warned. "The villagers will need to be able to clear it when they come back."

Scopes gave him a wounded look.

"All right, all right. You know what you're doing." Michael looked at the setup one last time. On one side of the trail was a small chasm crammed to the top with trees, saplings and brush. It would take many hours of machete work to hack a path through that. On the other side was a rough, steep hillside that climbed into a stubby peak—even more impassable.

Scopes had dug into the loose dirt where the slope was steepest, setting a charge that should take a bite out of the mountain. What was up would come down. And cover the trail.

If they were lucky, the renegade soldiers would never know how much trouble he'd gone to on their behalf. If their goal was to make straight for the border, they'd use the trail to the west of the village and never see the avalanche Scopes dumped on this one.

Michael believed in luck. He courted it. He didn't rely on it.

Scopes was laying the fuse. "Don't make it too short," Michael said. "I know you like to watch your babies go off, but I'd like fifteen minutes between us and whatever goes flying."

Scopes sighed and reeled out a little more fuse. "You got it."

A minute later they were moving up the winding trail, the fuse burning merrily behind them. They didn't run, just kept a good, steady pace, walking quickly enough to catch up with the villagers.

"I still think you shoulda let Banner do a few fly-bys," Scopes said. "Let him open up the guns on his bird a few times, and those sons of bitches would think twice about making trouble."

"Try to remember that we're assisting in the peaceful evacuation of civilians—a deviation from our original orders, but one that doesn't put egg on Uncle Sam's face. Strafing a bunch of former soldiers on the losing side of a war is another story."

Scopes's assessment of those "former soldiers" was obscene, and one Michael agreed with. "Think the Colonel will let Banner bring back the big bird?"

"I heard a rumor once that the Colonel does have a heart."

Scopes snorted. "Can't believe everything you hear. But those kids…"

Michael nodded. However much trouble he and Scopes might be in for expanding on their orders so drastically, they could still hope the Colonel would agree to provide nonaggressive emergency backup—for the children. The Cobra was big enough to lift most of them if things went south—and if it got here in time. "He's going to be plenty unhappy with you and me, though."

"Yeah, yeah. You gave me the pitch already. So maybe I lose my stripes. Wouldn't be the first time. I'll get 'em back." He glanced at Michael. "Colonel's gonna come down harder on you than me, anyway."

"That's the price I pay for getting to wear those pretty silver bars on my dress blues."

"I know how much you like looking pretty for the ladies. Speaking of which..." He cleared his throat. "You were putting out some pretty strong signals about the Reverend."

"I knew you could take a hint." Since Scopes's idea of subtlety meant substituting PG-rated equivalents for the obscene part of his vocabulary, Michael's "hint" had consisted of threatening to tie Scopes's tongue around his throat if he gave A.J. a hard time.

"Yeah, well...I just wondered if you and she were, like, a permanent thing."

"Thinking of trying your luck?"

"No, no, nothing like that. Though she is a looker. I just never saw you get all touchy about a woman before."

"I plan to marry her."

Shock held the other man silent for a few minutes. "You set the date?"

"Not yet. She turned me down."

"Well, hell."

"Yeah." Michael stopped, looking back. "Shouldn't the charge have gone off by now?"

"Pretty quick. So, she got someone waiting back home for her or something?"

Michael supposed he should be flattered that Scopes thought the only reason a woman would turn him down was a previous involvement. "No, she's a widow whose husband was shot to death in front of her. She's got a problem with guns." There was a good chance that she'd see him use his again, soon. If Scopes's boom didn't close the trail off as thoroughly as they were hoping... Michael's lips tightened. "How long was that fuse?"

Scopes grinned. "Hey, I'm good, Mick. Watch this. Five, four, three..."

The ground walked. Sound slapped his ears. On the other side of the mountain, dust rose into the air.

"No, no, *niñita,* that wasn't devils after us," A.J. bent to comfort the little girl who'd run to her, screaming. "Remember? Señor West told us how his big boom would make the earth shake."

The little girl sniffed and nodded.

Several other children had crowded close to A.J. and Sister Andrew. Most were looking back along the trail, where the dust thrown up by the explosion was slowly settling, falling out of sight behind the mountain's shoulder.

"I wish I could have seen it," Manuel said sadly.

She suppressed a grin. The boy had certainly tried. Good thing Sister Andrew had insisted on a head count. "Then maybe it would have been you flying up in the air, not just some dirt." She straightened. "Come on. Let's keep moving."

The villagers directly ahead had stopped, too, exclaiming over the explosion. Gradually, those in front started moving again, and A.J. and the children could, too. They were among the last in the long, winding stream of people.

There were only two donkeys. An old man with a bad leg rode on one up near the head of the caravan. The other donkey dragged a travois carrying a woman too ill to walk. On that animal's back were strapped Señor Pasquez's precious record books; as the *tepec,* he acted as a sort of justice of the peace and county clerk combined. Births, deaths, marriages—all became official when they were recorded in his books.

Everyone else walked at the pace of the slowest among them.

Trees grew right up to the edge of the left side of the trail, a crowded vertical weave of trunk and limb. To the right was a slope so rocky and lacking in soil that it was nearly bare, a rare emptiness in the forest that allowed a trail to grow instead of trees. On that side, sunshine shone down on rocks and small, tough plants, including a scattering of the tiny blue-white flowers she'd seen in the clearing that morning.

A.J.'s heart stumbled when she thought of the clearing and Michael and what had happened between them. She wanted to climb that rocky slope and bathe her head in the sunshine. She wanted to stop right here and wait for Michael to catch up because her heart was already hungry for the sight of him. And she wanted to hide from him.

Most of all, she thought wryly, she wanted to make her mind stop racing around and around and biting itself from behind.

Sister Andrew, who walked just behind, must have noticed her agitation. "There is no point in rushing the first part of our journey," the old nun said kindly, using English. "It would only tire some too much to continue later."

"My mind knows that, but my feet keep wanting to hurry."

"Mmm. You are afraid of the soldiers?"

"Aren't you?"

"Time enough for fear if I see them coming. Right now, there's just the sunshine, the children, the way my bunion aches." Her eyes were merry in their nest of wrinkles. "When you get to be my age, you have to conserve your energy. Borrowing troubles before they appear tires a person."

"I suppose so, but I don't know how to stop. My mind's doing the hamster thing—you know, circling round and round the same thoughts, going nowhere."

The sister studied her face a moment. "Thoughts of the soldiers?"

"Not entirely." A.J. hesitated. She was sorely in need of counsel, but didn't know how to bring the subject up. "Sister...you know that Michael isn't really my *novio?*"

She chuckled. ''If there is one thing that can chase thoughts of many dangerous men from a woman's mind, it is one particular man. Yes, I'd guessed you two weren't engaged. But I think you have feelings for him.''

''I'm in love with him.'' Saying the words out loud, she discovered, was a relief. ''But...''

''Why do we always find 'buts' to stick on love?'' She shook her head. ''Never mind. I interrupt too much. Go on.''

''I don't know. There's this great, big 'but' hanging over me like a dark cloud, but I don't know what it is. He asked me to marry him,'' she confessed in a low voice. ''I said no. I thought it was his...well, his violence that bothered me, but—''

''His what?'' The sister rolled her eyes like a teenager. ''Oh, I expected better of you. No, no, don't color up. Old women have silly expectations.''

''I don't think Michael is like the soldiers we're escaping, or anything like that. I just...'' She bit her lip. ''I saw him shoot a man—a man who was going to kill us. He did what he had to do. I know that, only I can't seem to get that image out of my head.'' *The man falling, dying...*

''Hmm.'' They walked on in silence for a minute before the sister continued. ''I am used to dealing with children, so forgive me if I shape my advice into a silly game. I want you to imagine something for me. Imagine that you have a gun in your hands right now—feel the weight of it, the cold metal. Now, what if one of those soldiers came out from behind that tree—oh! Right there!'' She pointed, acting out alarm so realistically that A.J. jolted and looked. ''And he has a gun. He's pointing it at little Manuel. No—at me. What do you do?''

''I—I guess I'd point my gun at him, tell him to stop.''

''And if he didn't? If you saw that he was going to kill someone, and the only way you could stop him would be to shoot him?''

A.J. swallowed. The sister's game didn't feel silly at all. "I'd shoot."

"You would accept that stain in order to prevent another evil. But what if you didn't see him before he shot? What if he killed me, left me bleeding at your feet—but then you pointed your gun at him. It's a much bigger gun, and he is afraid. He drops his gun and surrenders. What do you do? Do you still shoot him?"

"I..." A.J. took a shaky breath. *Gunfire—harsh, unbearably loud. Blood. Dan's blood, splattering her, the wall, the floor...and rage.* Blind, consuming rage. "Oh, God. Dear God."

"What is it, child?"

"My husband. Two years ago, he was shot. Killed. I watched him—saw him fall. His blood...I think, if I'd had a gun then, when that man shot him, I might have—I would have—"

The nun stopped and put her arm around A.J., turning them both gently away from the children. "My dear, I'm so sorry. When I played my little game, I had no idea you had such horrors in your memory."

"It's...all right. I just..." Only then did A.J. realize she was crying. "I didn't know. I never let myself think—" She hiccupped. "Think about it. I didn't want to know. I—oh, I hate to cry."

"We hate to have splinters removed, too, but we're the better for it." Callused fingers wiped the tears gently from Alyssa's cheek. "You are all right now?"

She nodded, unable to speak. It was so obvious now. She wasn't repulsed by Michael's violence. She was repulsed by the echo it set up in her, the festering fear that she was capable of much worse than what he'd done. That she might be able to kill—not in defense, but out of the blind need to strike back.

She hadn't wanted to see her own ugliness, hadn't wanted to taste again the desperate hate that had exploded in her when Dan was killed. Now that she had…she drew a shaky breath. "I'm okay. I'm better." Wobbly, with a sourness in the pit of her stomach, but better for having faced what she'd tried so hard not to know. "I need to think about…all this."

The nun smiled. "Children give us little opportunity for reflection, I'm afraid, but there are moments between wiping noses and—ah, look. Here comes your young man."

So he was. Michael and his sergeant had rounded the nearest curve in the trail and were less then fifteen feet away.

He moved so beautifully, with the easy, ground-eating pace of a man who refuses to waste energy he would need later. A man with the strength and stamina to keep going long after others had flagged or failed. Her heart swelled at the sight of him.

He was frowning. "What's wrong?"

Belatedly she realized her face must show the effects of her tears. Well, no point in pretending her cheeks weren't wet. She dried them unselfconsciously. "Nothing. We heard the explosion. Did it go okay?"

"The lieutenant wouldn't let me stay to watch," Scopes said sadly.

Michael's frown didn't waver. "The rest of you had better catch up with the others. Alyssa and I will be along in a minute." Then he waited, obviously expecting to be obeyed.

He was. A.J. tried to ignore Scopes's smirk as he and the sister moved on ahead. "You do the 'officer in charge' thing very well," she said.

"You should see me when I have a whole troop to order around instead of a few dozen women and children. Now—tell me what's wrong."

"I'm okay. Really," she insisted. "Sister Andrew was just…removing a splinter."

"If you've got an open wound—"

She smiled. "A spiritual splinter. I'll tell you about it later." This wasn't the time. She needed to think, to absorb and understand what she'd learned. And he didn't need his attention divided right now. Still… "I'm glad to see you," she said, and impulsively stretched up to place a soft kiss on his mouth.

That startled him—but surprise didn't keep him from sliding an arm around her waist, drawing her closer and returning her kiss. When he lifted his head, pleasure had replaced surprise in his eyes—a deep pleasure, which hinted at more than the simple flare of desire.

Though that was there, too. "I'm glad to see you, too." He brushed her lips lightly one more time, then slid his hand down to grasp her hand. "Come on. I'm on duty. We'd better catch up with the others."

She liked, very much, knowing she could make him smile that way. They started walking together, and it felt rather like their first days together. And very different. "Good idea. Who knows what Manuel has decided to investigate?"

"Hmm. Think I should warn Scopes to make sure Manuel doesn't get into his pockets? He keeps a different set of goodies on hand than I do—fuses, wire, explosive caps."

Her eyes widened in alarm. "Michael, you don't think—"

"Hey, I'm just kidding." He frowned. "Mostly kidding."

"He was really fascinated by the explosion."

They exchanged a glance and, in unspoken agreement, walked faster.

Twelve

For the next couple of hours, Michael coursed up and down his ragged column like a sheepdog with a big, unruly flock, his walking stick in his left hand, his CAR 16 slung over his shoulder. And fought the desire to drag Alyssa off into the bushes and take her, hard and fast.

The degree of his desire—and his frustration—baffled him. Sure, danger could be an aphrodisiac, but there wasn't much to do right now but walk and wait, with none of the adrenaline-drenched rush of action. Yet he went right on wanting her with a deep, dragging ache.

Something had changed.

He couldn't put his finger on what was different. He just knew something was. The change was there in the way she smiled at him every time he passed her while checking out the rear. It had been there in her kiss.

Her kiss. He shook his head slightly, trying to clear it.

He'd just conferred with Pasquez again. The *tepec* assured him his people could keep up this pace—such as it was.

They'd discussed the route in more detail. They should reach a river in an hour or so, and could make good time once they forded it; the northern bank was rocky and bare for the most part. They'd continue along the river for about three miles before the trail parted ways with the water, winding up to a narrow pass. The climb there was steep, and the pass was going to be one hell of a bottleneck, but there was a small meadow on the other side where the villagers could camp...while Michael and Scopes took positions at the pass.

Michael was headed for the rear now, hoping Scopes had returned. As expected, they'd lost radio contact with Boise and Smiley, so Michael had sent his sergeant to reconnoiter their back trail, see if there were any signs of followers. There shouldn't be. Not yet. It ought to take the renegades at least half a day to either dig out the trail or hack a new one through the gully—but Michael didn't like depending on what *ought* to be true.

He rounded a curve in the path, working his way upstream through the flow of people, and saw Scopes moving toward him. Scopes saw him and gave a quick hand signal—all clear. Michael breathed a little easier.

The two of them moved as far to the side as possible, letting the others flow around them. ''No sign of 'em,'' Scopes said.

''Good.'' Michael took out his map and brought Scopes up to date on their route. ''We have to make that pass before nightfall.'' Michael refolded the map. ''There's a steep drop on one side.''

''Couldn't take it in the dark, then. Not with the kids.''

''The renegades could. If they're feeling hasty.''

They exchanged a glance. ''Guess we'll be seeing some night duty, then.''

''Yeah.'' He shifted the strap of the CAR 16. ''I'm going to the rear, make sure we don't have any stragglers.''

The sergeant chuckled. ''Is that what you're doing? And here I thought you wanted to see A.J.''

Michael's brows lifted. ''Her name's Alyssa.''

''She said to call her A.J. Real nice woman, even if she is a preacher,'' he said tolerantly. ''Got a pair of legs on her that won't quit, doesn't she?''

Michael sighed. ''What did you say to her?''

''Don't get all bent out of shape. I know how to be respectful. You go on back and tell her hi, and if you'll take my advice—''

''I don't want your advice.''

''Sweet talk her off into the bushes. You're wound about as tight as a man can get without snapping something, and nothing relaxes a man like a good—'' The look on Michael's face must have been hint enough for once, because he stopped, frowned, then went on testily, ''I wasn't being disrespectful. She could probably use—ah, a little relaxation, too. She smiled real cheery and all, but she's bound to be getting frazzled, the way those kids hang all over her.''

Michael started to snap something about minding his own business—then closed his mouth. Scopes was right about one thing. He was wound tight. Normally he wouldn't get bent out of shape by his sergeant's decidedly casual notions of what constituted respect. ''After I see Alyssa, I'll check the back trail.''

''Sure thing. Look, if you're too shy to take her off in the bushes, just drop back behind the rest. Hold her hand and look at each other all moony-eyed awhile.'' He winked. ''Ain't as good as the other, but it might help.''

He sighed. ''You've got the column for now, Sergeant.''

Scopes tossed him a cocky salute. ''You say hi to your lady for me. And don't hurry back.''

Michael wished, as he made his way past babies being carried, older children bickering or playing, young women and older women, that Scopes had kept his mouth shut for once. Taking Alyssa—into the bushes, or anywhere else—was on his mind too much already.

Then he rounded a curve in the trail and saw her. Scopes

had been right. She was a child-magnet. A toddler was in her arms; Manuel walked alongside her, no doubt peppering her with questions, while two older girls followed, obviously including her in their conversation.

Then she looked up and saw him, and her face lit up. And his focus narrowed to her. Only her.

When he joined her, though, the children were too delighted with the novelty of his presence to let him talk to Alyssa. He took the toddler from Alyssa to give her arms a rest, dissolved the two girls in giggles with a couple of compliments, and patiently explained to Manuel why some things burned and others exploded when touched by fire.

His eyes met Alyssa's. Some things, he thought, could do both—burn and explode, over and over again. Maybe Scopes had been right about two things. He wanted time with her alone. Not long. A few minutes...what could it hurt? "Think the sisters could handle the kids for a few minutes?" he asked causally in Spanish. "I'd like to talk to you."

"Well..." She glanced behind her.

Sister Constancia was nearest; she made a shooing motion, smiling. "I'll take the little one for a while," she said, and Michael transferred the sleepy toddler to the nun's soft, strong arms.

Then he took Alyssa's hand and started walking back down the trail, away from the others.

"Is something wrong?" she asked, her forehead creasing.

"No. I just wanted to be with you."

"Oh." That pleased her. Color rose in her cheeks and her eyes glowed. She pushed her hair behind her ear. "How's your leg holding up? It's still got a hole in it."

"Not such a big hole." In truth, it ached, but the muscle hadn't been damaged as badly as he'd feared. It had been infection rather than the wound itself that had crippled him; with that cleared up, he had almost normal use of the leg again. "How are you holding up? If you've been carrying that little girl for long, your arms must be tired."

She chuckled. ''Think cooked spaghetti, and you'll have the idea. I thought I was in good shape until recently, you know.''

''You are.'' He stopped. They'd rounded a curve in the trail, and the others were out of sight. ''In damned good shape, I mean.''

She slid him a teasing glance. ''So are you.''

The invitation he read in that glance couldn't be there. Not now, not here. But his unruly body didn't care about the time and place. *Down, boy.* He took her other hand to keep himself from grabbing anything he shouldn't. ''You seem...different. Almost lighthearted.'' Which was a damned silly thing to say, considering their circumstances.

''I do feel lighter. I told you that Sister Andrew removed a spiritual splinter...that's part of it. Then, too, I've been trying to follow her advice about living in the moment, not borrowing trouble.'' She grimaced. ''Easier said than done, of course. Especially...'' She paused. Her chin came up a fraction, and she finished calmly, ''Especially when the man I love has a habit of getting himself shot while protecting everyone but himself.''

There was a roaring in his ears. Weakness in his legs. A dippy, dizzy swirling in his mind, and a terrible hunger in his gut. ''Alyssa?'' He groped for sense, or at least for words, but came up empty. Except for her name. ''Alyssa.''

Her fingers tightened on his. She looked a little pale, but met his eyes steadily. ''You must have guessed. After the way I gave myself to you, you must have guessed.''

''I...'' He wanted to hear her say the words, say them directly to him. He needed that—but how could he tell her? How could he ask, just come out and ask, if she was sure—if she really *loved* him—he groaned, grabbed her face in both hands, and kissed her.

She opened to him. Molded her body up against his in instant welcome, and all he could think was *more*. He needed more, needed all of her. He ran his hands over her, back to waist, hips to buttocks, and groaned.

A.J. had never felt anything like the storm of need that raged inside Michael, spilling over onto her with every sweep of his hands. Where had this come from, this raw, shaking power? Had she truly loosed it by letting him know she was in love with him? Now, drawn into the center of the storm with him, she could only gasp for air, and shudder in reaction when his fingers dug into her hips and he ground himself against her.

He tore his mouth away. "I need…let me have you, Alyssa." His mouth quested over her face, her throat, somewhere between plea and demand in its urgency. "Will you let me?"

He said "let me." She heard "love me." Silently she gave—comfort, with the sweep of her hands along his back. Permission, with the press of her lips. And love, with everything in her.

He shuddered. Went still, as if struggling to contain the storm—but it broke, crashing over them both.

His hands raced over her, finding buttons, snaps. His mouth followed. By the time he backed her around a tree and up against its smooth bark, her shirt hung open and her breasts were wet from his mouth. And she was on fire.

Her own hands trembled, then tore at the stiff, stubborn button above his zipper. He cupped her with one hand, kissing her, thrusting his tongue deep in taunting mimicry of what they wanted. Needed. The low sound that came from her throat sounded suspiciously like a growl. He jerked her zipper down.

His gun slid from his shoulder, thumping against her arm. He froze.

The gun didn't matter, not the way it had before. Not the way she'd made him think it mattered. She had to be sure he knew, so she took the strap and eased it off his arm herself, her eyes meeting his.

Something wild surged in his eyes. Quickly he set the

weapon on the ground, then held her face in both hands, and kissed her.

The buttonhole on his pants finally gave up its button, but she couldn't get to his zipper—he was dragging her pants and panties down. Her heart pounded, her blood rushed. *Now,* it beat. Now, now, now. Cloth bunched awkwardly at her feet. *Shoes,* she thought—stupid, blasted, in-the-way shoes—but he solved the problem by jerking the material over one shoe, and off that leg.

She tugged down his zipper, took him into her hands. He groaned, his neck going rigid, then slid his hands beneath her bottom, lifting her. His easy strength sent another tremor of hunger through her. The trunk was hard and round against her back. Her bare leg came up automatically, hooking itself around him as he lifted and positioned her—and thrust inside.

The suddenness jolted her. "Michael?" She scattered kisses over his face, his neck, whatever she could reach, and with her hands tried to slow him, to soothe them both.

He groaned and began to move. Quick, hard thrusts—but the position didn't let him come deeply enough inside. She moaned in frustration, trying to shift, to find a way for him to penetrate deeper. Already his thrusts were quickening, the tempo building, and she was ready, so ready—but couldn't get the pressure *there,* where she needed it. She hung on the very edge of explosion—then his hands moved, shifting to her thighs, opening her legs more fully, and when he slammed against her this time, it was right. Perfect.

She cried out, her body bucking with the force of the climax. He thrust one more time, his head thrown back, and she felt the hot spurt of him deep inside. The world went blank.

Birdsong. That was the first thing she noticed in the slow, languid return of sense. Then the deep, shuddering breath he drew as they sank, together, to the earth, stopping when he reached his knees, so that she straddled his lap. His head dropped forward, his forehead resting on her shoulder. His chest heaved as if he'd just finished a marathon.

She leaned her head against his. How silly they must look, she thought, smiling. Her pants and panties were still bunched up around one ankle; his were around his knees. Passion was such an undignified business, glorious and messy.

She stroked his hair, cherishing him, feeling a deep calm descend now that the storm had passed. He'd needed her so badly, and that need had taken the shape of passion. But it wasn't only her body he'd needed. She was sure of it.

She spoke very softly. "I love you."

He wrapped his arms around her and held on tight. And said nothing at all.

He'd taken her up against a tree. A tree, for Pete's sake. Michael couldn't believe he'd dragged her off the trail and taken her up against a tree.

God, it had been wonderful. He was grinning as he tucked in his shirt and zipped his pants. He draped an arm over her shoulder, watching with interest as she fastened her pants, then pulled her shirt together. "Need any help with those buttons?"

"What buttons?" she muttered, head down as she fastened her shirt "You popped half of them off."

"Uh-oh." He ought to regret that. He should at least make an effort to stop grinning like a fool.

She slid him a reproachful glance. "Everyone is going to guess what happened to my buttons."

"Hmm." Since he couldn't think of anything reasonable to say, he opted for silence.

She loved him. It was still sinking in. Of course, she still hadn't said she was going to marry him—but if she loved him, surely that would be the next step.

It took only a couple of steps to be back on the trail. He shook his head, amazed all over again at himself. At least they were well behind the others. No one would have seen or heard...but there were those buttons. The missing ones.

For some reason that made him grin again. Primitive and

base as it might be, he liked the idea of everyone knowing she was his. He glanced at her, his arm tightening slightly on her shoulders.

Her eyes were heavy-lidded, nearly closed. Compunction struck him. "Tired?"

"Shh. I'm enjoying a bath fantasy. It involves a deep, deep tub filled to the brim with hot water and bubbles. Lots and lots of bubbles."

"I wish I could give you that bath, and the time and safety to enjoy it." He wanted to give her everything she wanted, everything she needed. And had so little to offer...

"Oh, the fantasy will do for now." But her eyes opened, smiling with amusement into his. "At least my fantasies are harmless. Manuel has started fantasizing about explosions."

His brows drew down. "Is it fantasy, or trauma?"

She chuckled. "Oh, fantasy in this case, I'm sure. He's so fascinated by explosives that he thinks every cloud of dust he sees is another of your big booms."

Her words settled uneasily in his mind. "Every cloud of dust...Alyssa. When did he see another cloud of dust?"

"I guess it was about thirty minutes ago. Not long before you joined me, actually. That's what he was telling me about. I was trying to convince him it couldn't have been another explosion he'd seen, since you'd only set off that one, but he...what is it?"

Half an hour ago, Scopes would have been on his way back, having nearly caught up with the "column" once more. Michael himself would have just left Pasquez about then. He hadn't seen any telltale rise of dust, but the terrain could have hidden it. "Dammit to hell! I didn't think of it. Not once did it occur to me."

"What? Michael, what is it?"

"They could have had explosives, too. The renegades."

He questioned Manuel, and the others who had been in about the same location at the time. Two others—a ten-year-old girl and an older woman—reported seeing a sudden, dirty haze rise into the air over the shoulder of the mountain. He hurried to find Scopes.

His sergeant greeted him with a grin. He was chewing on a twig—an old campaigner's trick to keep the mouth from drying out when you couldn't stop to drink. "Hey, you don't look relaxed. Didn't you—" He cut himself off, his tone changing completely. "What's up, Mick?"

"If the bastards behind us tried to clear the trail using explosives, would we have heard the blast?"

His teeth clamped down suddenly on the twig, snapping it in two. He spat out the piece in his mouth. "Depends on how far away we were, whether they buried the charges, how deep, what they used."

"Half an hour ago, Manuel and a couple of others saw dirt rise in the air back toward the village."

"Hell."

That about summed it up.

They reached the river quickly, urgency lending energy to even the oldest and youngest among them. The children didn't understand what was wrong, but they knew their mothers were frightened and kept up the newly quickened pace for the next hour.

But inevitably, some began to flag, and the pace slowed. Michael tried to get Pasquez to speak to his people, persuade them they *had* to hurry, especially here where the going was relatively easy. But this time the old man set his jaw stubbornly. "We don't know those devil men are on this trail. A cloud of dust—what does that mean? Anything. Nothing. You are young," he said, and sighed. "Young and impatient. Old legs cannot keep up with yours. The worst of the trail is still ahead, when we climb up to the pass. The little ones and the old ones like me must save our strength for that."

Michael had to bow to the old man's greater knowledge of his own resources. Logic said the *tepec* could be right about the dust cloud, too—but Michael's instincts were shrilling.

He'd cursed himself once, briefly, for having sent the helicopter off. If he'd kept it near, he could at least have stayed in radio contact with Boise, known for sure what was happening back at the village. He'd cursed himself, too, for not having considered the possibility the rebels might have explosives, but not for long. It was a waste of time and energy to indulge in regrets. And realistically, he'd had no reason to think a bunch of ragtag rebels might have explosives. His sergeant might never leave home without them, but Scopes was the exception to a number of rules.

He could only hope the rebels didn't have anyone as knowledgeable as Scopes. A poorly planned blast could have made matters worse instead of better. Otherwise…well, at least he had some experts at praying on his side.

Three of those experts were just ahead of him. Alyssa looked relaxed. She was holding little Rosita again, talking and smiling with three boys. Every now and then she glanced over her shoulder to say something to one of the nuns, who walking slightly behind her.

And every time she did, her gaze strayed farther back. Checking out the trail behind them.

She looked up as he approached, her lips curving in a smile much too saucy for a minister. "Hi there, soldier."

"Hi, babe. Got a minute for a lonely man in uniform?"

She chuckled. One of the boys grabbed Michael's hand, asking to be carried. He looked tired and fretful, poor kid. Michael lifted the youngster, tucking him on his hip the way he'd seen the women do. The little boy made a surprisingly warm and comfortable burden.

What would it be like to have a child of his own?

Quickly he shut the thought off. Until they got through this, he couldn't afford to think about the future. The odds were against him having one.

"I saw you looking over your shoulder," he said quietly to Alyssa, using English so the children wouldn't understand. "Don't worry. No one will get past Scopes without us knowing about it."

He'd sent Scopes behind to play rear guard. It was a position he would rather have taken himself, but his sergeant's pithy comments about the weakness in Michael leg having seeped into his head had made him agree that Scopes was more fit for that duty.

Alyssa shifted Rosita. The little girl had fallen asleep, and her cheek was damp and sweaty where it had been cushioned by Alyssa's breasts.

His burden, too, was drowsy, laying his head on Michael's shoulder. He really ought to put the boy down. He needed to keep his arms free…in a minute he would, he promised himself. There was a surprising comfort in the small burden.

"How far back do you think they are?" she asked, low-voiced.

"Maybe still at the village."

"Don't coddle me."

It had been a pretty feeble effort, but dammit, there was so little he could do for her. "We can't know for sure. It depends on how well their blast cleared the trail and how much of a hurry they're in. We've been making about two miles an hour. Chances are they'll make three miles an hour. Could be more," he admitted. "If they have some reason to hurry."

"And how far do we still have to go?"

"The pass is only about four miles from here…horizontally. Unfortunately, a lot of that distance is up a steep slope. Pasquez says we should reach it around five."

She was silent. He figured she was doing the math. Five o'clock might be too late. "They have no reason to hurt us," she said at last. "If their goal is the plantation and they're in a hurry, messing with us would just slow them down, make them waste ammunition."

He nodded. He could at least give her that hope—and it wasn't unreasonable, given what she didn't know about what had happened at the other village. And wasn't going to know, if he had anything to say about it.

Nausea touched Michael's gut. It wasn't an unfamiliar

feeling, before battle or after one. Death was never pretty. But the way some of those people had died…his arm tightened on the small, drowsy boy he held.

"Michael?" She touched his arm. "You okay?"

He shook himself mentally. "I was having a little tactical chat with myself. Nothing important."

"I've got some tactics to suggest, if we ever make it to a bed."

She made him smile—which was just what she'd had in mind, he could tell. Her own smile widened, her gaze playing come-hither with his. So he flirted back and walked a little farther with the young boy in his arms, stealing these few moments. Finally, though, he had to bend and put the boy down. *"Lo siento,"* he murmured at the boy's protest.

He straightened. "I have to keep my arms free. And I really should drop back. The rear guard is supposed to march at the rear, not wander along chatting."

She glanced at the gun slung on his back and nodded. No protests. No begging him to be careful. Whatever fear she felt, she kept to herself.

Gallant. That was the word for her. "Have I told you that you're a lot like one of my men? Only prettier, of course. And a helluva lot sexier."

She pushed her tangled hair behind her ear and grimaced. "You aren't picky, are you, Lieutenant?"

"Yes, I am," he said softly, drawing a fingertip along her cheek. He would make sure she made it home to savor that bubble bath she'd fantasized about, and sleep safely in her bed. Even if he wasn't there to share it with her. "Very picky. About some things."

Thirteen

She'd thought she was tired before. Three hours later, A.J. knew the full meaning of the word. She was hot, dirty, sweaty—and sticky between her thighs from that glorious, hasty coupling against a tree.

The thought of it made her smile, but her smile faded quickly. He hadn't said he loved her, but he'd made it clear he needed her, that she was special to him. That was enough…wasn't it?

A.J. shifted her arms, adjusting the weight of the child on her back in a futile effort to find a way to ease the strain. She hurt. Back, shoulders, arms—they'd gone from aching to trembling, with occasional sharp, stabbing pains. No surprise. Sister Constancia had taken Rosita from her when they stopped at the river for a short break so A.J. could carry four-year-old Sarita. Sister Andrew was carrying little Carlos. Dimly, that worried A.J.; the grade was steep here, and while the nuns might be used to hard work, they were twice A.J.'s age.

But there wasn't anything she could do about it, so she concentrated on putting one foot in front of the other. Since they'd started climbing, her thighs and calves had joined the mass of aches that made up her body. She'd be lucky if she could stand upright tomorrow.

Assuming she made it to morning. A.J. glanced over her shoulder and saw nothing—nothing except the sisters, some of the older children, and green. That all-pervasive, choking green. When she faced forward again she saw more green, along with the broad back of Señora Valenzuela, who had come to the rear to help with the children, bless her.

She didn't see Michael, hadn't seen him since the all-too-brief rest by the river when he'd nearly caused a mutiny by insisting everyone lighten their loads before tackling the steep slope. Since the bulk of what they'd brought was food, and everything else was essential, they'd refused.

Even the nuns had resisted the idea. A.J. had told them quietly that they must trust God to provide—but that He wouldn't provide earthly food for dead children. Sister Andrew had nodded grimly and instructed the older children to abandon their packs so they could carry the little ones.

Michael hadn't wasted time arguing. Instead, he'd started going through their packs, throwing food into the river—and he'd very nearly been attacked by the people he was trying to save. Then Señor Pasquez had joined him, calmly tossing corn, flour, beans and dried fruit onto the ground.

There had been some grumbling, but the example of their *tepec* had encouraged the rest to lighten their packs. Maybe they were glad now, she thought, catching at a tree trunk to help her up a particularly steep bit.

Since then, Michael had dropped farther back, out of sight. Guarding their rear. She was so afraid for him....

Up ahead, someone exclaimed loudly. Others began chattering up, but A.J.'s Spanish wasn't good enough to sort out what had them all excited. "What is it?" she asked Señora Valenzuela. "Can you hear?"

"Shh..." The older woman was badly out of breath, so she stopped, listening. "Ah, praise God! They have reached the pass, those at the front." She beamed at A.J. "We are nearly there, and no devil-men."

The news heartened them all. A.J.'s muscles didn't stop aching, but she found it easier to ignore the pain and press on.

The pass didn't mean safety for Michael. For the rest of them, yes. The pass was narrow. Two men with automatic weapons like those Michael and his sergeant carried could hold off forty men there, if need be.

But eventually, those two men would run out of bullets.

Maybe the rebels wouldn't come. Maybe their blast had gone wrong, and they'd never even started down this trail. And if they did come, surely they'd give up when they saw how lethally the pass was defended, long before Michael ran out of ammunition. Surely the—

Gunfire screamed, shattering her thoughts, making her stumble. *Michael!* Instinctively she started to turn.

"Go!" Sister Andrew's hand at her back wasn't gentle. "Go and go quickly, unless you want to take the baby on your back into the middle of *that!*"

She went. Tears came. She ignored them as well as her screaming heart, scrambling up and up—toward the shouts of the others, the crying of children, a woman's scream of fear. Little Sarita was sobbing with terror in her ear, her legs clenched tight, her arms nearly strangling A.J.

And from behind, gunfire. A sharp burst, several individual shots, another burst—from a different spot?

Scopes is back there, too, she reminded herself. Michael isn't alone. God, please God, keep him safe, keep them both safe....

So suddenly it was like stepping outside from a crowded room, the trees ended. Rocks surrounded her now on both sides, towering high on the left and well above her head on the right. Rocks and dirt slid beneath her feet and she nearly fell, nearly lost the precious burden on her back, catching Sarita at the last moment as she slipped, her poor little legs unable to hold on. She made herself slow down. The breath heaved in her chest.

And she heard it. Disoriented, she couldn't identify the sound, though she'd heard it before—a thrumming, mechanical noise, getting louder by the second. Coming from—the sky?

She looked up. And a great, army-green helicopter flew into view over the tops of the rocks on her left—heading toward the shooting.

Thank you, thank you, thank you!

''Praise God,'' Sister Andrew murmured, adding more practically, ''Keep moving. They're still shooting.''

The trail leveled then sauntered down, an easy slope now, widening as it descended. A.J. was still moving quickly, with rocks high on either side, when gunfire erupted again—this time a huge, steady stream of it, coming from the air.

The copter. It must be firing on the rebels. A.J.'s breath hitched. The safety she'd prayed for had come in the shape of death—for some.

The fusillade cut off as suddenly as it had started. Behind her, Sister Andrew was murmuring a prayer in Spanish for the souls of those killed by that hail of bullets.

A.J. drew a deep breath. Death had been dealt back there—for whom? How many? Michael was all right, she told herself. He had to be. And life lay on the other side of these rocks.

The rocks led them into a wide, grassy clearing surrounded by towering pines. People flooded into it ahead of A.J., most of them hurrying, a few pausing to look over their shoulders. Some crossed themselves. Children cried, and everyone clustered together, seeking comfort in closeness.

Confusion reigned. No one knew what to do.

Then the helicopter appeared over the ridge. It hovered just above the clearing, impossibly loud, the wind from its blades huge, alien. People scattered.

As soon as it had a clear space, it set down. The big doors in the side opened and men spilled out. Men in uniform, government troops—but not the U.S. Army. They wore San Christóbal's brown uniforms, and they hit the ground running, heading back toward the pass.

The cavalry had come to the rescue.

Michael had plenty of reason to bless whatever luck or foresight had moved him to send the helicopter back to the base. Banner had gone straight to the Colonel, ready to plead his case. Rather to his astonishment, the Colonel had nodded, told him to get the big Cobra ready—and then he'd gotten on the phone.

Seems the San Christóbal government had urgently requested U.S. support in rounding up the strays from *El Jefe*'s army, but the brass at the top couldn't get a green light from the president. They had, however, been authorized to provide limited technical support.

The Colonel had decided that flying a squad of San Christóbal troops right to the spot where the biggest bunch of rebels were known to be qualified as damned fine technical support. The U.S. had the helicopter and the knowledge of the rebels' whereabouts—that was the technical part. The natives could supply the troops. He'd called his counterpart in the San Christóbal army and set it up.

Michael couldn't help thinking it would have been nice if the troops had arrived about ten minutes earlier.

His bearers nearly tipped him out of the stretcher on the steepest part of the climb to the pass. White-hot fire exploded in his shoulder. As soon as he could breathe again, he started cursing.

"Might want to tone it down," Scopes said from beside him. "Here comes your lady."

Alyssa. He managed to lift his head and saw his sweet,

gentle Alyssa nearly mow down two of the soldiers in front of his stretcher, getting to him. ''Michael! Oh, God, they told me you'd been shot.''

''Hey, I'm okay.''

She shuddered. Scopes dropped back before she could shove him out of the way, too, and the men carrying him started moving again. He reached for her with his left hand—his right arm was strapped to his side—and she took it, walking alongside the stretcher.

He let his head fall back as he drank in the sight of her—huge eyes, dirty cheeks and all. There were smears in the dirt. She'd been crying. Over him?

''You are *not* okay, damn it,'' she said fiercely.

''I will be,'' he said. ''But you're a mess.''

Her laugh broke in the middle. ''Not half as much of a mess as you are.'' Her gaze skittered over his shoulder—which, he knew, did look pretty bad, with all the blood. ''When the soldier who told me you were hurt said you wanted to see me—he said to *hurry.*'' She gulped.

Dammit, the idiot had made it sound like he was on his deathbed. He stretched out his free hand. She took it. ''I asked them to bring you so I could propose again.''

She stared at him blankly. ''Now?''

The pain in his shoulder was getting worse. Hard to see how that could be, but it was. ''I told them they couldn't load me on the copter until you married me.''

''You what?'' She glanced around frantically, as if looking for someone with the authority to override him. Scopes just shrugged. So she spoke quickly in Spanish to the men carrying him, telling them not to listen to the idiot on the stretcher—get him to medical help, and do it *now.*

They looked uncomfortable, and apologized.

''I'm afraid I'm the hero of the moment,'' Michael said. ''They don't want to go against my wishes.''

One of the men, who may have understood some English, broke in then in Spanish, urging her to do as the *Americano teniente* wished—and quickly, please, before he lost any more blood.

What little color she'd regained fled from her face.

"I'm not dying," he said as firmly as he could—though it came out more breathless than he would have liked. "I just want to get married. Now." She shook her head, but more because she was dazed than in refusal, he thought. "I'm sorry I don't have a ring, but..." He had to stop and catch his breath when the angle shifted as they moved downhill. That hurt. "I asked the corporal to find someone else, too. If he...good. Here he is."

Señor Pasquez joined them, huffing and puffing. "I hurried," he said, "but I may have to perform the ceremony sitting down. My legs...ah," he sighed, and smiled. "The bride is here. Good."

"You have your book, to make it legal?" Michael asked.

"I will write it in the register," the old man promised. "Now, you are ready?"

Michael looked at her and waited. She'd said she loved him. He was pushing her hard, but he *had* to. When that copter had lifted up over the peak that held the pass, he'd been down, his gun arm useless, with blood running out of him like water from a burst pipe.

Now that he had tomorrow back, he meant to spend it with Alyssa. No waiting around, giving life a chance to throw more surprises at him. There were going to be some problems...a few of them swam dizzily through his mind. He blinked, realizing he'd faded out for a moment.

Hell. Get married first, sort things out later. His hand tightened on hers. "Alyssa?"

She took a deep breath. "Yes. All right. I'm ready."

He made it through the simple ceremony, though toward the end black dots were dancing in front of his eyes. He stayed conscious when they carried him to the helicopter, though his head was swimming by then. Before they lifted his stretcher onto the floor of the copter, though, he very sensibly passed out.

A.J. spent the first two hours after her wedding with sound battering her eardrums. The chopper was very loud, even with the earplugs Banner had handed her.

She couldn't hold Michael's hand because the corpsman attending him and the IV needed to be there. She stayed close, but he wouldn't know that. He didn't regain consciousness. When they landed in Panama at the small base that was their destination, he was still out cold.

Four hours later she was airborne again—this time in a DC-9. This time Michael had a paramedic and a nurse with him, and a lot more equipment—a full hospital bed that clamped to the side and deck of the plane. Oxygen. A heart-rate monitor. And the IV, of course.

He did wake long enough to insist she call his brothers. He gave her his brother Jacob's phone number, then he slipped away again.

The copilot put the call through for her. She sat on the jumpseat behind the pilot, headphones on her ears and lights blinking at her from the bewildering console and listened to a phone ringing in Dallas, Texas.

"Yes?" a female voice said.

"I—is this Ada?" For a moment, curiosity swamped everything else.

"Yes. Do I know you?"

She had to smile at the tart inquiry. "No. I need to speak to Jacob West, please."

"You and everybody else today. All right, just a minute while I fool with these buttons. Don't know why they needed to put in such a fancy phone," the woman muttered. "Here. I think this one will—"

Silence. She was just beginning to think she'd been cut off when a deep, masculine voice said, "West here."

"Jacob West?" Her heart was pounding. She tucked her

fingernails into her palm, squeezing, fighting to stay in control. She had to deliver the news calmly.

"Yes."

"This is Reverend Kelleher." No, that wasn't right, not anymore—but she'd sort all that out later. Right now she had to tell this man... "I'm calling about your brother Michael. He's been...hurt."

His quick, indrawn breath was barely audible. His voice remained cool and steady. "How bad?"

She squeezed her hand tighter, the nails digging in. "His condition is stable. He's being flown to Houston for surgery."

"What kind of surgery? Dammit, tell me what's wrong with him. Now."

In spite of everything she could do, the tears were starting. "He was shot. The bullet did—they say it did very little damage on entry. They think it might have been a ricochet." *Get it said*, she ordered herself. Tears or no tears, she had to say it. "But it lodged near his spine. Th-there's danger of paralysis. That's why they didn't want to operate at the base in Panama. He wants you and Luke to be there."

A.J. stood by the window in the nearly empty surgical waiting room, holding her elbows, keeping her arms locked tight to her body. She had the silly idea that if she let her arms hang loose, something inside her would break free and she'd come apart.

The glass was dark, though she could see lights. Lots and lots of lights. After so many nights when the only light came from the moon and stars, Houston, with its noise, crowds and millions of artificial lights, was a little overwhelming.

But then, she was easily overwhelmed right now.

She'd called her parents shortly after they wheeled Michael into surgery. They'd been overjoyed to hear from her and would be here as soon as possible, but it might be a couple of days. They'd both come down with the flu. Her father had been ready to jump in the car anyway, but A.J. had told him firmly she didn't need their germs, knowing that would work better than any pleas to wait until they were up to traveling.

It was lonely, though, waiting by herself....

''Reverend Kelleher?'' a man's voice said.

She turned slowly, still hugging her arms close. ''Not exactly.''

Four people were crossing the room, heading for her—two men and two women. One man looked like a male model, only better. There was too much charm in those easy, perfect features for such a plastic profession. The other man was taller, older, with a face that might have been shaped by a hatchet, not an artist's chisel. One of the women was older, a tiny, skinny woman in baggy jeans, with a frizz of unlikely yellow hair around her leathery face. The other was flat-out beautiful.

''Try to be exact,'' the hard-featured man snapped. ''The nurse said you were the minister who arrived with my brother Michael. Are you or not?''

''Jacob.'' The beautiful woman put a hand on his arm.

So this was Michael's oldest brother, the one he thought so much of. He was a big man, well over six feet, broad through the shoulders and chest. ''I used to be Reverend Kelleher. I just remarried. I'm not used to my new name yet.''

''Pleased to meet you, Reverend,'' the tiny woman with yellow hair said. ''Now, tell us about Michael.''

''He's in surgery.'' And had been for what seemed endless hours, though the clock assured her only fifty minutes had passed.

''Excuse me, but you look about to fall down.'' The woman with Jacob West put her hand on Alyssa's arm. ''Have you been with him all this time?''

She looked polite but puzzled, as if she wasn't sure why Michael might have—or want—a personal chaplain in attendance. It made A.J. smile. "Yes, I was there when—when—my, but you're gorgeous." The inappropriate comment made her flush. "Excuse me. I'm not thinking straight."

The woman laughed. "That's perfectly all right. Oh—we haven't introduced ourselves, have we? I'm Claire, Jacob's fiancée. This good-looking reprobate is Luke, his brother. And this is Ada." Her smile indicated the yellow-haired woman, who was studying A.J. with a frown on her face.

"You do look all done in, honey," Luke said kindly. "Maybe you should sit down awhile."

Honey? A.J. shook her head, trying to clear it. She knew she looked worse than "all done in." Someone—she couldn't remember who—had given her a fatigue shirt to replace the one she'd worn for so long. The one with the missing buttons. Tears stung her eyes. "So you're Luke."

"Yeah." He tipped his head to one side thoughtfully. "You're not here as a minister, are—"

"I am going to have to sit down," a soft, breathy voice said. "I just can't stand hospitals. Never could. The energy here is terribly distressin'—all those sick people."

Jacob turned, frowning. "What kept you?"

"Cami had to stop off in the ladies' room," the younger, smaller of the two women who'd just entered said. She had a round, friendly face, a trim figure clad in jeans and a purple top—and an incredibly bright green cast on her wrist. She was half supporting the other woman, a pretty blonde with big curls, big eyes and a simple little silk dress that had probably cost several hundred dollars.

"I swear," the blonde said in that little-girl voice, "a faintness comes over me every time I set foot in a hospital. I have always been sensitive that way. But I had to come. I just had to."

The woman with her wrist in a cast rolled her eyes but kept her voice soothing. "Sit down for a few minutes and you'll feel better."

"I have to know how he is first. Poor Michael. If he should

be paralyzed—oh, it just doesn't bear thinkin' of, does it?'' She sniffed delicately. ''I do assure y'all, I will still marry him, even if he never walks again.''

''I'm sure you will,'' Ada said tartly.

Heat, then cold, chased over Alyssa's body. She heard herself speak as if from a great distance. ''What did you say?'' She started toward the blonde. ''Who *are* you?''

The woman blinked very fine, thick eyelashes. ''Why, I'm Cami Porter, Michael's fiancée. And you are…?''

Alyssa licked her suddenly dry lips. ''Alyssa Kelleher…West. His wife.''

''Calling Cami with the news was not one of my better ideas,'' Jacob admitted, shoving his hands in his pockets.

''I'm damned if I can see why you did it,'' Michael snapped.

''I wasn't thinking straight. Why else would I have called your fiancée to let her know you were undergoing major surgery?''

Michael had run out of breath before he'd run out of curses after learning about the scene in the waiting room yesterday. He rubbed his chest gingerly now. Breathing hurt. Everything hurt. Getting kicked by a mule would have to feel a lot better than he did right now.

But they'd gotten the bullet out, and without doing any lasting damage. He was sure he would feel really good about that…eventually. When his life wasn't totally screwed up.

''It was quite a scene,'' Luke said reminiscently. ''One thing you have to say for Cami—she does know how to wring every ounce of drama from a situation.''

''Don't worry about her threat to call her lawyer,'' Jacob said. ''My lawyer will handle that. The prenuptial agreement is tight. She's not entitled to a penny unless you marry her—which, obviously, you won't be doing now.''

''I don't give a damn about Cami, her lawyer or the money! Alyssa…'' God, what she must be thinking, feeling...his left hand tightened into a fist. She had to give him a chance to talk to her. To explain.

"She waited," Luke pointed out. "Stuck it out the whole time, waited until you were in recovery before she let Jacob whisk her off to a hotel to get some rest."

"She would." It didn't mean anything, except that Alyssa wasn't the sort to run out on a man when he was down—even one she must think had used her. "Hasn't been back since, though, has she?"

Luke and Jacob exchanged uneasy glances. Alyssa had left the hospital yesterday morning shortly after dawn, when Michael was moved to recovery. None of them had seen or spoken with her since.

"I explained to her about the will," Jacob muttered. "When I was driving her to the hotel."

"I'm sure *that* helped." She must think he'd married her because of the trust, that devil-inspired, thrice-damned trust.

"She probably slept the clock around," Luke said. "By the time the surgeon came out to tell us you'd made it through okay, she looked worse than you do right now."

"Yeah. Maybe. Look—"

The door to his room opened, and hope burst, full-blown and painful, in Michael's heart. But the woman who came in wasn't Alyssa.

Ada set the plant she'd brought on the dresser opposite the bed, then put her hands on her hips, sharing her frown with each of them equally. "All right, you can all clear out now. I'm going to talk to Michael."

Luke and Jacob protested, but neither could stand against Ada when she was in a mood. And she was definitely in a mood.

"You will remember that he's convalescing?" Jacob said from the door, scowling in a way that had been known to send investors scurrying for cover.

"I'm not going to beat him up," she said tartly. "Now, go on, get out of here."

As soon as the door closed behind them she turned to Michael, her hands on her hips, and shook her head. ''Maybe now you'll be ready to give up all that gallivanting around you do, playing with guns and trying to save the world.''

''Maybe.'' He felt too weary to pick up their usual argument.

She made a *tch* sound and came up to the bed. ''You scared the bejabbers out of me, boy,'' she said gruffly, and touched his cheek once, lightly.

A measure of peace entered along with her touch. Ada wasn't a hugger, wasn't one to stroke or nurture in the usual ways. But she'd always been there, she'd always cared, and he and his brothers had always known that. ''Sorry about that. I'll try not to do it again.''

''Well.'' She nodded once. ''Enough of that. Time to straighten out this mess you've made. Of all the lame-brained, idiotic—proposing to that Cami creature has to be the stupidest thing I've ever seen you do. And you've done some damned stupid things,'' she added darkly.

''It seemed like a good idea at the time.'' He couldn't explain, not without giving away why he and his brothers were marrying in such haste—and Ada wasn't supposed to know what they were doing for her.

She propped her hands on her skinny hips. ''I suppose you're just as stupid as Jacob and Luke, thinking I don't know what's going on.''

''Ah—''

''Oh, I'm used to male stupidity—have to be, after all those years with your father. But I don't know what I've ever done to make the three of you believe *I've* got beans for brains. How any one of you could think I wouldn't figure out why you all three suddenly developed this overwhelming yen for matrimony, I will never know.''

He opened his mouth, realized he had nothing to say, and shut it again.

She gave another sharp nod. ''Good for you. Not much

point in trying to make yourself sound like anything but a fool. Of course, I have to give you and your brothers credit—once you decided to do the thing, you found some powerful women to tie the knot with.'' She smiled smugly. ''What little sense you do have, you got from me, not your father.''

At last she'd said something he knew how to respond to. ''True.''

''Now,'' she said, dragging over a chair and sitting next to his bed. ''We had better figure out how you're going to keep that pretty thing you married from running the other direction when she hears your name.''

''I've screwed it up,'' he said quietly. ''Worse than my father ever did, I think.''

''Oh, not worse. First thing is, you have to tell me if you love her or not.'' She gave him a sharp look. ''I'm guessing you do.''

The word sent up strange shock waves inside him. ''I...does it matter? Even if I manage to convince her I care, love doesn't fix anything, cure anything. How many women did my father love over the years?''

''Too many.'' Her voice was uncharacteristically soft, a little sad.

''Love is...'' He didn't know what it was. That was the problem. ''It complicates things.''

Now she snorted. ''No, love is simple. Everything else is complicated. You start out with love, you've got something simple and strong to return to when life gets messy. I'll say one thing for your father—the old fool did get that part right. Only problem was, every time things got complicated, he started all over again with another woman instead of sticking it out, building on the love that was already there. He never could get it through his thick head that you can't close a circle if you start drawing it all over again every time you get confused.''

He shook his head, smiling at her fondly. He had no idea what her circles had to do with the mess he'd made of his own life—he and Alyssa hadn't even gotten started in their marriage before everything fell apart. "Well, my mind's going in circles. Does that count?"

"You're paying attention to the complications, not the important stuff." She stood. "When you see Alyssa again, pay attention to what you feel, not what you think. Your biggest problem right now isn't the way your wife and your fiancée tripped over each other yesterday. It's the fact that you can't say out loud, even now, that you're in love with your wife."

There was a soft tap at the door. It swung open. "Hi," Alyssa said quietly. "Jacob told me you had company, but I thought you might not mind a little more."

"I'm on my way out," Ada said. She paused, patted his hand once—a little awkward, as usual, with the gesture of affection—and left.

Alyssa stood near the doorway, her eyes uncertain. She was wearing a dress. That came as a small shock. He'd never seen her in anything but the pants and shirt she'd worn in San Christóbal. The dress was a simple knit, narrow and belted at the waist, in a sunny sky blue that matched her eyes. Her hair was different, too. The curls had been partially tamed by being pinned into a chignon, but some of them were escaping, frisking around her face. He cleared his throat. "You clean up pretty good." *Beautiful,* he thought. She looked so beautiful to him.

Her mouth crooked up on one side and she moved a farther into the room. "I guess this is the cleanest you've ever seen me. I think," she said, smoothing a nervous hand down her skirt, "this is when I'm supposed to ask how you're feeling. For old time's sake, tell me about your leg first."

He smiled, but it hurt. Old time's sake? That's what you said to someone you hadn't seen in a long time, someone who wasn't part of your life. "I haven't noticed any problems with my leg since I got the new hole in my chest. Alyssa..."

She turned to study the plants and flowers set in a row

along the dresser. "My, you have quite a garden started here. I'm afraid I didn't bring anything."

She wasn't going to make it easy on him. Well, why should she? "I'm sorry," he said simply.

She didn't turn. Her shoulders were stiff. "I remember when you told me you deserved an explanation. I do, too."

"Jacob said he told you about the trust, and why...why I thought I had to marry quickly."

"Oh, that part's been explained." She turned suddenly, her eyes flashing. "The part I want to hear from you is why you never mentioned it. Why you never mentioned *Cami.*"

"You wouldn't have married me if I had." His chest was hurting. Bad. He pushed the button that made his bed lift anyway. He didn't like being flat on his back, and he needed to see her face better. "I never wanted her. From the first time we kissed after seeing the butterflies, there was only you."

She swallowed. "And after I told you I loved you? You didn't think I deserved to know about a little detail like a fiancée then?"

"There wasn't much time for explanations." He started to lift a hand toward her, winced and let his arm drop. "And I didn't want you to think I'd married you to dissolve the trust. I didn't...that's not why."

She looked away, then down, both hands smoothing the unwrinkled surface of her dress. When she met his eyes again, hers held a hint of—amusement? Surely he was mistaking that gleam.

"I know that," she said. "Jacob told me that if you'd wanted to throw a spanner in the works, you went about things just right. He isn't sure if our marriage is even legal, which could make dissolving the trust tricky. Especially if Cami sues for breach of promise the way she's threatening to do."

"God save me from helpful brothers," he muttered.

''Look, I'm holding you to it. Our marriage. I don't care what the courts say—you're mine, and I'm not letting you go.''

''Michael.'' She sounded—exasperated? Not angry, not hurt—but rather like Ada when she was lecturing him. Now she came over to the bed. ''I believe you, you know. I...when I first heard, I was shocked, hurt...but I knew you hadn't lied to me. Not with your words, not with your actions.''

She believed him. Believed *in* him. For one terrible instant, his eyes stung. He swallowed, fighting to get himself under control. ''I'm not like your Dan,'' he managed to say. ''I can't be the kind of man he was, the kind of husband he was.''

''No, you can't.'' She sighed. ''One of the hardest things for me has been letting go. I didn't want to be anyone other than the woman who had loved Dan, the woman he'd loved. But his death changed me. Time changed me. I had trouble admitting that.'' She took his hand then, and smiled at him. ''You aren't like Dan. You're wonderful just as you are—exactly the kind of man I need in my life now.''

He could swear his heart started beating again at that instant. Whatever it had been doing before hadn't done the job right, apparently, because only now did oxygen and life flow through his body again.

''We'll marry again, if that's necessary for legal reasons. But...but there's something you haven't said. Something important.'' She hesitated. ''I need the words, Michael.''

''I...I've never said them to a woman. Maybe not to anyone,'' he admitted. He couldn't remember. Had he ever told his father he loved him? His brothers? His mother? Maybe, when he was very small.... ''I don't know about love,'' he said a little desperately. ''I don't know if I can do it right.''

She said nothing, just stood there, her hand warm and comforting in his, her gaze steady. Waiting.

''Hell,'' he muttered. All right, he could do this. ''I love you, all right?''

Her hand tightened suddenly on his. "Was that so hard?"

"Yes. No," he corrected himself immediately. There was an odd warmth, a looseness, in his chest. "No, it was really...kind of simple, wasn't it?" The warmth spread, reaching his neck, his jaw, widening his mouth into a smile. "I love you," he repeated, the smile stretching into a big, silly grin.

She made a sound between a laugh and a sob, bent and took his face in her hands, and kissed him. "I love you, too."

This time he managed to get his arm to work. He had to, had to feel her hair, touch the silky skin along her throat. "We'll work the rest of it out. All the details." They had the basics, the place to start from—love.

"Sure we will. First things first, though." She lifted her head, her eyes wicked and happy. "You'd better get yourself well as soon as possible, because you owe me a wedding night, soldier—with a bed. I insist on having a bed this time."

He laughed.

Epilogue

Christmas Day, at the West mansion

"Mmm." Michael pressed a kiss to the side of her neck. "Have I told you how sexy you look in those robes, Reverend?"

Alyssa laughed. "And I'm staying in them, too. There are twenty people downstairs, waiting for me to marry your brother."

"He's too late." He'd tugged the robe to one side and was bending his attention to the sensitive place where her neck met her shoulder. "I already married you."

She turned in his arms, looping hers around his neck. "So you did. Twice." And gave herself up, for the moment, to his kiss.

On the advice of Jacob's attorney, they'd gone through a second ceremony as soon as he was released from the hospital to make sure there wouldn't be any problems with the trust. Cami had ceased to be a problem as soon as Michael signed over a portion of the money he would soon inherit to her—an action that had disgusted Jacob, but neither Michael nor Alyssa wanted to drag things out. Nor did they care about the money. Cami might be walking away with a small fortune, but Michael, it turned out, was going to have a large fortune. Very large.

Large enough to do a lot of things more important than taking his ex-fiancée to court. The village of Cuautepec was going to have a new school, for example, complete with a teacher. They'd already received the goats and chickens. And Sister Andrew was looking into establishing a pottery, using clay from the river and the kiln and supplies Michael had promised.

And that would put only a small dent in the money.

Someone pounded on the bedroom door. "Hey, you two—stop necking," Luke called. "We need to get Jacob married before he starts gnawing on the woodwork. Or the guests."

Reluctantly, Michael lifted his head. "I intend to finish this discussion later. In bed."

She grinned. That tree along the trail would always hold a special place in her heart, but there was no denying that beds were more comfortable.

He picked up his cane and started for the door. Luke had given him the handsome ebony walking stick topped by the snarling head of a wolf for Christmas. In another couple of months, he probably wouldn't need it anymore.

When he was medically cleared, he might rejoin his team. Or he might not. He hadn't decided, and she wasn't pressuring him. They both still had a lot of adjustments to make, a lot of decisions about how to shape their life together.

It would work out, she thought as they went into the hall. They were very different people—in some ways. But both wanted to live lives in service to others, however differently they'd chosen to serve. And they loved each other.

Sometimes it really could be that simple.

"There you are." Luke spoke from the stairs, relief and humor in his voice. "Jacob is driving us all crazy."

"The ceremony isn't scheduled to begin for another fifteen minutes," Alyssa said mildly.

"Tell my brother that. He wants to get married, and he wants to do it *now.*"

She exchanged a smile with Michael. That had been his approach, too.

Her parents were there, as were the parents of Luke's wife, Maggie, and Claire's mother and stepfather. Luke and Maggie had arrived early that morning with the boy they were planning to adopt so they could stage a massive paper-tearing spree. Luke had been an extravagant Santa—which, from what she'd learned from Maggie, was a miracle all by itself. He'd brought dozens of gifts for Maggie and the boy, and several for the rest of them, too.

Alyssa and Michael had exchanged a single present—the rings they'd bought each other, two simple gold bands. And Ada had given them all a wonderful present when she'd returned from her latest treatment—a glowing bill of health from the doctor, along with her threat to "be around long enough to tell all of your children the truth about you."

"Have I mentioned that this is a very odd house?" Alyssa asked as they started down the stairs. The finial at the bottom was shaped like a snarling lion, and that was the least of the house's peculiarities.

"Most people think so," Michael said cheerfully. "Uh-oh. Battle stations. There's Jacob."

He certainly was. The cool, controlled man she'd met at the hospital, the businessman whose icy control and acute sense of timing might eventually make him richer than his father had been, looked ready to jump out of his skin.

She told herself that ministers weren't allowed to giggle.

"At last," Jacob said, heaving a sigh of relief. "Everyone is ready."

"Claire isn't going to vanish if you don't marry her in the next five minutes," Michael said, amused.

"I know, but—" He reached up to jerk at the knot of his tie. "I just want to get it done."

He'd twisted the tie crooked. Luke chuckled and straightened it for him. "If I'd known how much fun it would be to watch you come apart like this, I'd have encouraged you to get married years ago."

"Wouldn't have done you any good. I didn't know Claire then," Jacob said simply.

A few minutes later, Alyssa stood in front of friends and family, both new and old, and opened the book. Snow was sifting down lightly outside; it would probably melt as soon as it touched down, for the weather wasn't cold. A Christmas tree glowed merrily at the other end of the room. A scrap of red ribbon, missed in the hasty cleanup, dangled from the chandelier.

It was that bit of red ribbon that undid her. After all she'd been through, all these others had been through, to have arrived safely to this day—miracles still happen, she thought, and sniffed.

Oh, dear, she thought, blinking rapidly. Claire and Jacob didn't want to be married by a weepy minister.

Alyssa's mother sat at the piano, playing the old, familiar music as the bride started her slow walk on her stepfather's arm. Claire was certainly a beautiful woman—but her physical beauty was secondary now, eclipsed by the radiance of a bride who walks forward to join the man she loves.

She stopped in front of Alyssa and took Jacob's hand.

Oh, my. Alyssa struggled to blink away the happy tears filling her eyes. Ada was already crying, she saw. And a couple of others were, too. Then her gaze met Michael's.

She smiled. *Miracles call for a few tears,* she thought. "Dearly beloved," she began, tears blurring the words, but her voice clear and firm. "We are gathered here today..."

* * * * *